THE HORSE AT THE GATES

by

DC Alden

A CIP catalogue record for this title is available from
the British Library

ISBN 978 0 956 90802 5

Tyler Press
Unit 3608
PO Box 6945
London W1A 6US

www.tylerpress.co.uk

This hollow fabric either must inclose,
Within its blind recess, our secret foes;
Or 't is an engine rais'd above the town,
T' o'erlook the walls, and then to batter down.
Somewhat is sure design'd, by fraud or force:
Trust not their presents, nor admit the horse

Virgil's *Aeneid*

Be not fainthearted then; and invite not the
infidels to peace when ye have the upper hand:
for God is with you, and will not defraud you
of the recompense of your works...

Qur'an

Prologue

'Tell me, what will happen after the bomb, after the chaos that will follow?'

The young student whispered the question as he leaned across the restaurant table, careful to shield his mouth with the palm of his hand as he'd been taught. His contact, Javed Raza, a burly field operative with Pakistan's intelligence agency, waved the young man back into his seat and summoned a waiter with a snap of his fingers. He had arrived at the popular Islamabad restaurant only moments ago and understandably the boy was eager to press him for information, but the meeting had to appear casual, just two friends meeting for lunch. Raza made sure he sat facing the street and draped his crumpled suit jacket over the back of the chair.

'All in good time, Abbas,' he said, scooping up a menu. Raza saw the boy frown as the waiter delivered a carafe of water to the table. Ah, the impatience of youth; he knew the feeling, the thrill of a forthcoming operation, the excitement as the details of the target unfolded. He should be feeling the same but today he wasn't himself. Maybe it was the weather; it was damned hot, the sky a clear blue, the sun a relentless white orb baking the city. He poured a tall glass of water and raised it to his mouth, his lips barely moving. 'Be patient. Eat. Then we talk.'

The waiter took their order and hurried away. Raza fanned his sweating face with a folded newspaper and watched the street. Their table was outside on the pavement, set deep in the shadows of the Haleem Cafe's striped awning that offered some protection from the midday sun. Nearby, the lunchtime crowds squeezed through the bazaar's narrow streets. Businessmen jostled for space alongside burqa-clad women while street vendors lounged outside garish shops and ramshackle stalls, smoking cigarettes and touting their wares with oft-repeated mantras. The noise was incessant as voices battled with each other, with the taxis and motorbikes that revved and honked their way through the human tide. Laughing children ducked and dodged through it all, oblivious to the crowds, mocking the curses that followed them, ignorant of the hardships the future held for them – if they were lucky, Raza observed.

His dark eyes narrowed as a passing military foot patrol cut a path through the throng, weapons held across their chests, suspicious eyes peering beneath helmet rims. Islamabad had barely been touched by the violence spreading around the country yet there was nervousness in the soldiers' movements, a sense of urgency that fuelled their swift passage through the narrow confines of the bazaar. Raza watched the crocodile of green helmets bobbing through the crowd until they were lost in the distance.

The food arrived in short order, delivered to the table in steaming bowls; spicy lamb biryanis with alu subzi potatoes, taftan bread and chapattis, with a side order of shami kebab for the boy. They ate in relative silence, watching the ebb and flow of the bazaar as the tables around them filled with lunch goers. Raza could only manage a few mouthfuls then pushed his plate away, the nausea that had plagued him all morning robbing him of his appetite. Finally the table was cleared and the carafe refreshed. Raza produced a small white tablet from a pill box and slipped it under his tongue, washing it down with a glass of water as the waiter delivered a pot of coffee to the table.

'You are unwell?' Abbas asked, pouring them both a cup.

'It's nothing. The heat.'

'It's barely thirty-five degrees.'

Raza ignored the observation. He pushed his coffee cup to one side and leaned forward, his thick, hairy arms folded on the table. 'So,' he began, his voice low, his eyes scanning the other diners, the passers-by, the street vendors, 'you are prepared?' Although both men spoke fluent Punjabi, they slipped easily into Arabic.

'Yes,' replied Abbas, burping loudly as he drained his cup, 'I have made my peace.'

Raza noticed that the boy's green eyes shone brightly, sensing the adrenaline that pumped around his body, like a fighter seconds before the opening bell, energised, powerful, a machine of violence waiting to be unleashed. He'd seen this before, in others, those that had been chosen for missions from which there would be no return.

'Your courage is an inspiration to others. Your family will be proud.'

Raza watched the boy stroke his thick beard and lower his eyes. He stared at the table cloth a moment, then looked up and said: 'They have no knowledge of this.'

'Have no fear,' Raza assured him, 'they will be informed.'

'They are poor. I am their only son.'

'Arrangements have been made. They will be compensated handsomely.'

The boy's eyes closed momentarily, the guilt lifted from his shoulders. It was only right. The parents were farmers, scratching out a living from the stubborn soil of the Siran Valley. Like most parents they nurtured a hope that their young son, blessed with an aptitude uncommon for his lineage, would support them during their advancing years. It was not to be, the boy drawn to the cause in his first semester at the University of Engineering & Technology in Khuzdar. There he'd been marked for interest, cultivated, schooled in the necessity for global Jihad. Normally such an intelligent asset would not be wasted on a single operation, but today was different. Like no other.

'Tell me, Mister Javed. After the bomb. What will happen?'

Raza spoke quietly, his eyes watchful. 'It will not be as you imagine, my young friend. The armies of Allah will advance without weapons and the battles will be bloodless, fought in the polling booths and government chambers of the west. It is true, many will die today and most will be brothers and sisters of the faith...' Raza paused, studying the boy before him. 'You seem untroubled by this.'

'The cause is worthwhile, is it not?'

'More than you realise.'

'Then it is not for me to pass judgement, only to execute the mission.'

Raza leaned back in his chair and regarded Abbas with a satisfied eye. The candidate was much more gifted than the usual batch of ignorant goat herders and mental cases who rarely hesitated to sacrifice their young lives for Allah. 'Where is the vehicle?'

The boy pointed a slender finger towards the eastern end of the bazaar. 'Some distance away, just as you instructed.'

'Let's walk.'

The bill was settled and the men left the restaurant, plunging into the river of bodies, allowing the swirling current of humanity to carry them along, indistinct yet disconnected from the herd. The boy walked slightly ahead, subtly shouldering a path through the crowd. He was acting like a bodyguard Raza realised, protecting his master from the worst of the throng. None challenged his sharp elbows, his garb and purposeful movement brooking no argument. Despite the waves of nausea Raza smiled with satisfaction. The boy would not disappoint.

Ahead a small group of western missionaries, all women, clustered around a young blind girl and a smaller boy squatting between two ramshackle market stalls. The children were filthy, their clothing threadbare and soiled, their thin faces streaked with dirt. The boy was maybe six or seven, a begging cup held tightly in his grubby hands. The missionaries clucked around the urchins like mother hens, soothing and pawing them with their bare hands. Westerners were a rare sight in Pakistan these days and Raza felt the anger rise in his chest. Infidels, stubborn in their flawed beliefs, meddling in the affairs of others, their smooth words and fake smiles luring the afflicted and the dull-witted towards the Christian faith. One of them unknowingly blocked their path, a small pale woman with grey hair tucked beneath the rim of a white baseball cap. As if he'd read his mind, his young companion stiffened his arm and elbowed her roughly aside, much to Raza's amusement.

They left the bazaar behind them, and Raza was thankful to be free of the stifling press of humanity. He held his jacket over his arm as the afternoon sun beat the earth, hammering the asphalt roads and dusty pavements. He took a crumpled handkerchief from his pocket and mopped his clammy brow, wincing as a sharp pain shot up his arm and pierced his neck. The boy hadn't noticed, striding ahead and clearly untroubled by the heat, dressed as he was in a white, full length disha dasha, his bald head protected from the sun by a knitted kufi. They turned off the main road and into a shady side street where the battered Toyota pickup waited. Raza almost sighed with relief.

They climbed inside, rusted door hinges creaking loudly, Raza fumbling with the air conditioning as the boy coaxed the engine into life. The dark blue pickup threaded its way through quiet back streets and out onto Jinnah Avenue where it merged with the heavy eastbound traffic. As the Toyota cruised along in the near side lane Raza watched the passing landscape, the roadside advertising hoardings, the flame trees that lined the busy avenue, the looming towers of the city's financial district, glass and steel facades sparkling beneath the hot sun.

'Look around you, Abbas, look how our country tries to mimic the west, how our leaders crave their acceptance, how they flood our markets with western goods, undermining the laws of sharia with their twisted values.' He glanced to his right. The boy said nothing, his eyes glued to the road. 'Europe is another matter,' Raza continued in a low voice, massaging the ache in his left arm. 'Their governments and institutions are slaves to political correctness. Their leaders are wary of our growing power, our willingness to defend our beliefs with violence, but are too shackled by their liberal ways to challenge us. Instead they appease us with weak words and fear in their eyes. Ah, here we are.'

Ahead, through the dirt streaked windshield, Raza saw the Aiwan-e-Sadr, Islamabad's Presidential Palace, squatting majestically between the Parliament and the National Assembly buildings. For a moment Raza ignored the numbness in his hands. For the average citizen the regal cluster of modern architecture ahead represented absolute power and authority in Pakistan, yet for those like Raza it offered nothing more than a charade of stability, the corrupt politicians inside seeking to paper over the cracks of Pakistan's fractious existence, to smother its deep religious and political divisions. Raza despised those that occupied the buildings' marble halls.

'A house of cards,' he hissed through his teeth, 'ready to fall.' He pointed through the windshield. 'Turn here.'

The boy yanked the wheel to the left and soon the Toyota was cruising the shaded streets of the Markaz district, less than a mile from the Presidential Palace. At Raza's instruction he turned again, pulling the vehicle up onto the driveway of a residential property. The house was non-descript, a white-washed bungalow with red roof tiles set back from the road, the door and windows secured behind steel grills, the type of dwelling fancied by a senior government worker or moderately successful businessman. Raza looked up and down the street, shielding his eyes from the glare of the sun. Nothing moved, not a single person, a vehicle, or even a stray dog. The risk of being seen was minimal, yet decades of clandestine operations and covert training dictated his movements whether he like it or not. He climbed out of the pickup, making a struggle of getting into his jacket, his chin held low, sweeping an arm across his sweating face. Then he was in the shade of the arched portico, a set of keys in his hand. He unlocked the heavy brass padlock that secured the steel security gate and swung it wide. The varnished wooden front door behind it was opened and Raza led the boy inside, flicking on the lights. Bare bulbs glowed overhead, revealing a large open living area, whitewashed walls, the floors covered in simple stone tiles. The windows were boarded on the inside with thick sheets of plywood. There were no pictures, no furniture to speak of. They passed a kitchen to the left, empty, cupboard doors left open like mouths waiting to be fed. A short hallway led them to a rear bedroom and Raza unlocked the door with a thick brass key. Inside, the room was in darkness, the window sealed with another sheet of plywood. There was no bed, only a table, barely visible in the gloom, an indistinct lump on its surface. Raza ran his hand around the wall and found the light switch. An overhead strip light hummed and blinked into life, washing the room in its harsh industrial glare. A green military rucksack occupied the table top. A very large rucksack.

'How many people does it take to create chaos?' asked Raza rhetorically, checking the snap-locks on the rucksack for signs of tampering. 'Long ago, nineteen martyrs armed with box cutters crippled the world's largest superpower in a matter of hours. London and Madrid suffered similar chaos when a mere handful of our soldiers - ' Raza's words caught in his throat. His head swam, then his stomach lurched violently. 'Wait here,' he commanded.

He walked quickly along the corridor to the bathroom where he performed two tasks. The first was to throw up, his knuckles white as his hands grasped the cool rim of the sink. After his exertions he let the water run, splashing his face and neck. He stood upright and looked in the mirror. Not good, he realised. His brown skin had taken on a grey hue, the rings beneath his eyes darker than usual. The collar and front of his shirt were soaked, the thick hair on his chest visible through the damp material. He didn't have much time.

The wave of nausea temporarily sated he moved on to task number two, which required him to stand on the toilet seat and reach up into the small roof space above. From the dark recess he retrieved a thin aluminium briefcase and headed back to the bedroom on rubbery legs.

'You are unwell,' the boy said. This time it wasn't a question.

'It does not matter.' He placed the briefcase on the table and snapped open the locks. Inside, cushioned within thick foam compartments, were two brushed-steel tubes with distinctive red caps. 'You recognise these?' he asked. The boy snorted, almost indignantly, Raza noticed. Such confidence. He spun the briefcase around and the boy ran a finger along the grey foam, lifting out the bridge wire detonators from their compartments and inspecting them with a practised eye. He nestled them carefully back inside the foam then turned his attention to the rucksack.

'It is not as I expected.'

'These things rarely are.'

'It looks smaller.' The boy unzipped a fastener around the outside of the rucksack and removed a green nylon flap. Behind it was a panel, the writing on its green casing clearly Urdu. 'One of ours,' he remarked.

Raza nodded. 'Based on the Russian RA-One One Five tactical model. This one was originally intended to take out the Indian naval base at Karwar. The design is crude. No timing mechanism, no remote detonation…'

'A martyr's weapon,' the boy finished. He embraced the rucksack in his arms and dragged it towards him. He unfastened the top snap locks with well-practised fingers and rolled the nylon material down, partly revealing the smooth metallic tube inside. He peeled away several Velcro flaps until the inspection and access panels were visible, then stood back. Raza watched him run a hand along the metal casing of the warhead. 'It is a thing of beauty,' he said quietly, almost reverently.

Raza stepped forward and lifted the foam panel containing the detonators out of the briefcase, revealing a comprehensive and sophisticated set of screwdrivers and a pair of small electronic devices that he didn't even pretend to understand. He pushed the case towards the boy.

'You have all you need?'

The boy ran a finger over the screwdrivers then removed the devices, checking power levels and murmuring approvingly. '*Insha'Allah,* yes. Everything.'

The older man sighed, mopping his sweating face and neck with his handkerchief. 'Good. Then I must leave.' He checked the digital Timex on his wrist. 'The President will begin his address to Parliament in one hour and twelve minutes. You should detonate the device at exactly two forty-five.'

The boy checked his own watch and nodded. Already Raza could see his mind was elsewhere as he laid his tools carefully on the table in a precise and specific order. There would be no cries of *alahu akbar* here today, no other jihadi proclamations or exhortations of violence. They were both professionals, men of faith to be sure, but professionals first and foremost. He left the boy alone, closing the bedroom door behind him.

Raza secured the front of the house, the boy now sealed safely inside. He started up the Toyota and backed off the driveway, idling by the pavement as he searched the street for inquisitive eyes, for waiting army trucks or hovering helicopters. There were none. He jammed the vehicle into gear and headed north, towards the Pir Sohawa Road, the winding, twisting route that would take him up over the Margalla Hills and beyond the range of the blast.

He'd travelled less than two miles when the pain gripped him, his chest constricting as if a steel wire had

10

been curled around his torso and violently tightened. He cried out and swerved the Toyota off the road, the front tyres bouncing over the kerb as it slewed to a halt in a cloud of red dust by the roadside. He clutched his chest, arms wrapped around his body, then turned and vomited onto the passenger seat. He finished retching after several moments, cuffing silvery strands of bile from his mouth as sweat poured down his face. He needed help, fast. Cars drove by him on the road, oblivious to his plight, the pickup stalled deep in the shade of a stand of eucalyptus trees. He considered calling an ambulance but that was pointless. The hospital was less than a mile from where the boy now worked. No, he had to get away.

He pulled himself upright and leaned back in his seat, moaning softly, willing the pain to pass. Through the windshield his eyes searched the densely wooded hills before him, seeking the road that would lead him to safety in the valleys beyond. Another wave of pain jolted him sideways, pulling him down onto the passenger seat, his body settling into the puddle of bile and barely-digested lumps of food already congealing on the cracked leather. With a trembling right hand he reached into his trouser pocket, his thick fingers desperately seeking the familiar shape of his pill box. He withdrew it, flicking open the lid as another knife of pain stabbed his chest. He fumbled the box, spilling the contents out into the foot well below him before he could catch one. He panted heavily, his lungs labouring under the strain, his damp face resting on the hot leather of the door panel, a thin string of saliva dangling from his lower lip. He stared down at them, a constellation of heart pills arranged against the backdrop of the rubber matting, as distant as the milky way itself, and equally pointless. The sound of the nearby traffic faded to a distant hum as he stared up through the windshield, the blue sky barely visible between the dark leaves of the eucalyptus. The thick overhead covering swayed back and forth, the branches bowing and waving before a gentle afternoon breeze. The motion seemed to calm him and the pain gradually subsided, his damaged heart slowing its frantic, erratic rhythms. His breathing retuned to something like normality, yet still he could not move. Instead he lay still, staring at the shifting trees until they blurred, then disappeared.

His eyes snapped open, his heart quickening, the palpitations increasing. His breath came in ragged gasps and once again he felt the first ripples of pain fanning out around his body. Something was wrong. He was still alive. With a dangerous effort he dragged his left arm from beneath his body. The blue LCD display of the Timex pulsed before his eyes – fourteen forty-three. He let his arm drop, moaning in temporary relief. The pain ebbed and flowed across his chest, his arms, his neck, getting sharper with each wave, building towards its deadly finale. Raza settled onto his back and waited for it to be over, briefly wondering what Paradise would be like. He hoped it would be as he'd been taught, that the rewards for martyrdom would be as described, that his heart would be whole and strong once more. He hoped it would be all of that.

Through the windshield the branches ceased their rhythmic swaying as the breeze suddenly faded, then died. Everything became still. With his good arm Raza tried to shield his eyes as the sky overhead suddenly brightened, turning from blue to a dazzling, burning, searing white.

The leaves vanished. The trees, vaporized.

The two-megaton detonation wiped the administrative heart of Islamabad off the face of the earth, killing the President, the Senate, all of the National Assembly, plus every other living organism within a two mile radius. Beyond that, roads melted and tall buildings were levelled, the blast wave rolling across the flat plain to the west and destroying everything in its deadly path. Thousands died in an instant, thousands more were buried, blackened and burned.

High above the earth, in the cold vacuum of space, orbiting satellites and remote sensor platforms recorded the light pulse and the resulting heat bloom, downloading real-time images and digital data to frantic controllers in scores of monitoring stations across a dozen countries. World leaders were woken, or interrupted, or whisked to emergency facilities, depending on their proximity to the ruins of Islamabad. The Indian government was first to denounce the ghastly event, immediately denying any involvement while ordering their armed forces to go to full nuclear alert. The world held its breath and waited.

While the radioactive fallout drifted on the wind and settled across the Pothohar plateau, the political fallout was carried around the world. Governments squabbled, diplomacy failed.

Pakistan disintegrated, descending into all out civil war.

Heathrow, Middlesex

'Eight minutes out, Prime Minister.'

Gabriel Bryce cursed silently, gripping the tan leather armrests a little tighter as the pilot's voice hissed inside the soundproofed cabin. Around him the sleek executive helicopter continued to buck and dip as it headed west, buffeted by a strong head wind and violent rain squalls. He glanced at the two close protection officers opposite, noting the tension in their bodies as the helicopter chopped through the deteriorating weather. He took small comfort in the fact that he wasn't the only one trying to conceal his anxiety.

Timing could be a real bastard, Bryce observed. His first helicopter trip in weeks just happened to coincide with a major storm front sweeping in from the Atlantic. Devon and Cornwall had already taken a battering and soon it would be London's turn. The experts said the worst was due in about six hours which offered Bryce a sliver of optimism. By then he should be safely back in Downing Street, tucked up inside the warmth of his apartment.

The helicopter dropped suddenly, the sound proofing in the passenger cabin failing to smother the roar of the engines overhead as the pilots fought to correct the stomach churning plunge. Bryce's mouth was dry, his heart thumping in his chest. He knew he was in capable hands, that the pilots were experienced, that the state of the art helicopter was fitted with every safety device imaginable, yet still he felt powerless, exposed – scared, if the truth be told. He was a terrible flyer, simple as that.

It was the fear of crashing of course. Not the crash itself but those terrible moments, sometimes minutes, before an aircraft hit the ground, when the crescendo of human howls competed with the ear-splitting scream of the engines, the bone rattling vibration of a failing airframe, the abject terror on the faces of the passengers. He'd imagined it many times, visually aided by his fascination for air crash investigation programs. Why he did it, he didn't know, but he regretted watching them every time he boarded an aircraft.

He recalled the collision near Heathrow, almost twenty years ago now, between a British Airways triple seven and a Qantas airbus, one of the big double decked ones. Both planes had a full passenger manifest, the airbus loaded with jet fuel after takeoff a minute or so before. The collision had lit up the night sky, the burning wreckage raining down across the town of Windsor. The footage was still replayed on TV occasionally, the impact captured by dozens of local authority CCTV cameras. Bryce recalled a number of charred corpses had the audacity to land within the grounds of the Royal castle, an event that generated almost as much official outrage as the circumstances of the collision itself.

Yet it had changed things completely, the third runway scrapped, the plans for a new airport dusted off and speedily implemented. Now, London International straddled the Thames estuary, billions over budget and four years overdue, but an example of what could be done if the political will and the necessity were there. All it took was a tragedy on an unimaginable scale for it to happen.

The helicopter shuddered and lurched to the left and Bryce strangled the armrests once again. He felt a hand on the sleeve of his overcoat.

'Almost there,' soothed Ella. His Special Advisor sat in the seat beside him, completely unruffled, bundled up in a black North Face parka, her blond hair tied back in a loose pony tail, her blue eyes blinking rapidly behind rimless designer glasses. Bryce could tell she was faintly amused by his aversion to flying, so he focussed his mind on other matters instead.

'What's the latest from NASA?'

Ella fished inside her parka and produced her cell. She massaged the touch-screen with practised ease. 'Still no contact. They're saying it could be a software failure with the communications code package, either on the craft itself or at the deep space site in Mojave.'

'Poor bastards,' Bryce muttered, 'all that way and we don't even know if they survived the trip.' The thought put Bryce's own fear of flying into perspective. The first manned mission to one of Jupiter's moons, the three man crew rocketing through space in medically-induced comas, all contact with the tiny craft lost, the deadline for mission failure fast approaching. 'We'd better prepare something, just in case.'

'I've got Sam working on it.'

'Good. Anything else?'

Ella scrolled down the screen, flicking each line of news feed with a soberly painted fingernail. 'The storm is hogging the domestic headlines. Floods and wind damage down in Cornwall, channel crossings cancelled, blah blah. The usual pieces. Nothing else worth mentioning.'

Bryce grunted an acknowledgement. Their journey tonight had been a clandestine one, descending into the tunnels beneath Whitehall, their footsteps echoing along dimly lit subterranean chambers until they emerged into the pouring rain outside the old Admiralty building on the Mall. The car that idled by the pavement whisked them unescorted through the sparsely populated streets of Victoria and across the river to Battersea power station. In the shadow of the derelict structure the executive helicopter waited, rotors already turning. Within a few minutes Bryce could feel the strength of the approaching storm as the aircraft battled through the sky across west London. At least it was dark, he thought. He didn't care to see the towering wall of black clouds as they headed towards them.

'One minute,' announced the pilot over the intercom, and Bryce began to relax a little as the aircraft dropped lower and the turbulence subsided. Chain link fencing flashed beneath them, then a jumbled collection of flat rooftops. The nose of the helicopter tilted upwards as it flared for landing opposite a single storey building, cloaked in darkness and fronted by a tarmac apron. Bryce glimpsed a solitary figure sheltering beneath the overhanging canopy, then he was lost in a storm of spray as the aircraft settled onto the tarmac. The bodyguards were already unbuckling their belts and Bryce saw the tension in their faces, glimpsed the ugly black weapons concealed beneath their raincoats. There was a pause as the rotors wound down and Bryce saw the figure by the building head towards the helicopter, body bent over, the umbrella held like a shield against the weather.

The bodyguards piled out of the helicopter and stood guard on either side of the door, their eyes probing the night, raincoats flapping in the wind. Cold air rushed in, snatching the warmth of the cabin away as the man with the umbrella waited by the open door. His thin face had a well-worn look about it, the eyes sunk deep into their sockets, dark hollows under the cheekbones. The corduroy collar of his Barbour was turned up around his ears and a fine sheen of raindrops clung to its waxy surface. He held the umbrella aloft, his hands wrapped in black leather gloves, his eyes squinting against the rain. He had to shout to make himself heard.

'Welcome to Heathrow, Prime Minister. I'm Mike Davies, Chief of Operations.' He nodded to Ella. 'Miss Jackson. Follow me, please.'

Bryce stepped out of the aircraft. Silver sheets of rain swept across the tarmac, driven on by the relentless wind. He buttoned his coat to the neck and thrust his hands in his pockets, following Davies toward the unlit building where they huddled beneath the canopy. Overhead, one of its metal panels had worked loose and was banging a demented tattoo in the wind. Davies held open a filthy glass door and gestured them all inside. Bryce stamped his wet shoes on the floor, the sound echoing around the darkness. Should've worn something a bit sturdier, he realised.

Davies stooped to pick up a large flashlight by the door and swept its powerful beam around the immediate area. Bryce saw they were in a small terminal building, quite obviously abandoned. The place was devoid of furniture, the floor a mixture of cracked tiles and threadbare carpet, the walls sporting chipped and discoloured patches of paintwork where a myriad of signage once hung. Most of the external windows were boarded up, the surrounding walls heavily stained by water damage, the wind squeezing through the inevitable gaps and moaning through the building. Overhead, rain hammered on the roof and buckets lay scattered around the floor, catching the leaks from above. The place was to all intents and purposes derelict, an unused concrete shell located at the far edge of what was once the world's busiest airport.

'This is Security Station Four. It used to be the old VIP terminal,' explained Davies. 'We've had one or two snoopers since we opened for business but they never get further than the fences.'

Davies led them through the building, the sound of their footsteps competing with the wind, the cone of light bouncing in the darkness. They filed into a short corridor, at the end of which was a heavy looking grey door emblazoned with a black stick figure being zapped by a large bolt of electricity. The words beneath read: *Danger of Death – No Entry To Unauthorised Personnel.*

Davies tapped the sign and smiled. 'More subterfuge.' He produced a swipe card and waved it against a section of the wall close by. The door clicked. Davies placed a hand on it and pushed.

'Please follow me.'

'Wait here,' Bryce ordered the policemen. He ushered Ella through the door and closed it behind them. Another short corridor, this one lit by a single overhead strip light, the walls grey cinderblock. The smell of decay and damp was gone, replaced by warm air, a low electronic hum. Davies led them into a dimly lit corridor, a glass partition running along its length. Behind the glass was a high-tech control room, dozens of brightly lit monitors and coloured lights glowing in the darkness. Bryce estimated there were a dozen or so people scattered around the windowless walls, dressed in civilian clothes and monitoring banks of surveillance screens, the bright wash throwing their faces into stark relief.

'Don't worry, they can't see you,' Davies informed them. He tapped the glass with a knuckle as they headed toward another door at the end of the corridor. 'All this is one way. The operators in there are monitoring the accommodation areas on the old runways.'

Bryce watched the watchers as they filed past. He paused behind an operator and the first thing he noticed on the screen was the lack of activity, no doubt due to the late hour and the terrible weather. The camera angles were varied; most were high, some were low, some wide angled and others narrowly focused. There were interior shots of brightly-lit communal rooms and long, empty corridors with doors on either side stretching into the distance. There were night vision cameras in shades of ghostly green, probing dark and muddy alleyways and deserted open areas. Litter seemed a common feature in almost every shot, spilling out of plastic bins, piled in corners or tumbling through the barren dreamscape. A sudden movement caught Bryce's eye, a distant camera capturing a man ducking out of an accommodation block, a burqa-clad woman trailing behind him. The man unfurled a striped umbrella on the muddy steps of the block, then headed out into the night, stepping carefully around the puddles, making no attempt to share the shelter of the brolly with the woman behind him. She hurried after him obediently until they were out of sight.

'What a charmer,' observed Ella.

They followed Davies up a metal staircase to his first floor office, originally an observation deck the Operations Chief explained as he closed the door. A single desk occupied a space near the far wall, alongside two metal filing cabinets. The other walls were decorated with a multitude of large scale maps of the Heathrow site, except the wall that looked out over the runways. That one was made of a single sheet of glass and Bryce was drawn to it, Ella falling in beside him.

'Jesus,' she breathed, shaking off her coat.

'Indeed.'

It had been just over eighteen months since Bryce had last visited the site, almost two years since

Islamabad was destroyed by the nuke. Back then he'd given a short speech over at Terminal Five, emphasising the need for the countries of Europe to join together, to give aid and comfort to the refugees who'd travelled so far and suffered so terribly. Thirty prefabricated temporary accommodation blocks had been erected, clustered around the old taxiways and aircraft stands of terminal five, each housing two hundred people. He'd welcomed the new arrivals, drank coffee, posed for photographs and then returned to London, his duty done. It was supposed to be a temporary arrangement, a short term fix; considering the international pressure being brought to bear, the civil war in Pakistan was not expected to last this long. Yet it had, the violence spreading across the country, the refugees continuing to flee westwards, transiting through the Gulf States to Egypt where over two million people still languished in desert camps outside the cities. From his elevated vantage point Gabriel Bryce stared out across the expanse of Heathrow and shook his head; it was hard to imagine that an airport once existed here at all.

Beyond the waiting helicopter below, beyond the double chain link fence that surrounded the terminal building, the Heathrow Relocation Centre sprawled into the distance, a seemingly endless landscape of prefabricated flat rooftops marching toward the dark horizon. The two storey structures covered the disused runways, the aprons, the taxiways, the grass verges, crammed together into every available space. Halogen lamps clustered on steel towers glowed above the rooftops, rain sweeping through their bright shafts of light. The nearest accommodation blocks were five hundred yards away, curving into the distance in line with the well-lit perimeter fence. Rubbish piled against the chain link and strands of material fluttered in the wind, caught in the crown of razor wire that topped the fence. Distant lights glowed in the old terminal buildings.

Bryce turned away from the window, pulling off his overcoat. He was dressed casually, grey slacks and a black turtleneck sweater. 'Quite a sight when you see it up close,' he remarked.

Davies hung his coat on a stand behind the door. 'You should see it in the daytime. It's more like a city.' He took a seat behind his desk, inviting Bryce and Ella into empty chairs opposite.

'Looks deserted out there,' Bryce observed.

'Friday's a busy day for the population here. Prayers, followed by all sorts of meetings and sit downs. The main arrivals hall in Terminal Five is being used a mosque, as are the ones in the other terminals, plus there are several more scattered around the site. We've estimated they're cramming in between five and ten thousand in each of the main buildings, nose to socks.'

There was a tap on the door and an Asian man entered, a tray of coffee and biscuits held before him. He wore a navy Border Agency fleece zipped up to the chin, partly obscuring his wispy beard. He nodded politely while Davies cleared a space on his untidy desk and began pouring the coffee. Bryce shot a look at Ella as the man backed out of the room. Davies caught the exchange as he passed around the mugs.

'Don't worry, Taj is my right hand man, one of my senior interpreters. Very high clearance.' The security chief leaned back in his chair. 'Well, you can see the operation has grown immeasurably since you were last here. As I explained on the phone, we're struggling to cope.'

Bryce sipped at the steaming liquid as he registered the untidy mess of papers on Davies' desk. Behind him, a high spec printer beeped continuously, spitting out sheets of paper. 'I was aware of a certain level of pressure on resources here Mister Davies, but nothing like you described during our conversation.'

'The place is falling apart, Prime Minister. To all intents and purposes we've lost control.' Davies unlocked a desk drawer and removed a single sheet of paper. He handed it to Bryce. 'This is why I couldn't talk on the phone.'

Bryce gave Davies a puzzled look then began to read:

Originator: DAVIES, Michael, Chief of Operations, Border Agency, Heathrow Relocation Centre, Middlesex. CONFIDENTIAL SECURITY INCIDENT REVIEW – NOT FOR CIRCULATION - EYES ONLY.

12-01: 661/541 - Female stoned to death by large crowd of male assailants between blocks 227 & 228, sector 14.

11-02: 1025/445 - Two security officers seriously assaulted in sector 09 during routine patrol. Personal protection equipment, swipe cards and radios stolen.

29-03: 256/091 - Teenage girl doused with flammable liquid and set on fire outside maternity unit at Terminal 2. Three family members detained. Released due to lack of evidence.

27-05: 199/472 – Male killed during large disturbance at wedding ceremony in Terminal 4.

22-08: 088/190 – Two males found gagged, bound and hung in washroom in block 17, sector 3. Murdered by unknown assailants for alleged homosexual activities.

Bryce looked up, his face pale. 'These incidents happened here?'

Davies crunched on a biscuit and nodded. 'All in the last eight months. I assumed you knew because detailed reports of each incident were sent to both my own superiors and to Minister Saeed. He ordered a blanket censorship.'

Tariq.

Bryce held up the sheet of paper between his thumb and forefinger, as if the contents were somehow contagious. 'What about the suspects? The witnesses?'

'Some of the incidents were captured on CCTV but Minister Saeed had the footage seized. He promised an internal inquiry but it's yet to happen. The casualties have been explained away as accidents, suicides, that sort of thing.'

'He's covered this up?'

Davies hesitated. 'Well, that sort of accusation is above my pay grade, Prime Minister. However, I can tell you that Minister Saeed's office makes very little attempt to liaise with Operations these days unless it's to restrict our effectiveness in some way. I've raised concerns with my own chain of command but I've been told in no uncertain terms to shut up and crack on.'

Bryce handed the sheet of paper back to Davies. 'This is unacceptable.'

Davies locked the paper away and swept a hand towards the window. 'The simple truth is, out there beyond the wire the rule of law is an imported one. They have their own leadership hierarchy, operate a working Sharia court system, manage their own disputes, you name it. One by one our integration programs have been scrapped and my staff no longer patrol the accommodation blocks or any of the public areas.'

'Why?'

Davies looked pained. 'Minister Saeed believes our presence intimidates the refugees.'

Bryce got up and went to the window. Rain continued to lash the camp, urged on by the strengthening wind. The roof above creaked before its power but Bryce was oblivious to the fast approaching storm.

'You've spoken to the minister directly about your concerns?'

'I managed to get a moment with him a few weeks ago. He told me in no uncertain terms that the running of the camp must not be interfered with.' Davies leaned back in his chair. 'I'm not sure if you're aware of the influence he holds here, Prime Minister. He gave a speech in Terminal Five the other week. You could hear the roar of the crowd from here. It was more like a political rally.'

Bryce pointed to Davies' computer screen. 'Can you show me the footage?'

The security chief shook his head. 'All monitoring systems in the terminal buildings are disabled when Minister Saeed visits. Privacy issues.'

Bryce stared across the dark expanse of Heathrow. This was getting worse by the minute. 'You were right to contact me directly, Mister Davies.'

The Chief of Operations took a sip of coffee. 'There are other concerns, Prime Minister.' He put his mug down and began ticking them off on his fingers. 'We have a rising birth rate that our medical facilities cannot cope with, we're seeing disease outbreaks, we've got tribal and family disputes, many ending in some form of violence. And we're losing refugees too, a thousand in the last six months, just disappearing into the night. Some we pick up outside the wire, most we don't. I haven't got the resources to combat it.'

Bryce thought he'd misheard. 'Escaping?'

'Every day. We can't cope,' Davies admitted, holding up his hands.

Bryce was finding it hard to take it all in. Control of the site had been lost, that much was clear, and Tariq had allowed it to happen. Worse, he appeared to be actively encouraging it. Behind him, Davies took advantage of the Prime Minister's silence.

'It's like a separate country out there, a country of over one hundred thousand. And rising.' Davies lowered his voice and Bryce had to face him to hear what he said. 'The fact is, it doesn't feel like a humanitarian effort anymore. It feels more like a siege.'

'That's dangerous language, Mister Davies.'

The security chief didn't blink. 'It's the truth.'

Bryce turned back to the window. So, the monthly brief he'd been receiving from Tariq's office was deliberately evasive, a smoke screen to hide the true nature of what was happening here. But why? He marched back to his chair and pulled his coat on, helping Ella into hers.

'I want a detailed dossier on what you've just told me. Include everything Mister Davies; media files, departmental communications, minutes of meetings, the lot. I'm putting a stop to this shambles.'

Davies hesitated, his hands folded nervously on the table. 'You're shutting us down?'

Bryce nodded. 'That's why you contacted my office, isn't it?'

'Sir, with all due respect, I'll need some assurances. Being a whistleblower doesn't exactly look good on one's cv. I've got financial commitments, a pension to consider - '

Bryce cut him short, snapping the collar of his coat around his ears. 'You'll be taken care of Mister Davies, you have my word. It's your superiors who may be seeking new employment opportunities.'

Davies rose from behind his desk, clearly relieved. 'I appreciate that, sir.'

'As soon as possible, Mister Davies.'

Outside, helicopter rotor blades beat the air, whipping clouds of spray across the tarmac. Thirty seconds later they were airborne, the nose of the helicopter dipping as it cleared the boundary fence. As they climbed higher Bryce settled back in his seat. The whole relocation program was experiencing a fundamental breakdown and refugees were still arriving, hundreds every day. Bryce felt a mixture of emotions; anger, confusion - and a lingering sense of unease. Davies had painted a picture of growing lawlessness, coupled with a burgeoning cultural assertiveness that was given legitimacy by Tariq's deep involvement. *Murders,* for God's sake. Something had to be done.

Next to him Ella said, 'You're kidding, right? About shutting down the program?'

'Does it sound like I'm kidding?'

Ella's eyes widened behind her frames. 'You can't. Brussels won't allow it and besides, EU immigration laws prevent us from excluding members of extended families already settled here in Britain. We're legally bound to accept them. We'd be overruled Gabe, and the press will hang you out to dry.'

'To hell with the bloody press,' Bryce seethed. 'People have been killed back there, Ella. This is exactly the sort of ammunition I need to block Cairo.'

The Special Advisor's face paled in the dim cabin. 'You're *what?*'

'Look, if we can't deal with a few hundred thousand refugees, what d'you think will happen if we ratify Cairo?'

'Jesus, think about what you're saying, Gabe. You can't block it anyway,' she warned, 'you've already signed off on the framework document. The wheels are in motion. They're building the bloody stage as we speak, for Christ's sake. It's too late.'

'Without my signature the treaty is a no go,' Bryce reminded her.

'But we *need* that deal,' Ella stressed. 'Egypt is sitting on top of some of the biggest oil and gas fields the region has ever seen and they're practically giving it away compared to our existing deals with Russia and the Gulf states. Accession is a small price to pay in comparison. We have to be realistic, Gabe.'

Bryce's nostrils flared. 'It's not the prospect of Egypt joining the EU that bothers me; it's the millions of refugees they're trying to unload on the rest of us.'

'Oh, please. Now you're beginning to sound like your own hate mail.'

'Rubbish.' Bryce found it difficult to filter the frustration out of his voice. 'Look, we've already given leave to stay to over four hundred thousand refugees, plus the hundred thousand back there at Heathrow still waiting to be processed, and tonight we've discovered that the whole place is a complete and utter shambles. No,' he declared, chopping the air with his hand, 'there'll be no more refugees. And no treaty, not until we get our own house in order.'

Ella took a moment to remove her glasses, polishing the lenses with the cuff of her sweater. 'And when are you thinking of dropping this bombshell?' she finally asked.

'As soon as Davies delivers that dossier. A week, maybe two.'

Ella slipped the glasses back on her face. 'Gabe, you need to think about things very carefully. All this could play straight into the hands of the far right, not to mention the Opposition.'

'And what about the murders? The security breaches? If that gets out before we get a chance to denounce it we'll look even worse.'

'Maybe you should talk to Oliver first, before you take this any further.'

Oliver Massey, billionaire former party treasurer and major financial contributor, was an old friend of Bryce's and still held significant influence over party strategy. Bryce had impressed Massey as a young MP, the textile magnate subsequently funding Bryce's campaign for party leadership and later donating a large percentage of his election-winning war chest. He was a good friend, yet a distant one, a very private figure who preferred the sunnier climbs of the Caribbean than the wind swept shores of Britain. Looking out of the rain-streaked window, Bryce didn't blame him. Yet Massey was a believer, one still convinced that his old friend was the right man for the job.

'He's aware of my doubts about Cairo, and shares them. He's prepared to back me whatever decision I make.'

'But you just can't - '

'Enough,' scowled Bryce. 'I won't be swayed on this, Ella. Your job is to keep on top of Davies, make sure that dossier shores up my decision. We need to spin it aggressively so when we do go public people fully understand the scale of the problem.'

Ella stayed quiet, knowing better than to argue with him when he had the bit between his teeth. His premiership had been a tough one, born on the back of a serious economic downturn and a failing power infrastructure. Ella was right, the country needed Cairo, but at what price? Super-cheap energy would certainly boost the economy but if they couldn't control the expected influx of impoverished refugees then the whole exercise was pointless. And there were other, darker repercussions to consider. Violence had begun to sweep the country, a spate of attacks that bore all the hallmarks of religious intolerance; two churches burned down in Lancashire, Jewish cemeteries desecrated, the Israeli embassy in London firebombed. Bryce had ordered a media blackout in an effort to quash any subsequent escalation but the warning signals were clear. There could be no more refugees, no Treaty of Cairo, until the situation had been brought firmly under control. The country, and Brussels, would understand.

Ahead, the sparkling towers of London shimmered in the night as the helicopter began its descent. 'When does Tariq get back from Istanbul?'

'Next week.' Ella reached for her cell. 'You want me to pull him out of the conference now?'

Bryce shook his head. 'No. The Islamic Congress will kick up a stink if we yank one of their guest speakers.'

'So, how do you want to play this?'

'We keep it to ourselves,' Bryce ordered, 'just you, me and Davies. As soon as the dossier's ready we go public.'

Ella turned the cell over in her hand. It was a nervous gesture, Bryce knew. 'What about Cabinet? You'll have to brief them.'

'No. I can't afford any leaks on this one.'

'That's a risky game, Gabe.'

'I'll chance it. I'm fed up with off-the-record briefings making the front pages.'

'And Tariq?'

'Screw Tariq,' Bryce snapped. 'This whole mess could sink us thanks to that idiot. As soon as we've got that dossier Tariq is out. Finished.'

Below, the ghostly luminance of Battersea's chimneys swept into view as the helicopter circled the power station to land. Bryce unbuckled his seat belt as the aircraft settled on the glowing pad. It was only after he'd stepped out into the rain swept darkness, as he settled into the back seat of the waiting car, that he realised he hadn't noticed the turbulence of the return journey at all.

North London

The man slipped past the shaven-headed bouncer and yanked open the heavy wooden door, careful to grasp the worn metal handle with only two fingers. The door swung shut behind him and he wiped his fingers on the leg of his jeans. The Kings Head public house was, as expected, a shithole. Situated at the heart of the Longhill estate in north-west London, the single storey concrete block sported mesh-covered windows, graffiti-daubed walls and a chalk notice board that promised satellite TV and home-cooked meals. The only thing cooked around here was heroin, the man speculated. In any case, the Kings Head was a focal point of dubious entertainment for the residents who occupied the surrounding concrete towers, and it was here he'd find the man he sought.

The inside was gloomy, narrow windows set high around the walls, beaming thin shafts of milky daylight across the floor. The man clamped his cell phone to his ear, faking a conversation while his eyes adjusted to the shadows. The bar was directly in front of him, enveloped in a layer of blue smoke. Smoking laws were unenforceable here, a pointless and potentially dangerous exercise for any local official who might be bothered to try.

To his left, along a short corridor, a dimly lit pool room reached towards the rear of the building. More smoke swirled over the tables, a heady mix of tobacco and cannabis leaking along the corridor. Young men drifted in and out of the table lights, feral street roughs with pale chins jutting beneath baseball caps and hooded sweatshirts. Pool balls cracked noisily, the air punctuated by harsh laughter and coarse street talk.

The man looked away, careful not to make eye contact with the players. To his right several tables and chairs were clustered together, their occupants bathed in the light of a huge TV. A cry went up, cruel encouragement for the horses that galloped across its high-def surface. Gambling, alcohol, drugs; the blatant sins that surrounded him made his skin crawl.

He charted a course around scattered chairs and heavily stained tables and crossed the open floor to the bar, his trainers rasping noisily on its tacky surface. He was confronted by a lurid assortment of pump lights advertising cheap lagers and a steel shutter hung above the counter like a guillotine. He finished his bogus conversation and slipped the cell back into his pocket. The landlord, a flat-nosed rough with heavily tattooed arms, glanced up from his newspaper.

'Yeah?'

'Lager. Small one,' he said, pinching his finger and thumb together. The landlord swept a calloused hand across the chipped bar, its surface decorated with a dizzying pattern of moisture rings.

'Name your poison.'

The man selected the only brand he vaguely recognised. It wasn't the type of establishment to flash notes around so he paid with small change, counting out a few coins and dropping them into the landlord's outstretched hand.

'Like a bloody homeless shelter in 'ere,' he scowled, fingering the coins. A ripple of course laughter erupted from the cluster of punters, briefly smothering the drone of the racing commentator. It faded quickly as the horses headed toward the start line for the next race.

The man made no comment. He carried his lager over to a quiet corner and sat down, leaving the grumbling landlord in his wake. He unfurled a *Racing Post* from his pocket and stared uncomprehendingly at the form pages, sensing his presence had slid back into welcome obscurity. He sipped his drink, careful not to grimace at the foul taste.

Thirty minutes passed. The man relaxed a little more, confident he was now a part of this miserable landscape. A casual glance in his direction would confirm that he was just another of life's hard-luck stories, crushed by the system, his only solace a few cheap beers and an afternoon watching the races. Still, it paid to be vigilant. Observation was his tradecraft, a skill that had kept him alive through countless operations in Europe and beyond.

Ten more minutes passed. Another groan went up from the horse-fanciers. One punter made a scene of ripping up his betting slip and tossing the scraps into the air like confetti. He pushed his chair back and sauntered across to the bar. It was him the man decided, recognising the target from the surveillance photographs: Daniel Morris Whelan, thirty-eight years old, medium height, slim build, shoulder length brown hair, a faded St. George's cross in blue ink tattooed on his neck.

He watched carefully as Whelan chatted with the barman and took a lager back to the table. He sipped the foam head, watching the latest odds ticker-tape across the bottom of the screen, then headed across the floor to the toilets. It was time.

The man left his newspaper on the table and casually followed Whelan into the gents, careful to push the door open with his shoulder. It was a foul-smelling convenience, the walls an urban collage of graffiti and right-wing political stickers, the single toilet stall to his right blocked and caked with excrement. Flies hopped and flitted across a thin barred window high on the wall and water dripped noisily, the sound echoing off the once-white tiles. The smell was overpowering. He held his breath and moved past the toilet stall. Whelan was in the far corner, urinating freely, his body swaying slightly as the overflow from the urinal splashed around his worn sports shoes. The other two receptacles were filled with cigarette ends, tissue paper and gobbets of phlegm. He saw Whelan turn, saw him register his unwillingness to use the blocked facilities.

'Cleaner's on holiday again,' Whelan quipped. He zipped his fly and wandered over to the sinks, where a stainless-steel wall tile served as a mirror. He didn't wash his hands. Instead, he pulled a comb from the pocket of his jeans, scraping his long hair back off his forehead and smoothing it down with his other hand.

The man stepped gingerly across the puddled floor and unzipped his fly. 'Bloody disgusting,' he muttered with unrehearsed venom. He saw Whelan study him in the mirror, taking in the jeans and the old combat jacket, the black hair cut aggressively short.

'You new round here?' Whelan ventured.

'Not really,' the man replied, his urine splashing loudly. 'Met a mate just down the road, got me a bit of work. Just as well coz I need the money bad. I'm still on parole.'

He noticed Whelan's eyebrows arch with interest. 'Really? Where were you banged up?'

'Winchester. Fourteen months. Violent Disorder, GBH.'

'Oh yeah?' Whelan rinsed his comb under a tap and slipped it into his back pocket. 'Well, you're in good company. Lot of ex-cons round here.'

The man zipped his fly then stood at the sink next to Whelan. No soap of course, or hot water. He rubbed his hands vigorously under the cold tap.

'That's what you get when you defend your country, stand up for what's right. It's all wrong, mate.' He wrung his hands dry and leaned on the sink, hoping his outburst would have the desired effect.

'Where are you from? Originally?' Whelan asked. 'You look a bit...well, you know.'

'My dad's Italian. From Naples.' He swiped a hand across his stubble covered face.

'Italy, eh? Proud fascist history you've got over there. What's your name?'

'Sully.'

Whelan held out an unwashed hand. 'I'm Danny. Fancy a drink?'

They huddled together in a gloomy corner, away from the TV screen and the luckless punters. The table surface was cluttered with empty glasses. Whelan cleared a space and rolled a cigarette, carefully sprinkling a few shards of cannabis resin along its length. He fired it up, tilting his head and blowing out a long thin plume of smoke.

'Fourteen months, yeah? That's harsh.'

'Proper stitched up,' grumbled Sully. 'Long story short, this Pakistani firm was running gear on the estate, heroin mostly. That shocked me at first because they're Muslims. You know, supposed to be religious and that.'

'All part of the jihad,' Whelan observed, sucking on his cigarette. 'It's not just about bombs and bullets.'

Sully nodded, his meticulously rehearsed story flowing easily off his lips. 'Anyway, they got my mate's sister hooked on gear, pimping her out to minicab drivers and that. So me and Calum – that's my mate – we went round to the flat where she was staying with one of them. We knocked on the door, and I could see the geezer behind the glass, right?' Sully leapt to his feet, a muscular arm pitching forward. 'BANG!

I heaved a lump of concrete through the door, caught him right in the face. Next minute we're inside yeah, giving the fat bastard a good pasting...'

'Sweet.'

'...then two others come running out into the hallway, so Calum does both of 'em with the pepper spray.'

'Beautiful. Burn their fucking eyes out,' purred Whelan.

Sully's devilish grin faded and he went quiet. He slumped back down into his seat, deflated.

'That was it,' he said quietly. 'Police turned up, we got nicked. Didn't want to hear our side of the story, didn't give a monkey's about Calum's sister. Hate crime, pure and simple. Feet never touched the ground. Fourteen months, no early release.'

Whelan pinched the end of his cigarette, balancing it carefully on the lip of the ashtray. He leaned forward on the table, his eyes focussed and alert, despite the booze and drugs.

'A familiar tale, mate. Country's had it.' He waved a nicotine stained finger between them. 'See, the government don't give a shit about people like me and you, don't care about *real* English people. We don't fit in to their bullshit utopian experiment. That's why we've got to stick together, know what I mean?'

Whelan turned, and Sully followed his gaze. No one was paying any attention to them. Whelan smiled and rolled up the sleeve of his faded grey sweatshirt. 'Check that out,' he declared proudly.

The three lions *passant* were tattooed on the inside of Whelan's left bicep. Unlike the blue smudge on his neck this tattoo had been expertly drawn, the colours bold and vivid, the mediaeval lions a clear and exact representation of early English heraldry, the initials *EFM* in angular black type beneath.

'Jesus, that's beautiful,' breathed Sully. He looked up. 'English Freedom Movement, yeah? Hard core, you lot.'

'Used to be, before the ban,' Whelan sighed, rolling his sleeve back down. He lifted his glass and saluted a small shield sporting the same three lions fixed above the bar. Sully hadn't noticed it earlier, barely visible amongst the faded Union Jack bunting that ran across the dark wood panelling near the ceiling. He took another sip of lager and snorted self-consciously. 'There's me going on about my troubles and here I am, sitting with a proper patriot.'

Whelan smiled, clearly enjoying the respect Sully was showing. 'Don't worry about it. We all do our bit. You've spilt blood, done your bird. Me, I've had run-ins too.'

Sully nodded sympathetically. He already knew about Whelan's brushes with authority; dishonourable discharge from the British army for illegal possession of explosive materials, a drink-driving offence whilst employed by the civil service, public disorder fines for the distribution of offensive literature. The list wasn't the longest he'd seen but it contained the three essential ingredients; military service, explosives and connections to racist organisations.

'Don't matter what we do or say, government just does what it wants,' Sully moaned. 'Take Bryce, for instance...'

'Fucking traitor.'

'...letting all them refugees come over here, giving them benefits and houses. Hardly any of them work. Take a walk around Brent Cross mall these days and you'd think you're in Karachi or wherever. Even the Maccy D's has gone Halal.'

'You wait. When they sign that Cairo treaty the floodgates will really open,' Whelan complained. He drained his glass. 'Fancy another?'

Sully nodded. 'Why not.' He watched Whelan amble across to the bar, returning a minute later with two more glasses of foul lager in his fists.

'Sorted.' He sat down and raised his glass. 'Here's to England. What's left of it.'

Sully gingerly sipped his brew. 'Cheers.'

They lapsed into silence. Whelan shoved his glass aside and began rolling another cigarette. 'You said your mate got you some work. Doing what?"

'Nothing much,' Sully shrugged. He rummaged in the front pocket of his jeans and pulled out a scrap of paper. 'He works for an employment agency. They don't hire ex-cons but he sometimes gives me jobs off the books. I've only been out of nick for six weeks but he's already sorted me out a couple of times. All cash in hand.' Sully smoothed the paper out on the table. 'This is it, the number of a bloke who runs a refrigeration company. Wants me to make a delivery, big fridge or something.'

'Drive and drop? I used to do all that,' boasted Whelan, lifting the glass to his lips. 'What's it paying?'

'A thousand Euros.'

Whelan choked on his lager, coughing foamy droplets across the table. He cuffed his wet chin. 'For delivering a fridge?' he rasped. 'Jesus, that's a nice touch. Why so much?'

Sully shrugged. 'No idea. My mate reckons it's a tax dodge but so what? A grand's a nice chunk.'

'A right result,' agreed Whelan, clearing his throat. 'Your mate at the agency, is he looking for anyone else? I used to drive for the civil service, important documents, that sort of stuff. I drive trucks, too. Learned in the army.'

Sully smiled apologetically. 'Not really. Bit risky, being off the books an' all that. He only does it for me because we're old school mates. Sorry.'

'No probs,' Whelan shrugged, 'Don't ask, don't get, right? I've got a few things on the go anyway.'

'Good for you.' Sully rose from the table. 'Another drink?'

'Sweet,' Whelan grumbled.

'Alright. I'm off for a shit first. Back in five, yeah?'

Danny Whelan's bitterness bubbled to the surface as he watched Sully lope towards the toilet. Another door slammed in his face. Every time an opportunity came along to make some cash it disappeared quicker than a fart in the wind. The horses didn't help, or the dogs. They bled him dry, along with the lottery and a bit of puff. By the end of the week his welfare credits were gone, sucked back into the system that supported both him and his dad in their twelfth floor flat near the Kings Head. It wasn't his fault he had no money. He'd worked a bit, in the army of course, then the government job. He'd still be there if it wasn't for that piss up after work, followed by the breathalyzer on Chelsea Bridge Road Then there was his mouth, always getting him into trouble. No-one understood him, see? They didn't realise what was going on around them, the Third-Worlders pouring into the country, mosques everywhere, good people arrested for protesting and speaking their minds. No-one wanted to hire a trouble-maker. Fine. If he couldn't beat the system then he'd take from it, bleed it as much as he could. But those welfare credits only went so far.

He thought his luck would change when he joined the English Freedom Movement. It was a proud organisation, cared about the direction the country was headed. True, there were a few boneheads amongst them but mostly the Movement was made up of decent folk, those that wanted an end to immigration and Britain's membership of the EU, a return to traditional British values and way of life. Danny felt at home amongst its ranks, always attending the monthly meetings and helping out where he could; membership drives, leaflet campaigns, ferrying some of the older members down to the seaside in the summer. He'd even brought his dad along once, the change of scenery and bracing sea air doing the old man a world of good. And then, a few short months after he joined, they passed the Hate Crime legislation and the ban was imposed, declaring the English Freedom Movement an illegal organisation. Meetings were cancelled, its members scattered to the four winds under threat of prosecution and imprisonment. Danny was absolutely gutted.

Still, he enjoyed flashing his tattoo to anyone who showed the slightest interest, revelling in the notoriety. But what exactly had he got out of it? At its height the Movement was an impressive network of patriots who didn't want foreigners cutting their grass or painting their houses. For new members like Danny jobs were supposed to come flooding in, all cash, never a penny going to Whitehall or Brussels. The Movement was better than the Masons he'd been told, guaranteed to find work for their own. But now it was gone, over, and Danny was once again on his own, left to fend for himself. Typical.

Not like that lucky bastard Sully. Danny glanced towards the toilets. He was still in there, doing his business. He glanced at the paper with the phone number, the ticket to a thousand easy Euros pinned beneath the ashtray where Sully had stupidly left it. A thousand Euros. Who was this Sully anyway? He wasn't a local, just a jailbird with a friend in the right place. Danny used to be in the Movement; where were his friends? Where were his connections?

Danny's fingers hovered over the scrap of paper, his eyes flicking toward the toilet door. He gulped hard. What if Sully caught him nicking it? He was a big bloke, with rough hands and lumpy knuckles, a fighter's hands. His face was chiselled, the sinews in his neck like rope, the cold eyes black and piercing. He looked like a mafia henchman, would probably batter Danny without breaking sweat. If he caught him. Worst way Sully would just call his mate at the agency, cancel the job. Or not. A thousand Euros – even Danny would risk a kicking for that.

He shot another look at the toilets, scooped up the scrap of paper and headed quickly for the pub door.

Sully could barely breathe. Locked inside the toilet stall, it was all he could do to stop from gagging. He'd tried to flush the toilet clean but the pathetic trickle of water from the cistern barely touched the sides. He couldn't even look at it. He'd seen worse things; bodies blown apart, corpses riddled with bullet holes and stab wounds, frozen cadavers high in the mountains of Kurdistan, but this was different. This was supposed to be a civilised nation. How could people socialise in such filth? It beggared belief.

He glanced at his watch. Finally. Ten minutes had passed, surely enough for Whelan to have taken the bait. He exited the stall with some relief, washing his hands vigorously under the tap. He took a moment to compose himself, counted silently to ten, then walked out of the door. He crossed to the bar, glancing over his shoulder. Whelan was nowhere to be seen. He ordered a bag of peanuts and went back to the table, taking his time to leaf through the *Racing Post*. When he was certain Whelan was long gone he stood up and made his way outside, blinking in the daylight as he left the Kings Head in his wake.

He walked briskly through the rubbish-strewn alleyways and headed toward the small park that bordered the estate. He gave a wide berth to a gang of hooded youths baiting two vicious-looking dogs and cut through a stand of trees towards the main road. He headed north towards Wembley, dumping the combat jacket into a rubbish bin along the pavement. This wasn't a typical operation; the people he'd met today were locked into a depressing cycle of poverty and violence, critical of the state yet dependant on it for their meaningless existence. Whelan was different, a man who sought to bite the very hand that fed him. Despite the hateful rhetoric and the bitterness there was a quality there to be admired, a rebellious spirit that in another time and place could have been put to good use.

The car was where he'd left it, a Golf hybrid, parked in a supermarket car park over a mile from the Longhill. He climbed inside and rummaged in his pocket for the key, mindful of the security guards that patrolled the neat ranks of vehicles. He started the Golf's engine, slipped it into gear and pulled out onto the main road. He wrinkled his nose in disgust, the stink of the Kings Head still wrapped around him, the stale odour of alcohol and smoke clinging to his clothes. He powered down the window to get some fresh air, his fingers drumming the steering wheel as he crawled through the traffic. Now that the pieces were in play he felt excited at the thought of what was to come. There was much at stake; lives would be lost, many of them believers, but every jihad involved sacrifice, whether intentional or not. It was the way of things, from the earliest days.

And the cause this time was more righteous than any before it. The Minister had described it best; he'd likened Europe to a piece of fruit, ripened by the sun, dangling seductively from a thin branch.

Soon it would be picked.

Guildford, Surrey

His close protection officers kept a discreet distance as Bryce approached the grave, easily distinguishable from its moss-covered neighbours by the glint of white marble and a colourful splash of flowers. Still fresh, noted Bryce. That would be Jules, Lizzie's green-fingered sister who lived a few miles from the cemetery just outside Guildford. He never brought flowers himself, mindful of Lizzie's hay fever and the discomfort it brought her. Jules was a decent woman but Bryce had never really clicked with the rest of her family, the pressures of his work and their strong Conservative values denying them the common ground that neither party had really sought.

Lizzie was different, the rebel of the clan, a political science student when they'd first met at Cambridge. The relationship had quickly blossomed into something more serious, the firebrand socialist and the daughter of a Tory Peer proving to be a real power-couple at Emmanuel College. Marriage followed shortly afterwards, the joy of their union tempered by the revelation of Lizzie's inability to conceive. She'd made up for the disappointment by enthusiastically supporting her husband through his career, from junior political analyst to head of the party's Policy Unit, after which he was elected to parliament for the Wiltshire seat of Swindon North. She never saw him enter Number Ten, the cancer that killed her discovered during a routine doctor's appointment less than eight months before the general election. The cruelties of fate; not God's will, as some of Bryce's friends had suggested, reasoning that a divine hand had other plans for the only woman he'd ever truly loved. Bryce believed that any God wouldn't be that cruel.

He squatted down and tidied the grave carefully, brushing away the twigs and fingering the wet leaf mulch from the inscriptions on the smooth white slab. The marble was cold to the touch, a sensation that Bryce always found mildly unsettling, a reminder of the frozen eternity of death, of the pale bones that lay a few feet beneath his fingers. His withdrew his hand and stood, his knees cracking painfully in protest. He took a few steps and sat down on a nearby bench, pulling his overcoat tightly around him and thrusting his hands deep into its pockets. At either end of the row his security people watched from behind dark glasses, ready to turn others away, selfishly guarding Bryce's quiet contemplation. Lately it was making him feel guilty, denying others access to their loved ones' final resting place. During his first visits he couldn't have cared less if the queue went twice around the cemetery, consumed as he was by grief. Yet now, as the years passed, he had become sensitive to the inconvenience his security arrangements inflicted on others.

As if on cue he saw an elderly lady turned away by one of his bodyguards. She was a small, sad looking woman wrapped inside a pale green overcoat, grey hair spilling out from beneath a matching woollen hat. Bryce watched her through guilty eyes as she shuffled a few yards away, a posy of flowers clutched to her chest, a large handbag dangling from a bony hand, as she waited patiently for Bryce to finish. He winced with embarrassment.

Despite the cold it was a beautiful day. A late September sun shone in the sky, a cobalt-blue dome that stretched from horizon to horizon, randomly dotted with tiny cotton-wool clouds. Closer to earth, birds flitted across an untidy mix of tilting headstones and cheerless stone angels, and dead leaves tumbled and scraped along the path, piling around his feet before scattering on a gusting breeze. It was only on days like these that Bryce visited, days when the sun shone. It was a poor excuse for his less than regular visitations but he truly hated winter here, the cemetery ringed by lifeless trees, damp soil under leaden skies, the depressing Victorian spectacle of organised bereavement. How he wished that Lizzie's family had opted for cremation.

He glanced toward the old woman again. Still she waited. He waved at the bodyguard to let her through, after which she had to suffer the indignity of having her bag searched. Bryce watched her as she walked stiffly towards a nearby grave, changing the flowers that wilted in a small vase. The memorial was a basic arrangement, a simple weather beaten headstone, a border of white gravel littered with dead leaves. A small Union Jack planted at the base trembled in the breeze, and a photograph in a silver frame lay propped against the stone, the soldier's proud pose faded by time and the elements. Bryce nodded politely to the woman and looked away.

The graves marched down the hill in solemn ranks toward a distant line of poplars that bordered the cemetery. Dozens more flags caught his eye, adorning the headstones of soldiers killed in the meat grinder that was Afghanistan. He shivered, burying his chin deep inside the cashmere folds of his overcoat.

And what had it all been for anyway? Despite the continued presence of the United Nations the Afghanis had returned to their feudal existence, the Mullahs once again ruling from the ruins of Kabul, the provinces carved up amongst the warlords, the poppy fields thriving. And the drugs continued to pour into the west, an unstoppable tide of misery that plagued Europe in ever more inventive chemical manifestations. It was just one more problem to be tackled, a growing list that was rapidly piling up outside Bryce's door. A drum began to beat behind his forehead and Bryce pinched the bridge of his nose to stem the growing headache.

He stared at Lizzie's headstone and whispered: 'Where are you when I need you, love?' She never answered of course. Lizzie had been dead for over four years now, and in truth she'd been his only real friend, a true companion. She was always at his side, beautiful, smart as hell, a pressure valve when things got tough. Bryce often joked that she should of been PM instead of him, but now there was no-one to laugh with, no-one to confide in, to lay down by his side. He was leader of a nation of seventy million inhabitants, surrounded by advisors, ministers and bodyguards – and yet he was alone. He still wasn't ready to meet anyone else, to endure the awkward first dates, to discuss Lizzie with another woman, to live with the guilt of never visiting this bleak cemetery again. It still seemed too soon.

He glanced to his right where the woman sat on the next bench, handbag resting on her lap. Bryce got to his feet and approached her, hovering a short distance away. The woman turned, raising a hand to shade her eyes from the bright sunlight.

'Good morning.' Bryce gestured to the bench. 'Do you mind?'

'Please,' the woman replied, inching further along.

She was well-spoken, in that bland, Home Counties way and subconsciously Bryce pegged her as a probable Tory. He perched himself on the edge of the bench and extended his hand. 'Gabriel Bryce.'

She took it, her hand dainty in his, her grip surprisingly firm. 'I know who you are,' she said. She didn't offer her own name, which Bryce regarded as loose confirmation of her political loyalties. She was also unfazed by his company, which was a rare experience for the Prime Minister. He didn't normally meet random members of the public and when he did they were carefully screened supporters or party members, sycophants in the main, the type of people who would queue for hours just to shake his hand or have their picture taken with him. This woman wasn't like that, and neither did she seem as old as she'd first appeared. Her skin, though lined with age, was coloured a healthy pink by the sharp air, her brown eyes bright and intelligent. Perhaps it was bereavement that had aged her, knowing the debilitating effect that loss can have on a person's health. Her clothing was smart but old fashioned, the woollen coat and knitted hat neither waterproof nor insulated against the cold. Bryce guessed she was in her sixties.

He indicted the nearby headstone. 'Your son?'

'Gavin. An only child.' The smile never made it to her eyes, Bryce noticed. 'He'd be in his thirties now.'

The faded picture propped against the cold stone showed a young man wearing full dress uniform, his back ram rod straight, his hands placed stiffly on his knees, chin tilted upward towards the camera. His face was frozen in that serious boy soldier expression, pride and vulnerability all in one, his eyes barely visible beneath the gleaming peak of his service cap. Bryce said: 'Afghanistan?'

The woman nodded. 'Part of the peacekeeping mission. Such a waste, all those lives, don't you think? You know, it still pains me to see world leaders fawning all over those Taliban creatures. Such a betrayal.'

Bryce felt a little uncomfortable, recalling last year's visit to Downing Street by the robed and turbaned delegation from the Islamic Emirate of Afghanistan. 'I know it sounds harsh, but that's the reality of politics, madam. Every conflict ends with dialogue and compromise, if only to prevent more loss of life.'

The woman sniffed, sitting a little straighter on the bench. 'I'm not a fool, Mister Bryce, I understand the way the world works. I just don't think it was worth losing my boy over. Any of those boys.' She nodded toward her son's grave. 'His best friend Miles ended up in a hospital near Birmingham, one of those ghost wards for veterans. It sounds like a terrible thing to say but I'd rather Gavin be here, in his grave, than rotting in one of those godforsaken institutions.' She turned and fixed Bryce with a cold stare. 'You really should do something about them, you know. Disgusting places.'

Bryce knew about the ghost wards, where damaged and distressed servicemen and women lived out their days in NHS isolation units dotted around the country. The spectres that roamed their halls had been long forgotten by the media and quietly ignored by politicians, any political capital to be gained from their recognition spent long ago. Bryce himself had never visited one.

Before he could muster a suitable response the cell in his pocket began to vibrate. 'Excuse me.' He glanced at the screen, then up the hill towards the cemetery access road where Ella stood watching him. She held up her arm and tapped her wrist. Bryce waved and got to his feet.

'Time I was going,' he announced. 'Pressures of work and all that.'

The woman looked away. 'Of course.'

'I'm sorry for your loss.'

'And I for yours,' said the woman, and Bryce thought she meant it. He'd only taken a few steps when her voice called after him: 'Do you despise this country, Mister Bryce?'

He stopped and turned around. 'Excuse me?'

'Our culture, our values. Do you despise them? If you intend to sign that Cairo treaty then you must.'

Bryce offered a confused smile. 'Why do you say that?'

'Because it's the truth.' The woman nodded towards her son's grave. 'That's a temporary headstone, the second this year. The others were smashed, Gavin's picture torn up, the flags trampled on. I'm not the only one.' She waved a hand around the cemetery. 'Most of the other soldiers' graves have been vandalised too, and the Jewish ones. The police say its kids but everyone knows it's not.'

Bryce shrugged his shoulders. 'I'm afraid I don't have - '

'Jihad, Mister Bryce. That's right, and I don't mind saying it, although most people are either too blind or too stupid to see it. Our cities are changing every day, slowly but surely, and Cairo will be the final nail in the coffin.' The woman regarded Bryce for a moment, then said: 'I've offended your socialist sensibilities, haven't I? It's interesting, without your teleprompters and prepared speeches you people are lost for words. Is it because you know I'm right, Mister Bryce?'

It was strange to hear such uncomfortable language from a respectable looking woman but despite that, her words resonated with him. He remained silent as she produced a tissue from the sleeve of her coat and dabbed at her nose.

'Politicians always make the mistake of confusing opinions with facts, and facts can be so politically inconvenient, can't they? It's no wonder people are leaving.'

'Leaving?'

'Yes, leaving. Emigrating.' Her sharp eyes narrowed as she studied his face. 'Don't insult my intelligence, Mister Bryce. We've all seen the queues outside the embassies in London. Two families in our village have already gone. It seems everyone knows somebody who's left, or is thinking of leaving. People are fearful of the future here, that's why they're moving away.' She nodded toward her son's headstone. 'I'd go myself but I can't leave my boy.'

In fact, the figure for last year's émigrés was five hundred and seventy two thousand, Bryce recalled, but who knew if those were all migrants or holiday makers or others simply returning to the land of their birth. The system had stopped recording the details decades ago.

'I wouldn't believe everything you read,' he lied. Next to him the woman's face flushed, her heavily veined hands twisting the straps of her handbag.

'Don't patronise me, Mister Bryce. Those two million refugees camped in the Egyptian desert will have the right to become EU citizens if that terrible treaty is signed and we both know where most of them will be headed.'

'Well, that's not strictly - '

'And why won't the Arab nations or Turkey take them? It's always us, isn't it? I'm a Christian, Mister Bryce. I believe in charity, in helping those less fortunate than ourselves, but the system won't be able to cope with so many people. If you sign that treaty it will mark the beginning of the end.'

Her eyes bored into him, her lower lip trembling. Bryce could feel her anger and was momentarily lost for words. It had been a long time since he'd encountered such animosity from a member of the public, certainly not since his days as a young MP, door knocking around shabby council estates. He glanced again towards the grave she visited, her only child, lying dead beneath her feet all these years. Was it any wonder she was bitter?

'These are complex issues, Madam.'

The woman chuckled without humour. 'Yes, of course, silly me. How could I possibly understand them?' She got up from the bench and took a few steps to her son's grave, kissing her finger tips and laying them gently on the headstone. 'And besides,' she said, stepping back onto the path, 'I'm just a law abiding taxpayer whose family has lived here for centuries. On what planet would someone like you ever have the interests of someone like me at heart?' Before Bryce could reply the woman said, 'Good day, Mister Bryce,' and turned away.

A minute later Ella appeared at his side, jabbering away into her cell headset, the wind whipping at her hair, at the faux fur collar of her beige overcoat.

'Who was that?' she asked, following his gaze.

'Nobody.' Bryce watched the woman as she departed, the sound of her footsteps snatched away on the freshening breeze. He could feel Ella's eyes on him. 'What?'

'Are you alright, Gabe?'

'Of course. Why'd you ask?'

Ella shrugged her shoulders. 'Nothing. You look a bit pale, that's all. Tired.'

'What do you expect in this bloody job.' The woman was distant now, a small figure glimpsed between the landscape of headstones. Then she was gone. Bryce sighed. 'Let's go.'

The sleek ministerial convoy waited along the access road, engines purring quietly, exhaust plumes condensing on the cold air. Doors swung open as Bryce approached, and sharp eyed men in bulky overcoats scanned the terrain for trouble. He was about to duck inside his BMW limousine when he heard a faint chant carried on the wind. A large group of people had gathered at the main gates of the cemetery, placards held high. Black-clad policemen in riot gear lined the road, herding them towards the opposite pavement.

'Who are they?'

'Students mostly, plus a sprinkling of pro-refugee supporters,' explained Ella. 'They arrived a little while ago in a coach. There's about forty of them, well organised, a camera crew, nicely printed placards etcetera. Someone must've tipped them off that you were here.'

'No bloody privacy anymore,' Bryce fumed. He ushered Ella inside the BMW, a bodyguard closing the door behind him. He was glad to be out of the cold, embraced once more by the heated interior and the soft leather. He wriggled out of his overcoat as Ella keyed a button and raised the central glass partition, sealing the rear passenger compartment with a soft *thunk.*

'I've issued a D-Notice,' she announced, snatching the ear piece from her head. She winced as she caught several strands of hair in its rubbery hook. 'Ow! Stupid thing. Anyway, they can't use any footage of you at Lizzie's grave or otherwise.'

'Good.' Bryce watched the Range Rover ahead move off, then the smooth power of the BMW kicked in as it accelerated after it. They approached the main gates at speed, the ranks of headstones on either side a grey blur, the faces of the curious flashing by. Then the BMW was through the gates, turning past the police motorcyclists that blocked the road, past the chants of the protestors, most of them hidden from view behind a line of police vans, their screaming placards dancing an angry jig above the roofs - *No More Borders! Justice for Refugees! Yes to Cairo!*

'You think they know something's in the wind?'

'Not a chance,' Ella replied. 'If they did there'd be thousands of them.'

Ten minutes later the convoy curled up the slip road and onto the A3 motorway towards London. Bryce settled into his seat, the BMW's passage almost soundless in the Kevlar-cocooned interior. He stared out of the window, watching the traffic flash by as the convoy ate up the miles towards the capital.

'Tell me about tomorrow.'

'The press conference is scheduled for five-forty five,' Ella informed him, 'followed by the Cabinet meeting at six-fifteen. I've laid on a few extra bodies for the communications office too. We're bound to get swamped afterwards.'

'Fine.'

Ella paused, toying with the cell in her hand. 'There's still time, Gabe. We can justify the Heathrow suspension but stopping Cairo is going to be a bloody hard sell. If you brief Cabinet beforehand they'll be more inclined to support your decision. Cutting them out of the loop like this will just piss them off.'

Bryce shook his head. 'My mind's made up, Ella. This way the Heathrow dossier will have maximum impact, both here and in Brussels.'

'It's risky. I'm getting a ton of calls already, demanding to know what the press conference is about. There's a lot of frustration out there.'

'Stall them. Once we go public they'll understand.'

Ella glanced at the back of the driver's head, at the bodyguard next to him. Despite the soundproofed partition she lowered her voice. 'Have you thought about the repercussions, Gabe? I mean *really* thought about them?'

Bryce exhaled noisily. 'Don't patronise me, Ella. I've thought of nothing else this past week.'

'Because DuPont is going to go absolutely ballistic when this breaks. The other leaders will too. We're not the only ones who need that gas and oil. Most of Europe's economies are depending on it.'

'I know that,' Bryce snapped. He took a breath. 'Look, all we're talking about here is suspending the treaty, not scrapping it. We need assurances, that's all. Guarantees. Same applies to the relocation program.' Bryce was silent for a moment, then he turned and said: 'What about Tariq?'

His Special Advisor tapped her cell. 'I've scheduled five minutes in your office just before the press conference.'

'It won't take that long.'

Ella frowned. 'Strange, he's barely been seen since he returned from Istanbul. Even Rana's being cagey about his movements.'

'She's covering,' Bryce said. 'Anyway, it's irrelevant. Tariq's history.'

Outside, a police motorcycle outrider shot past the car, square jaw jutting beneath his black visor. 'The next few weeks are going to be hell,' Ella muttered.

Bryce reached over and gave her arm a reassuring squeeze. 'Don't worry, we're doing the right thing. Tomorrow is about hard choices, plain and simple, and it's my job to make those choices. It's why people voted for us.'

Ella looked away. 'I hope to God you're right Gabe, I really do.'

Bryce saw her reflection in the glass and knew she was worried. Privately he was too, but what other options did he have?

The convoy continued northwards, the outriders carving a path through the afternoon traffic. Bryce took advantage of the silence, staring out of the window as he contemplated firing his Communities minister. Tariq had once been a trusted comrade, rallying Britain's burgeoning Muslim community behind Bryce's election campaign, earning his place in Cabinet with his intelligence and unswerving loyalty, a dependable mouthpiece both at home and in Brussels. He was passionate, a team player, and yet there had certainly been a cooling of their relationship in recent months, Tariq distancing himself from the intimacy of their ideological bonds, succumbing instead to the growing power of the Islamic Congress of Europe, aligning himself with pro-Cairo factions in the European parliament. It was understandable; Tariq was seen as the major conduit of Islamic influence and opinion in Bryce's government and Bryce had encouraged it for his own political purposes, yet somehow it had led to the debacle at Heathrow. Despite the betrayal he would miss Tariq's counsel and powerful cultural influence. A hard man to replace, indeed. Something else he had to work on.

Outside, the green fields of Surrey yielded to the urban sprawl of the south London suburbs. Rain drops tapped the window, slithering across the thick glass like tiny tadpoles of mercury. He thought of the woman back at the cemetery, her bitter words, her warning about Cairo. Wherever she'd got her information from, and Bryce guessed it was from an uncensored blog somewhere, her facts were essentially correct; the treaty had to be stopped. The problem would be, for how long?

Sirens wailed as the convoy slowed and the traffic became heavier. Bryce looked beyond the warehouses, beyond the industrial units and the suburban rooftops that lined the motorway to where the sky met the earth.

In the distance, far to the east, storm clouds gathered on the horizon.

Luton

Thirty four miles to the north, Danny Whelan swung the wheel of the truck in a tight arc across the car park then stamped heavily on the brakes. He crunched the gear lever into reverse, the warning signal beeping loudly, and backed the vehicle smartly towards the covered loading bay. He watched his wing mirror carefully, as one of the mosque staff waved him backwards. *A loading bay! Jesus, how big was this place?* Too big, he decided. Still, he had a job to do.

The truck was where the bloke on the phone had said it would be, an unmarked white Ford Cargo parked on the edge of an industrial estate near Kings Cross station. Danny had arrived by pushbike, unwilling to use the CCTV saturated London transport network. The estate was deserted, the surrounding business units barred and shuttered, the morning sun still loitering beyond the horizon. He waited in the shadows for a minute or two, half expecting to see an enraged Sully pacing around the truck, waiting for Danny to show up and give him a beating. But there was no Sully, no one around at all, and Danny was relieved, if not a little surprised. After all he'd stolen the job from under Sully's nose and yet no one seemed to be bothered, not Sully, his mate at the agency nor the bloke on the phone. Strange. Danny dismissed the thought; who cared, as long as he got paid, right?

He locked his bike against a railing, found the keys behind the fuel tank and climbed into the cab, still thinking the whole deal was a bit suspect. His doubts were soon laid to rest when he saw the money, ten crisp one hundred Euro notes tucked inside an envelope in the glove box. Danny's heart sank when he inspected the paperwork - *a mosque?* – and he was half tempted to take the money and piss off, but common sense got the better of him. If he played his cards right this could be the start of a regular gig and besides, all he had to do was deliver a fridge to a mosque. As long as no-one found out, so what?

Danny didn't really think about it on the journey north, humming away to the radio as the truck rumbled along the M1. It was only when he turned off the motorway and saw the distant gold dome dominating the skyline that his mood changed. The Luton Central Mosque was huge, almost as big as the one being built in the east end of London. Danny remembered complaining about that one, an afternoon of drunk-dialling Stratford council to voice his protest. Every leftie do-gooder he spoke to was full of praise for it, talking about serving the needs of a diverse community, the celebration of different faiths and all their other bullshit. What about my community? Danny had raged from inside the public phone booth, what about our needs? As usual he was threatened with prosecution, heard the tell tale clicks on the line as the conversation was recorded and the trace begun. Opinions weren't allowed anymore; the Thought Police were always watching, always listening. Bastards.

He engaged the hand brake with another sharp hiss of compressed air and jumped down from the cab, slamming the door behind him. The loading bay was situated at rear of the building, set deep in the shadow of the mosque walls. Danny's eyes were drawn upwards to the roof. There, gleaming in the afternoon sun, the golden dome thrust upwards into the sky, visible for miles around as it rose above the surrounding suburbs. For a moment Danny just stood there, quietly impressed by the sheer scale of the construction.

He vaguely remembered something about it on the news, Bryce and his entourage of flunkeys padding around in their socks, waffling on about its importance in the community, blah-blah, bullshit, bullshit. He also remembered the Prime Minister's female staff, forced to wait outside in the rain, polite smiles fixed on their faces while inside they seethed at the insult to their feminist sensibilities. Fucking hypocrites. But there was no doubt about it, the Luton mosque was big, could probably hold thousands of worshippers. And as buildings went, Danny grudgingly admitted that it was an impressive sight. Not beautiful or anything, not like St. Pauls or Westminster Abbey, but it had lots of marble columns and arches and skinny little windows. And CCTV cameras, he noticed.

He clambered up onto the concrete loading bay, dusting off his jeans as the mosque worker in a white robe stepped forward, hand outstretched.

'My name is Imran. You have paperwork?'

Danny pulled an untidy collection of printouts from his back pocket and handed them over.

'It's all there, bruv. Delivery note, itemised bill, the lot.' He scraped his long hair back and removed a self-rolled cigarette from behind his ear. It had just a little touch in it, enough to give him a buzz, but not enough to get him nicked. He fumbled for a lighter until he realised Imran, or whatever his name was, was staring at him.

'Smoking is forbidden.'

Danny removed the cigarette from his lips and replaced it behind his ear. *Taking the piss,* he sulked. Normally he wouldn't swallow shit from someone like him but he needed this job to go smooth and besides, the bloke was a big lump. Head like a coconut, shovels for hands and a wide set of shoulders straining at the stupid dress he was wearing. Best not to wind him up.

Imran pointed at the truck. 'Open, please.'

Danny poked a fat green button and a battered metal tailgate lowered itself onto the loading bay with a loud hydraulic whine. He squatted down and unhooked the latch. With a grunt of effort, he heaved the shutter door upwards and stepped back.

'There you go, Abdul,' Danny smiled, pointing at the chest freezer strapped to the side of the truck's interior. 'One refrigeration unit. It's all yours.'

It was big, woven in clear plastic shrink-wrapping like a giant insect cocooned in a spider's web. Danny was glad he didn't have to shift the thing himself. It was already loaded when he picked up the truck in Kings Cross but he'd definitely enjoy watching this miserable twat struggle with it.

Imran glanced at the unit and sighed heavily. He turned to Danny. 'Very big, yes? Please, you help? No-one here.' He waved an arm around the deserted loading bay.

Danny glanced at the cars parked in the reserved spaces nearby. A Mercedes MPV, an Audi, couple of big four-by-fours; someone was here all right, they just didn't want to get their paws dirty. Well screw it, he needed the money more than the grief. Danny forced another smile.

'No sweat, Abdul.'

Inside the truck he released the restraining straps and manoeuvred the unit towards the tailgate, relieved the thing was on wheels. Even so it was heavy, and Danny thought that a little strange. After all, fridges were normally pretty light, only the compressor units giving your average fridge a bit of weight. But this unit felt different. Abdul watched him as Danny struggled to manoeuvre the wheels over the lip of the tailgate. Lazy bastard. He braced his arms and pushed with all of his strength.

'Whoa! Watch your toes!' warned Danny belatedly as he shoved the unit hard over the tailgate and onto the loading bay. Imran saw it coming and stepped deftly out of the way. 'Really takes off when you get your weight behind it, eh?'

Imran said nothing, steering the front end towards a set of large double doors. Despite himself, Danny was intrigued. He'd never been inside a mosque and he wasn't sure what to expect. He knew there was a main hall where everyone knelt down and prayed, that much he'd seen on the TV. *Oops, someone's dropped a contact lens,* was his favourite joke, though no-one seemed to laugh at that one anymore. Still, it'd be something to tell the others down the King's Head. On second thoughts maybe he wouldn't. You never knew if -

'Stop!' barked Imran as they crossed the threshold. He pointed at Danny's white Adidas trainers. 'Please remove. Forbidden.'

'Yeah, yeah,' moaned Danny, hopping around on each leg as he slipped off his trainers, his socks making damp footprints on the concrete. He placed his shoes on the tailgate then glanced up, straight into the lens of a CCTV camera. I get it, he realised, the rest of 'em are up in the office, laughing their beards off at the stupid Infidel. And I bet old Abdul speaks fluent English too. Mugging me right off.

'Keep me socks on, can I?' he moaned sarcastically. He'd been stitched up, sure, but he kept his mind focussed on the money and together they steered the unit inside. Danny's head swivelled left and right as they rumbled along the corridor, stealing a glance inside the rooms along the way. They passed a large kitchen, deserted, only the cold light of a fly-catcher filling the room with its electric blue glow. Further along they passed a bare storeroom, empty shelving fixed to its walls. In fact, the place had an air of desertion about it, Danny realised. The corridor was devoid of life and quiet, almost silent, like a proper church. Just ahead, Imran held up his arm and called a halt. Danny straightened up.

'I think I've slipped a bloody disc,' he complained, rubbing the small of his back.

The big Muslim ignored his banter. 'In here,' he commanded.

Danny sighed and swung his end around, wheeling the unit carefully around the doorframe into another storeroom. This one was also empty.

Imran held a finger to his lips. 'Quiet. Prayers,' he whispered, pointing at the wall. Danny listened carefully. He could hear it now, the low drone of voices coming from the other side of the grey cinderblock partition. Must be the main prayer hall. He could imagine them all in there now, arses in the air, bobbing up and down like a load of brainwashed robots. He lined the unit up along the wall then dusted off his hands.

'There you go, Abdul. All sorted.' He made a move for the door then looked down, puzzled. 'Hang on, you've got a problem here. There's no power along that wall.' He pulled the unit away from the cinderblock and crouched down. Nothing. Then he studied the unit itself, running his hands over the thick plastic. 'That's weird. Doesn't seem to be a power cable.'

Imran waved Danny towards the door. 'No problem. Come.'

Intrigued, Danny continued his search, dropping to his knees and peering beneath the unit. 'No compressors either. Why's it so heavy then?'

He straightened up and studied the other walls. 'You got no sockets in here at all. How you going to juice the thing up?'

'You are fridge expert?' Imran hissed. He held out a thick arm and ushered Danny out of the room. 'Leave it, we fix later.'

Danny shrugged. 'Whatever, bruv. Just trying to help, yeah?' He wasn't about to break into a sweat over this idiot. Besides, the job had been done and now he just wanted out of the place. Back in the corridor his finger scribbled on the air. 'Just need your autograph now, Abdul. You've got the paperwork, remember?'

'Wait here.'

Imran veered away and entered a room on the other side of the corridor. Danny took a step towards the door and looked through the small glass window. Abdul was hunched over a desk, scribbling on his paperwork while another couple of beardies were packing several large crates with files and computer stuff. Across the room, someone else was clearing out a book shelf. Abdul's face filled the window and the door swung open. Danny stepped back, a wry grin on his face.

'Moving out already?' he teased. 'What's up, Abdul? Not paid the rent?'

For a big bloke he moved bloody fast, Danny later recalled. A large hand shot out and grabbed his shirt, pulling him tight to the big man's barrel chest. The other shoved the signed invoice roughly into his shirt pocket. Danny recoiled as Abdul's hot breath wafted in his face, the stench of garlic and onion filling his nostrils.

'My name is Imran. *Im-ran,*' he growled. He shoved Danny away, then waved his hand dismissively. 'Take truck and go.'

Crimson faced, Danny swivelled on his stockinged feet and marched out to the loading bay. He fumbled with his trainers, cursing under his breath as he squeezed them on. He tried to fasten his crumpled shirt until he realised two of the buttons were missing. Taking a deep breath and summoning up as much dignity as his boiling emotions would allow, Danny hopped down from the loading bay and climbed behind the wheel of the truck. Thirty seconds later he was steering the vehicle beyond the gates of the mosque and out onto the main road, deliberately forcing a minibus full of worshippers to swerve out of his way.

Fat bastard, he raged silently, laying his filthy paws on me. He breathed heavily, his thin face still flushed with anger as he gunned the truck through busy traffic. He gripped the steering wheel hard as he imagined his bloodied fists pummelling Abdul's face, raining blow after blow as the bastard pleaded for mercy through split lips and broken teeth. No-one messes with Danny Whelan.

But deep down, Danny knew that was all it'd ever be, a violent fantasy. He wasn't like the other blokes, the hard core ones who went looking for trouble, orchestrating violence against ethnic gangs and left wing rent-a-mobs. Even in his youth he wasn't much of a fighter, more of a periphery sort of geezer, someone who got in a few boots after the others had taken the victim down. Like a jackal, in one of them wildlife programs he liked so much.

Coward, his inner voice mocked. And it was true. Danny knew blokes who would've cracked Abdul the minute he got stroppy, the sort of people who would never back down, even if it meant ending up in intensive care. There were some like that in the army, a couple in the Kings Head, rough fuckers with short fuses, always ready to take offence, even quicker to unleash a whirlwind of fists and kicks. Or a knife. Danny kept well clear, circling them like they had leprosy, unwilling to mix in their company. Nutters. But at least they could hold their heads up high. Not like him. Fucking church mouse.

He fired up his cigarette, the tobacco and narcotic mix assuaging his anger and numbing the shame of his rough treatment at the hands of an immigrant. *Concentrate on the money,* he advised himself. A thousand Euros was a lot of dough. He had to use it wisely, not waste it on gear or gambling. Well, maybe he'd burn a couple of hundred of it, as a little reward to himself.

As he idled at a red traffic light he was gripped by a sudden flash of panic. What if Abdul made a complaint, grassed him up to the fridge bloke? No, he decided, they'd got their delivery and besides, Danny could always chalk it up as a misunderstanding. You know, a cultural thing. Twat didn't speak English proper anyway.

As the traffic thinned and the miles rolled beneath the nose of the truck, Danny saw the blue sign for the M1 motorway and veered aggressively across the carriageway, heading south. He'd be back in London in an hour, home in two. I'll give Carlos a bell, he decided, score a quarter of the grade A gear, the real mellow stuff that filtered out all the bullshit. He'd wash it down with a few pints at the Kings, maybe shoot the shit with the boys, spend a little of that hard earned dough.

After the day he'd had, he'd certainly earned it, hadn't he?

Downing Street

'Are we ready?' Bryce asked.

He buttoned the front of his suit jacket, checking the Tag Heuer Monaco on his wrist as he adjusted the cuffs of his shirt. It was almost time. He felt energised, ready to face his audience, but as he envisaged the expected storm of criticism that would surely follow his speech his nerve momentarily faltered. He was about to turn into a road he'd never travelled before, with no way of knowing where it would lead him. He refocused his thoughts as Ella fussed around him, all business.

'Your speech has been uploaded into the teleprompter and these are your notes, just in case.' She handed over a small white card. 'The press are waiting and most of the Cabinet are here too.'

Bryce raised an eyebrow. 'And Tariq?'

'Running late,' Ella informed him. 'He's at Millbank right now, finishing up a meeting.'

'Well, in that case he leaves me no choice. I have to sack him in absentia.' Bryce shook his head. 'Arrogant bloody fool.' He began rummaging through the neat stacks of folders and documents piled on his desk. 'Where the hell did I put that Heathrow dossier?'

'In your safe.' Ella pointed to the opposite wall with a soberly painted fingernail.

'So I did. Where's Davies now?'

'I've got him squirreled away downstairs. Sam's briefing him before the media eat the poor man alive.'

Bryce nodded and crossed to the wall safe. His private study was situated on the first floor, a reasonably sized room tucked away at the rear of the building, a quiet bolthole where Bryce could escape the unrelenting demands of office. He liked its size and its light, its lack

71

of formality. It was modestly furnished with a mahogany writing desk and a red leather Chesterfield sofa along one book-lined wall. The opposite wall boasted three large French windows that overlooked the rose garden below, a unique selling point for any study in Bryce's opinion. It was quiet, cosy, and in the depths of winter a fire burned in the grate at Bryce's feet.

The slim wall safe was mounted inside the chimney breast, hidden behind a hinged replica of Aivazovsky's 'The Ninth Wave'. Bryce had a fascination for seascapes, stemming from the sailing holidays of his youth and his all too brief flirtation with off shore racing during university. There was never any time for it now and he often missed it. He studied the painting for a moment, the castaways clinging to a broken mast, helpless as the sea threatened to engulf them; today, he thought he understood how those people felt. He punched a code into the safe's keypad and the thick hatch swung open. Bryce turned around. Rana Hassani's tiny figure stood in the study doorway.

'The relocation program is to be suspended?'

Bryce shot a glance at Ella who immediately moved to intercept the Deputy Communities Minister. 'I'm afraid the Prime Minister can't see you right now, Rana. If you would - '

'Well?' Hassani demanded, dodging Ella's outstretched arm.

Bryce retrieved the dossier and closed the safe door. 'Where did you hear that?'

'So, the rumours are true,' she glowered.

Bryce struggled to keep his own temper in check. 'Rana, this is neither the time nor the place for this and besides, you're overstepping the mark here.'

Saeed's diminutive deputy stood her ground. 'Prime Minister, with respect, I don't think you've thought this through.'

'Really?' he bristled, waving the dossier in the air. 'I think when you've heard the contents of this report you may reconsider that opinion. Now, if you'll excuse us.'

Hassani didn't move. 'I'd like two minutes of your time.' She tilted her veiled head respectfully. 'Please.'

Bryce took a deep breath. 'Fine,' he relented, 'two minutes.'

Behind Hassani, Ella shook her head vigorously. Bryce ignored her as he took up position by the window. The sun had already set, the sky a palette of deepening blues, the few clouds to the west brushed with streaks of pink and red. He looked down, where the evening shadows invaded the garden. The lawn was immaculate, the flower beds still quite colourful despite nature's autumnal assaults. He looked beyond the perimeter wall and over the black steel spikes towards St. James Park, where stubborn leaves clung to the trees, shivering in the evening breeze. Nearby, scattered groups of tourists gathered in small knots on Horseguards Parade. The historic square once heaved with tour parties, all flocking to London in their millions to visit its multitude of attractions. Now it appeared desolate.

Two families in our village have already gone...

'Prime Minister,' Hassani began in a quiet voice behind him. 'The relocation program is a humanitarian effort on an unprecedented scale, a challenge that we here in Britain have met with resounding success.'

Bryce turned to face her. 'I'm afraid that's not the case - '

'Let me finish,' Hassani commanded, holding up her hand. Bryce fumed silently. True to form she'd completed the predicted mood swing from respectful colleague to irritating nuisance in one small sentence.

He'd look forward to sacking her too, if he ever got a word in.

'Suspending it, or whatever it is you intend to do, is not only illegal, it will also damage international relationships, especially across the Islamic world. Furthermore it will cause great distress among the seven million Muslim voters right here in Britain. To even suggest such a course of action is unethical, unconstitutional and quite simply unacceptable.' Her voice had risen steadily as she spoke, the last word delivered just short of a bark. Before Bryce could answer, the Communities deputy continued her lecture.

'Both Britain and Pakistan have enjoyed a long history together and many of the refugees see Britain as a spiritual home. To deny them the opportunity to come here is an abuse of their human rights. The program must continue, so that displaced friends and relatives may be welcomed into the bosom of the Pakistani community. It is our duty to - '

'A duty we can ill afford,' Bryce cut in. He took a deep breath, knowing he had to tread carefully. 'Rana, I sympathise with your argument but it's a fact that the refugees have travelled through some extraordinarily prosperous countries to arrive at the gates of Europe. As well as a *temporary* suspension, I intend to pursue agreements with the Gulf states, encourage them to accept a share of the burden until the situation in Pakistan is resolved.'

Hassani's eyes bored into him. 'The refugees are a burden to you?'

Bryce chewed his lip; this debate was going nowhere. He glanced at his watch. 'Your two minutes are up.'

'I strongly advise you to reconsider your position,' Hassani urged, wagging a slender finger at the ceiling. 'Much hatred has been directed towards the refugees and this suspension will only fuel such loathing, a state of affairs you will be held responsible for.'

Ella stepped between them, towering over the tiny minister. 'That's enough, thank you Rana. I think you've made your point. Now, if you don't mind, the Prime Minister has a press conference to attend.' She glared at Ella then left the room, leaving the door wide open. Ella swung it closed it behind her.

'Jesus Christ, that bloody woman.'

Bryce stared at the door. 'How the hell did she find out?'

'Must be someone at Heathrow, one of Davies' team probably.'

'I warned him, no leaks.'

'If Rana knows then so does Tariq.'

Bryce let out a long sigh. 'Well, in a few minutes everyone will know.'

'She's right about one thing. The Muslim community will see this as a bad day for them.'

'Which reminds me.' Bryce produced a piece of paper from his jacket pocket. 'A short list of prospective candidates to replace Tariq, all with the necessary credentials. Go over it, would you? Let me have your thoughts?'

Ella plucked the paper from his fingers and scanned it quickly. 'I will.' She stood in front of Bryce and her hand reached out and smoothed the lapels of his jacket. 'You look very nice,' she smiled. 'Very handsome.'

'Ella - '

'I can have an opinion, can't I? If I can't have you then at least allow me that.' Bryce said nothing as she picked a thread of lint from his shoulder. She smiled and squeezed his hand. 'I'm always here for you, Gabe. You know that.' Bryce saw the pain of rejection flash momentarily in her eyes, then she blinked several times and took a deep breath, once again in total control. 'Ready to face the mob?'

'As I'll ever be,' he smiled grimly.

'Then let's go. We're late.'

They left the room, striding past Bryce's apologetic private secretary and out onto the landing. As Ella trotted down the Grand Staircase, its walls lined with portraits and photographs of previous Downing Street incumbents, Bryce paused beside his own image. It was a moody black and white study of sincere statesmanship, his thick grey hair swept back off his suntanned forehead, the sharp lines of his tailored suit more Vanity Fair than The Labour Review. Bryce studied the photograph intently, unsure if he recognised the man who held his gaze with such confident ease. It was an old picture, taken before Lizzie fell ill, when life promised to deliver everything he'd ever worked and hoped for, halcyon days that were now nothing but a distant memory. Feeling faintly unnerved, he headed quickly downstairs after Ella.

His Special Advisor carved a path through the expectant faces packed into the corridor outside the State Dining Room where the press conference was being held. Most were familiar; Cabinet ministers, their expressions ranging from curiosity to indignation, anxious advisors sporting glowing cell earpieces and a sprinkling of Downing Street staff, all drawn by the mystery of the moment. They pressed against the walls to facilitate the Prime Minister's smooth passage, a few quiet words of greeting and encouragement following him along the corridor. Ahead, the bright glare of the press conference beckoned, the buzz from the assembled press corps rising as they neared the room. Ella peeled away at the threshold and the chatter died away. 'Good luck,' she whispered and took up position just inside the room. Dossier tucked beneath his arm, Bryce took a deep breath and swept through the mahogany doors into the glare of the TV lights.

The roller shutter rattled slowly upwards, the mouth of the warehouse gaping open to reveal nothing but blackness. The silver Ford delivery van emerged almost silently from the dark interior, lights extinguished, the driver a vague shadow behind the wheel. In his rear view mirror he saw the swarthy man lower the shutter then melt into the darkness of the warehouse. The driver shifted in his seat and concentrated on the road ahead, steering the vehicle through the narrow backstreets of Waterloo, only flicking the lights on when he spotted a lone car approaching. He sat a little straighter then, accelerating to a reasonably sedate speed, unwilling to draw unnecessary attention to himself or the van. He cruised past empty industrial units and scruffy local authority tenements, past brightly-lit convenience stores and boarded up pubs, until he reached the roundabout at the southern end of Waterloo Bridge. From there he headed north across the river Thames. He glanced to his left, where the lights along the embankment were strung like pearls, curving towards the Palace of Westminster and the seat of power in Britain.

'Good afternoon,' announced Bryce, settling behind the lectern. There was an enthusiastic chorus of replies from the press corps packed within its wood-panelled walls, pens poised expectantly above notepads, recording devices held aloft. He took a sip of water and cleared his throat, blinking into the bright TV lights arranged across the back of the room. He glimpsed his reflection in the teleprompter next to the lectern, the lighting catching the expensive sheen of his grey Hugo

Boss suit and the rich red of his perfectly knotted silk tie. He looked every inch the European statesman he was and today he would prove how seriously he took that role. Words glowed on the teleprompter, scrolling slowly upwards.

'For some months now the focus of this government has been centred on divisions in international relations. As I speak here today, US and Chinese warships eye each other suspiciously in the south China sea as the localised military build up accelerates. In the Middle East, Iraqi and Iranian citizens are digging nuclear fallout shelters, a depressing phenomenon not witnessed since the darkest days of the Cold War of the last century. Closer to home, Polish terrorists persist in their attacks on Russian interests as the New Soviet Army sends more and more tanks toward their neighbour's frontier. In short, the world is witnessing worrying divisions. I have spent many months, both here and abroad, attempting, along with my colleagues in Brussels and the United Nations, to pull people round to a common position. Today, that is still the goal of this government, the search for peace and greater understanding amongst the international community, under the guidance and governance of the United Nations.'

Bryce took a moment to allow the weight of his words to percolate amongst the journalists around the room. He caught the eye of the well-known lead anchorman from the Islamic News Network, his arms folded tightly across his chest, his dark eyes glaring at him from the back of the room. Perhaps he knew what was coming, Bryce speculated, but it hardly mattered. In a few moments the whole of Europe would know.

'But the quest for peace should begin at home, for how can we lecture others on peace when the concept is an alien one for some of our own citizens?'

Bryce glanced down, flicking over the cover of the dossier. He frowned, his eyes scanning the words uncomprehendingly. Something was wrong. A low murmur began to fill the room, banishing the awkward silence.

Bryce held up a hand. 'I'm sorry, there seems to be a slight - ' His voice trailed away. He was looking at an intelligence briefing document, not the Heathrow dossier. Bryce realised he'd picked up the wrong bloody report, distracted by Rana's interruption and the similarity of the buff coloured unmarked binders. He turned to Ella and shook his head. She peeled away from the wall and marched forward. Bryce held his hand over the microphone as the chatter in the room rose.

'I've picked up the wrong report. I've got to go back upstairs.'

'I'll go.'

'It's in my private safe. I'll be a couple of minutes, tops.'

Ella nodded and summoned Bryce's press officer to the lectern with a curt hand gesture. 'Go. Quickly.'

Bryce leaned into the microphone. 'Ladies and gentlemen, my apologies. Slight hiccup with my documentation. I'll just be a moment, then we'll continue.' He scooped up the intelligence brief and left the room quickly, Ella marching behind him, a buzz of mild confusion trailing in their wake. In the lobby he paused at the foot of the staircase and turned to Ella. 'Wait here.' He took the stairs two at a time, heading towards his private study.

The silver Ford idled in traffic beneath Big Ben, the Victorian tower reaching towards the deepening blue of the evening sky. Ahead, Parliament Square was thronged with hundreds of protestors. A huge inflatable pyramid dominated the square, lit from inside, its steep nylon flanks decorated with pro-Cairo messages, most in English, others in Arabic swirls. Hundreds of flags and banners fluttered in the evening breeze, declaring their support for the treaty, the refugees, the Islamist fighters in Pakistan, the Palestinians in Gaza. Braziers flickered in the half light, illuminating the faces of the people gathered around them. Most were women, heads covered with veils or shrouded in Burqas, seeking warmth as the men chanted nearby, their fists raised in unison, their angry voices competing with the hum of the traffic.

The Ford entered the square, the rush hour traffic circling the protestors like Apache Indians surrounding a wagon train. The Ford inched its way across the busy lanes, indicating its intention to turn into Whitehall. The driver slowed just before Downing Street where a large crowd had gathered outside the black steel gates. They were mostly tourists, attracted by the history, by the steady procession of ministerial cars and the rows of high-tech satellite broadcast vans lining the pavement outside the Ministry of Foreign Affairs. Armed police officers in black body armour and Kevlar helmets eyed the van as the driver stopped for the obligatory security checks. He powered down the window and held up his ID card for inspection, the policeman giving a thumbs up to an operator behind the bomb proof glass of the control booth. The anti-vehicle trap was lowered, the black gates swinging open. The driver smiled and drove into Downing Street. He had no reason to fear the security checks or any other inspection, his familiar face and the van with the imposing black crest of the Government Mail Service emblazoned on its sides ensuring a trouble free passage into the most famous cul-de-sac in the world.

Bryce closed the study door behind him and marched across the floor to the wall safe. Stupid of him, really. He should've checked, made sure. Still, he'd only be a moment and the press corps were clearly intrigued by his forthcoming announcement. The safe beeped its approval of the correct code and the door swung open. He extracted the Heathrow dossier, thumbing through the pages to check its contents. Satisfied, he placed the intelligence brief back inside the grey metal womb of the safe and sealed the door. He swung the Aivazovsky back in place, once again admiring its composition, its vivid colouring. He made a sudden promise to himself: when all this was over, when the country was back on an even keel, he would make time, to once again hear the snap of a wind-filled sail, to feel the shifting deck beneath his feet, to taste the salty air on his tongue. No excuses, no postponements. A day out, someday soon, to ride the swell of the sea.

He pushed the painting home, feeling the click of the magnetic catch, then turned to leave the room, the Heathrow dossier clutched in his hand.

Along Downing Street's narrow confines, shadows deepened and lights began to glow as the warble of evening birdsong competed with the steady throb of the city. Government workers hurried purposefully up and down the cul-de-sac, the door to Number Ten opening and closing with industrious regularity. A police officer stood guard outside, pistol on his belt, hands behind his back, his boots treading a tiresome path up and down the pavement. The press corps gathered behind steel barriers across the street, camera lenses trained on the Prime Minister's residence. They chatted quietly, the banter often punctuated by a peal of laughter or the chirp of a cell phone. The silver

Ford glided by them all, camouflaged by its banality, a regular fixture in Downing Street's landscape. It reached the end of the cul-de-sac, swinging around to face the Chief Whip's office in Number Twelve before reversing, then heading back up the street. It purred to a halt outside Number Ten, the driver obscured by tinted glass, his lips moving in quiet prayer.

At the top of Downing Street the tourists still gathered behind the security gates, posing for photographs as commuters hurried past them, dodging, weaving, eager to return home after another busy day. Across Parliament Square the quarter bells of Big Ben heralded the approaching hour as the giant minute hand crept towards its summit. Many people heard the first chime of the great bell, its familiar peal ringing out over London, announcing the hour of six o'clock.

No-one heard the second.

The sudden pulse of white light was brighter than a thousand suns. Microseconds later a tremendous detonation ripped through the air, the pressure wave punching its way through the walls of Downing Street, through the Cabinet and Foreign Ministry buildings, hurling concrete, metal and flesh before it. Debris was thrown hundreds of feet into the sky, chased by a roiling ball of flame that reached high above the rooftops. Buildings shook and windows and ear drums were blown out for hundreds of yards around. As the earth trembled a choking cloud of smoke and dust rolled across Whitehall, enveloping everything in a yellow fog, blinding and suffocating as it spilled across the roads and pavements. In the dreaded lull that followed a rainstorm of twisted steel and stone crashed to earth, showering the streets with deadly wreckage.

As the dust swirled alarm klaxons wailed into life across central London, filling the air with their chilling moan. In Downing Street an enormous crater, several yards deep and filling rapidly with water from a cracked main, marked the spot where the silver Ford had parked only a moment before. Building facades on both sides of the street had been ripped away, exposing shattered interiors where small fires glowed, and a snowstorm of paper drifted on the dust-filled air.

High above the rooftops, thousands of startled birds wheeled above the carnage in a black, screeching cloud.

Aftermath

Bryce regained consciousness slowly, his vision wavering between darkness and a strange, blurred world he didn't recognise. He preferred the darkness. It was somehow warmer, more comforting, but a pounding ache in his lower jaw denied him the beckoning shadows. He opened his eyes, slowly, painfully, cuffing away the dust that clogged them. The first thing he saw were his hands, black with soot and cut in numerous places. He felt dizzy and nauseous, and everything sounded muffled, like his ears were blocked. After several confused moments he realised he was lying on his back on the floor of his study. But that was wrong, surely? The ceiling above was scarred and pitted, the crystal chandelier that usually hung from the centre of the room missing, his books scattered around him, covered in dust and filth, competing for space with jagged floorboards and splintered furniture.

He forced himself to inspect the damage more carefully. Plaster had been stripped away from the shattered ceiling, exposing wires and cables that swung lazily like jungle vines. He turned his head. The windows overlooking the garden had been punched out and a gentle breeze swirled dust and soot around the remains of Bryce's study. Through the blanket of partial deafness he heard the sound of roof tiles slithering and scraping above, then watched them sail past the windows before crashing onto the patio below. And he could smell gas. That wasn't good. As his ears began to clear his first lucid thought was a gas blast. He tried to move, then realised he couldn't. He was trapped.

He struggled against a rising tide of fear and forced himself to study his immediate environs. He was surrounded by debris, enclosed by it, his suit covered in dust and blood. He took a deep breath that caught in his lungs and he coughed violently for several moments. He tried another, the ache in his chest signifying some sort of internal injury. He moved his arms slowly, shrugging off the plaster and pieces of timber until he could move his upper body freely. He ran his hands over his torso, probing carefully until he winced. A broken rib, perhaps two, on his right side. He moved his right leg, drawing his knee up. No pain, good, thanks no doubt to the heavy desk that partly shielded his body. His other leg wouldn't move, trapped beneath a jumble of debris. He pulled weakly at his trouser leg but the limb was well and truly wedged. He noticed a large beam close by, lying parallel to his body, a heavy steel one, covered in thick black soot. Another few feet and he wouldn't be breathing at all, that was for sure. The ache in his face persisted and he found his jaw, feeling carefully for damage. His fingers came away slick with blood. He turned and spat several times, trying to clear the dust and blood from his mouth. He probed his gums, his tongue slipping between the gaps where his teeth were a short time ago. No wonder his whole head was splitting in pain. Bryce's mind reeled as he tried to piece together the last few moments. He remembered hurrying back to the study, to retrieve the Heathrow dossier. Then he'd turned to leave when –

What, exactly? He recalled a flash of light beneath the door, an ear splitting bang, an earthquake that shook the ground beneath his feet. He'd felt the floor drop away only to rush back up and meet him. Then the world turned black.

He had to get out of here. He pulled at his left leg again, but it was well and truly jammed beneath a pile of thick timbers sporting rusted, twisted nails. As his hearing returned to something like normality he became aware of the sound of breaking glass and distant sirens. He thought he could still smell gas. That must have been the cause of the explosion. He had to get outside.

He called for help, the words rasping between toothless gums, his throat still thick with dust. He doubted anyone more than six feet away could hear him. He spat again, more blood, more dust. He pushed himself up into a sitting position, an inch at a time, mindful of the broken ribs and their proximity to his lungs. He lifted his chin, peering over the piles of rubble across the floor of his study – and his eyes widened in horror, his jaw sagging painfully in shock.

Number Ten was devastated. The explosion had ripped a gaping fissure from the front of the building and every window had been blasted away. The floor to his study was still intact, along with a section of the landing outside, but beyond that the building was ruined. He searched for his secretary, saw her desk overturned, debris piled against the rear wall as if swept there by a giant's broom. He thought he saw something pale amongst the carnage, a limb perhaps. He called again, the sound whistling through the gaps in his teeth, but no-one answered. Panting for breath he turned away, looking across the street where the exterior wall of the Ministry of Foreign Affairs had been peeled away by the blast, revealing blackened rooms and broken furniture. It reminded Bryce of a macabre doll's house. On one of the floors a large table hung by two of its legs from the shattered floor above. As he watched, the floor timbers groaned and gave way, sending the table crashing to the ground in a cloud of dust and rubble.

Closer, the staircase inside Number Ten marched up towards the roof as it had always done, the stairwell walls cracked and exposed but still standing, the balustrades dangling like broken teeth all the way to the top floor where most of the roof was missing. Bryce was stunned, his head moving back and forth as he struggled to make sense of the scale of the damage. He vaguely recalled being told that Number Ten could withstand this sort of thing, that the famous front door alone took at least eight men to carry it, such was the strength of its construction. Bryce couldn't even see the thing, the front of the building gone, the gap wide enough to drive several trucks through.

His arms felt weak and he eased himself back to the floor. He fought the shock, forcing himself to relax. Nearly everyone had been downstairs; Ella, the Cabinet, the press, Downing Street staff. Why couldn't he hear their shouts, their cries for help, for God's sake? *Am I the only one left?* He heard more sirens but they still seemed distant. Where were the emergency services? Minutes had passed, maybe more. It was getting darker, he was alone, trapped, with no way of -

He fumbled painfully inside his jacket, his fingers feeling for the cell phone buried in his pocket. He fished it out, checked its smooth silver body for damage. The screen sported a small crack but amazingly the device had survived, the coloured icons glowing in the gloom and the swirling dust. He thumbed the contacts button, scrolling through the list until the saw the name, the only senior minister he knew for sure wasn't in the building. He tapped the screen, lifted the device to his ear. A click, a hiss, then the wonderful sound of a distant ringing tone.

Above the sirens wailing in the street outside, above the shouts that echoed around the marble atrium and the continuous squawk of radio transmissions, Tariq Saeed's sensitive ear picked out the soft warble of his cell, the small device vibrating in his hand as his entourage of aides and security personnel swept into the lobby of the Euro Tower on Millbank. The pulse rippled up his arm and he glanced at the screen as he continued marching towards the bank of elevators ahead.

Then he stopped suddenly.

Around him the scrum of policemen braked sharply, boots squeaking on the polished floor. Saeed paid them no mind. Alive? Impossible. He was too close to the blast, had to be dead. Someone else, then? Doubtful. *Consider every eventuality, plan for every improbability,* he reminded himself. He muted the ring and turned to a senior police officer alongside him. He waved the device in the man's face.

'The cell network. Should it still be operating?'

The policeman shook his head. 'The order has already been passed, Minister. Transmitter towers are being shut down as we speak.'

'Then make it happen faster. The terrorists will take advantage of any chink in our armour.'

'Immediately, Sir.'

Saeed headed towards the elevator that waited to whisk him up to the Emergency Management Centre on the twenty-second floor. As armed guards crammed into the lift around him, the index finger of his right hand found the power button to his cell phone and held it down.

Call ended.

Bryce was confused, his head pounding. It rang, he was sure of it. Before he could punch the button again he heard a shout, then footsteps crunching through the rubble below. His heart leapt. He raised himself up, calling for help until his chest hurt, the word sounding like *help* through his broken teeth. He peered over a pile of bricks towards the shattered staircase as a head bobbed into view, then a set of shoulders, the form indistinct, masked by dust and cast in shadow. It was a man, wearing civilian clothes.

'Where are you?'

Bryce raised his arm, above the lip of the desk, above the rubble. 'Over here!'

The man scrambled towards him, stepping carefully over mounds of shattered bricks, splintered timbers and broken plaster.

'Thank God,' Bryce breathed.

'Don't move.'

Bryce obeyed, the man's manner immediately authoritative. He was in his late thirties, Bryce judged, his dark hair cut short and flecked with grey, the pale line of an old scar curving beneath his right eye. He wore a black polo shirt and khaki trousers, the ones with pockets down the legs. Quickly and carefully he cleared a space next to Bryce, kneeling down and shrugging a small rucksack off his back.

'Thank you,' Bryce gasped, 'thank you.'

'My name's Mac,' the man announced, snapping on a pair of purple latex gloves. An intricate tattoo covered his left forearm and a black digital watch glowed on his wrist. 'Where are you hurt?'

'My ribs. I think they're broken.' Bryce pointed to his bloody jaw. 'I've lost some teeth. And my leg's trapped.'

Mac probed his head just above his right ear. Bryce winced. 'You've got a nasty cut on the head, too. Did you lose consciousness at any time?'

Bryce nodded. 'I think so.'

'O.k., just relax,' Mac said. He ripped Bryce's shirt open at the torso, running his fingers gently over his ribcage. 'Can't feel any breaks. Does it hurt when you breathe?'

Bryce nodded. 'A little.'

'Bruised probably.' He rummaged inside his rucksack, retrieving a small green medical kit. He cleaned and dressed the head wound, wrapping a bandage around Bryce's skull and securing it tightly. He opened a bottle of water, then gently eased Bryce's head to the side. 'Take a swill, spit it out.'

Bryce did as he was told, watching the bloody mixture congeal in the dust below his chin. He felt Mac's fingers holding his jaw, the other hand gently pushing balls of cotton wool into the gaps in his teeth.

'No photo shoots for you for a while,' he said. He inspected Bryce's leg then carefully shuffled along on his knees, testing the weight of the timbers, straining to move them. He produced a torch from his rucksack, waving it beneath the pile of debris, scanning the limb.

'Can't move it but I don't think you've suffered any major damage. Wiggle your toes for me.'

Bryce did as he was told, feeling the digits moving in his shoe. 'I can move them. That's good, right?'

Mac nodded. 'Yep.' He stared up at the ceiling, the sky above. Bryce followed his gaze and the sound of a helicopter filled the air. It buzzed into view, not far above the roof, the noise of the rotors hammering the walls, churning up a dust storm that whipped debris around the remains of the room. Dangling cables twisted violently and paper funnelled into the air. The searing shafts of a search light lanced through the building at crazy angles, slicing through a sandstorm of dust and debris. Mac leaned over, shielding Bryce with his body until the sound of the rotors receded.

'Fucking morons,' Mac cursed, spitting dust from his mouth. 'Probably a news crew. Could have brought the building down.' As if to punctuate Mac's words a sudden avalanche of debris thundered close by and dust billowed up from the remains of the lobby, filling the room with choking black filth.

'Got to get you out of here,' coughed Mac. 'I need help, though. That leg won't move and neither will those timbers.' Mac swiveled around, his neck craning above the rubble. 'Where the hell is everyone?'

'I thought – aren't you part of the emergency services?' Bryce stuttered, 'a doctor perhaps?'

Mac shook his head. 'No, I'm just a civvy. I was in the tube station at Westminster when the bomb went off. Ran over, to see if I could help. Everyone else ran the other way, police included. They must know something we don't.'

Bryce lifted his head off the floorboards. 'Bomb?'

'I'd lay money on it,' Mac said. 'I had to skirt the crater to get in here. Bloody massive. Car bomb, no doubt.'

'But I can smell gas.'

'That's residual, probably. It also explains the lack of response from the fire and ambulance teams. They're worried about secondary devices.'

Bryce stared again at his saviour. 'You sound like you've got experience in all this.'

Mac pulled his own cell from his trouser pocket. 'Ex-Royal Marine. Two tours in Afghan, one of them with the UN during the Kabul uprising. Car bombs were two a penny back then.' He held up his phone. 'See, no signal. They've cut comms, as a precaution.' He tucked the device back into his pocket then stood up, taking a careful step towards what was left of the landing.

Bryce panicked. 'Where are you going?' His eyes caught a movement above, something bright drifting past the shattered roof, darting beneath the blackened rafters. A burning ember floating on an updraft, soon joined by another, then several more. A plume of smoke funnelled past the jagged breach. Something was on fire. Bryce stared in horror at the mountain of dry timbers, the piles of books that surrounded him. 'Listen Mac, I don't care what you have to do, just get me out of here.'

Mac saw the embers too, sniffed the air. He didn't say a word, just stepped over Bryce and tried again to shift the timbers that pinned him. He strained and struggled, teeth clenched, the veins in his neck bulging, sweat glistening on his face. Nothing moved.

'Jesus Christ,' he panted, slapping the dirt from his hands. 'I can't shift it. The floor's partially collapsed beneath your leg. I think that's what saved it, but all this shit on top has got it trapped.' His head swivelled this way and that, searching. He picked up a thick piece of timber, inserted it next to Bryce's trapped limb and braced his hands along its length, like a power lifter about to explode into action. He blew his cheeks out hard and attempted to stand, back straight, knuckles turning white as he gripped the wood. Bryce felt a timber against his leg shift slightly. Glowing embers began to swirl through the building, a swarm of deadly fireflies that drifted on the evening breeze, tumbling through the debris and settling on the dry kindling that lay all around.

Bryce's eyes widened in fear. 'Jesus Christ, hurry up Mac!'

✫ ✫ ✫

93

Millbank

Tariq Saeed stood silently at the window on the twenty-second floor of the watching the pall of dense black smoke rise above the Westminster skyline. Despite the chaos around him he was distinctly unruffled, his black hair neatly parted to the side, his beard trimmed close, immaculate in a navy blue pinstripe suit and a pale blue tie that matched the colour of his eyes, as if he'd picked it out for that very reason. He hadn't of course. The blue eyes were a physical characteristic that occasionally brought him personal shame, a reminder that somewhere in his distant past an ancestor - a woman no doubt - had disgraced herself and the family name by laying with a foreigner. Or perhaps she'd been raped, a common enough occurrence during Europe's sordid colonial escapades, but a disgrace none the less. Honour decreed that death should have followed, preferably by the hands of a family member, and yet somehow the infected gene had been passed down through the generations, bestowing on Saeed a childhood of playground bullying, an adolescence of female interest, an adulthood of envy and suspicion. He stood out from the crowd, both physically and intellectually, had married a beautiful woman, siring three healthy boys, all blessed with their mother's dark brown eyes. If they could see him now, if they were old enough to understand what was in his heart, they would feel pride in their father's achievements.

Behind Saeed, the Emergency Management Centre was packed with dozens of officials; a gaggle of bureaucrats from the Civil Contingencies Secretariat, a cabal of senior police and fire officers, MP's and stry of Defence personnel, suits and uniforms, ,athered in tight knots as they regarded the solitary figure by the window. Saeed sensed their sympathy but it was more than that. There was also respect, for Tariq Saeed, Minister for Communities and Social Cohesion, was now potentially one of only two surviving Cabinet members. Or so everyone assumed.

The best laid plans of mice and men, Saeed mused, balling his fists behind his back. His eyes wandered across the darkening skyline. He could make out Big Ben and Westminster Abbey, a triumvirate of famous spires jutting upwards through the haze, but beyond Parliament Square everything was blanketed by clouds of dust and smoke. Flames glowed like angry coals in the darkness as night crept across the city.

Saeed inched closer to the glass and looked down. Far below, behind twirling strands of blue and white tape strung across the street, Millbank itself was choked with fire engines, ambulances and police vehicles, a sea of blue and red flashing lights all desperate to race into Whitehall. Across the river the south bank was similarly clogged, and on both sides of the Thames, thousands of civilians streamed away from the area. It would be a long journey for many; all modes of transport had been shut down, trains, tubes, buses, everything. London was at a standstill.

'Sir, we must make a decision.'

Saeed glanced over his shoulder. The senior emergency service personnel were standing in a loose half-circle behind him, frustration etched across their faces, the urge to begin rescue operations an almost tangible thing. As Saeed opened his mouth to speak, another distant boom rumbled across the skyline. He turned in time to see a fireball rolling skyward over Whitehall. The uniforms surged towards the windows, crowding around Saeed. He bristled at the physical proximity.

'Could be another fuel tank erupting, or a gas main letting go,' ventured a Fire Chief.

'Gas supplies to the whole area have been shut off,' confirmed another voice.

'Residual fumes in the pipes, then. Or maybe storage tanks. Has anyone any idea how many fuel storage tanks there are in government buildings?'

'That's your domain,' sniffed Robin Chapman, the Metropolitan Police Commissioner, 'you have inventories for this sort of thing, no?'

The Fire Chief turned on him. 'Now wait just a minute - '

They continued to squabble as Saeed looked on. Chapman was a typical choice for the Met's top job, a political appointee rather than a policeman, a Common Purpose graduate whose successful rise up the ladder had been moulded by Saeed and others in return for unswerving loyalty. There were many like him in positions of power right across the country.

'Enough!' ordered Saeed. He turned away from the window. 'We have to assume that was another bomb.' His voice was smooth, his accent polished and eloquent, the result of private schooling and a Cambridge degree that had long since buried all traces of his immigrant upbringing.

'If we don't start rescue operations soon, the casualty list could be far higher than it already is,' argued the chief operations officer of the London Ambulance Service, a small, thin man with receding grey hair. Saeed saw the man's face boil with frustration. 'Those buildings are old, many of them still have original timber frames. If those fires take hold we could have casualties burning to death. The Prime Minister himself may be - '

'Don't you think I've considered that?' snapped Saeed. 'If they've managed to hit Downing Street we have to assume they can and will hit elsewhere. How do we know Parliament hasn't been targeted? How do we know they're not waiting to detonate further devices as we rush to help?'

'It's a chance we'll have to take,' the chief retorted. 'This time wasting is costing lives.'

The comment was greeted with a vigorous head nodding and murmurs of agreement. Saeed sensed the tide turning against him.

'You're right,' he admitted, pointing a finger at the pall of smoke in the distance. 'But we all agree this is a sophisticated operation. Someone out there is watching, waiting for us to make our move. I'd like to make sure it's as safe as possible. The army has - '

The doors to the room suddenly flew open and the imposing bulk of Jacob Hooper, Secretary of State for Defence, swept into the room, his entourage of advisors and assistants trailing behind him like pilot fish. His grey suit was covered in dust, his white shirt and red striped tie caked with soot, his shoes scuffed and dirty. He came to a halt in the middle of the green carpet, waving a document above his head.

'This is more than just an isolated incident,' he bellowed. The voices in the room died away. 'There's been another bomb, a few minutes ago. A device was detonated at the Luton Central Mosque.'

All eyes turned toward Saeed. 'What did you say?'

Hooper shook his large, balding head, laying a meaty paw on Saeed's shoulder. His quiet words dripped with sympathy. 'I'm afraid it's true, Tariq.'

Saeed cupped his hands over his mouth. When he spoke his voice barely rose above a faint whisper. 'Friday prayers. The mosque would've been packed.'

'Yes,' Hooper soothed, 'we must brace ourselves for many casualties.' He turned to face the room, the document once again raised above his head, a thin sheaf of papers bound in a clear plastic cover brandished like a religious artefact before devoted worshippers. 'Cell phone conversations, intercepted less than six hours ago. They refer to a *spectacular*, quote unquote. There's also mention of the Prime Minister and the timing of this afternoon's press conference.' He lowered the folder, slapping it into the chest of a loitering assistant. 'This is a truly horrendous day. We must act, and act swiftly.'

'Then let us begin rescue operations immediately, Minister.'

Hooper stared at the Ambulance chief, at the other senior officers gathered around him. 'You understand the dangers?' he asked.

'We've discussed them,' Saeed interrupted, brushing dusty fingerprints from his shoulder. 'They're prepared to accept the risks.'

'The counter IED teams are not far away,' Hooper pointed out.

'We can't wait, Sir.'

The Defence Minister waved his hand. 'Then go. And take every precaution,' he boomed as the chiefs hurried en masse towards the doors. The corridor outside bulged with armed police. Saeed waited until the last one had gone and the doors were closed. He turned to Hooper, inspecting him carefully. 'Are you alright, Jacob?'

Hooper swallowed hard and nodded. Tiny grains of dust from his head drifted towards the carpet. 'I'm fine, thank God. Your phone call was incredibly fortuitous.

Another few minutes and we'd both have been inside Downing Street. Makes me sweat just thinking about it.' He patted the dust from the sleeves of his jacket then said: 'We need to talk, Tariq.'

'Yes. There's much to discuss.'

Saeed looked over Hooper's shoulder. The room was quieter now, the lights dimmed as a security measure. Hooper's entourage loitered nearby, deep in discussion. Every phone in the room was in use, glued to the ear of a pale faced MP, their voices urgent, fearful. Civil Contingency people and assorted government workers crowded around the conference table at the far end of the room, heads huddled together, their voices laced with the whisper of uncertainty, their assistants scribbling furiously on electronic tablets that glowed in the diffused light. Several police officers were stood in front of a huge map of London covering one wall, discussing security measures. Others came and went, low level flunkeys and secretaries, moving urgently, seeking purpose, craving the stability that had been so violently snatched from them by the Downing Street bomb. Saeed could smell their fear, could see the unspoken pleas for help in their eyes as they regarded the two most senior members of government still walking and talking.

He felt a hand on his arm as Hooper guided him away from his entourage towards the window. The power had been cut to Whitehall and Big Ben was a black shadow in the distance, shrouded behind a veil of smoke. Beyond was a deep red glow, as if a meteorite had fallen from the sky and destroyed Downing Street along with everything around it.

Then Hooper spoke, glancing down to the street below where a procession of emergency vehicles, blue and red lights flickering in the darkness, moved slowly towards Parliament Square. 'There's no constitutional model for an event like this. That said I've spoken with Brussels and three of the Lord Justices of the Supreme Court. The Prince of Wales has agreed with their recommendation that interim authority be passed to me to act on the Prime Minister's behalf until the situation becomes clearer. As my most senior minister I expect your full support Tariq.'

'You have it, Jacob.'

'We'll need help. The democratic process must be maintained.'

'We have a majority in both Houses,' Saeed pointed out. 'Your authority will not be questioned.' He fished inside his jacket pocket and produced a sheet of paper. 'I've taken the liberty of compiling a list of MP's from across the political divide to replace the casualties. Some have previous Cabinet experience.'

Saeed watched Hooper as he scanned the list, the fat fingers stroking the heavy jowls, the bulbous eyes that sat too close together, the bushy brows that arched above them. He truly was an ugly man, Saeed concluded. And predictable.

'Yes, very good,' Hooper said. 'We should all meet at the earliest opportunity.'

'I'll arrange it. In the meantime Brussels has allocated several floors here in the Euro tower, to temporarily house the new administration, which means the police will have to block off the surrounding streets as a security measure. As a consequence the general public will be denied access to the area. The Tate Gallery will have to close I'm afraid.'

Hooper waved the information away, his gaze fixed on the destruction in Whitehall. 'The least of our concerns.' He was quiet for a moment, then he said, 'While we're on the subject Tariq, I'd like you to take charge of security, liaise with the police and security services. The perpetrators of these hideous acts must be caught, and caught quickly. Tensions will be running high across the country, particularly in your own community. We must nip any unrest in the bud. You'll be my point man on this. In effect, my Deputy Prime Minister.'

Saeed paused, then said: 'Shouldn't we at least wait until the emergency services have begun rescue operations? My appointment may seem a little presumptuous.'

Hooper turned, a grim frown knotting his brow. 'Take a look out there, Tariq.' He tapped the glass with a thick finger, where distant flames leapt above the shattered rooftops and black smoke towered into the night sky. 'Downing Street is gone.' Hooper turned to face him. When he spoke his words resonated around the room, ensuring that everyone – including Saeed – acknowledged the authority in his voice. 'This is no time for half measures, Tariq. We must act quickly and decisively. The country is depending on us.'

Saeed nodded his head in acceptance. Yes, he concluded, the man really was predictable.

The darkness was almost complete, the smoke thicker, the glow of the fire visible beyond the shell of the study wall. Bryce coughed and spluttered, holding a handkerchief over his nose and mouth. All the while Mac worked away on his hands and knees, a desperate shadow that tugged and pushed and pulled, burrowing at the thick knot of debris and fallen timbers trapping Bryce's leg. He grunted with the effort, swearing violently as he lacerated his hands once again. His latex gloves were in shreds and he pulled them off, hurling them to one side.

The evening wind shifted, kicking up the dust, drawing the smoke up through the building like a chimney. Behind Mac, through the gaping brickwork, Bryce glimpsed a tongue of flame. Then another.

'Jesus Christ, Mac, the fire's getting closer.' Mac said nothing, moving around the heavy desk and attacking the timbers from another angle. 'Mac? Did you hear me?'

Bryce heard the whimper in his own voice, the fear constricting his vocal chords, his shattered teeth and bleeding gums sucking at the words. At any moment Mac would realise the futility of his efforts and save his own skin, scrambling back down the shattered staircase, leaving Bryce to his fate. He was going to burn to death, like an accused witch, the flames igniting his clothes, scorching his flesh –

'Mac, for God's sake - '

Quiet!' he yelled. Bryce cringed as he watched Mac scramble across the debris towards him. He flinched as he knelt down, felt his hand being grabbed and squeezed. Bryce could feel the warm blood, imagined the cuts criss-crossing his hands.

'I won't leave you, got it? But you've got to help me, work your leg free when I say. Ignore the pain or we're both dead.'

Bryce nodded several times, his eyes flicking from Mac to the orange light that played across the shattered walls, dancing through the building towards them.

He watched Mac stumble around the dark lump of his desk, saw him duck out of sight for several long, agonising seconds, then reappear with a thick piece of floor joist in his hands. He scrambled over the piles of debris towards his trapped leg, setting his feet wide apart above the spot where the limb disappeared beneath the wreckage, his body a dark silhouette backlit by hungry flames that glowed devilishly around the pockmarked walls. He winced as Mac plunged the stake deep into the debris, felt the timbers shift around his leg, squeezing the limb, clamping it to the floor.

'Mac, please!'

'Wait!'

The younger man leaned on the end of the stake, pushing down. Bryce felt something shift, the weight suddenly easing off his kneecap. Hope blossomed.

'That's it, Mac! Keep going!'

Mac tugged the timber out and stabbed it back into the pile, twisting, digging deeper. He pushed down again, using his body weight, levering the debris upwards. Bryce moved his leg. Pins and needles raced up and down the limb as the blood began to flow. He reached down, balling the material of his trousers and pulling his knee towards him, his calf scraping across wooden splinters and rusted nails. He ignored the pain, the tearing of flesh. He was out, free.

Mac allowed the pile of timbers to crash back down and scrambled over to Bryce.

'Let me see.' He panted, bending over the limb. The trouser leg was shredded, the skin slippery with blood. Bryce felt Mac's hands working the flesh, the bones, the joints. 'Any pain?'

Bryce shook his head. Smoke swirled around them, black smoke, noxious, choking. Through the gap, the fire leapt upwards, hungry, searching.

'On your feet!' Mac ordered. His strong hands gripped the lapels of Bryce's jacket and pulled. Bryce pushed himself to his knees. The jacket caught on a nail and Bryce shook it off. Mac lifted him up under the armpits then dragged him across the wreckage of his study. Bryce stumbled, then focussed on his footsteps. He saw his books, scarred and blackened, splintered furniture he barely recognised. Mac's hand pulled him mercilessly. He tripped, put his hand out to break the fall, sinking to the elbow in broken plaster and other debris. He pulled himself up, his collar ripping as Mac grabbed his shirt and yanked hard. Back on his feet, Bryce discovered his shoe was missing, the sock wet with blood. He didn't feel the pain, only the heat from the fire, roaring up from the lobby, curling hungrily beneath the first floor landing where they now stood. He threw an arm up over his face.

'The stairs, quick!'

Bryce staggered after Mac, the heat forcing the men against the wall of the staircase. Broken glass cracked and crunched underfoot. Bryce glanced down. Former Prime Ministers stared back at him, their faces lit by a fiery glow. He stumbled down a few more steps then collided into Mac. For a moment he almost felt safe, skulking behind the broad shouldered man in front, protected from the worst of the heat. The fire was less than fifteen feet away, consuming what remained of the lobby, roaring up towards the roofless sky. Timbers cooked and splintered, cracking in the heat. Bryce glanced toward the interior of the building, where corridors and state rooms once existed, now a dark grotto of unspeakable devastation. Smoke and flames belched from within.

'We have to jump the last bit,' Mac shouted. Part of the staircase was missing, the ground twenty feet below. 'Get in front of me. I'll lower you down.' Mac shuffled around the small section of landing they were standing on, twisting Bryce so his back faced the street. Bryce could feel the heat of the flames now, prickling his shirt. He panicked, gripping Mac's outstretched hands with his own.

'I can't!'

'You can! Climb down, now. Don't worry, I've got you.'

Bryce did as he was told, sliding towards the edge of the landing and lowering his body over the lip. He looked down, over his shoulder. The familiar black and white tiles of the lobby were submerged under a sea of rubble and jagged floor joists. He hung over the edge, feet dangling, Mac's face above screwed in effort, the sweat pouring off his face.

'Let go! Drop!'

'I can't!' Bryce shouted, staring at the debris below.

'Yeah, you can,' Mac replied, prising Bryce's fingers from his wrist. Bryce dropped hard, crashing on to the rubble. He yelped in pain, rolled through the dirt and soot. Fear forced him to his feet, the intensity of the flames pushing him backwards until he realised he'd stumbled out into Downing Street itself. Bryce caught himself on the edge of the crater, a giant hole that marked the epicentre of the blast. He was rooted to the spot, shocked by its enormity, then Mac was beside him, pulling him from the edge, pushing him onwards over hillocks of brick and rubble. On the other side of the street the Ministry of Foreign Affairs was an inferno. They were caught inside a cathedral of destruction, the flames all around, towering towards the night sky. Mac gripped his hand with strong fingers, dragging him over the rubble.

They reached Whitehall a moment later, the suffocating heat left behind them. Bryce slipped from Mac's grasp and fell. Slowly he pulled himself up, his mind struggling to comprehend the scale of the damage. Whitehall was covered in debris, the asphalt road barely visible under a carpet of wreckage; huge chunks of masonry, twisted metal, a sea of shattered glass glinting in the firelight. Vehicles lay abandoned in the street, their doors flung open in haste, the nearest ones overturned and engulfed in flames. Bodies littered the scene like piles of sack cloth, some limbless, some half buried, torn and shredded clothing, bags, footwear - the detritus of instant havoc wreaked upon an unsuspecting populace surrounded Bryce. Even the streetlamps had been decapitated by the blast.

Then Mac was at his side again, yanking him upright by the armpits, cursing, pushing him away from the burning TV vehicles, from the inferno of the Foreign Ministry. Thick smoke swirled and eddied on the evening breeze, the air tainted with the stench of burning rubber. Bryce could taste it in his mouth, on his tongue. He heard a shout, then a scream that echoed around the shattered buildings. The sound unnerved him. His eyes bulged in fear.

'Keep moving!' Mac shouted.

'Which way?'

The smoke seemed to be getting thicker, a choking black ceiling above them. A dark shape loomed out of the smoke from behind a burning police car. The man hopped past them muttering angrily, his leg missing below the knee. His hair was singed off and his clothing shredded, exposing more wounds that leaked a frightening volume of blood. Before either of them could react the man had disappeared, lost behind a veil of smoke.

'Jesus Christ,' Bryce whispered.

Mac grabbed his hand, squeezing it tightly. 'We can't help him. Just keep moving.'

Bryce felt himself being dragged forward again. He had no strength left, his legs like iron weights, his lungs devoid of oxygen. His head swam. All he wanted to do now was lie down, just for a minute. He couldn't go on, couldn't take another step. He was about to let go of Mac's hand when another sound reached his ears, the sound of a distant siren, getting louder, penetrating the fog of his mind. He felt Mac's hand tighten and suddenly the smoke parted like a curtain before them.

A sea of blue and red lights stretched across Whitehall, filling Parliament Square and washing the Houses of Parliament in colourful strobes. Dozens of figures raced towards them, silhouetted against the lights, the sound of their running feet rising to a crescendo, a stampede of help and assistance. Bryce sank to his knees, exhausted, the relief a palpable thing. He felt a hand on his shoulder and looked up. Mac's hair was matted with filth, his face streaked with soot. The smile carved through the dirt, through the blood and grime.

'Here comes the cavalry,' he grinned, all traces of anxiety gone from his voice. 'About bloody time, eh?'

Bryce tried to laugh but it caught in his throat. Tears streaked through the dirt and then the uniforms were on them like a wave. Urgent hands reached down for him, lifting him bodily off the ground, moving him swiftly away from the flames and the rumble of collapsing timber and masonry. His senses were assaulted, the acrid smell of burning, the garbled chatter of radio transmissions, the multitude of voices jabbering in an unintelligible chorus around him. Sirens wailed and helicopters buzzed somewhere above. He felt suddenly claustrophobic, hemmed in by a scrum of uniforms, medical green and police black, the cold contact of their clothing abrasive against his raw flesh. Some held Perspex shields overhead, protecting him from further assault like a cohort of Roman Legionnaires surrounding their wounded General. Bryce was a rag doll in their hands. His head lolled back and he stared upwards, beyond the helmets and visors, the ring of screaming voices and anxious faces, up to where a faint dusting of stars glittered in the night sky. He thought it was the most beautiful thing he'd ever seen.

The sirens grew louder and blue and red strobes pulsed brightly, lighting the scene with their flickering luminance. He felt himself being lowered onto a stretcher, then lifted again, and slid inside an ambulance. Door slammed and paramedics in masks and clear plastic glasses loomed over him, slicing the clothes from his body. They tore the dressing from his head, the cotton from his mouth, wiping and swabbing, checking pressures and pupils and beats per minute. They swayed in unison as the vehicle headed away from Whitehall at speed, engine roaring, sirens clearing the way. He stared up at the ceiling, at the alien beings that surrounded him, peering, probing, puncturing his skin with drips and needles and other medicines.

Slowly Bryce began to relax. He'd live, of that much he was certain. Sure, he was sliced and diced, battered and bruised, but he sensed there was nothing dangerously wrong. The paramedics, in their cold and frighteningly impersonal language, confirmed it. Bryce could tell by the reduced speed of their industry, the soothing words and smiles.

He let the motion of the ambulance calm his shattered nerves. He'd survived. And it was all thanks to one man.

Saeed and Hooper were locked in intense discussion when a commotion from the corridor suddenly filled the room. There were shouts of excitement as a large group of suits and uniforms spilled through the double doors, Commissioner Chapman at their head.

Saeed recognised most of the civilians, Labour MP's and party apparatchiks, their assistants weighed down with folders and paperwork. The word had gone out, the ruling classes drawn to the new hub of power. He watched Chapman march towards the window, braided cap tucked beneath his armpit. He was breathless, the words tumbling from his mouth.

'He's alive! The Prime Minister has been found!'

Faces beamed around the room. Saeed heard a sob of relief, saw the unbridled joy on the faces of the underlings. Some of the women hugged each other, others dabbing moist eyes with balled up tissues. He regarded them with barely disguised contempt, stifling his own personal roar of frustration. 'What's his condition?' he snapped.

The policeman's smile faded. 'It's serious, multiple injuries. They're taking him to King Edward the Seventh. It'll be a while before we know any more.'

'Any other survivors?' Hooper inquired, his arms folded behind his back. 'Senior people?'

'Most of the buildings in Downing Street have suffered severe damage and the place is an inferno. It doesn't look hopeful,' Chapman warned.

'In that case we're still in crisis,' Hooper reminded them.

'There's more,' the Commissioner continued. He handed a folder to Hooper. The Defence Minister gave Chapman a quizzical look then flicked open the cover, glancing through the thick sheaf of eight by ten colour stills.

'Our first breakthrough,' the policeman explained, quiet excitement in his voice.

Hooper arched a bushy eyebrow. 'Already?'

'This man was captured on surveillance cameras at the Luton mosque yesterday morning. He delivered a large container, an industrial refrigeration unit we think.'

'I thought the mosque was destroyed,' Hooper said.

'I'm afraid that's the case,' confirmed Chapman, 'but the security feeds were backed up off site. Counter Terrorism Command tracked the vehicle back to London via its GPS. Local CCTV shows the suspect used a pushbike to leave the area. We lost him near Paddington.'

Saeed glanced over Hooper's shoulder, saw Daniel Morris Whelan glaring directly into the camera lens, the smudge of a tattoo on his neck.

'That artwork looks distinctive. Do we know who he is?'

'We're running the images through facial recognition and a team is trying to secure DNA evidence from the vehicle. It's a matter of time.'

'What about the Downing Street bomb?'

'A different matter,' Chapman explained. 'Judging from the small amount of aerial footage we've been able to view, the crater suggests a car bomb, which means the vehicle was an official one. Somehow the terrorists gained access to Whitehall. The Downing Street security system has been destroyed so we'll have to interrogate the Whitehall feeds. Again, it's a matter of time.'

'An inside job,' Saeed concluded.

Chapman gave a curt nod. 'Without doubt.'

Hooper passed the folder back to the policeman. 'Use every available resource you have, Commissioner. Minister Saeed is acting Deputy Prime Minister so you will liaise with him in future. I want these bastards flushed out.'

The room had filled with people again, the news of Bryce's survival injecting the air with the hum of quiet optimism. Every seat around the conference table was now filled and human traffic in and out of the room gathered apace as messengers made up for the lack of cell phone coverage. Saeed's mind drifted, again wondering how Bryce had survived. The van's floor and side panels were packed with military grade explosive, every nook and crevice, every void and space. The vehicle's suspension had been specially modified to take the extra weight, the driver a Christian convert who'd yearned for Paradise. The van was directly outside Number Ten when it detonated, but Bryce had slipped away a moment before, a problem with his speech. Despite that, despite the years of structural strengthening and fortifications, Number Ten had folded like a house of cards in the ensuing blast. Saeed had monitored the live transmission from a room downstairs, until the picture from the press conference had disappeared in a storm of static. Even he had been momentarily unnerved by the sheer force of the blast, the rumble felt beneath his feet, the windows of the Euro Tower rattling violently. Yet Bryce had survived, an eventuality he'd forced himself to consider. And plan for.

He studied the faces around him, the streams of officials that were now pressing into the Emergency Management Centre. There were more MP's now, military men in dust covered uniforms, Commissioner Chapman and a host of other senior police officers, EU delegates and their assistants. Even the Director-General of the BBC, plus board members from Sky, Reuters and Bloomberg had been summoned. If a bomb went off in this room the country really would be in trouble, mused Saeed. He watched Hooper acknowledge the new arrivals, saw his eyes register the size and importance of the growing audience. He leaned into the Defence Minister's ear. 'Jacob, you should say something.'

'You're right.' Hooper buttoned his jacket, brushing the dust from its flanks and lapels. Saeed gestured for the heavy wooden doors to be closed and the chatter in the room faded to silence as Hooper cleared his throat loudly. Behind Hooper, beyond the glass wall, the sky to the north glowed a deep red.

'Ladies and gentlemen, we are in the grip of a crisis as unique as it is terrifying. Whitehall has been decimated by a bomb, as has the Luton central mosque.' Some of the new arrivals gasped in disbelief. Saeed studied their faces, expressions and emotions that ranged from fear and uncertainty to outright shock. 'Casualties are unknown at this time,' continued Hooper, 'but the death toll is expected to be considerable.'

'We must act!' screamed the MP for Solihull, standing behind the conference table to Hooper's right. He thumped the wooden surface with a balled fist. 'The full weight of the law must bear down on these vile racists!' A murmur of agreement rippled around the table of politicians and Hooper acknowledged them with a grin nod.

'My Right Honourable colleague is correct. Something must be done to combat the deadly threat we face and I can tell you now that evidence is already beginning to emerge. From the Luton incident we have a face, and a vehicle, and soon we will have a name. Now, it's obvious that the clear intention of these terrorists was to decapitate the government and spark civil and religious unrest. They have failed on the first count and we must work hard on the second to ensure that our communities are protected, that the ambitions of these murderous bigots are thwarted and each and every one of them is brought swiftly to justice.' Hooper paused for a moment, as if searching for the right words. Saeed sensed the building tension, the fear that was so obvious a few minutes ago slowly turning towards determined anger.

'We have to protect what remains of our government,' Hooper boomed, his voice resonating like a operatic virtuoso. 'In light of the severity of the situation and the condition of Prime Minister Bryce, President Dupont in Brussels, our own Lord Justices and the Prince of Wales himself have all endorsed my temporary status as head of government until the situation becomes clearer. I hope I can count on each and every one of you for your support.'

Saeed watched the back of Hooper's head, the folds of flesh pressing together as his polished dome swept the room, his suspicious eyes seeking out possible dissenters. There were none. Saeed caught the mood amongst the audience, the subtle nodding, the resolute faces. Britain had lived with terrorism in many forms over the years and the spectre of a dangerous enemy within had always been firmly entrenched in the nation's consciousness. Now it was taking shape once again, given form by the glowing wreckage beyond the window, the bodies that lined the pavement in Luton, the CCTV images of persons unknown.

Saeed saw Anna Reid, the Solicitor General, press through the crowd and pause before Hooper. She was a tall woman, thin, with collar length black hair and a severe fringe. Her boss was missing somewhere amongst the rubble of Downing Street, which technically made her the acting Attorney General. Saeed believed that for many in the room the crisis also had its upside, a sudden promotion being the obvious and immediate benefit.

'Jacob, I think I speak on behalf of the room when I say that you have our full and unequivocal support,' gushed Reid.

'Thank you, Anna,' Hooper smiled, shaking her outstretched hand.

'Thank you, Prime Minister.'

The words hung in the air, like an unfamiliar odour requiring immediate categorization. Saeed watched the crowd for a reaction but there was no obvious one, simply a bovine acceptance of the situation. A camera flashed, the handshake a physical representation of the transition of power, captured for immediate dissemination to every media outlet across Europe. Saeed almost smiled; there was tomorrow's front page right there. And by the time the sun rose, Bryce's head might just as well have been found in a gutter. The King was dead, long live the King.

And there was something else too. In less than an hour Millbank had become a nexus of power, the new administrative heart of the country. Already Downing Street and what it had represented was passing into memory, a moment of huge psychological significance for those around him. Soon there would be a scramble for desk space, with whole floors being hastily rearranged while computer networks were reconfigured and new equipment filled the cargo elevator. Outside, the security cordon was tightening its grip around the building, the surrounding streets. Whitehall had been emptied, a sinking ship whose passengers sought the comfort and security of Millbank, desperate to be a part of the new government that was taking shape right before Saeed's eyes.

The events of today would be met with approval in the east. In the private villa along the Turkish coast, in marbled halls across the Middle East, the men of power would talk favourably of Saeed and what he'd accomplished so far. There was still a long way to go, many years in fact before the plan came to full fruition, but such was the speed of the power shift he'd witnessed today, Saeed was now convinced he'd see it in his own lifetime. His heart almost sang at the thought of it, of the pride his children would feel, the esteem his name would be held in throughout the Ummah.

Only Bryce remained a problem. A sudden recovery, the resumption of power, the continued opposition to the Treaty of Cairo, all could tip the scales in the wrong direction. Bryce had to be sidelined, hindered, his name and reputation devalued to a point where he was no longer considered to have any meaningful input in a future administration. And it had to be done carefully, subtlety, so that the name of Gabriel Bryce became an uncomfortable and embarrassing topic of debate and discussion. Saeed already knew how, the necessary pieces already in place. The trick was to convince Hooper who stood a few feet away, pumping hands and revelling in his new status.

Saeed finally allowed himself a careful smile as he joined in with the ripple of subdued applause. Power was such a corrupting influence, a drug that, once savoured, demanded to be fed. Hooper was already a junkie and Saeed felt it too, yet his rise to power had been engineered for a much higher purpose, a divine quest that rose above the sins of vanity and personal gain.

And Bryce stood in the way of that. But not for long.

North West London

Danny Whelan stood silently in the doorway of the kitchen watching his father tackle a stack of dirty dishes. Like most of the other rooms in the old man's twelfth floor apartment the kitchen was cramped and narrow, a single row of top and bottom kitchen units, an upright fridge, a stainless steel sink next to the window, all immaculately clean. The opposite wall was bare, except for a clock with old fashioned numerals and a calendar. Danny glanced at the picture for September, a photograph of a turreted castle, the flag of St. George fluttering above its ramparts. The thick stone walls were framed by harsh, snow capped peaks, the castle itself seemingly suspended in mid air above a mist covered field. Beneath the stirring image, the text read: *Scenes of England, reproduced with kind permission for the English Freedom Movement.* A familiar bitterness welled up in him then, a reminder of the legacy that the Movement had bestowed on him; a tattoo he generally kept covered and a calendar that would soon be out of date. But right now those were the least of his problems.

The old man was hunched over the sink, thin arms covered in soap suds as he worked his way through the soiled plates and saucepans. His white cotton vest hung loosely off his bony shoulders, his baggy grey sweatpants gathered in concertina folds around the worn carpet slippers.

'Thanks for dinner, Dad.'

The old man didn't look up, his attention devoted to the removal of a particularly stubborn stain on a chipped brown pot. 'That's alright son. Nice to have a decent bit of fodder for a change.' His voice was hoarse and scratchy, a lingering symptom of the chest cold he'd recently endured. Danny tutted and turned away, returning a minute later with a well worn sweatshirt.

'Put this on. You'll catch your bloody death again.'

The old man wiped his hands on a tea towel and wrestled the sweatshirt over his head. Danny moved to help him, pulling it down around his waist.

'There you go, pops.'

'I can manage.' Whelan senior rolled up the sleeves and plunged his hands back into the soapy water, getting to work on a heavily stained coffee mug, one with the England football team logo and 'FIFA World Cup China 2026' stamped on its side. Danny remembered it well, the so-called English players lined up for the opening match in Beijing, not a single white face amongst them, and no one making any effort to sing the national anthem. Bloody disgrace. If it wasn't his dad's mug he'd have chucked it over the balcony ages ago.

'What are you up to then?'

'I was thinking of going out for a while,' Danny replied.

The old man's hands froze in the water. 'You be careful out there, son. They're rounding people up, shipping them off to the detention centre at Camp Hill. It's on the news.' He wheezed, smothering a cough with the back of his hand. He placed the mug carefully on the draining board.

'I've got to find out what's going on, pops.'

'Watch the TV, then.'

'No, I mean what's *really* going on. On the street.' Danny thrust his hand into the pocket of his jeans and pulled out a fold of money. He laid two of the notes down on the counter. The old man's eyes flicked between the money and Danny's face.

'What's this?'

'Some more money from that job. For food and stuff. Bit towards the bills too.'

The old man stared at the notes. 'If you get caught you'll be in a lot of trouble. Me too, probably.'

Danny shook his head and forced a smile. 'Only a couple of people know I'm staying here. I'm still registered at the hostel, remember?'

'You can always come back, son. This is your home, where you grew up.'

'I get more housing credits if I'm in that shithole, which means sooner or later they'll have to give me my own place. I'm just working the system, pops.'

The old man picked up the tea towel again, bunching it up as he dried his hands. 'What did you have to do for that anyway?'

'I told you, a delivery.'

'What sort of delivery?'

'A fridge. Big bloody thing it was too, one of them industrial ones. Nearly broke me back.'

'Where to?'

'Eh?' Danny felt the blood rushing to his cheeks, a jolt of fear triggering the sudden pounding of his heart.

'The fridge. Where d'you deliver it to?'

He remembered Abdul's dirty breath, the big hands that twisted his shirt collar, that shoved him hard and sent him sprawling through the mosque. He remembered the news bulletins the following night, seen through a haze of blue smoke and chemically dulled senses, the shattered dome, the lumpy white sheets lined along the pavement, the wailing relatives. He swallowed hard. 'Just some place outside London.'

The old man picked up the money, his fingers savouring the crispness of the paper. 'Jesus, two hundred Euros. That's lovely, son.' He opened a cupboard above him and placed the notes beneath a stack of small plates. 'I can't say we don't need it. Just be careful, alright?'

Danny didn't answer, instead watching his father close the cupboard door, using the tea towel to wipe away a few damp fingerprints on the handle. Danny gently took the cloth from his hand and got to work on the pile of dishes next to the sink. He worked in silence as his father ran a broom across the floor. When Danny had finished he wiped the draining board dry, polished the taps then slapped the tea towel over his shoulder.

'There. All sorted.'

The old man smiled. 'Thanks, son. So, where are you going?'

'The Kings, probably.' He turned towards the window. Outside, tower blocks marched across the estate, the roof mounted wind turbines turning lazily in the evening breeze. The city sparkled under the night sky, the view one of the only benefits of living on the Longhill Estate. Up here they couldn't smell the rubbish strewn alleyways or see the graffiti on the walls. Instead the signs of social deprivation were audible, the bickering families, the jumbled drone of televisions, the muffled thump of music, the pitiful whine of housebound dogs. For the last two days Danny had filtered it all out, had smoked enough resin to knock out a bull elephant, but the nightmares had penetrated the fog of drugs, the blanket of sleep that had wrapped itself around his body. He'd thrown up in his bedroom last night, taking care not to disturb his dad as he rinsed out the wastepaper basket in the bathroom, his hands shaking, his body covered in a light sheen of sweat. He'd curled up beneath his duvet, shutting the world out as the news from Luton grew more terrible each day.

He could hand himself in right now, tonight, tell them what really happened, but would they believe him? He'd be arrested for sure, interviewed over and over again, spend weeks on remand in a category double

'A' nick while they tried to corroborate his story. Danny knew they wouldn't have much luck doing that; a bloke called Sully with no last name, a cell number that was now disconnected, a lorry with an envelope full of cash in the glove box. Anyone with half a brain would know something was dodgy. And there was Downing Street too, the bomb going off at exactly the same time as Luton, the news full of right-wing conspiracies. So he'd be charged, a trial would follow, the country howling for justice. His defense lawyer would be state appointed, in other words useless, and whoever was getting done for this one would go away forever. The thought chilled his bones.

'You all right son?'

Danny turned away from the window, saw his dad stroking the grey stubble of his chin, his rheumy eyes troubled. 'I'm fine,' he lied. 'Think I'm coming down with that bug that's going around.'

'Stay in then.'

'I've been stuck indoors for two days, dad. Fresh air will do me good.'

The old man tapped the side of his neck. 'Well make sure you cover that up. Police ain't mucking about now, not with the Prime Minister in hospital and half the government dead. I told you, Camp Hill is filling up, lot of your old mates in there I expect.'

'Ex-mates. I don't see anyone from the Movement anymore.'

'Just as well,' the old man muttered, 'I never really took to that lot.'

'You had a good day out that day, down at the seaside.'

'Yeah, that was nice,' his dad admitted, 'but they're a weird bunch, talking about what they would do if they was in power. Nasty stuff, some of it.'

'That's called politics, dad.'

The old man frowned, wagging a bony finger. 'Don't patronise me, Danny. I might be old but I'm not stupid. Would you want to see old Jaz thrown out of his newsagents, deported back to a country he's only been to once?'

'Well, I - '

'Where would you get your scratch cards then? Or your paper? Nearest shop is on the high road. Oh yeah, you couldn't go there either coz your mates would've chucked them out too.'

Danny held his hands up. Normally he would've launched into one of his impassioned speeches about race and immigration but he had other things to worry about now. 'Alright, pops, I get it. Anyway, it's not about blokes like Jaz.'

The old man took a step forward and laid his hand on Danny's shoulder. 'All this bitterness and hate won't get you anywhere, son. You've got to make the best of your life, find a bit of happiness, any way you can. If your mum were alive she'd tell you the same.'

Danny felt a sudden wave of emotion choking him. The words lingered behind his lips, like caged birds waiting to be released in an explosion of wings. The urge to unload the whole story on his dad was almost overpowering but Danny knew that would only make things worse. The stres and worry would probably make his dad ill, and worse, he'd be incriminating him too. He didn't trust himself to look his own father in the face so he stared at his shoes instead. 'You're right, dad. I'm pretty bloody useless ain't I?'

He felt his father's fingers squeeze his shoulder. 'No you're not, son. You've had a few problems, had a bit of bad luck, that's all. You're still young. There's still plenty of time to turn your life around.'

'Sure there is.' Danny patted his dad's hand and eased it from his shoulder.

'Be careful out there, son. Cell's on if you need me.'

'I'll be careful,' Danny mumbled. Out in the hallway he grabbed his coat and a tatty baseball cap off the hook by the front door. He paused for a moment, watching the old man settle down in the living room, the light of the TV flickering off the wall, the sterile sound of canned laughter. He stared at the door to his bedroom, where the small rucksack lay beneath his bed, stuffed with clean clothes and a wash kit, the rest of the money and his passport. The letter to his dad lay in a drawer, hastily scrawled in the dead of night, stained with tears of guilt and drug induced self pity. He stood there a moment longer, wracked with uncertainty, then closed the front door behind him. It wasn't time, not yet. He'd give it another night, a few more hours to think up a plan, make a decision.

Run...

He shook off the thought as he trotted down the stairs, past the terminally broken elevators in the lobby and out into the night. He pulled the baseball cap low over his brow, navigating the concrete alleyways of the estate, fading in and out of the street lamps and their weak pools of stored solar lighting. He heard it before he saw it, the low hum of the propellers, then the blink of a red collision light as the bulbous nose crept into view above the nearest tower block. He kept his head down as the unmanned airship drifted slowly overhead, its platform of cameras and sensors scanning the streets below, the ghostly white letters that read 'POLICE' clearly visible on its inflated black flanks. Danny ducked inside an unlit lobby until the drone of its propellers had melted away. It was the second one he'd seen that day, unusual because the blimps normally flew over a couple of times a week.

Run, Danny...

He turned the corner towards the small parade of shops, their shutters covered in unintelligible scrawls of coloured spray paint. Danny ducked inside the Kings Head, acknowledging the bouncer in the shadows of the doorway with a familiar nod. The pub was busier than usual and he loitered near the door for a few moments, soaking up the vibe like a swimmer testing the water. There was no tension in the air, no strangers lurking, no sudden crash of glass, of shouted commands to *Stand Still! Don't Move!* He scanned the faces, hoping somehow that Sully would be there, knowing he wouldn't.

The lights in the pub were out, the tables around the room basking in the warm glow of flickering tea-lights, illuminating the crooked smiles and easy banter of the regulars. Shadows danced around the walls and music thumped quietly in the background. Despite everything Danny found himself warming to the ambience, a welcome change from the usual undercurrents of tension and violence. The scene reminded him of a distant New Years Eve, during his one and only tour of Afghanistan, most of the camp bedded down for the night, the tent lit by a small gas lantern. He could still see the grinning faces of his mates around the card table, the clink of bottles as they saw the New Year in, cocooned within the confines of the camp, in the warm embrace of their friendship. He missed those times, those friends.

He pulled off his baseball cap and sauntered over to the bar, squeezing between the drinkers, the small camping lamps hanging from the overhead shelves lighting its length. The landlord nodded.

'Alright Dan?'

'Sweet. What's with the candles?'

The landlord pulled a pint of lager and pushed it in front of Danny, leaving a wet trail across the bar. 'Saving energy, bruv. Bills are sky high at the minute, so I'm cutting down on my overheads.'

Danny passed over a ten Euro note and sipped the froth from the glass rim. 'Decent crowd this evening.'

'Yeah, funny that,' observed the landlord, scanning the note under an ultra-violet reader. 'Give 'em a national crisis and a few candles and suddenly everyone's a happy camper.'

'Sort of reminds me of when I was in Afghanistan,' Danny began, warming to the subject. 'New Years Eve twenty two, it was. Bloody cold that night, if memory serves - '

The landlord had already drifted away to serve another punter further down the bar. *Ignorant bastard,* Danny fumed silently. For a minute there he'd felt a little better, his thoughts momentarily distracted from the shit he was in. Still, his job tonight was to keep his ear to the ground, see if the police had been nosing around the estate. He had to stay focussed.

He moved away from the bar, pulling off his coat and sitting down at a table on his own. He found half a daytime spliff in his pocket, puff-lite as he jokingly called them, and considered sparking it up. He frowned, his resolve already crumbling as he smoothed the spliff between his fingers. He was supposed to stay alert, not get stoned. Besides, hadn't he had enough lately? Then again it would help him relax, calm his frayed nerves. He clamped it between his lips. Fuck it, why not? He lit it with the tea-light on the table, exhaling slowly and rocking back in his chair, his eyes roaming the room, his ears catching snippets of conversation around him.

Despite the soothing buzz of the drug, Danny realised how much he hated the Longhill, how much he detested himself and the shitty choices he'd made that saw him homeless and unemployed at thirty eight years old. He'd love to leave this place but where else could he go? He'd been out of work for ages, no decent qualifications and a few convictions on his record. Not exactly an employer's dream. So like it or not the Longhill was his home, a familiar stamping ground where he was known and reasonably respected.

And there was his father to consider too, his health not being what it was. Despite having a useless shit for a son his dad rarely complained, allowing Danny to sleep in his old room instead of that miserable hostel, cooking and washing for him without charge or complaint. His dad had been proud of him once, when Danny had joined the army, when he landed the government job. His photo was still up on the living room wall, the one of him in his dress uniform, next to the one of mum. Happier times, that's for sure.

But what if he had to leave, to run as the voice inside him urged? He had his passport, a bit of money, but he'd be picked up the moment he tried to leave the country and the cash would soon run out. To say his options were limited was an understatement. He took a long toke of the spliff to numb the bitterness that bubbled inside him. What a loser he'd turned out to be, discipline gone to shit, a mere shadow of the man he once was, all those years ago when he took the oath and wore the uniform. He closed his eyes and again the memories returned, the camaraderie, the friendships, the laughs. If he concentrated hard enough he could almost smell the dry air of the Afghan desert, taste the tang of jet fuel in his mouth, the roar of the helicopters as they -

The overhead lights suddenly blazed into life and the poker pod in the corner announced its garish presence with a neon flash and a loud, melodic jingle. A cheer went up around the bar.

'Bill's been paid!' someone joked to a chorus of laughter.

'Check your phones. Special announcement on the news,' explained the landlord, pointing to the TV on the wall. The sudden change of vibe only worsened Danny's mood. He pulled out his cell, saw the Public Information message flashing in his inbox, saw the others around the bar doing the same.

'Turn it up,' a voice yelled.

The landlord stabbed at the remote control with his thick fingers. 'Hang on, for Christ's sake.'

News channels scrolled across the screen until a cry went up and the familiar logo of the BBC appeared. The crowd pressed in, dragging their chairs noisily across the floor and settling down in front of the wall-mounted TV. *News update, every fifteen minutes,* announced a scrolling banner. There was nothing else, just the usual countdown to the hour superimposed over a rotating globe and surrounded by the animated stars of the EU. The familiar theme of the BBC News filled the pub as the landlord toyed with the remote.

Danny finished his smoke and dropped the butt on the floor, crushing it beneath his trainer. The stopwatch graphic reached zero and the music finished on a long, piercing scrape of strings that Danny found slightly unnerving. His heart began to beat a little faster. He looked over his shoulder where he noticed the roughnecks from the pool room had drifted into the main bar, baseball caps and hoods pulled low over glowering faces. He turned back as a sterile newsroom filled the Hi-Def, a sombre-looking man in a suit on one side, a Hijab-wearing female newsreader on the other.

'Typical!' protested a voice in the crowd. He was silenced by a wall of *shh's*.

'*Good evening,*' greeted the man in a serious tone. '*This is the latest government news bulletin, brought to you by the BBC London News desk.*'

'*The Interior Ministry has announced that the Emergency Powers Act remains in force across the country and restrictions on public assembly and movement are currently active. A full copy of the Act has been made available for download and members of the public are advised to familiarise themselves with its provisions.*'

'It's what?' another voice mocked. A derisive cheer erupted around the bar. The landlord hissed for quiet, straining to hear the rest of the announcement. It was several seconds before the laughter faded.

'*And now for a news update,*' continued the woman, adjusting her glasses, the navy-blue veil framing her oval face. '*Prime Minister Hooper has met with President Dupont and representatives from the Islamic Congress of Europe in Brussels to discuss the security situation and the threat to Muslim communities across the continent. In a statement issued earlier today both President Dupont and Prime Minister Hooper have pledged to tackle rising Islamophobia and are considering amendments to existing hate crime legislation, a move welcomed by leaders of the Congress. In a communiqué issued by the EU Commission a short while ago...*'

Danny choked on his lager, coughing violently. He rocked forward on his chair, thumping the glass on the table. 'Jesus Christ, more legislation,' he shouted at the screen. 'Won't be able to breathe without getting nicked - '

'Keep it down,' growled the landlord.

'*...after an extended session in the European Parliament, during which Turkish MEP's called on the British government* *to reconsider its long standing opposition to the Treaty of Cairo as a gesture of reconciliation towards greater European harmony. In London the new Cabinet was formerly approved by British and EU officials and during a short speech outside the Euro Tower in Millbank, Deputy Prime Minister Tariq Saeed welcomed the Turkish statement and declared that the new government was dedicated to the European Union's policy of expansion and peaceful integration. Later, Minister Saeed and several other senior figures visited the King Edward the Seventh hospital in Marylebone, where Gabriel Bryce is undergoing treatment for injuries sustained in the blast. A hospital spokeswoman announced his condition as serious but stable...'*

'Peaceful integration? What a joke,' spat Danny. He shoved back his chair in disgust and headed towards the lavatory. Bloody BBC, he seethed. Ministry of Propaganda more like. He waded across the piss-covered floor and relieved himself, a familiar vein of anger replacing the fear and apprehension that had plagued him since Luton. He remembered a time when veils were only seen during the BBC's Middle East hour, or during Rama-bloody-dan. Now they were everywhere, even on kid's shows.

He wandered over to the sink, checked his reflection. He looked tired, dark circles framing his bloodshot eyes. That would be a lack of sleep and the recent excess of dope. His hair needed a cut and a shave wouldn't go amiss either. Maybe tomorrow. Yeah, it was probably a good move anyway, smarten his act up, change his appearance a little, just in case. He yanked the lavatory door open and stepped out into the bar.

'...a powerful compound used almost exclusively in military applications, according to government forensic officers. So far the death toll at Luton has reached one hundred and four with two hundred and seventy injured, many seriously. Over

forty of the dead were Egyptian tourists who'd travelled from London on a day trip to visit the mosque...'

Danny froze, fear gripping his insides like a cold vice. The shattered remains of the Luton Mosque filled the screen, its walls reduced to piles of smoking rubble, the dome tilted at a jarring angle. He looked around the bar. Everyone was riveted to the news bulletin.

Run, Danny...

On the screen the image changed to an aerial shot of Whitehall, the road clogged with police vehicles, ambulances and digging equipment. The Foreign and Cabinet Offices were reduced to piles of blackened rubble and ant-like figures scurried over the debris that was once Downing Street. Only a few walls remained, the teetering brickwork propped with steel supports. In the daylight, the size of the bomb crater and the sheer scale of the devastation brought a gasp from the punters around the bar.

'...according to Counter Terrorist Command, and has uncovered strong links between the explosives used in both the Luton attack and the blast that destroyed Downing Street, resulting in the deaths of a further one hundred and seventy eight casualties, many of them serving members of the government. Police have issued an image of a man wanted in connection with the attack. Thirty-eight year old Daniel Whelan, from London, was captured on CCTV cameras at the Luton Mosque shortly before...'

Danny was horrified to see his picture flash up behind the newsreader, superimposed over a shot of the hostel in Acton as a dozen armed police officers poured inside the shabby building. He dragged his eyes away from the TV, saw the drinkers around the bar looking at each other in disbelief.

'Was that Danny boy?'

'Can't be..'

'…they've made a mistake, bruv..'

'…he's here somewhere…'

Lost in the shadows Danny moved towards the main door, head low, legs like jelly, squeezing behind the punters still glued to the news broadcast. He glimpsed the landlord's puzzled face, the eyes that registered the empty table, the jacket over the chair, the glass of unfinished lager. The roughnecks stood in a tight group in the middle of the floor, pool cues in hand, heads swivelling around the room, bodies like coiled springs. The bar was quiet, the mood of the crowd still doubtful, yet Danny felt the sudden change, the tension that charged the air like static electricity. He kept moving, shoulder to the wall, head down, avoiding all bodily contact. He reached the main door, pushed it open, moving past the oblivious bouncer as the newsreader's words chased him from the premises:

'...*right-wing organisation, with previous convictions for the distribution of banned literature. The Metropolitan Police has offered a substantial reward for information leading to Whelan's arrest. Meanwhile, tributes to the victims of the Luton attack continue to pour in from across the Islamic world...*'

Run, Danny, RUN!

Cold fear snapped at his heels. Danny twisted through the graffiti-strewn labyrinth of the estate, arms and legs pumping, trainers slapping noisily on the pavement, his heart pounding as he sprinted through canyons of grey concrete. He reached his block in less than two minutes, yanking open the security door with a fumbling hand and staggering against the wall inside, his breath coming in heaving rasps.

Then he heard them.

The rumble of feet on the pavement, the whoops of excitement echoing around the towers. They were coming for him, knew where his dad lived. He was trapped. *C'mon, Danny, think!*

He stared through the mesh-covered door and saw the first of them running towards the tower block, the roughnecks coming hard and fast, pool cues in their hands. On instinct Danny threw himself back against the wall and made for the elevator control room a few yards away. The lock was always broken, the machinery within providing a warm environment for users to get fucked up in. He ducked inside and pulled the door to, punching the overhead light switch. He held his breath in the darkness and peered through the smallest of cracks as the roughnecks bundled inside the building, ignoring the broken lifts and heading up the stairs, a blur of hoodies and baseball caps, the air punctuated with chilling howls and guttural cries. He watched the last of them flash past, the stampede receding as they climbed higher up the stairwell. Young and reasonably fit they may be, but twelve floors was an effort for anyone.

Danny listened carefully until he was sure the lobby was deserted. He crept out of the machine room and back onto the estate, sick with fear, the guilt of leaving his dad at the mercy of the pack compounding his anxiety. He couldn't think about that now, had to get away fast.

He dropped down a flight of stairs into an underground car park, a black, rubbish-strewn chamber lit only by ghostly shafts of yellow light, a graveyard of stripped-down, burnt-out vehicles. He hesitated only for a second then moved through it quickly, bounding up another concrete staircase at the far end. Another alleyway, then he was lost in the darkness of the park, loping across the open space and into the trees on the other side. He stopped, crouching in the bushes, his breath coming in painful heaves. He heard more shouts, saw another posse hunting him, flashlights probing around the tower blocks, flicking across the open spaces for signs of flight. Danny edged further back into the undergrowth, watching their frantic movements as they charged along balconies and thundered down staircases, their cries of frustration echoing across the park, desperate villagers armed with flaming torches, seeking out the monster in their midst.

He'd seen enough. He turned his back on them, on the Longhill estate and the life he knew, and disappeared into the trees.

King Edward the Seventh Hospital, London

Somewhere in the darkness Bryce heard a noise. It was an indistinct sound at first, a low murmur lurking somewhere on the outer edges of his consciousness. Then he heard another sound, rather like the first, but pitched slightly higher. Voices. Yes, that was it, voices, out there in the shifting shadows. He could hear them talking, the words unintelligible, muffled, like they were speaking under a blanket. He felt himself moving towards them, the blackness slowly turning to grey, then a milky whiteness. The voices belonged to two dark shapes, directly ahead, very close. They spoke quietly, almost whispering, and Bryce still couldn't make out what they were saying. Other indistinct objects suddenly morphed into familiar forms. He saw a large TV, a picture frame on the wall, an empty chair by the window. The voices fell silent. Bryce slowly turned his head, heard the familiar metallic clatter of his chart at the end of the bed, caught a glimpse of a man leaving the room, the door closing with a soft click. His eyes snapped fully open and he balled his fists, rubbing the sleep from them, yawning loudly as he finally returned to the land of the living.

Which was funny, because he didn't feel very alive. In fact, since he'd been in hospital he'd felt disconnected from the real world, drifting in and out of consciousness, a sensation rather like an out of body experience, he imagined. He felt no pain, only fatigue. He couldn't stay awake longer than an hour or two, his limbs like lead, his eyelids often struggling to stay open. He was told he needed to rest, the cocktail of drugs that seeped into his veins fighting the infections, bolstering his immune system, feeding his battered body. Rest, the consultant ordered, rest the nurse insisted, rest the orderly advised. All he did was rest.

He turned towards the window where the view was distinctly uninspiring, a windowless building blocking out most of the natural light, the brickwork streaked with rain patches, the thin sliver of sky above grey and forbidding. The room itself was comfortable enough, if a little too warm, with all the trappings a private hospital offered. There was a wall mounted TV opposite his bed, a sofa and two chairs for visitors, a fridge, a well-appointed private bathroom near the door to his right. Tasteful artwork adorned the walls, a mixture of Edwardian landscapes and eclectic post modern pieces, and an abundance of flowers from well-wishers filled vases on every shelf and sideboard. A luxury dressing gown with a royal crest embroidered into the breast pocket hung from a hook behind the door and Bryce yearned for the strength to stand upright, to wrap the garment around his body and venture outside his heavily guarded room. If only he had the strength.

He'd lain immobile for over a week, surrounded by IV drips and clear plastic tubes, wired up to meters and monitors that recorded his pressures, beats and temperatures and God knew what else. He had a needle feeding fluids into a fat vein in his left hand and a crescent of tiny suckers clamped to his chest monitored his heart. A catheter was inserted in his penis (he was glad he'd been unconscious for that one) and a large dressing covered the wound to his thigh. To the left of the bed an impressive bank of electronic equipment displayed a confusing array of information that Bryce didn't even pretend to understand. Instead he was just thankful to be alive.

During his brief periods of consciousness he'd seen the images on TV, the devastation of Downing

Street, the horror of Luton. It was worse for them, the worshippers at the mosque. Politicians represented the establishment, a target for all manner of terrorists over the centuries, but to destroy a mosque, a holy place, where men, women and children gathered in the eyes of God – Allah, he corrected himself – was unthinkable. How people could ever contemplate such an act was beyond Bryce's comprehension.

He'd seen Jacob Hooper on the newscasts, a natural choice for temporary leader given the circumstances, but perhaps a little overbearing. Yet it was Tariq's presence at Millbank that bothered him. He'd proved himself to be unworthy of high office, was on the brink of back bench obscurity and now there he was, either at Jacob's side during the press conferences or making statements in the heavily guarded Houses of Parliament. Deputy Prime Minister indeed. It was wrong.

Bryce often chastised himself for such unpleasant thoughts when he should be rejoicing that his old comrade had survived. And the new Cabinet, well, there were some good choices and some strange ones. Nearly a quarter of the newly promoted ministers were Muslim MP's, some of them blatantly unqualified for such high office Bryce believed, yet it wasn't his decision and clearly the continuity of government had to be maintained. Besides, Bryce consoled himself with the fact that the Muslim community would be reassured by such a strong presence in the heart of the administration and he looked forward to meeting them all on his return, if only he could keep his eyes open long enough to ever get out of bed.

The door opened and the orderly Suleyman entered, manoeuvring a trolley beside Bryce's bed. He had the typical complexion of a Turk, olive skin and black eyes, with a permanent shadow of a beard on his face and neck. He greeted Bryce with a warm smile.

'Morning, Mister Gabriel,' he beamed in a cheery London accent.

'Suleyman.' He wore a maroon tunic and black trousers, a gold coloured plastic name badge pinned above his left breast pocket. Bryce guessed that he took part in some kind of recreational sport, the wide shoulders and muscular arms testament to a regime of intensive physical activity. He really should ask him about it, after all Suleyman seemed to be a permanent fixture in his room these days. Setting the brake on the trolley, the younger man tilted his head to one side and gave a small bow. 'Breakfast is served.' He removed the stainless steel plate cover with a flourish, a small ring of steam rolling up towards the ceiling. 'Porridge, scrambled egg, juice. No hot beverages, I'm afraid. Doctors orders.'

'Lovely,' Bryce replied without enthusiasm. The drowsiness and the protective gum guard he wore combined to slur his words. He plucked the guard from his mouth and made a conscious effort to form his speech coherently. 'Suleyman, someone was in here a minute ago, doctors I think. Who were they?'

The Turk frowned. He glanced around the room, as if the people Bryce referred to could still be there. 'In here?'

'Yes, a few moments ago. Perhaps you passed them in the corridor? Or maybe they're still at the nurses' station?'

The orderly shook his closely cropped head. 'I don't think so. There's only me and nurse Orla on duty today.'

'What about the policeman outside? He must have seen them.'

Suleyman shrugged and cocked a thumb over his shoulder. 'There's no one out there. Shift change I think.'

Bryce tutted. 'Well, someone was here. Maybe they were consultants.'

'Probably,' the orderly agreed, pumping up the pillows behind Bryce's shoulders. He positioned a tray across Bryce's lap and served up the food, placing a plastic spoon in his hand. 'Come on, eat up,' he smiled.

Bryce toyed with the food, forcing himself to swallow several mouthfuls. It was a struggle. Although the eggs were delicious and the orange juice freshly squeezed, Bryce didn't feel very hungry. It was as if he'd just come out of a coma, his head still thick with sleep, his stomach not quite ready to begin digesting food. What he wouldn't give for a strong pot of tea or coffee, anything to blast away the fog of fatigue that smothered his brain. Caffeine aside, what he wanted was a chance to wake up, get a little fresh air before breakfast perhaps, maybe some exercise. Any exercise in fact.

He pushed the eggs away as Suleyman fussed around the room, emptying the wastepaper basket and tidying the magazines on the coffee table. Fatigue notwithstanding, Bryce certainly felt better. The pain that had wracked his body had been reduced to a few minor aches, the excruciating sensitivity of his missing teeth soothed by the remedial dental repairs. His ribs no longer hurt, the broken nose would soon be reconstructed and he could move his leg a little more every day. The cuts and lacerations across his body had all been cleaned and dressed many times. He was healing nicely he'd been told. Before too long he'd be back in charge, sitting behind the Prime Minister's new desk on the twenty-sixth floor of the Euro Tower on Millbank. He was looking forward to his first day, although things were never going to be the same.

There'd been so much death. Friends, colleagues, Downing Street staff. Many of the Muslim victims had already been buried and he'd briefly caught Rana Hassani's funeral on the news, the streets of Slough swamped, the noisy outpouring of grief, the anger of the young that had resulted in the firebombing of two pubs near the town centre. There'd be more funerals to come, a public service to commemorate the deceased, a day of national mourning, proposals for the bomb site. So much to do, so much to take care of. Bryce wanted to be a part of it and yet his enforced banishment to a heavily guarded private hospital ward was somehow comforting, cocooned as he was from the chaos of the world outside.

He thought of Ella, lying in her own personal Hell. She'd been found in a bathroom, buried under a mountain of rubble. When Bryce had gone upstairs to retrieve the Heathrow dossier she must have used the opportunity to answer a call of nature, an action that had saved her life. She was one of only a few survivors from Downing Street and yet she had failed to regain consciousness. The last he'd heard she was still in a deep coma in the intensive care unit at St. Thomas'. Her injuries were extensive, the news bulletin had reported, not least those to her spine. Tears of frustration had stained Bryce's cheeks. Why did he have to hear everything from the news? Where was Hooper? Why wasn't he being briefed during his periods of lucidity?

He was about to ask Suleyman to turn on the TV when the door opened and nurse Orla entered the room. She wore a uniform of light blue, a crisp double buttoned tunic and trousers that strained against her heavy frame, and her hair was knotted in a tight auburn bun at the nape of her neck. Bryce didn't care for her too much. He thought her attitude was a little stern, almost indifferent. As if to reinforce that view, nurse Orla didn't utter a single word as she marched around his bed to inspect the monitors. Her practised fingers danced across the displays, and she made the *mmm* sound several times. Bryce noticed all medical professionals seemed to make that noncommittal, faintly annoying sound. Perhaps it was taught to them in medical school, the students spending whole lessons on how to make patients feel ill at ease.

'Well nurse Orla, what's the prognosis?' Bryce began, hoping to stir up a little banter. She didn't answer. Bryce glanced at Suleyman who ignored them both, concentrating intently on arranging the flowers in their vases. 'Nurse,' Bryce repeated, injecting a little authority into his voice.

Finally she turned towards him. Her narrow, freckled face seemed locked in a permanent frown and she looked a little irritated at the interruption. 'Yes, sir?' Her accent was Irish, not the harsh vowel sounds of the province but the gentle cadence of the far south. Before Bryce could speak she tutted loudly and picked up his temporary dental work sitting on the sideboard, inspecting them closely. 'They've done a grand job with those teeth.'

'Nurse.'

'What is it?'

'I had a couple of visitors a few minutes ago. Who were they?'

'Visitors?' she echoed. She seemed as puzzled as Suleyman at the suggestion. 'You've had no visitors since the day before yesterday. Prime Minister Hooper and Minister Saeed stopped by. Quite a day that was, I can tell you.'

'Doctors, then. Consultants. They were looking at my chart.'

Orla straightened up, hands on her wide hips. 'No, you've made a mistake. Access to this room is strictly controlled. Sure, I'd know if anyone had been in here.'

'I saw them,' Bryce insisted. 'They left when I woke up.'

She glanced at the fob watch dangling from her tunic. 'You were asleep?'

'I'm always bloody asleep!' he snapped. Orla stared at him like an aggrieved school mistress and Suleyman's duster froze on the window sill. Bryce took a deep breath and kept his voice calm. 'I'm sorry about that. A little frustration, that's all. I feel so doped up I can barely stay awake.'

'It's called the healing process,' Orla reminded him, patting his arm as if he were a child. She turned her attention back to the monitors as Suleyman sprayed window cleaner on the glass in short puffs of mist. Bryce spoke to her ample backside.

'I realise that, it's just that I'm feeling a lot better and I need to keep my brain active if nothing else. You say Minister's Hooper and Saeed were here?'

'Yes. And the photographer.'

Bryce jerked upright. Orange juice slopped across the tray. 'A photographer? Please tell me they didn't take any pictures.'

Orla shrugged her shoulders. 'Of course she did. It was all official and above board. The Prime Minister said the country had a right to - '

'I'm the Prime Minister, for God's sake!'

'Well, in any case they wanted to send a message to the terrorists, that they'd failed.' She removed the tray from his lap and placed it back on the trolley.

'Although they didn't print the most flattering picture of you, I must say. You looked quite ill.'

Bryce fumed, balling the sheets up in his fists. How dare they publish pictures of him without permission. What the bloody hell was Jacob playing at? 'Why don't I have a phone in here? Bring me a phone, would you? I need to make a call.'

Orla shook her head. 'I don't have that authority, sir.'

'Well find me someone who has!' Bryce yelled.

'Try not to get yourself excited,' warned Orla. Before Bryce could answer she spun on her heel and headed towards the door. 'I'll see what I can do,' she said over her shoulder.

Bryce's head swam, the world before his eyes momentarily shifting on its axis. He clamped them shut until the giddiness faded. His heart thumped in his chest and his pulse quickened, banishing the fatigue. It felt good. Beside the bed the monitors flashed and beeped their disapproval. Suleyman diplomatically ignored the outburst, using a long feather duster to clean the TV on the wall.

'Turn that on, would you Suleyman?' The Turk wiped a finger across the touch screen, coaxing the unit into life. 'Were you here when this photographer was taking pictures?'

'No, no,' Suleyman insisted, shaking his head as he flipped through the mini-screens on the menu. He saw a news icon and stabbed it, the image filling the TV. 'I was downstairs with the other staff. There were lots of very important people here, lots of police too. All the streets were blocked off outside.'

Bryce waved a hand for silence as the picture on the TV changed to a reporter standing outside the Houses of Parliament, a large umbrella held aloft as rain and sleet lanced across Parliament Square. Big Ben loomed above him and the famous building behind was ringed with huge slabs of concrete and razor wire. Armed police stood guard behind the barricades, black uniforms glistening in the rain.

'...*in parliament behind me, where the Egyptian delegation is meeting behind closed doors with government officials to finalise details of the energy bill, expected to come into force if, as expected, Prime Minister Hooper endorses the Treaty of Cairo. Deputy Prime Minister Tariq Saeed said earlier today that he was hopeful Britain would soon announce its intention, particularly in light of the recent attempts by neo-Nazis to...*'

'Tariq,' Bryce whispered.

'Excuse me, Mister Gabriel?'

'Nothing.' Bryce pointed to the screen. 'Tell me Suleyman, what do you think of this treaty?'

The Turk studied the reporter huddled beneath his umbrella as he tapped the feather duster lightly in his hand. 'I think people are fed up with being scared. The country's in a mess. People want stability, see the economy pick up. Cairo will be good for all of us.'

'What about the refugees in Egypt?' Bryce argued. 'Aren't people worried about the sheer numbers that will enter Europe? The potential strain on public services?' He lowered his voice. 'The tensions it could cause?'

Suleyman dismissed the idea with a shake of his head. 'Not really. My mum and dad came over when I was a boy, knuckled down, paid their bills. Same for a lot of Turks when we joined the EU. In my tower block in Newham there are nearly two hundred families, most of them from different parts of the world, and everyone seems to get along. You said once that this was a country of immigrants, remember that Mister

Gabriel? Well, you're right. There's no British anymore, we're all just Europeans.'

'So you support the treaty then?'

'Who doesn't?' the Turk shrugged, 'Apart from the terrorists that is.' He waved the feather duster across the screen then turned and smiled at Bryce. 'Oh, I nearly forgot.' He bustled over to the trolley and bent down, retrieving a parcel from the lower shelf. He handed it to Bryce. 'Arrived yesterday.'

He'd received a mountain of get well gifts in the last few days; a veritable forest of plants and flowers, video messages from world leaders and media personalities, a ton of mail from ordinary people. He'd barely had a chance to look at any of it. This would be the first one he'd unwrapped himself and it was a welcome distraction. The package was quite heavy, the thick padded envelope unceremoniously ripped open at the top and marked with a 'SCANNED AND PASSED' security stamp in bold red letters. The front of the package bore his address here at the hospital, and turning it over he saw no return address on the back. He ripped the envelope all the way open and withdrew the contents.

It was a book, a beautifully bound volume with a dark blue spine inscribed with gold lettering. Bryce turned it over. *Chasing the Rainbow – A History of Around the World Ocean Voyages*. The cover showed the bow of a yacht, buried deep in the trough of a huge grey wave, black storm clouds pressing down above the mast. It was a powerful image, frightening even, and Bryce guessed it was somewhere in the Southern Ocean. He thumbed through the glossy pages and something dropped into his lap. It was a small card, the words on it handwritten in a neat block of text. It read:

Hello Prime Minister,

Tried to visit you last week but apparently I don't have the necessary clearance. In any case I hope you're recovering well. They ran your biog on a news program the other day and I noticed you were a keen sailor in your youth, so it seems we both have something else in common as well as surviving a major terrorist attack. I thought I'd leave this book with you. It's a cracking read and maybe when you're feeling better it'll inspire you to take to the water again, get a bit of sea air. Always works wonders for me.

Get well, good luck.

Mac

He turned the card over in his hand. The logo on the front was a clear outline of a yacht, the words 'Boat Delivery Specialists' beneath, an email address and telephone numbers. Bryce flipped the card over and re-read the message, deeply moved by the gesture. The first call he made would be to Mac, not only to thank him for the book but for his life too. He hadn't had the chance to do that yet and it bothered him greatly. Without Mac he'd have been a charred corpse in the rubble.

The door opened and nurse Orla marched back into the room. She paused at the foot of Bryce's bed and cleared her throat, her hands folded in front of her.

'I'm afraid I can't get hold of anyone right now, sir. Your call will have to wait.'

'It can't,' Bryce said. 'Let me have your cell phone. I'll cover any cost.'

Confusion clouded Orla's face. 'I don't - '

Bryce held out his hand. 'Don't be ridiculous. Your phone. Please.' He saw Orla glance at Suleyman, as if she were seeking permission. Bryce frowned. 'Why are you looking at him?' He turned to the Turk. 'I'm getting nowhere here. Let me have your phone, please.'

Suleyman shook his head slowly. 'Nurse Orla is right, she doesn't have the authority and neither does the hospital.' He waved her away and Orla hurried from the room. Suleyman put down his duster and came over to Bryce's bed, squeezing his muscular frame into a chair. He leaned back, crossing one leg over the other. Bryce was confused.

'What's going on? And since when does an orderly give orders to a staff nurse?'

The Turk smiled. Rain drummed on the window. 'Minister Saeed has expressly forbidden any contact with the outside world. For now.'

Bryce thought he'd misheard. 'He's what?'

'It's about your personal safety, sir. There's been some threatening phone calls, here at the hospital. A security guard has been arrested, as well as a kitchen porter. We're monitoring suspicious activity in the apartment block across the street.' Suleyman leaned forward, shoulders bulging beneath his purple tunic. The chirpiness had disappeared, replaced by a voice that was measured, serious. Authoritative. 'Minister Saeed believes that an infiltration exercise is in progress. That another attempt may be made on your life.'

Bryce's eyes narrowed. 'Who are you, Suleyman?'

The orderly kept his voice low. 'I've been sent here to watch over you. On Minister Saeed's orders. He insisted you be looked after.'

'I want to speak to him.'

'He's coming here, very soon.'

'You're looking out for me?' Suleyman nodded. 'Then who were the two people checking my chart when I woke up? Why did they run off?'

The Turk pushed himself out of his chair and pressed the call button next to Bryce's bed. 'You sure you weren't dreaming? An after effect of your medication?'

'Don't patronize me. I know what I saw.'

Suleyman ignored him as nurse Orla reappeared. 'Let's get him settled,' he ordered. As Orla busied herself next to the bed, the Turk took the card from Bryce's fingers, slid it inside the book and placed it on the trolley. 'I'll put this with your personal effects. Let me know when you want it.'

'What I want is to make a bloody phone call.'

'Not possible.'

'I'm not asking. Don't forget, I'm the Prime Minister.'

'Well, technically that title now belongs to Jacob Hooper.' Suleyman shrugged his shoulders and smiled. 'Hey, don't shoot the messenger, Mister Gabriel. I'm following orders, that's all. Now, Minister Saeed will be here in the next few days, so I suggest you rest until he gets here. Then you can talk.'

'No, I want my phone call, dammit. Are you...you... can you...'

The words trailed away. His mouth felt thick, his tongue heavy. He turned his head, watched nurse Orla as she regulated the drip chamber, saw the glistening droplets feeding into the clear plastic tube, spiralling down into his body. Suleyman turned off the TV and gathered his cleaning materials, placing them on the trolley. Orla pulled the sheets over Bryce's chest and slipped the mouth guard over his upper gum.

'Get some rest, now.'

Suleyman stood beside her, looking down. 'Don't worry Gabe, I'll be watching your back.'

He heard them chuckle, the voices sounding distant, as if Bryce were at the bottom of a deep well, two dark silhouettes far above him. He opened his mouth, tried to speak.

'Suleyman...'

'What do I keep telling you?' the voice echoed. 'Call me Sully.'

The lights dimmed and he heard the wheels of the trolley squeaking out of the door. Then there was silence, only the distant patter of the rain on the window registering in his dulled senses. His eyes closed once, then twice, waves of fatigue pounding the shoreline of his consciousness.

Then the world turned black.

Hertfordshire

As the single-decker bus approached Radlett train station, Danny emerged from a stand of trees by the side of the road and jogged toward the bus stop, only turning at the last moment to flag the vehicle down in the wash of its headlights. He wore a high-visibility orange raincoat with 'NETRAIL' stencilled on the back in large black letters, the collar turned up against the early morning drizzle, a black beanie hat pulled low over his eyes. The bus rattled noisily to a halt at the stop and the doors hissed open. Danny climbed aboard.

'How far you going?' he asked the driver, a scowling young Asian man with spiky gelled hair and a gold ear stud. He pointed above his head, his hands wrapped in black fingerless leather gloves.

'Read the front. Watford general.'

'Right,' Danny said. He smiled, eager to avoid confrontation. 'That's fine.'

The driver sucked his gums loudly and gave Danny a filthy look. 'Tap in, then.'

Danny fished the travel card from his pocket and wiped it across the reader. It was the first time he'd used it and his heart almost skipped a beat as the digital display momentarily flickered before announcing his authority to travel. The driver closed the doors and floored the accelerator, sending Danny scrambling for a hand hold. He glanced over his shoulder, saw the driver's challenging stare in the rear view mirror. Danny smothered his anger and walked towards the back of the bus. There were several other passengers scattered throughout the seats, most wearing medical uniforms of one sort or another. Early hospital shift, Danny assumed.

He found an empty seat at the rear of the bus, sliding down low and folding the collar of the raincoat around his face. The other passengers paid him no attention, wrapped in their own thoughts or watching the news on one of the on-board TV screens. The newsreader droned on about a protest march planned for London, then the progress of the Egyptian treaty talks with other European leaders in Brussels. Danny's heart suddenly leapt when his own picture flashed up on the screen, superimposed over footage of the decimated Luton Mosque where bodies were still being recovered. Danny felt sick, with fear mostly but also with revulsion at the sight of small body bags being stretchered into waiting ambulances while mourning parents screamed and beat their chests. He hated Muslims, of course he did, but not like this. He rubbed a hand across the dark growth on his face and up over his severe and uneven haircut. Relax, he told himself, no-one will recognise you in a hurry.

He yawned, stretching his legs beneath the seat. The past week had been both physically and mentally exhausting. From the Longhill estate Danny had jogged for half a mile before climbing over a fence and scrambling up a railway embankment. It was the best way to leave the area he decided, avoiding the streets, the CCTV, the forces that hunted him. The railway line was deserted, the occasional train announcing its presence long before he saw it, and was easily avoided. He kept his ears open for police blimps too, but never saw one.

The crew hut had been occupied when he first encountered it, a long, singly storey portacabin adjacent to the tracks, just past the station at Neasden. He'd waited in the undergrowth, listening to the muffled voices, watching the flickering light of a TV beyond the mesh covered windows. After a while several orange-clad workmen piled outside and boarded a small engine on a nearby service track. With a loud clanking and a flash of electrical discharge the engine tooted its horn and headed off into the darkness.

Danny circled the portacabin carefully, creeping around the outside then peering through the grimy windows until he was satisfied the place was empty. The door was unlocked and he moved inside quickly, listening for several moments in case someone was still there. In the corner the TV was switched off, an almost empty percolator of coffee steaming on the kitchen unit. There was a range cooker and a microwave, a couple of battered sofas and a table piled with newspapers. To the left was a door that led to the washroom. Danny found a pair of scissors in the kitchen drawer and got to work on his hair, scooping the cuttings from the sink and scattering them outside. He found a pair of navy-blue work dungarees hanging on a hook near the shower and changed into them, stuffing his jeans down into a waste bin. He drank the coffee and helped himself to some bread from the overhead units, a single slice of cooked ham from the fridge. He chewed the food slowly while he weighed up his options. Cheated out of their prize, someone on the Longhill would have called the police by now. The estate would be crawling, his dad's flat torn apart. The guilt almost choked him but he had to avoid the authorities. The longer he stayed on the run, the more chance that the real terrorists were nicked. The portacabin was isolated, far from the streets, a source of warmth, food and fresh water. It was worth the risk.

After midnight a fine drizzle had begun to fall. Danny found an orange hi-vi raincoat amongst a dozen others on a coat rack beside the door and ducked outside. Behind the portacabin was a thick copse of birch and ferns and Danny decided to explore it, wading through the damp undergrowth. Deep in the trees, in a small clearing, he found what he was looking for. The mound of gravel was covered in weeds, a wheel-less barrow overturned on its summit. The pile of railway sleepers stood adjacent to a set of rusted tracks that were choked with vegetation. A disused spur, leading to who knew where, unused, forgotten.

He manoeuvred the sleepers until he'd created a chamber, a deep crawl space where he could keep dry, where the thermal imaging cameras couldn't penetrate. Next to the sleepers he found some sackcloth and made himself a bed inside the chamber. Returning to the portacabin he stole a few newspapers from the untidy pile on the chipped coffee table, a plastic bottle of fresh water and a toilet roll. Lying inside his hide, listening to the rain drumming on the wood above him, he felt safe. Now he had a chance to grab some sleep, to feed himself, to think about his next move.

The sound of the returning engine snapped Danny out of a fitful doze. He threw off the raincoat he was using as a blanket and crawled outside. It was still dark. Through the trees he saw the night crew stretch and yawn, grab their personal bags and trudge away in a long, luminous line towards the station at Neasden. The next shift arrived after daybreak, enjoyed a noisy, good natured breakfast and headed off on the service engine. Danny discovered fresh food in the fridge and helped himself to the older stuff, knowing each shift would blame the other for any discrepancies. He washed, trimmed his hair a little more, allowing the stubble on his face to grow. Back in his den he leafed through the state-owned *Guardian* to pass the time. There was a lengthy article about him, the photo a sneering police mug shot that highlighted his dishevelled appearance, the lank hair, thin face and dark circled eyes that glared at the camera lens. A drug user, criminal, waster – terrorist. The article picked his life apart, his unremarkable education, his service with the Logistics Corp, the drunk driving episode and subsequent sacking from the civil service, the arrest for leafleting with the banned English Freedom Movement. The article depressed him, his life laid bare, every major event analyzed, summarized and concluded. It was all tied nicely together, all so convincing that even Danny believed it. And worst of all was the picture of his dad being bundled into a van. He almost wept.

One night turned into two, then four. During the day he would stay close to the hide, wary of helicopters and blimps, scuttling beneath the sleepers when he thought he heard one approaching. He kept his cell off, knowing someone, somewhere would be waiting for its unique signal to appear on the grid, for his position to be triangulated, then targeted by men with dogs and guns. He dozed restlessly in his den, like a fox waiting for the world to darken, hoping that each passing hour would see the hunt slacken, the investigation move in a different direction. But the newspapers told a different story, the constant images of death and destruction, his picture everywhere, the country clamouring for justice. As the sun set on his fifth day in hiding, Danny realised they'd never stop searching for him. He had to run, get away as far as possible. To do that, he would need help.

The whistle of the service engine echoed through the trees. Danny heard it rumble past, headed up the track with the latest night shift. He broke down his den, dumped the sacking in the undergrowth, the papers in the waste bin. He filled his water bottle, took a little food and some fruit and stuffed it all into a carrier bag.

As an afterthought he rummaged through the personal belongings of the night shift. He found a pair of heavy duty cutters and a pre-pay travel card, then extracted a couple of twenty Euro notes from two separate wallets. In a final criminal act he took a black beanie hat from a hook by the door and headed off into the night, reasonably confident his temporary stay would never be discovered. He tramped noisily along the stones by the side of the tracks, the orange raincoat turned inside out, following a branch line that curved northwards. After a mile or so he dumped his ID card and cell phone in a deep rabbit hole along the embankment. The embedded chips frightened him, mindful of the urban myths about remote tracking. He felt naked without them but now he was on the run his paranoia cut deep.

The night was quiet, the sky clear and littered with stars. The track was deserted, not a single train interrupting his silent journey north. Where the line bordered houses and main roads Danny moved carefully, crouching, crawling, keeping to the shadows of bridges, walls and trees. Gradually he left the lights of the city behind, relaxing a little as the track wound its way northwards through fields and woods. Lights shone to the left and right, isolated farms, houses, darkened industrial estates. The only living things he saw now were wary foxes and darting bats.

Ten miles beyond Neasden the railway line dipped into a high sided embankment and disappeared into a tunnel that ran beneath the M1 motorway. Danny stood at the mouth, unnerved by the inky blackness of its unknown length, the proximity of the walls to the track. Too dangerous, he decided. He'd have to go around.

He struggled up the heavily wooded embankment, finally reaching the summit where exhaustion overcame him. He curled up on the damp ground, the raincoat wrapped tightly around his body, falling asleep just as a weak sun broke the horizon.

The bug woke him some time later, humming beside his ear, its tiny legs brushing his skin. He rolled over with a start, slapping his face in revulsion. He sat up wearily and yawned, his limbs aching from the cold, his eyes red-rimmed and gritty. The daylight gave him a clearer view of his surroundings. He was deep in the undergrowth, fenced in by a few spears of sunlight slicing through the overhead canopy. He took a swig of water and got to his feet, stretching languidly. He was on fairly even ground but a short distance away through the trees was a steep embankment that dropped towards the motorway. There were no paths nearby, no bridleways or trails. The wood was bordered by the train line on one side and empty fields on the other. For now he was reasonably safe. He'd wait until nightfall before moving again.

He explored the undergrowth, finding the dead branches and ferns required for a rough bed. When he was finished Danny studied his handiwork, enjoying a rare moment of satisfaction in recalling long-forgotten woodland skills. He lay down on the thick bed of ferns and slept fitfully during the afternoon. Later, as the sun began to set, he got up and watched the traffic on the M1 from the safety of the embankment. The road was busy but there were no obvious police patrols to be seen. There were no junctions nearby either, which meant little or no CCTV coverage. He hoped. He returned to his rough bed and waited a while longer, dozing as the sun disappeared beyond the horizon.

The woods were dark when he woke again, startled by a sudden movement in the bushes nearby. He looked around, his head swivelling right and left, trying to locate the source of the noise. Nothing. The gloom between the trees was barely penetrable, cloaking whatever lurked there. Danny scrambled to his feet, cursing his irrational fear. He brushed himself clean and scattered his temporary bed with a few lazy kicks. It was time to push on.

He side-stepped carefully down the steep embankment, using the trees to slow his descent, then crouched behind a bush at the roadside. The rush hour traffic had thinned out as the evening wore on, until the gaps in the traffic were wide enough for Danny to risk it. Choosing his moment carefully, he hopped over the metal crash barrier and ran across the motorway towards the woods on the far side, scrambling up the opposite bank as the nearest car flashed past. He kept on going, climbing a wooden fence and crossing a field of long grass until he found the train tracks once more. He trudged on, headed north.

Before dawn he left the line just south of Radlett station, climbing a wire fence and landing on an empty footpath at the southern end of the empty high street, deserted in the pre-dawn stillness. He'd heard the bus before he saw it, quickly deciding to take a chance and continue his journey in speed and comfort. He was far enough away from London now and he felt the need to test his disguise, check the credit on the travel card. Despite the awkward bastard of a driver he'd boarded the bus unnoticed, just another early morning commuter in his rail worker's uniform. No-one was looking for a rail worker. Yet.

He sat quietly in the rear seat watching the countryside flash by, fields of green and brown, the sky a dark grey. The TV droned on, the vent beneath his muddy trainers blasting diesel tinted warm air, the motion of the bus dulling his senses. Danny's head lolled once, twice. He slid lower in the seat as the drowsy cocktail lulled him into a deep, dangerous sleep…

He bolted upright, disorientated, his chin damp with saliva, a painful crick in his neck. Blue lights throbbed across the windows and a siren wailed deafeningly close. They'd found him. Panicked, he grabbed the handrail and stood, swaying awkwardly as the bus veered across the road and braked sharply. He lost his balance, glimpsing the ambulance as it swept past, and tumbled along the aisle to the floor. Helping hands came to his aid immediately, supporting him as he climbed to his feet.

'Y'alright, dear?' smiled a large black woman, her teeth as white as pearls, her nurses' uniform visible under a bright yellow raincoat. Her trained eyes bored into Danny's, searching for signs of damage or illness.

'Sure,' he replied, turning away from the intrusive stare. 'Lost my footing. Clumsy idiot.'

'If you're going to have an accident it might as well be on a bus full of nurses,' she chuckled. Danny thanked her again and looked out through the windscreen. Up ahead, the dark hedgerows and fields came to an abrupt end, dissected by the lights of a sprawling industrial estate on one side and row after row of terraced housing on the other.

'Where are we?' he asked the woman.

'Watford. Ten minutes to the hospital,' she smiled. 'You sure you're o.k.?'

Danny nodded and returned to his seat, rummaging in his carrier bag for the water and gulping several mouthfuls. He wasn't that far away now, about eight miles the other side of town. A short time later the bus turned into the car park of Watford General.

Danny hopped off the bus and weaved through the ranks of parked vehicles towards the bicycle shelters, the orange coat bundled under his arm, plastic carrier bag dangling from the other. It wasn't long before he found the perfect candidate, a well-used but serviceable all-terrain model. The CCTV post was a short distance away, the black bulbous eye of the camera dome hanging like a ripe berry from the curved neck. He was partially hidden beneath the shelter but he had to be quick. He snapped the cheap lock with the stolen cutters and wheeled the machine across the car park, plastic bag dangling from the handlebars. The sun was starting to rise as he pedalled away from the hospital, heading for the north-east of town where the bicycle hummed along the empty footpaths of Cassiobury Park, cutting across the Grand Union canal and crossing the bridge over the M25 London orbital.

After his brief brush with civilisation it was a relief to be swallowed up by the countryside once again. The sun climbed into the morning sky, its rays chasing the pre-dawn mists from the fields. As he coasted down an empty lane, Danny felt far removed from the Longhill estate, from the stink and poverty, from the integrated camera systems that tracked every movement, from the surveillance blimps that hovered over the skies of London. Out here things seemed clean, fresh, a place where English people toiled over English soil, where the peal of village church bells sounded across the fields and birdsong warbled in the hedgerows. England, my England. Danny smiled.

The house he sought wasn't far away. He'd googled it many times, heard rumours of the meetings that were once held there, meetings that mapped out a new future for Britain. He'd even borrowed a mate's car once, driving up here just to see it, his envious eye noting the high walls, the gravel driveway that curved towards the Georgian mansion whose distinctive chimneys climbed above the surrounding trees. He hoped – no, prayed - the man was still there.

He cycled through the village of Marshbrook, a collection of small shops with whitewashed walls and dark timber beams that sported neither security grills nor graffiti. Even the pavements were free from litter. A tractor rumbled past in the opposite direction, the driver waving cheerfully. Danny kept his head down, pedalling past the village pub where a middle-aged woman on a step ladder tended to a row of hanging baskets. Two early morning joggers bounced across the road in front of him, their faces flushed with effort, a blur of expensive trainers and lurid running gear. Then he was through the village, the well-kept high street surrendering to fields and hedgerows once again. The lane he sought was the last turning on the left, just beyond the edge of the settlement.

Danny leaned into the corner, the tarmac of the road giving way to a well-worn dirt lane. There was an open field to the right and the houses of the rich to the left, set well back from the lane itself and partly hidden by walls and trees, exclusive dwellings where privacy was highly valued and earnestly defended. Danny felt like a trespasser.

At the end of the lane a pair of black spiked gates set into a high wall barred any further passage. Danny climbed off the bike, rivulets of sweat running down the sides of his thin face, his t-shirt beneath the orange raincoat damp from exertion. Through the bars of the gates he saw thick banks of rhododendron bushes lining the gravel driveway towards a stand of tall cedars. He could just make out the roof of the distant house.

A sudden breeze made Danny shiver. What if the man had moved? What if one of the villagers had recognised him? And yet he had no choice other than to push the intercom button next to the gate.

'State your business,' ordered a voice from the tinny speaker.

Summoning all his courage, Danny pulled off the raincoat and lifted the sleeve of his t-shirt, exposing the *lions passant* tattoo to the camera that scrutinised him from above the gate. There was silence for several long moments, then the same voice said: 'Wait.'

A couple of minutes had passed before the dog appeared, a German Shepherd, its paws slapping the gravel as it bounded towards the gates. It skidded to a stop just before the bars, its brown eyes locked on Danny, a low growl rumbling in its throat. Danny took a step back, despite the barrier between them. The dog, sensing his fear, bared its yellowed teeth silently. Not once did it bark. Danny, despite his nerves, was impressed. This was a well-trained animal, not like the snapping, vicious fighting dogs that strained at their owner's leashes back on the Longhill. Suddenly, to Danny's horror, the gates hummed and swung inwards.

'Inside. Be quick about it.'

Danny froze as a man emerged from the thick bushes beside the gates. He looked a little younger than Danny, his fair hair cut short, a camouflaged jacket over jeans and green wellingtons. In his arms he cradled a black shotgun, a police-issue Mossberg if Danny wasn't mistaken. The voice, bearing a slight west country twang, was the voice on the intercom.

'Don't worry about Nelson, he won't harm you as long as you do as you're told. C'mon, let's go. Bring the bike inside.'

Danny pulled his raincoat back on and wheeled the bike through the gates, keeping it between him and the loping Alsatian. The man whistled and Nelson darted away, back around the curve of the driveway. Danny followed him, past the huge rhododendron bushes, the well kept lawns and open spaces where dead leaves had been raked into wet piles. The smell of wood smoke hung on the air and birds chirped noisily from the trees above. Around the walls tall evergreens screened the estate from prying eyes.

The house loomed ahead. Danny thought it was amazing, like a footballer's house, or a movie star's. It had big double doors, a porch with white columns and a huge lantern overhead. It was old – no, period Danny corrected himself - but it had been beautifully restored, the stonework and window frames painted a brilliant white, the walls a shade of soft green that blended in with the surrounding grounds. At a right angle to the house two cars were parked in the shadows of a large car port, a white Bentley Continental and a more practical Nissan pickup. Even the car port construction matched the house, with some sort of accommodation above. Danny was impressed, and not a little intimidated. He continued across the drive, wheeling the bike towards the main door.

'Not that way, round the back. And leave the bike.'

They skirted the side of the building, following a neatly-cut path through the cedars to the terrace at the rear. Danny was impressed by its sheer size and opulence. The tiles underfoot were limestone, the terrace dotted with flower pots and tubs of every shape and size. Garden furniture was stacked in neat piles and covered with green plastic tarpaulins and tropical plants ringed the terrace like a Mediterranean hotel. A flight of wide steps led down to another terrace level that housed a large, empty swimming pool, dead leaves littering its tiled base. Further away, beyond a wooden perimeter fence, the ground sloped towards a shallow valley and the distant, sun dappled Hertfordshire countryside. From the rear of the house there wasn't a single dwelling as far as the eye could see and overhead, white clouds drifted across a clear blue sky, chased by a gusting wind.

Danny was impressed by the house, the huge terrace, by the unrestricted view. There was a sense of security about the estate, as if the world had been shut out behind the high walls and was forbidden entry. For the first time in a long time, Danny felt safe.

'Twenty four acres, in case you're wondering.'

He turned. A man beckoned him from an ornate wrought iron table, a big man, bald, tanned, his eyes shaded by designer sunglasses, his imposing bulk wrapped in a navy blue Barbour jacket. He didn't get up as Danny approached, the remnants of a hearty breakfast scattered across the table in front of him. In his fist he held a large cigar, the smoke whipped away by the wind. Danny's armed escort whispered in the man's ear while Nelson settled down beside him, head between its paws, relaxed but watchful as Danny waited a few yards away.

'Cheers, Joe,' the man said in a harsh London accent. 'Get rid of the bike, please. And that awful jacket.'

Danny quickly pulled his raincoat off and handed it to Joe who trudged back around the side of the house.

'Joe's my sister's boy. She's fucking useless, heroin addict, but he's a smart lad, looks after my interests.

Ex-army, like you. Lost a lot of friends over in Afghanistan, all on the same chopper. One of the only survivors. Very sad that, don't you think?'

The man waved Danny into a chair opposite and he eyed Nelson warily as he sat down on the cold metal seat. His thin body shivered in the wind. 'I didn't mean to disturb you like this, Mister Carver. I didn't know where else to go.'

Raymond Carver, ex-chairman and founder of the English Freedom Movement, laid a reassuring hand on Danny's arm. Danny looked down at the thick, well-manicured fingers that patted his goose pimpled skin. His eyes travelled upwards, past the heavy gold Rolex, to the chunky gold necklace that nestled in the dark hair beneath his open neck shirt. He'd only ever seen the man once before, from a distance, at a rally in a field in Kent. Ray Carver was a big man in the flesh, a hard man, a street fighter in his younger days, a businessman, politician, self-made millionaire. Danny had never been more intimidated.

'Don't worry, Danny. Can I call you Danny?'

Danny nodded, searching the older man's craggy face, his eyes impossible to read behind the gold rimmed sunglasses. 'Sure, Mister Carver.'

'Let's cut the formal bullshit, shall we? Ray or Raymond, whichever you like.'

'Ok.'

Carver puffed several times on his cigar, studying the tip that glowed like a hot coal. 'No-one knows you're here, right Danny? You didn't tell anyone you were coming? Anyone at all?'

'Didn't have a chance even if I wanted to, Mister – I mean Ray. Some people in the village saw me though.'

Carver leaned back in his chair, blue smoke swirling around his mouth. 'Oh, I wouldn't worry about them.

Many of us share the same ideals if you understand my meaning. We live quietly, discreetly. Privacy is highly valued in Marshbrook.'

'That's good.'

Carver held out his hand. 'I need your ID card. And your cell phone.'

'I dumped them.'

'You know they can track those things, don't you? It's the chip.'

Danny looked bemused. 'Yeah, I – can they?'

'Course. Where exactly?'

'Where what?'

'Where did you dump them? C'mon, quickly.'

So Danny explained. When he finished Carver nodded several times, apparently satisfied.

'How did you get here, son?'

'I walked, mostly.'

Carver stared at him for a moment and then said: 'Bullshit.'

'I swear, Mister Carver. I followed the train lines for most of the way. And a bus.'

Carver leaned forward, tapping the grey embers of his cigar into a large cut glass ashtray. 'Police have got every transport hub covered across the whole country. Your picture's everywhere; TV, news billboards, papers. It even flashed up on the Bentley's console the other day.'

'That's why I cut my hair, let my beard grow. I was careful, Mister Carver. I stayed out of sight.'

'Ray.'

'Sorry. Ray.'

The older man balanced his cigar in the ashtray and dragged his chair closer to the table. He produced a small notepad and pen from his pocket, flipping it open to a blank page. 'Alright, Danny. From the moment you decided to run, I want to know what happened. Every route you took, people you saw, where you slept, ate, took a shit, everything. From the beginning.'

Danny told him, his thin arms wrapped around his body. He was freezing, the sharp breeze gusting across the terrace, cutting through his damp t-shirt and filthy dungarees. Carver seemed oblivious to his shivering, to the tremble in his voice, scribbling away on the pad as he recorded every detail of the escape. He's a careful man, Danny told himself, knowing the interrogation was necessary. Because that's what this was, an interrogation. Carver had asked the same questions several times, forcing Danny to repeat himself through chattering teeth. He willed himself to concentrate, focussing on his answers, recalling the details of his journey north. Carver referred to his notes constantly, his inquiries delivered in a quick fire fashion.

'The bloke on the bus, the driver. What was he wearing again?'

'An earring,' Danny chattered.

'What else? You mentioned something else.'

'Er, gloves. With no fingers. Like weight training ones.'

'Colour?'

'Black.'

Danny watched Ray mark a line of notes with another small tick. That was a good sign. If Ray felt safe then he'd be more inclined to help him, right? He had to be totally honest, one hundred percent kosher. For thirty minutes Danny answered every one of Ray's questions with as much speed and accuracy as he could muster. Eventually Carver said: 'You're sure that's everything?'

'Positive.' Danny shivered violently, his arms tucked inside the bib of his dungarees. He was silent for a moment, then he said: 'I didn't do it, Ray. I didn't know it was a bomb.'

Carver shrugged, shoving the notepad in his pocket. 'No-one's accusing you Danny.'

'The people on my estate, they were hunting me like a dog.'

'Every one of them a fucking Judas,' Carver spat. 'Forget them. You can't go back there anyway.'

'Mind your blood pressure, Raymond,' giggled a voice from the French doors. Danny saw an older woman step out onto the terrace and waddle towards them, her silver hair cut fashionably short, a heavy parka wrapped around her voluminous frame. Like Ray she was well tanned, her ready smile dazzlingly white.

'There she is, ear wigging again,' Carver chuckled. 'Danny, this is my wife, Tess.'

'Missus Carver,' trembled Danny.

'Tess will do just fine,' she smiled. In her hand she held a black puffer jacket, the other shading her eyes from the bright sunlight. Her wrists were heavy with bangles that chimed musically as she moved.

'Where's your sunnies?' Carver frowned. 'All that squinting will make your lines worse.'

She turned towards Danny and pulled a face. 'He's such a flatterer, isn't he? Here, you must be freezing.' Danny almost snatched the jacket from her outstretched hand and tugged it on over his t-shirt. He sat back down, tucking his chin deep inside its warm folds. He felt Tess's eyes on him.

'Well, it's nice to meet you, Danny,' she said. She held out her hand and Danny grasped it, mumbling an embarrassed greeting. 'Love the new look by the way.'

Danny ran his hand across his stubbly head. 'I didn't really - '

'Don't worry, I'll tidy that up for you. Cut hair for a living years ago. That's how I met Ray. Course, he had some back then.' She gave her husband's head an affectionate rub.

'Any news?' Carver asked his wife.

Her smile disappeared and she nodded gravely, as if announcing the death of a sick relative. 'It's all about Cairo now. The French came in with a deal sweetener late last night, something to do with future power station construction. Media are all over it.'

Carver snorted loudly, clamping his teeth around the soggy end of his cigar and firing it up with a gold lighter. 'And so it begins,' he growled, coaxing the burning tip with pursed lips.

'We're not done yet, Raymond.'

Carver looked at his wife, smiled, and took her hand in his, kissing it gently. 'Ever the optimist, that's my Tess.' He cocked his head toward Danny. 'What about our guest?'

'Item number three on the BBC, five on Sky. Cairo's knocked him off the top slot.'

'That's good. What else?'

'Joe's taken the pickup, gone to have a look around the village and beyond for any unusual traffic and suchlike.'

'I want him to take a trip into Watford, check for any activity around the hospital. Danny got off a bus there,' he explained. 'The law will be all over that place if they've got a sniff.'

Tess pulled a cell from her pocket. 'I'll ring Joe now.'

Carver shook his head. 'Not on the phone, love. From now on, no phones, no texts or tweets, nothing. Mundane, everyday stuff only.' He turned to Danny, exhaling a thick waft of smoke. 'O.k., son, you'll stay here for now, keep out of sight. Tess'll tidy you up, sort your hair out. Keep the beard though. Later on we'll talk about the next step.' Carver reached out, patted Danny on the arm. 'You're among friends now.'

'That's right,' echoed Tess, 'you're quite safe here.' She brightened suddenly, tucking her hands beneath her armpits and stamping her fur-booted feet. 'God, it's freezing. I'm going to run upstairs, sort out some clothes for our guest.'

'Good girl.'

Tess leaned over her husband, planted a wet kiss on his head and waddled back to the house before disappearing inside. Danny thought he could still hear her bangles even after the door had closed.

Carver stubbed out the cigar in the ashtray then glanced at his Rolex. 'Come on, I'll show you to your digs.' He got to his feet, hitching the waistband of his jeans up beneath the bulge of his belly. He pointed to Danny's feet. 'Kick those things off before you come in the house, son.'

Danny slipped his filthy trainers off and padded after Carver through the French doors, delighting in the unexpected warmth of the floor tiles, then marvelling at the size and the hi-tech, marble opulence of the kitchen. He followed Carver through a huge reception room where every wall, every shelf and sideboard seemed to have some reference to historical England, from the medieval paintings and antique maps that littered the walls to the ornate bookshelves crammed with gold-leafed, leather bound volumes. In the wide entrance hall a gleaming suit of armour silently guarded the main door, the symbolic shield with its three lions *passant* clamped between its metal gauntlets. Carver rapped the shield with his knuckles as he passed.

'Look familiar?' he chuckled.

'Yeah,' replied Danny, rubbing his arm self-consciously.

'Never was one for body art myself. You know tattooists are supposed to report political artwork to the authorities, right?'

Danny looked pained. 'Yeah, but the bloke was kosher, Ray. Known him for years.'

'What, like the others on your estate?' he sneered over his shoulder.

Danny didn't reply. Instead he said: 'Lovely house.'

'Car dealerships aren't the cash cow they used to be,' said Carver, grabbing a set of keys from a hook behind the front door. 'Got out at the right time. Sold the lot.'

Danny hobbled painfully behind Carver across the gravel driveway then up a flight of stairs behind the car port. Carver unlocked the door and led him inside, pushing the sunglasses on top of his head.

'This is the guest suite. You'll be comfortable here.'

Danny looked around the self contained apartment, at the modern furniture, the neat kitchen with its full complement of hi-tech appliances. There was a single bedroom with a view that looked over the grounds behind the house. 'Are you sure, Ray? I don't want to cause you any trouble.'

Carver's cold grey eyes regarded him unblinkingly. 'Keep it clean, that's all I ask. Now, there's a phone in the kitchen with a pre-programmed number for the house. Don't use it unless it's an emergency. And for fuck's sake, don't call anyone. Understand?' Danny nodded. 'There's some books and magazines on the shelf there and you've got the TV. It's fully cabled up. Don't browse the net, though, not for anything. Tess'll bring a bit of shopping over later so you can cook some grub. When it's dark we'll go for a walk around the grounds, stretch your legs, get a bit of fresh air. Get to know one another.'

Carver picked up the TV remote and switched it on. He handed it to Danny. 'There you go.' The TV hummed into life. Long range images of the southern end of Whitehall filled the large screen, a LIVE caption running in the top right-hand corner. It was an unrecognisable landscape of shattered and blackened buildings shrouded in clouds of dust. In the foreground, covering the grass in Parliament Square, a small village of white tents had been erected. The newsreader filled in the blanks; the temporary structures housed rescue management, a casualty clearing station and a provisional morgue.

Carver shook his head. 'Every time I see that it makes my heart break.' The scene on the TV switched suddenly to a press conference, the caption reading: Millbank, London. The camera was fixed on several empty chairs positioned behind a table with the European Union flag draped across it. In the foreground the press corps gathered, heads bobbing at the bottom of the screen. An explosion of camera flashes announced the arrival of Prime Minister Hooper. He took the middle seat as senior European ministers occupied the other chairs.

'Here we go,' Carver announced ominously. On the screen an aide scampered forward, activating the microphone on the table in front of Hooper, then retreated out of sight.

'Thank you all for coming,' the Prime Minister began. 'I want to start by offering my condolences to the families of the victims whose bodies were discovered in Whitehall this morning…'

'Over two hundred now,' Carver reported. 'Let's see how long it takes before they mention you.'

'…these systematic attacks in an effort to destabilise the country. As a nation, as a continent, as Europeans, we cannot allow this to happen…'

'Bollocks,' Carver growled.

'…and therefore the regional government of the United Kingdom has taken the decision to join our European partners and ratify the Treaty of Cairo, a historic piece of legislation that will further harmonise our nations and bring peace and economic prosperity to the continent. Anything less will send a signal to our enemies…'

'Peace in our time, eh?' scoffed Carver. The broadcast lasted for another few minutes and then the scene changed to a reporter standing in front of the pyramids outside Cairo. Behind him a giant stage was in the final stages of construction. 'Jesus, look at the size of that,' Carver exclaimed.

'…a huge demonstration here in Cairo later today, in response to the attack on the mosque in Luton. The British government, in line with other EU countries, has called for greater understanding between communities across Europe and President Dupont himself has demanded the drafting of new legislation that will protect Europe's Muslim citizens from…'

'What a surprise,' Carver sneered, 'more bloody laws. Remember the fuss over ID cards? Never, they said. Now you carry one or else. DNA databases, remote hacking, international arrest warrants; people laughed at me years ago when I warned them. Now they're the norm.' He snatched the remote from Danny's hand and turned off the TV. 'That's enough of that. Still, you're off the top slot, which is good.'

Danny stared at his own reflection in the TV screen. Coming here had solved his immediate problem but the truth was he was placing the lives of a retired couple in serious danger. If he was caught here they'd all go to prison for sure. So what if he'd been a member of the Movement? Did that give him the right to just turn up, impose on these people who clearly felt sorry for him, felt a duty to help, regardless of their own safety? No, it was a stupid idea. Despite the fuss over Cairo there was still a manhunt in progress, a price on his head, a fortune to be made for the right person who knew of his whereabouts. All it took was one phone call and it'd all be over. No, he had to keep moving. Somewhere, deep inside, he still had a little pride left.

'Listen Ray, thanks for your hospitality but on second thoughts I should get going, maybe tomorrow, after it gets dark. I don't want to take the piss but I'll need some supplies. You know, food, a bit of money.'

Carver frowned. 'What?'

'Just to tide me over until I find somewhere else. I don't want to get anyone into trouble. You could all go away for this.'

Carver took Danny by the arm. 'Nonsense, son. No-one's asking you to leave and besides, you're safer here than out there.'

'They know I was in the Movement, Ray. They might come here, question you and Tess.'

Carver shrugged his large shoulders. 'So what? The Movement was disbanded a long time ago and I swore an oath in front of my barrister and a county court judge, disassociating myself from the organisation and all and any of its members. You must remember that, Danny. It was all over the news.'

Danny stared at his stockinged feet, damp and black with dirt. 'I remember.'

'You think I was a traitor too, right son?'

Danny shook his head. 'I didn't know what to think, Ray. I was gutted, I remember that much. I'd not long joined, see.'

'It was the right move,' Carver explained. 'The authorities were clamping down on nationalist groups anyway, so it was only a matter of time. I pre-empted their bullshit, resigned my chairmanship, took a legal position. I protected myself, Danny, sang from their poisonous multicultural hymn sheet. I even made a donation to the Pakistan Relief Fund, signed the pledge alongside that Muslim MP down in Watford. D'you know how much that hurt? No, they won't come here.' Carver laid a meaty paw on Danny's thin shoulder, his eyes like steel pebbles, his large frame blocking out the light from the window. 'And even if they did, they'd never find you.'

Danny wilted under the stare, the weight of Ray's arm. He felt suddenly frightened. 'They won't?'

'Positive,' Carver said. Then he smiled, and Danny was relieved to see those impossibly white teeth again. Carver waved his arm around the room. 'I've still got friends out there Danny, sympathisers, ex-Movement people, people in authority. I'd be warned if the law started sniffing around.'

Danny took a deep breath and blew out his cheeks. 'That makes me feel better, Ray. As long as you're sure.'

'Course I am. All we do now is keep our heads down and wait. We watch and listen, see which way the wind blows. Cairo's bumped you off the radar, which means big changes are coming.'

'What sort of changes?'

'Let's just see what happens, son.'

They heard footsteps outside and the door to the apartment swung open. Tess breezed into the room, a stack of neatly-pressed laundry tucked beneath her numerous chins. 'Ah, here you both are. Danny, these are for you, some of Joe's clothes.' She loaded the pile into Danny's waiting arms. They smelt of lavender and soap. 'There's a plastic bag under the sink in the kitchen. Bag up all your old stuff and leave it outside the door. That'll go on the bonfire.'

Carver nodded. 'Grab a shower, get some rest, son. Tess'll bring some food over in a bit.'

Danny nodded his thanks. Tess left the room and Carver followed her. As he neared the door, Danny said: 'Are you really retired, Ray? Is the Movement really dead?'

Carver stared at him for a moment then shook his head. 'Never has been.' He tapped his chest with a finger. 'You can't turn off what's in your heart, right?'

Danny nodded. 'Where will all this end?'

'It won't end, not as long as there are people like you and me, Danny. You've managed to slip one of the biggest man hunts this country has ever seen, covered your tracks in London, made it all the way up here without drawing attention to yourself. You're smart, a quick thinker. In fact, when I look at you I see a bit of myself there.' He slipped the sunglasses back over his eyes and pointed towards the window. 'One thing you can be sure of; whatever happens out there, people like me and you, we'll go down fighting. You're a bloody hero, son. Now, get yourself some rest. You've earned it.'

Exhausted, Danny peeled off his socks and slumped onto the sofa. He'd been called a lot of things in his life, but never a hero. As Carver's footsteps clumped down the stairs outside Danny stretched along the deep cushions, the beginnings of a smile creasing his face.

✳ ✳ ✳

Chequers

A pale sliver of sky to the east offered the first promise of daybreak when the alarm warbled on the bedside table. Saeed slapped it off and yawned, stretching his long limbs and kicking the duvet off. In the bathroom he washed himself from head to toe then dressed, slipping a fresh white gown over his head. He crossed the bedroom carpet in bare feet and opened the curtains. The gentle valley sloped away to the south, cloaked in mist and bracketed by dark woods, the sky above paling before the rise of the sun. Somewhere a bird called, heralding the dawn. It was time.

Saeed knelt down on the prayer mat and closed his eyes, clearing his mind of all distractions. He breathed deeply, preparing himself for *Salat,* the first of his five daily prayers. His lips began to utter the quiet litany, his forehead brushing the mat as his mind, body and soul united in worship. He felt it then, as he did every day, the connection to his fellow Brothers, knowing that across the country they too were performing their own rituals, welcoming the new day. Only today that feeling was stronger, considerably so. For Saeed, this new dawn promised so much more.

Mentally and spiritually prepared, he dressed casually in a black sweater and green corduroy trousers and made his way downstairs to breakfast. Saeed rubbed his hands briskly as he entered; the dining room was empty and felt as cold as a tomb, lit from above by a large chandelier that washed the dark panelled walls in its harsh light. A white jacketed steward suddenly appeared behind Saeed, like a Victorian parlour trick, and took his order of toast and fruit juice. Saeed watched him disappear behind a well-disguised panelled door

177

as he sat down at the long breakfast table. Thankfully he ate alone, the daily papers spread across the white table cloth before him. He allowed himself a satisfied smile as the preparations for Cairo dominated the front pages, a compliant media taking up the treaty torch with impressive gusto. Saeed made a mental note to thank the media barons personally.

He took coffee in the library next door, where a log fire roared invitingly in the grate. He sat in a wing backed chair by the window, watching the sun rise above the woods, the mist rolling back before its watery rays. A dog barked, the sound muffled through the thick glass, and a black shape darted from behind the walled garden, streaking out into the field beyond. A bird rose from the grass in its path, cawing in annoyance as the Labrador raced after it, leaping into the air all too late. Another movement caught Saeed's eye and Hooper's rotund shape appeared from behind the wall, following the animal into the field. Saeed finished his coffee and went to fetch his coat.

Outside the air was brisk and scented with morning dew, with wet grass and damp earth. Saeed wrinkled his nostrils in disgust as he zipped his parka to the neck and trudged along a stone path in a pair of green wellington boots. He was an urbanite by nature and hated the countryside, with its rank odours and cloying dirt. In winter everything was cold and wet, in summer the air hummed with a million insects, crawling, stinging, laying eggs. Saeed shivered, partly from the cold, but mostly from the proximity of nature.

Hooper, on the other hand, was a man in his element. Saeed watched him striding across the wide field behind the house, a walking stick in his hand, calling to the lunatic animal that darted and panted and chased all manner of unknown tormentors. Hooper's two bodyguards trailed a short distance behind, heads swivelling this way and that, coats open, hands free. One of them saw Saeed and called to Hooper, who stood and waited. Saeed flinched as the Labrador spotted his approach and scuttled towards him, legs pumping through the grass, pink tongue lolling from the side of its mouth. He cringed as the unclean animal reared up on its hind legs and attempted to greet Saeed with its slavering mouth.

'Buster! Get down!' Hooper bellowed. The animal complied, spotting yet another unseen quarry somewhere across the field and sprinting after it. 'Sorry about that,' Hooper smiled. 'He tends to get a little excited in the morning. Millie used to walk him around the park at home, always on a leash of course. Out here he goes wild, absolutely loves it.'

Saeed fell into step beside Hooper, wet grass clinging to his boots, the two policemen keeping a discreet distance behind them. 'You've made quite a home up here, Jacob.'

Hooper's face was flushed pink by the sharp air, by the brisk pace he set across the field. 'Is that disapproval in your voice, Tariq?'

'Of course not, but it does make some things a little difficult, that's all. There's been some talk amongst the Cabinet, a suggestion that perhaps Chequers is not the most convenient place from which to govern the country.'

Hooper swiped the long grass with his walking stick. 'I'm not here out of choice Tariq, you know that. Millbank is too cramped, too many interruptions, plus we've got the bloody press corps camped out in the lobby, all of whom seem to think I should drop everything for a quick soundbite every time I'm passing through. It's absolutely ridiculous. Besides, this was your idea,' he pointed out. 'Chequers is secure, plus it has all the necessary comms and media links. I can get a lot more done up here.'

Of course you can, Saeed didn't say. In a few short weeks Hooper had become accustomed to life at the Buckinghamshire estate, as Saeed predicted he would. Hooper was born of country stock, his elderly father still presiding over several dozen acres of Lincolnshire countryside serviced by a regiment of foreign workers who toiled away the summers in huts of corrugated iron, separating pea from pod, broccoli from stalk. It was where Hooper had grown up, cementing his love of all things outdoors, a love that took him into the armed forces where he finished an unspectacular career as a lieutenant-colonel in the Logistics Corps. Politics followed, the move to London permanent after he met his future wife at a party in Chelsea. The woman had turned out to be as nakedly ambitious as Hooper and equally at home in the country. In the end, the choice had been a simple one.

And Chequers certainly fitted the bill, an estate of historical import and period elegance, of manicured grounds and attentive staff, where the perimeter was patrolled by serious men with automatic weapons and a state of the art helicopter squatted on a landing pad to the north of the house. Chequers offered status, Hooper's wide-eyed father clearly impressed as he shuffled around the grounds, the Hooper clan drinking and laughing long into the night as they revelled in their new found prominence. The wife had taken to the role of First Lady like a duck to water, the transition from reasonably sized terraced house in Putney to the impressive pile of Chequers made with an ease of entitlement that surprised even Saeed. He'd heard her sharp voice several times around the house during his visits, either berating the staff or acting as an unofficial tour guide to her designer-clad friends from London.

The house was divided into two parts, Hooper's substantial living quarters in the east wing and the more formal west wing, where the Prime Minister conducted the business of state. Cabinet meetings were now held in the main drawing room, the ministers ferried from London by motorised convoy or helicopter. Hooper had become accustomed to meeting by video-link too, a particular annoyance to those who had to endure his overbearing nature and abrasive people skills. There were also rumblings in Brussels, the Commission dismayed by Hooper's isolation, his particular form of governance. Saeed had become his protector, shielding the Prime Minister from the vast majority of criticism, coaxing his European colleagues, his fellow Cabinet ministers, Party members and not least the press to accept their leader's fledgling efforts, to understand his inexperience, his fear of another terrorist attack in the close confines of the capital.

Yet Hooper was right, Chequers had been Saeed's suggestion, but a calculated one. Hooper could no more resist the temptation of ruling the country from his own private estate than an alcoholic with money in his pocket could walk past a supermarket selling cheap alcohol.

Saeed turned to look over his shoulder. The policemen were some way back, the house shrinking into the distance as Hooper continued his morning constitutional. The demented dog flew between them once again, yapping and panting, before circling the security team and sprinting past Saeed's leg and out toward the tree line.

'Buster!' Hooper bellowed after the fleeing animal. He tutted and turned to Saeed. 'So, what's the word from our conspiracy theorists? Any new revelations there?'

'There's a rumour that Bryce was about to tender his resignation.'

Hooper arched a bushy eyebrow. 'Really?'

'The pressure of the job is huge, of course. Then there was the visit to his wife's grave the day before. Not unusual but significant, given the timing. The truth is we may never know. The only other person who may be able to shed light on what was going through his mind was Ella and she's still in a coma.'

'What about the man himself?'

'You've seen him, Jacob. He's still quite badly injured and in no fit state to communicate coherently. The point is, whatever Gabriel was about to announce it hardly matters now. We need to move on, concentrate on the future. There's much to be done.'

'Still, it's strange. The sneaky visit to Heathrow before the bomb, that Border Agency guy, Davies, killed in Downing Street. What the hell was *he* doing in Number Ten?'

Saeed's fingers stroked his meticulously manicured beard. 'Like I said, a mystery.'

'What I don't understand Tariq, is that Heathrow was your responsibility. Surely Gabriel would have mentioned something to you?'

'Well, he didn't,' insisted Saeed. 'The program is running fine and Davies has been replaced. We can only guess at what Gabriel was up to.'

'Well, they were up to something,' Hooper decided, watching his dog nosing along the distant tree line. 'I only found out about the Heathrow thing from one of the security team. Common knowledge amongst that lot, I'm told.'

Saeed watched the watchers, their trained eyes searching the fields and trees for potential threats.

They missed nothing, saw and heard everything. He'd have to be careful, changes would have to be made. 'As I said, it makes no difference now, and this continued speculation will only hinder our progress. We need to put the whole thing to bed, so as far as Gabriel's press conference is concerned we should push the resignation line, drip feed it to the media.'

'Think we can get away with it? Could be a hard sell.'

'Trust me.'

'O.k., I'll leave that in your capable hands.' Hooper took a step closer, his eyes watching the tree line where the shadows still lingered. 'What about these terrorists, Tariq? Are we still in any danger?'

'The current threat level has been lowered to severe and the police and security services remain on a heightened state of alert. We're continuing to round up right-wing activists and other potential troublemakers. Some have been charged for various offences but none in connection with the attacks. However, this Whelan character is still on the run. CCTV caught him jogging past a petrol station in Neasden a couple of days after the bomb. Since then nothing. Either he's gone to ground, or he's managed to flee the country. The police believe he'll pop up on the grid sooner or later and I'm inclined to agree with them. The main thing is we push on with our work.'

'Yes, yes' nodded Hooper. 'What about the bomb itself? Any news on that?'

'Forensics have established that both devices employed a military grade explosive of a type used by almost all European forces so it'll be hard to track down its exact origin. We know Whelan delivered the bomb to Luton and he almost certainly had a hand in the other, due to the timing and his previous employment as a government courier. The question remains: how did he get the explosives in the van? The police are still working on it.'

'The driver?'

A Christian convert, his devotion to Islam, like the cancer that ate away at his bones, a closely guarded secret from family and friends. He'd died for Saeed, for the cause, a true martyr.

'Just another victim. Apparently there was nothing to bury.'

'Poor bastard.'

A flurry of birds took to the air, exploding noisily above the tree line. The dog's manic barking echoed across the fields.

'Both President Dupont and President Bakari are keen to discuss the running order for Cairo,' Saeed mentioned. Hooper grunted a vague reply, stamping towards the trees. Saeed studied him closely, allowing the man to brood for several moments. Eventually he said; 'Jacob, what's the matter?'

Hooper came to a sudden halt and spun around. 'The truth? Cairo's the bloody problem,' He thrashed at the long grass with his walking stick, cutting through the wet stalks like a scythe.

'Excuse me?'

'It's going to clash with the reparation talks in Washington. I'm in a real bloody quandary.'

'We've already decided, the Foreign Secretary will attend the talks. After all, they're only preliminary discussions. A deal isn't expected.'

'Yes, but as head of state I really think I should be there.'

And Saeed knew why. As an act of good will Hector Vargas, the American President and billionaire media mogul, had decided to attend the opening session at the United Nations in New York, alongside the delegation from the Islamic Emirate of Afghanistan, in the latest round of war reparation talks. Tensions in the city would be high, demonstrations planned by veterans groups and others, the world's media focussed on events in the Big Apple rather than the done deal in Cairo. Then there was the memorial service for the three Jupiter astronauts, missing presumed dead, planned for the same week in Washington D.C. Vargas would be attending, along with NASA officials, former astronauts and a sprinkling of Hollywood and other media personalities. Hooper's presence at the talks would no doubt secure him an invitation to the service, a scenario he'd clearly considered. The fat buffoon was drawn to the glitz and power that emanated from Vargas and Washington like a moth to a flame.

'You'll be the only head of state from Europe there, Jacob.'

'Yes, but we were a major contributor to the mess in Afghanistan. I think it would send the right signals to Kabul, show them we intend to take these talks seriously, that we stand by our obligations.'

Saeed pretended to consider Hooper's argument, then said: 'Mmm, I see your point. It would also send a clear message to communities across Europe that you're sensitive to the plight of the Taliban government and the Afghan people. Yes,' Saeed nodded enthusiastically, 'on balance your presence in the States could reap some added diplomatic rewards right here in Europe.'

Hooper shifted from foot to foot, as if he was about to break into an excited jig. 'What about Dupont? Do you think he'll buy it? I can't afford to piss him off.'

Hooper waited with bated breath as Saeed performed a master class of contemplation. When he thought the man was about to burst he said: 'I doubt he'd object. In fact, if we spin it right, I'm almost certain that everyone will see your trip to Washington as a positive step towards greater understanding. I'll get an announcement drafted to that effect. In the meantime we should contact the U.S. ambassador, inform him of your intentions.'

'Yes, yes, of course,' blustered Hooper, barely able to contain his excitement. 'So you'll go to Cairo in my place, Tariq? You've no personal objection?'

'On the contrary, it'll be an honour to sign the treaty. We must speak to Dupont at the earliest opportunity so changes can be made to the program.'

'See to it, would you?' Hooper's eyes took on a faraway look, a self-satisfied smile creeping across his rotund face. 'I've only ever been to the White House once, and that was as a tourist. Boiling hot summer, just after we got married. Millie and I took photos outside.'

'And now you'll probably be a guest.'

'Jesus Christ, she's going to wet herself.' Hooper saw the disapproval in Saeed's eyes. 'Sorry, Tariq.' Embarrassment quickly forgotten, Hooper brushed past his deputy and headed towards the house. 'We should start back. There's work to be done.'

Saeed followed him, trudging the damp path of their tracks across the field. One of the policemen pulled out a radio and held it to his mouth, alerting someone, somewhere, of their imminent return.

Hooper turned and walked backwards, waving the walking stick above his head. 'Buster! Come here, boy!' The dog duly responded, bounding from the trees. As it raced through the grass, Saeed could see something in its mouth, something grey and white. 'What's that, boy?' Hooper said, slapping his legs as the animal skidded to a stop a few yards away. It dropped the wood pigeon from its jaws, the corpse a mess of blood and feathers.

'Good boy!' Hooper congratulated the animal, squatting down and rubbing its head and flanks. The dog raced away towards the house, ecstatic. Saeed thought Hooper, bursting with equal excitement, would run after him.

'There's something else, something we haven't thought of,' he warned. Hooper stood up, brushing his wet hands on his trousers.

'What?'

Saeed glanced at the policemen who watched them from a distance. 'It's delicate.'

'Don't worry about them, they can't hear us,' Hooper reassured him, his bulbous eyes flicking over Saeed's shoulder.

Saeed kept his voice low anyway. 'What if Gabriel regains consciousness in the very near future?'

'He's done that already,' Hooper reminded him.

'I mean full consciousness, all his faculties. If the doctors and consultants declare him fit he could spike Cairo.'

'He wouldn't dare,' growled Hooper. 'It's been through parliament, a declaration of intent has been signed. Brussels has begun preparations, tens of millions of Euros already spent. We can't go back.'

'But he could stall the process, postpone it even. Legally he'd have that power - as Prime Minister.'

Hooper's face darkened, his finger poking his own chest. 'I'm Prime Minister now, remember? Things have changed, we have a new government. The country's moved on for God's sake.' He snorted angrily through his nostrils, then he stepped closer and said: 'Can he do that? Constitutionally, I mean. Can he take back any sort of control?'

'Of course he can,' Saeed warned, scrunching his face into what he hoped was a convincing mask of concern. 'He could do what he likes, call a reshuffle, seek a vote of confidence from the parliamentary party. The country would marvel at his recovery, and he would use that emotion for political gain. You've seen him, Jacob. If anything, Gabriel Bryce is a pro.'

Hooper's jowls flapped from side to side. 'No, Brussels would overrule.'

'Not immediately. Constitutional processes have to be allowed to run their course. He could do a lot of damage before then.' Saeed paused, allowing the scenario to take firm root in the man's imagination, saw Hooper's eyes shift from left to right as anxiety gripped him, his hand involuntarily rubbing his shiny dome. 'And of course there's the Washington trip. Gabriel would spike that in a heartbeat. He's no fan of Vargas.'

'Fuck!' Hooper lashed the grass with his stick, the decapitated heads of wild flowers tumbling through the air. Saeed let him stew for a while, watching him turn towards the distant house, contemplating a life without the privilege, the prestige and the power he'd become accustomed to. Finally Hooper said: 'There must be something we can do, some clause, a legal precedent perhaps?'

'I've spoken to the Attorney General about this. If Bryce passes a physiological examination and is declared fit, all this goes away.' Saeed swept an arm around the estate. He saw Hooper's eyes drink in the rolling hills, the distant mansion, and thought the man was going to burst into tears.

'But we've worked so hard, achieved so much in a few short weeks. Surely it can't be undone as easily as that?'

'It can,' Saeed assured him, 'you signed documentation yourself, Jacob. Your appointment is a temporary one in the event of Gabriel Bryce's full recovery, remember?'

Hooper's large shoulders sagged. He leaned on his stick and stared at the ground, crushed. The animal trotted back to its master and sat at his feet, tail wagging, eyes pleading. Hooper nuzzled the dog's neck. 'It's alright, boy.'

Saeed looked beyond Hooper to where the policemen stood waiting. They were some way off, well out of earshot. Saeed waved them on and they moved further towards the house.

'There's another way, Jacob. Another option.'

Hooper lifted his head. 'What? What option?'

Saeed folded his arms, stroking his beard as if contemplating a new strategy. 'The scene outside the King Edward hospital remains the same, does it not? Granted, most of the news crews have gone but mountains of flowers still block the pavements and clutter up the railings. Every other day there's a news item regarding Bryce's recovery, speculation on his future, a general assumption that eventually he will recover.'

'Go on.'

Saeed could hear the desperation in Hooper's voice, the faint spark of hope that glinted in his globular eyes. 'What if there's another incident,' he began quietly, 'another attempt on Bryce's life? Something that would jeopardize the safety of staff and patients, something that would keep the threat of terror firmly entrenched in the public consciousness? An incident that would give us no choice but to have Bryce moved to a secure, undisclosed location, for his own safety and the safety of the public.'

Hooper's heavy jowls paled. 'You want to blow up a hospital?'

'Don't be ridiculous,' Saeed snapped. 'What we're talking about here is a whisper of an operation, a hint of a plot, an unknown, unsubstantiated conspiracy to murder Gabriel Bryce in his hospital bed. Leaked to the media it would be enough to give us the authority to move him, and by default *remove* him from the public consciousness. The flowers would wilt and die, the last of the outside broadcast vans would pack up and disappear, the hospital administration would breathe a huge sigh of relief. Life would go on and Gabriel Bryce would fade into obscurity like a retired politician. Out of sight, out of mind.'

Hooper's tongue darted lizard-like between his moist lips. 'And move him where?'

'A ghost ward,' declared Saeed.

The Prime Minister's eyes widened. 'You want to shove him in one of those ghastly places? Are you mad?'

'Not mad, Jacob, simply prudent. Look, if you transfer him to another private hospital the problem remains the same. Bryce will continue to recover while our political aspirations wither on the vine. The moment he is able to sit upright and hold a coherent conversation, our vision for the future, *and* your travel plans, will simply melt away.'

Hooper grasped at the straw. 'Can we get away with it?'

'Of course we can. Gabriel Bryce's security and well being is paramount. No one dare challenge the decision once it's made.'

'No, I don't suppose they would,' Hooper muttered. 'Have you somewhere in mind?'

'There's a particular facility in Hampshire, a secluded, highly secure unit for some of our more unstable veterans. A private suite could be made available. The chief administrator there is an old university friend of yours, I believe. Duncan Parry?'

Hooper raised his eyebrows. 'Duncan? Really? Good God, I haven't seen him for years. He and I took history.' A smile crept across his face. 'Yes, quite a character with the ladies, if memory serves.'

'And there are many opportunities for the right people in the NHS executive. Do you think Mister Parry can be trusted to help us? Would he be willing to pursue improved career prospects in return for providing secure accommodation for a VIP patient?'

'I really don't know. I could talk to him,' Hooper offered.

'Better yet, why don't you have him up for a discreet dinner? I'm sure you've both got a lot of catching up to do.'

'That's a splendid idea,' Hooper beamed. Then the smile faded. 'But what about Gabriel? I mean, will he be looked after adequately? And what about visitors?'

'The facility is called Alton Grange and yes, it has a fully equipped medical and physiotherapy suite. Don't worry, Jacob, Gabriel will be well taken care of. As for visitors, we can issue occasional press releases charting his progress. We don't have to be specific. Security, you see.'

Hooper was silent for a long time. He crouched down, stroking the dog, as he contemplated his next move. Saeed could almost hear his mind ticking over. As the silence continued, Saeed began to wonder if he'd somehow misjudged the man. No, he corrected himself, it was impossible. The players, specifically targeted, had been studied for over two years, their lives disassembled, their psychological processes broken down and analysed. They'd been followed, photographed, monitored, their homes bugged, their financial and medical records obtained and pored over by teams of professionals, searching for psychoanalytic and social cognitive patterns, detecting the traits, uncovering the layers, then finally revealing the psychological buttons that could so easily be pushed.

The Alton Grange administrator, Parry, was a case in point. To his colleagues and friends he was a capable mid-level manager of a secure mental health facility with a stable home life and modest ambitions. The reality was somewhat different. He was, in fact, deeply embittered by his mundane position, a borderline alcoholic who rarely spoke to his wife, instead spending most of his free time trawling the internet under a host of on-line pseudonyms in search of violent sex movies. He was also a right-winger and no friend of Bryce's policies, his credit card transactions revealing a history of book and film purchases of dubious political content. What would a man like that do when the call from Hooper came? Turn down an evening's entertainment with the Prime Minister of Great Britain, a guaranteed promotion to Richmond House in Whitehall? Of course not.

And Hooper himself, ambitious but distinctly unqualified for high office, his promotion to Defence Minister a reward from Bryce for his intimidating tenure as deputy chief whip. He was a bully, unpopular with his staff at the Ministry of Defence, avoided by most of the Cabinet at social gatherings, surrounded by a few sycophants drawn to his physically intimidating presence, his loud voice and brusque manner. There wasn't much to go on in his personal life. He had no obvious vices, his two young sons in private schooling taking a large chunk of his income and modest investments. Their recent move from a little known boarder in Shropshire to the gothic spires of Charterhouse in Surrey was in keeping with Hooper's new found status, and therein lay his Achilles heel. Hooper's life was all about status, whether earned or bestowed it did not matter. He was driven by ambition, pushed further by a harridan of a wife who relentlessly goaded Hooper about the material worlds of her friends and their successful husbands, the off-shore accounts, the luxury power boats moored in the Mediterranean, the villas in Cap Ferrat and the Costa Del Sol. The Downing Street bomb had been a fortuitous event for the Hoopers. Saeed himself had heard the voice recording, the whispered intimacy after a short and rare bout of sex, the witch's words in Hooper's ear: *this is your moment, Jacob. Don't screw it up, for God's sake. For the boys' sake. You'll never get another opportunity like this...*

Hooper had responded accordingly, as the psychologists predicted he would. Power had been seized, ambitions fulfilled by the blood of others. Now all that remained was this crucial piece of the jigsaw. Once that was in place, the picture would be almost complete.

'How long will he be there? At Alton Grange?'

'Long enough, Jacob. The Attorney General has made it clear that once Cairo is signed there can be no return to the past. The only thing that matters is Britain's future, with you providing the necessary leadership. There's much work to be done, a new continent to shape, new partners to nurture and support. And a new Prime Minister's residence to be built. You'd have final approval of the design of course. Or would that be Millie?'

Hooper's face broke into a wide grin. 'You're right, what's past is past. Gabriel was a competent leader but new blood is what's needed now.' He clapped his hands and rubbed them briskly together. The dog got to its feet, tail wagging furiously. 'Set it all up, Tariq, let's get the ball rolling on this Alton Grange thing.'

'I'll need authorisation for various procedures. Protection Command will require briefing.'

'Do we have to involve the police?'

'Of course. They're providing Bryce's security. However, in the event of another incident, the security services can legally supersede police authority. I have good contacts at Thames House. Discreet operatives can be resourced.'

Hooper nodded silently for several moments then said: 'Sounds like a plan. O.k., draft the papers and I'll sign them.'

Hooper turned to face the sun that climbed above the tree tops, a milky white disc that gave little warmth but speared the trees and flooded the field in rays of golden light. 'This dawn marks a new day for British politics, Tariq, one that we'll remember for a long time.'

Saeed followed his gaze as the jigsaw piece slotted firmly into place. 'I'm sure we will, Jacob.'

King Edward the Seventh Hospital, London

The shouting invaded his dreams, the screams rising only to fade again, before rising once more. They were screams of anguish, a wailing that was both familiar and disturbing. The darkness turned to grey, building to a bright white as he drifted upwards through the layers of fatigue. The room swam slowly into view, the TV on the wall, the chairs and coffee table by the window, the brick wall beyond. It was all as familiar as a prison cell and in some respects not that much different. The screaming was louder now, more intense, yet Bryce was still finding it difficult to focus.

It wasn't normal to still be feeling like this. November was almost upon them, his wounds were much better, and yet some days he felt as weak and exhausted as he did when he'd first arrived. It was the drugs of course, the sedatives that were being fed into his system. At first he welcomed them, numbing his body from the pain of his wounds, his mind from the shock of the bomb, the miracle of his survival, the loss of so many friends and colleagues. Now it was different. His body was healing but his mind was still clouded, his thought processes often vague and confused, until it was too much of an effort to keep his eyes open. He wanted to shout at the consultants as they pored over his charts, at the nurses who cleaned and dressed his wounds, at Orla, who tampered with his drip as Bryce watched her through heavy lidded eyes. But he didn't possess the strength. He wasn't getting better, he was getting worse. And the screaming was getting louder.

Sirens. As Bryce finally realised what the awful sound was, the door to his room flew inwards and crashed against the wall. The overhead lights snapped on and a group of doctors marched in, flanked by several nurses. A policeman in black body armour and brandishing an automatic weapon yanked the curtains closed, shutting out the night. More policemen funnelled into the room and Bryce heard shouting in the corridor outside. The sirens were louder now and a red strobe light pulsed near the doorway. Bodies crowded around his bed and the he heard the coffee table tip over, spilling the magazines that Bryce had never read across the floor.

'What's going on? What's happening?'

Medical staff pressed in from all sides. Practised hands went to work, stripping the bed covers off, unplugging his body from the complex machinery, his veins from the mind numbing drip. 'Someone talk to me, please!' He saw a familiar face lingering behind the medical team, talking earnestly to a helmeted policeman. 'Suleyman!' The orderly stared at him for a moment then looked away. His purple uniform was gone, replaced by a dark roll neck sweater and a short bomber jacket. Then Bryce smelt something burning and suddenly the sirens and the flashing lights and the urgency all made sense. The building was on fire.

The doctors loomed over him, tugging at his eyelids, blinding him with pen torches, checking his vision with waving fingers. Bryce could see the hairs in their nostrils, caught the whiff of breath mints and tobacco. They spoke to each other in their own language, of pressures and pulse rates, of medications and observations. A stretcher trolley was wheeled next to the bed and firm hands gripped his limbs, supported his neck. *One, two, three, lift...*

Smoke drifted across the ceiling, faint wisps of white and grey. A blanket was thrown over him, a pillow placed beneath his head, transport straps secured around his chest and legs. Orla was at his side, a rain coat draped loosely over her uniform. They were going outside, probably into the car park, or down the street perhaps, a fire assembly point. Bryce almost smiled. At last he'd feel the cold night air on his face, in his lungs. The doctors, gathered together at the foot of his trolley like a stone faced jury, finally nodded their consent. Responsibility was passed, commands were issued in harsh voices and the trolley was set in motion. Sully appeared at his side, hands on the safety rail, guiding Bryce out of the room and into the corridor outside. If he had the strength Bryce would've cheered.

'Don't worry Mister Gabriel, we've got a security situation here. Just relax, everything'll be fine.'

Bryce replied with a satisfied smile. He didn't care what was happening as long he got to leave his room for a while. There was more smoke in the corridor, the squeak of rubber boots on the floor, more shouting. Alarm strobes pulsed on the walls and strip lights passed overhead like white lines on a road. Black helmets bobbed in and out of his vision and he caught a glimpse at the clock on the wall behind the nurses' station: 02:14. Orla looked down at him several times, concern knotting her brow. A stethoscope dangled from her neck, swinging like a pendulum as they trundled along the corridor. They turned left, then right, then the trolley bounced over something hard and suddenly he was inside a large elevator with walls of brushed metal and bright overhead lights. The doors rumbled closed, the chaos of the corridor left behind. Sully on one side, the nurse on the other, two policemen by his feet, weapons clasped to their chests, all silent as Bryce felt the elevator travel downwards. They were definitely going outside.

The elevator jerked to a halt and the doors clattered open. A computerised female voice announced *basement level* in smooth tones. Cold air filled the metal space and the trolley shuddered as Bryce was backed out over the threshold. The two police officers remained inside and one of them leaned forward and stabbed a button with a gloved finger. The doors closed and they were gone, taking the light with them. Bryce lay on the stationary trolley, alone in the dark. As his eyes became accustomed to the gloom he saw a low concrete ceiling overhead, festooned with metal pipes that snaked their way across its blackened surface. He could smell petrol fumes and the stale odour of cigarette smoke. He twisted his head and realised he was on a raised loading bay that overlooked a large underground car park. Sully leaned over him in the dark, fumbling inside his jacket pocket.

'I have to put these on. Don't worry, it's just a precaution.'

'Suleyman, I - '

'Sully. Just Sully, o.k.?' The Turk pulled a blue paper head cover over Bryce's thick grey hair, then secured a surgical mask over his nose and mouth. Finally, he slipped a pair of clear plastic glasses over Bryce's darting eyes.

'What's happening, Sully?' There was still a faint slur to his speech and his voice sounded muffled behind the thin paper of the mask.

'Try and be quiet. It'll soon be over.'

'What will?'

'Shh.' Sully held a finger to his lips. 'No talking now. At all.'

Sully turned away and Bryce saw the flare of a match. The Turk was leaning on a nearby railing, one foot propped on a lower bar. Orla stood next to him, bundled in her raincoat and smoking a cigarette. Neither seemed concerned about Bryce's health and that both reassured and troubled him at the same time. He heard footsteps, then a man's voice echoed around the basement, making it impossible for Bryce to hear what was being said. He recognised Sully's voice, then Orla's. Footsteps clacked across concrete and doors slammed. An engine started up, then another. Blue lights swept the concrete walls, the ceiling. Bryce strained his neck, saw a police vehicle drive off, followed by an ambulance with all its lights going, then another police vehicle. He watched them as they headed toward the far end of the car park and disappear up a ramp, their sirens screaming into life.

'Let's go.' It was Sully's voice. Bryce saw him move around the back of his head. The trolley's brake was released and he felt himself moving forward, his body dipping as the trolley rumbled down a shallow slope towards the floor of the car park. He felt Sully yank him short as a vehicle backed towards the ramp. Bryce noticed it wasn't an ambulance, more like a small cargo van. He was confused. He looked up into Sully's thin nostrils, his olive skinned face glowing a fiendish red in the brake lights of the vehicle.

'Sully, what's happening? Where are we going?'

'Somewhere safe,' he whispered, 'now be quiet.' The back doors swung open and the trolley bumped against the foot plate. Another man appeared, wearing some sort of uniform, overalls of an indistinguishable colour and a baseball cap. He helped Sully and Orla to lift the trolley and manoeuvre it inside. They climbed in behind Bryce, locking the wheels and fussing over a tangled web of nylon cargo straps as they lashed the trolley to the wall of the van. Bryce saw that the inside of the vehicle was empty, a dark coloured roof and walls, a ridged metal floor. The rear doors slammed shut and Sully positioned his backside on the raised wheel arch. The driver squeezed past the trolley and into the driver's cab and a moment later the van's engine purred into life. Orla leaned across him, gave Bryce a visual check, adjusting the blanket up beneath his chin. She looked over at Sully.

'He's fine. Let's get the heater on back here, though. It's cold.'

'I'll do it.' Sully banged his fist on the wall of the van. 'Let's go.'

The nurse stumbled as the van started rolling, then she disappeared into the front cab. Bryce wanted to quiz Sully again but realised that an answer wouldn't be forthcoming. Beyond his feet, the rear doors had no windows, the outside world a vacuum of visual references. Frustrated, Bryce decided instead to concentrate on what his senses were telling him, what he could hear, what he could feel. The van swung around and Bryce felt the nose of the vehicle lift as it powered up the underground ramp and out onto the street. Sirens filled the air, much louder now, and flashes of blue and red momentarily illuminated the interior of the van. He heard harsh, urgent voices outside and someone banged the side of the van twice, the metallic echo startling Bryce. The vehicle powered forward again, then slowed and stopped. More voices, the crackle of radios. He heard the nurse talking, her voice pressing, authoritative. He glanced at Sully who seemed oblivious to the external dialogue, his arms folded across his chest, his legs stretched out before him. Again Bryce noted the casual clothing, the dark jeans, the flashy trainers on his feet. What did that mean? Then the van was on the move again, accelerating cleanly this time, the chatter from the driver's cabin more relaxed. Shafts of yellow light drifted across the van's roof with soothing regularity, indicating steady progress along empty city highways. After a while Sully stood up and removed the articles from Bryce's head, dumping them on his lap.

'You'll need them later,' he announced, his body swaying with the motion of the van. Bryce ignored the comment, determined to coax his escort into some sort of conversation. 'I don't feel tired anymore,' he lied.

Sully sat back down. 'What?'

'I said I don't feel tired. Well, not as much anyway. I think this little trip has done me a bit of good.'

'That's nice.'

'What security situation?'

'Huh?'

'Back at the hospital, you said there was a security situation. Was it the fire?'

Sully stretched his legs out and yawned loudly. 'Something like that.'

'Can't you tell me?'

'Get some rest.'

'That's all I ever do around here,' Bryce complained.

Sully drew his legs up, leaned forward. 'The hospital's not safe anymore. You're being moved, as a precaution.'

'Where to?'

'That's enough, now. Just be quiet,' Sully commanded.

Bryce didn't argue, unsettled by Sully's behaviour. His voice was quietly disarming but the dark eyes said something else. Back at the hospital he'd always treated Bryce with courtesy, if not the respect that a man of his standing and authority should be accorded, but that was something to do with his security brief, Bryce supposed. Now his attitude had changed. He seemed indifferent, disrespectful even. Maybe it was the late hour, or maybe it was simply a shift in perspective.

After all, it was Jacob who now ran the country, Jacob who was always on the TV or splashed across the front pages, Jacob who delivered rousing speeches in the European Parliament, Jacob who waved from the steps of aircraft as he went about the business of government. Bryce was no longer Prime Minister, something he'd come to accept, but it was only a temporary state of affairs. Sooner or later he'd be well enough to hold the reigns of office once more, to lead the new Cabinet and take charge of the country once again. Or so he imagined.

The truth was, things were much different now. Even a cursory glance at a broadsheet, or a brief spell of channel surfing told him that much. The mood of the public had changed, shaped by an enthusiastic media that had given their wholehearted support to Jacob's fledgling government, a government that was aggressively pushing the Treaty of Cairo, promising a new era of economic prosperity and social harmony, a heady cocktail for any electorate to consume. And consume they had, the opinion polls reflecting an extraordinarily high level of trust in Jacob's administration, a new sense hope amongst Britain's many diverse communities. For Bryce, a return to power could be a hard sell.

And then there were the other stories; the rumours of his imminent resignation, his stubbornness over Cairo, his inability to act in the best interests of the country. The underlying message was subtle, repeated at every opportunity in punchy editorials and popular talk shows - Gabriel Bryce was bad for Britain, Jacob Hooper and Tariq Saeed good. His reputation had been subtly tainted by politically motivated editors and producers on the orders of their masters, reinforcing his lingering suspicions that bad news stories would be thin on the ground for a while. Unless they were about him, of course.

Bryce knew a smokescreen when he saw one. The country's dark undercurrents still existed, swirling and shifting beneath the sparkling surface of a new dawn. His would-be assassin, Daniel Whelan, was out there somewhere, plotting, conspiring with others no doubt, preparing for the next attack. The public were reminded to stay alert, to keep an eye out for suspicious activity, to monitor friends and neighbours, to report strange behaviour, racist comments, dubious mono-cultural gatherings. And all the while the relocation program continued apace, the evidence of its disturbing consequences buried in the rubble of Downing Street. Bryce had once been a master of media manipulation, had used it many times to further his cause. Now it was being directed at his own premiership, his own policies – even his personality. He'd been replaced in the public consciousness, no longer a world leader, just a broken man who once ruled a country where the electorate's eyes had been opened by better, wiser men. Bryce was to be pitied but ultimately forgotten.

The loud ticking of the indicator signalled an imminent turn. Bryce felt the van drift to the left and then the rhythmic thump of rumble strips beneath the tyres. They were on a motorway, or rather they were pulling off one. The van negotiated a roundabout and then drove for another few minutes before swinging to the left and finally stopping. There was a quiet discussion up in the driver's cab and then the door opened. Bryce felt cold air on his face, heard the sigh of the wind in the trees, then the door slammed. He heard footsteps outside, walking past the van, then fading to nothing. Orla's face appeared above his.

'How is he?'

'Inquisitive,' Sully said.

'I don't blame him.'

'Please, don't talk like I'm not here,' Bryce insisted.

Sully leaned forward. 'Well, officially you're not.' He slapped Orla's ample backside. 'Let's go. And keep it under seventy.'

She flashed him a smile and climbed back into the driver's cab. The vehicle swung around and Bryce presumed they were headed back to the motorway. He felt the surge of the engine as the hum of the tyres increased. Outside, the occasional sound of vehicles moving at high speed. Sully smiled in the dark.

'Not far now, Gabe. D'you mind if I call you Gabe? I hate using that *Mister Gabriel* shit.'

Bryce twisted his head, saw the defiance in Sully's eyes, the mocking smile that played around his mouth. 'Something tells me you're going to anyway,' he muttered.

'You're catching on fast,' chuckled the Turk. He leaned forward, elbows on his knees, hands clasped together. 'They found a device, back at the hospital. It went off on the floor below you. Apparently it didn't detonate properly, just caused a fire. That's why you're being moved.'

'What sort of device?'

'The sort that goes bang,' Sully replied. He leaned back against the side panel and folded his arms, yawning.

'So, where are we going?'

'Another facility. More secure.'

'Where?'

'Not that far.'

'Where exactly? Come on Sully, don't treat me like a bloody child.'

'Relax, Gabe,' Sully murmured in the dark. 'Everything's been taken care of. You're going to be well looked after.'

Bryce turned away and stared at the ceiling, confused, apprehensive. He was travelling on a motorway in the dead of night, in an empty van with no medical equipment and no police escort, to an undisclosed location. That told him one thing at least; physically, he was healing well. He felt better in himself, stronger, this sudden journey, while unsettling, somehow invigorating his body. Yet despite the disruption and the occasional blast of cold air his brain still felt slushy, though not nearly as bad as it had done. Probably because he wasn't on that God-awful drip anymore, he realised. It was never feeding him, it was actually draining his life force. He twisted his head to face Sully.

'I want to speak to the head consultant when we get there,' Bryce announced. 'About my treatment.'

Sully's deep voice murmured in the gloom. 'Sure. Just get some rest, Gabe. It'll be a while, yet.'

The journey passed slowly for Bryce. He stared at the roof of the van, the intermittent wash of headlights sweeping above him, the hum of the tyres beneath. He dozed several times, the gentle sway of the vehicle lulling him into a shallow slumber. Passing vehicles would rouse him again and once he heard a police siren wailing but the van rolled onwards.

His eyelids were half closed when the ticking of the indicator summoned him back to consciousness. He felt the van pull to the left and their speed begin to reduce. They left the motorway and now Bryce was fully alert, feeling every bump in the road, every turn, listening for every sound. Sully still dozed, chin on his chest, legs stretched out before him. Bryce felt the roads were getting narrower, the world outside more remote. The sodium glow of streetlights no longer lit up the interior and the rare passing vehicle sounded dangerously close. Soon there were no vehicles, only the gentle hum of their own passage and the scrape of passing bushes and low hanging branches.

'We're nearly there,' Orla suddenly called from the driver's cab.

Sully yawned and stretched, balling his fists and rubbing his eyes. 'How long?'

'SatNav says less than two miles.'

'Shit.' The Turk got to his feet, grasping the trolley to steady himself. His big hands found the restraining straps and tugged them hard, trapping Bryce's arms to his sides, his legs bound tightly together.

'Jesus Christ, Sully,' Bryce wheezed, 'what are you doing?'

'Relax. It's for your own safety.'

The Turk pulled the head cover back on, the surgical mask and glasses over his face. Bryce began to panic, his heart rate accelerating. He tried to wriggle free but found his limbs were firmly tethered. 'I don't care who you work for Sully, I'm ordering you to release me and tell me what the hell is going on.'

'I can see the gate,' Orla shouted.

'Slow down.' Sully reached into his pocket, took out a fat silver pen. Not a pen, Bryce saw, an auto-injector. Cold fear gripped him as the Turk's large hand clamped around his jaw and twisted his head to one side. 'Hold still,' he ordered, 'it's just a sedative.'

'No more drugs,' Bryce pleaded through Sully's fingers, 'please...'

He winced as a sharp pain pierced his neck, almost like a bee sting. Sully let him go, stepping back as he watched Bryce closely. 'For God's sake, Sully. I need to... need to...what...'

And then he couldn't speak, couldn't move his tongue. Ice gripped his body, freezing his head, his neck, his left arm. He could feel the icy fingers travelling downwards, towards his twitching feet, then they too stopped. He tried to move his right arm, curled his fingers briefly until they too were seized, rigid beneath the blanket. He was immobile, frozen.

He was paralyzed.

His mind screamed but no sound came from his mouth. He could hear himself breathing, the respirations loud inside his head, could hear the gentle beat of his heart as the drug calmed him, dispelling the terror, the anxiety.

Sully stood over him as the van veered to the right. 'He's deep. We're good to go.'

Bryce was aware of the van stopping, the chatter of the nurse, a man's laugh. Something hummed and whirred, a metal gate, rattling open. The van pulled forward, the sound of another gate opening and closing, more chatter. The van purred slowly along for a minute, turning one corner, then another, finally coming to a halt with a gentle squeal of the brakes. The engine shut off. They'd arrived.

For a moment there was silence and then Sully moved and the rear doors of the van opened, inviting an icy blast inside. Bryce could feel it on his lips, inside his mouth, but nowhere else. The rest of his body had shut down, like a slab of dead meat. His head lolled from side to side as the folding wheels of the trolley hit the ground. He stared up at a building, a dark, Victorian edifice where the windows were covered with steel bars, not a single light glowing in any of them. A prison? Then he was on the move again. Bright lights suddenly blinded him, neon strip lights, passing overhead. A strong smell of antiseptic invaded his nostrils. Not a prison then, a hospital, one where the paint on the ceiling was cracked and blistered. The trolley turned this way and that, then he was in an elevator, travelling upwards, the single light above blinking intermittently. More ceilings, more lights. Rubber doors flapped open and then he was inside a room, the strip lights turned off, a yellow glow warming a cold corner. A table lamp, he guessed. Then a voice said: 'At last, I've been up half the night. Are you alright?'

It was a man, a voice he didn't recognise. Orla answered him.

'We're fine.'

'It's all over the news, you know.' A figure loomed over him, blond thinning hair, heavy framed glasses, his face lost in shadow. 'How is he?'

'Ischemic stroke, less than twenty four hours ago. He's undergone thrombolytic therapy and we've got him on heparin. His vitals are strong and he's responding well.'

'Good.' The figure moved away. 'I suggest we move him up to observation for the rest of the night. Have you got his paperwork?'

Silence. Then Sully's voice, sharp, irritated. 'You're aware of this patient's particular requirements? You've been briefed, right?'

The new voice sounded indignant. 'I have, yes.'

'Then paperwork isn't an issue, is it? And he stays here. We'll move him after breakfast.'

'It's important he's taken care of. I have a duty of care to - '

'That's enough. We'll discuss this later.'

'What about the other staff?' Orla this time.

The sound of a throat being cleared. 'As far as they're concerned you're an assessment team from London. Nobody will pay any attention to you in this place, believe me. Now, I'll give you the full tour tomorrow but in the meantime I'll show you to your accommodations.'

'That'll be grand, Mister Parry,' Orla chirped.

'No names.' Sully again, annoyed.

He saw their shadows move past him and the light was snapped off, plunging the room into darkness. Footsteps echoed along the corridor outside and he heard Orla laugh, the sound brittle, eerie in the dark. Several minutes passed before Bryce realised he'd been abandoned. As his eyes grew accustomed to the gloom he could make out a paler square of ceiling, a reflection of light coming from a window somewhere, interspersed with black strips. Bars. A barred window. His mind reeled, confusion and fear tumbling together like clothes in a washing machine. Not a hospital then, but a prison. Or a mixture of the two. What could –

He felt his eyes widen, his throat constricting as fear flooded his consciousness. A psychiatric facility. The double gates, the barred windows, the smells, all pointed to the same terrifying conclusion. How was that possible? A mistake had been made, a horrifying mix up that –

No. Impossible. Sully wouldn't allow such a screw up. And this new conspirator, Parry, had been expectant, complicit. Then the thought struck him: he'd been kidnapped. Sully and Orla, others most certainly, had planned the fire, snatched him from the hospital, then drugged him, hiding him in this awful place. Fear stalked him, lurking in the shadows, threatening to engulf him. He closed his eyes, shutting out the nightmare.

Somewhere, a distant scream ripped through the silence.

✵ ✵ ✵

Hertfordshire

Danny swung the axe high over his head then brought it down sharply, splitting the thick log into two neat halves. He picked them up and tossed them into the back of the Nissan pickup parked in the trees behind him, deciding he had enough to stock the woodpile for another week. He swung the axe again, burying the blade into the ancient tree stump, then slapped the dirt from his hands. He walked around to the back of the vehicle, making sure the tailgate was firmly secured, then climbed inside the cab. He sat there for a moment as a chill wind gusted through the woods, scattering noisy waves of dead leaves before it. Overhead, skeletal treetops creaked and swayed, the blue sky above paling before the approaching rain front.

The sweat on his body began to cool and he pulled a green fleece over his t-shirt to combat the sudden chill, careful not to catch the hairs of his beard in the zipper. He scratched his face and neck, still unused to the sensation of a full beard. Ray seemed pleased with its progress though, the dark hair just about thick enough to partially cover the tattoo on his neck, helping to – what was the word Ray used? – oh yeah, *cultivate* a new image, one that would enable him to return to society apparently. But not yet. The closest Danny had come to the outside world since he'd been here was the odd walk around the village late at night. He was grateful for the opportunity, for the change of scenery, but the beard was part of the deal. The walkie-talkie on the seat beside him crackled into life.

'Come in, Lima One.'

His call sign. That was Ray, always super-careful. He scooped up the radio. 'Go ahead.'

'Finish what you're doing and come on up to the house. I've got something for you.'

'Sure. Just packing up now.'

He slipped out of the pickup and retrieved the axe, grunting with effort as he worked the blade from the stump. He was about to throw it in the back when a movement caught his eye. About fifty yards away, where the woods bordered the meadow, Joe trudged towards the house, a brace of dead rabbits strung from a pole carried across his shoulder, a rifle held loosely in his other hand. Nelson bounded ahead of him, a flash of brown and black fur darting through the trees. Danny froze, studying Joe as he skirted the edge of the woods. He didn't like the bloke, not at all, a miserable bastard, always mooching around the estate with a gun in his hand or acting as a bodyguard to Tess and Ray when either of them went out. A weirdo, for sure.

A while ago Danny had been mending a fence on the far boundary when he spotted Joe watching him from a firebreak in the woods. He just stood there, motionless, staring. Danny had waved but Joe just kept on watching. Embarrassed and faintly unnerved, he'd concentrated on looping the roll of wire around the fence post. Next time he looked, Joe was gone. Three days in a row he'd seen him in standing in that firebreak, gawping at him. Intimidating him.

So one day Danny asked Joe about Afghanistan. He mentioned that he too had spent time out there, but Joe had merely laughed, the first and last time Danny had ever seen him do that. He'd also called him a 'fucking blanket stacker' because Danny had served in the Royal

Logistics Corps, a unit not exactly famed for their battle honours. Joe was infantry, the Rifles, a different breed he'd explained as the laughter died and his fists bunched. He'd stood right in front of Danny, toe to toe, three inches taller and much wider, a big brute of a bloke who drove his finger into Danny's chest and told him to mind his own business. Danny had backed away from the encounter, frightened, apologetic, and they'd barely spoken since. Now Danny avoided him like the plague, the cold eyes, the blunt manner, the lurking threat of violence.

Maybe he was jealous. After all, Ray had taken Danny under his wing, had spent many hours discussing the future of the country, politics, the threat that Europe faced. Joe never did anything like that, just lurked around shitting people up. So, he was jealous. Yeah, that was it, Danny realised triumphantly, he was jealous. A big, jealous, miserable twat. *And* he never took that combat jacket off. Chill out bruv, the war's over.

Still, Danny remained hidden behind the tailgate until Joe had trudged out of sight. Then a thought occurred to him. Down through the trees, at the bottom of the valley, was the fire break. Danny had never been down there, had no cause to yet. So maybe he'd take a quick look, see what Joe was so interested in.

Danny checked his watch then set off through the woods, his boots kicking up piles of dry leaves. The ground began to fall away, sloping gently down towards the valley and presently the deciduous mix of oaks and birch gave way to a wide firebreak. Danny stepped out into the firebreak and froze, watching, listening. To his right the break led out into the meadow, the exact spot where Danny had seen Joe standing. To his left, the break continued, following the valley and curving out of sight.

The wood stood before him, tightly packed ranks of mature fir trees that climbed up the opposite slope towards the distant southern boundary of the estate. Danny scratched his head. Maybe Joe had just been walking the fire break, checking for fires or something like that. In November? Unlikely. Something else then. Suddenly a rabbit broke cover and hopped out into the open close by. It sat on its haunches, oblivious to Danny, its tiny nose twitching as it inspected the air. That was it. Joe was hunting rabbits. Danny made a clicking sound with his tongue and the rabbit darted back across the break. He watched it scoot between the trunks of the firs, losing sight of its bobbing white tail as it passed the wooden handle sticking out of the ground.

Danny frowned. He stepped across the firebreak and into the trees on the other side, the ground beneath his feet carpeted with layers of dead needles that muffled his passage. He ducked low, swatting the branches away from his face until he found himself in a small clearing. Here the air was dead, the earth cold and wet, a place where the overhead cover filtered out the daylight, creating pools of deep shadow.

The shovel was standing upright, its exact symmetry conspicuous against nature's random background, its blade buried in a pile of damp brown earth. Lying beside it on the ground was a pick, its metal head rusted, the wooden shaft dotted with spots of green mildew. Danny took a step forward then stopped. The ground in the clearing didn't look right, the earth dipping inwards and forming a shallow depression. Danny knelt down and looked closer. Small metal pegs ringed the clearing, pinning a dark green tarpaulin to the ground. He loosened a few of the pegs and threw back the sheet in a cloud of pine needles.

Danny stood up. The hole had been cut into a rough rectangle, about six feet long and three feet wide. It was deep too, and dank water had collected at the bottom, its oily surface reflecting Danny's looming shadow. It was a trench. He stroked his beard, wondering why someone, Joe probably, would dig a trench in such a remote spot. He looked again. No, not a trench, it was more like a –

He gulped hard and took a hasty step backward. A grave. There was no other explanation. The clearing was isolated, the ground soft, the tools left behind to finish the job. Joe had been digging a grave. Why?

A bird shrilled close by, startling Danny. He threw the tarpaulin back over the hole and pegged it, making sure he covered the mottled sheet with as much woodland detritus as possible. He headed back through the trees at speed, twigs and dry leaves snapping and crunching underfoot. He reached the dirt track where the pickup waited and slid behind the wheel, panting hard. Firing the engine into life, he steered the vehicle along the rutted woodland track and out onto a small access road that wound its way around the woods toward the main house. As the Nissan glided along the asphalt drive, Ray stood on the portico, waving him over. There were two unfamiliar cars parked beneath the car port and Danny steered the pickup alongside them. He headed towards the house, noticing the dark clouds that loomed overhead.

'What kept you?' Ray demanded, his hands thrust deep into the pockets of a pair of grey tracksuit bottoms. He wore a matching grey turtleneck sweater, a pair of gold rimmed reading glasses perched on his bald dome.

'Nothing,' Danny shrugged, his reddening cheeks hidden by the beard. He cocked a thumb towards the pickup. 'I brought some firewood.'

Ray's eyes flicked to the car port and back. 'Good. Go and freshen up then come and join us in the main reception room.'

'Us?'

'That's right. Couple of friends I'd like you to meet.'

Danny's heart skipped a beat. 'What friends?'

Ray chuckled. 'Don't panic, son. All will become clear. Chop, chop.'

Ten minutes later, showered and changed, Danny hesitated at the door of the main reception room, a comfortable space with deep sofas and a log fire that hissed and spat in the grate. Ray, sprawled on a sofa, his arms spread across the back, waved him inside. On the opposite couch sat two men, their eyes tracking Danny as he shuffled self-consciously across the carpet. One wore an oversized rugby shirt with the collar turned up, the material straining across his pot belly and falling over designer jeans. On his feet he wore a pair of expensive trainers, not normally found on men in their forties. *Tosser,* was Danny's immediate impression.

The other man was older, mid-fifties, his long sandy hair receding heavily and exposing a high forehead spotted with freckles. The straggly hair was tied back into a pony tail and he too wore jeans and a black t-shirt with 'Cannes Film Festival 2028' in silver lettering on the left breast. Neither of the men stood.

Ray nodded towards his guests. 'Danny, I'd like you to meet two very good friends of mine, Marcus and Tom.'

Danny stepped forward and took each man's hand in turn. The fat one, Marcus, had a strong grip, challenging almost. With Tom it was like shaking hands with a corpse.

'The famous Danny Whelan,' Marcus beamed. 'a real pleasure.' He waved a hand around the room. 'How are you finding life at Chez Carver? Not too uncomfortable I hope?' He roared with laughter at his own joke.

'Ray's been very kind,' Danny responded.

His host waved a hand in the air. 'Nonsense. Giving shelter to a patriot in need, that's all.'

All eyes turned towards the door as a rhythmic jingle announced the arrival of Tess. She sashayed between the sofas in a capacious mint-coloured frock, the thin material struggling to contain her ample, bra-less bosom. Danny looked away, embarrassed. He'd seem some lumpy birds in his time but this one had no shame.

'Refreshments,' she announced brightly, placing a tray of tea, coffee and biscuits on the table between them. She glanced at Ray. 'Got everything you need?'

'Yes, my love.'

She straightened up, apparently noticing Danny for the first time. She pinched a tuft of hair between her fingers at the back of his neck. 'Mmm, that'll need a little trim. Can't have you getting all scruffy again, can we? Someone might recognise you.'

'Course not,' Danny replied, rubbing his neck. He noticed Marcus smiling as he stared at Tess's breasts. 'You can do it tomorrow if you like.'

Tess studied him for a moment longer. 'No, today. Before your picture.'

'My what?'

Tess ignored him and jangled out of the room, closing the door behind her. Ray poured three cups, passing one each to Marcus and Tom. He didn't offer

Danny one, instead waving him into a chair as he settled back into the sofa. 'I wanted you to meet these two gentlemen Danny, not only because they're good friends of mine but also because they can help you.'

'Really?' Danny sat forward, elbows resting on his thighs, his fingers knitted together. Marcus and Tom stared at him from one sofa, Ray from the other. He felt uncomfortable, like he was on trial. His mouth was suddenly dry. Where was all this going?

Ray took a sip of coffee. 'Marc and Tom are men of influence and skill respectively. Highly valuable commodities in these troubled times.'

Danny stayed quiet, his eyes flicking between Ray and the other two. Marcus dunked a biscuit in his drink, a chocolate finger, waving the soggy end in the air. 'Think of us as magicians, Danny. Now you see him, now you don't.' His shoulders jiggled with amusement as he popped the biscuit into his mouth.

'We're artists.' Tom spoke for the first time, a Midlands accent, flat, monotone. His eyes roamed Danny's face in a way that made him feel distinctly awkward. What were these two, a couple of fags? Another time, another place, they'd have got a slap, especially the fat one, but he was in a different world now, Ray's world, so he forced a smile.

'You boys are starting to freak me out.'

Ray chuckled, placing his cup back on the saucer with a scrape of china. 'Take it easy, Danny. What they're telling you is true, they're both artists and magicians. And here's the good part.' Ray leaned towards him, his voice low. 'They're going to help give you a new life.'

'That's right,' Marcus beamed, 'we're here to work our magic.' Tom simply nodded in agreement.

'Let me explain,' Ray began, nodding across the coffee table. 'Marcus here works for the government - '

The fat man squirmed on the couch. 'C'mon Ray. I thought we agreed not to - '

'Relax, Marcus. Danny has to understand that he has our trust, as we have his. Right Danny?'

Danny smirked at fat boy. 'That's right, Ray.'

'Good. Now, as I was saying, Marcus works in government, has access to the issue of new National Identity Cards.'

Marcus arched an eyebrow. 'Stuffed yours down a rabbit hole, is that right Danny? Very wise under the circumstances, but you'll need a new one. That means a new identity.'

'Hence the beard,' Ray added, 'and it suits you, too.' Danny found himself stroking his bristly face. 'The beard is just part of it,' Ray continued. 'Marcus will record all the necessary details today, then start the process of getting you issued with a new ID card when he gets back to London. Before that happens, Tom here is going to do a little prep work. Tom?'

'That's right, Danny.' The older man tapped a large silver flight case clamped between his calves. It was the first time Danny had noticed it. 'What we're going to do today is change your appearance so Marcus can record your ID card image. Ray's right, the beard suits you, and I can see that the lifestyle here has improved your complexion and added a little volume to your facial bone structure.'

Danny frowned. 'Huh?'

'Tom works in the movie business,' Ray explained. 'Special effects. He's the man who made old Daniel Radcliffe look like a thirty-year old in that *House of Windsor* series.'

Danny was impressed. 'Really? He looked proper young in that.'

Tom smiled for the first time, his fingers dancing on the air. 'The magic of the movies, Danny. Now I'm going to do the same for you.' Tom hefted the flight case onto the coffee table in front of him and snapped the locks open. 'I've got a range of coloured contacts, pigmentation and hair dyes, all the usual tricks of the trade. And then I have this.' From inside the case, Tom produced what looked like a loose flap of skin the size and shape of a sock.

Danny's face wrinkled. 'Shit. What's that?'

'That, my friend, is pure magic,' smiled Tom. 'Self-moulding latex membrane, imbedded with a tiny microchip. Apply it once, mould it to suit, program the chip, and voila. You can wear it again and again without hours in the make-up chair. It simply reshapes itself to your original design. It'll even match your skin tone.' Tom jiggled the rubbery material between his thumb and forefinger. 'This particular sample will be used to subtly change the shape of your face. I've undertaken some preliminary computer modelling, based on the shots Ray took when you first arrived here. This little baby will build out your forehead and subtly reshape the bridge of your nose.'

Danny ran his hand across his face. 'I'm going to look like some sort of caveman, right?'

'Caveman,' laughed Marcus, polishing off the last of the biscuits, 'that's a good one.'

Tom looked pained. 'This is cutting edge technology, extremely expensive. I've gone to a lot of trouble to get this.'

'A lot of trouble,' Ray echoed, his eyes boring into Danny's. Then his face softened. 'Think about it, son - new face, new ID. You'll be able to come and go as you please, travel, even leave the country. Not bad, eh?'

Danny stared at Tom's case, at the neatly labelled boxes sitting snugly in their foam compartments. 'Yeah. I suppose.' He felt Ray's eyes on him again, then heard him say to the others: 'Gents, why don't you get set up in the study while I have a quick chat with Danny? I'll get Tess to wheel in some more refreshments.'

'Lovely,' smiled Marcus, heaving himself out of the chair. Tom followed him through the door and closed it behind him. Ray shuffled along the sofa until he was next to Danny's chair.

'Something's wrong.'

'It's nothing,' Danny mumbled, studying his fingernails. A shadow crossed the room, the dying sunlight finally yielding before the approaching storm. Then the rain announced its arrival, drumming the windows with heavy droplets.

Ray swept the glasses from his head. 'C'mon, son. Out with it.'

Danny got to his feet and moved towards the window. He thrust his hands in his pockets and watched the storm front sweep across the hills behind the house, opaque sheets of rain falling beneath steel grey clouds. The window frame rattled slightly as the wind gusted around the building.

'You've been good to me, Ray. You took me in when I needed help, gave me a roof over my head, fed me, clothed me. I owe you so much already. And now this.'

'What?'

Danny turned, pointing to the empty couch recently occupied by Marcus and Tom. 'This. ID cards, expensive make up. All this trouble you're going to, and for what? Look, I try and pull my weight around here Ray, but I'm hardly a professional handyman, am I? Took me a week to master the bloody chainsaw. I ain't worth the bother.'

'You're in the Movement,' Ray assured him, 'and we look out for our own.'

Danny stared out of the window. 'The Movement's dead.'

Ray got to his feet and crossed the room. He laid a hand on Danny's shoulder, squeezing it with strong fingers. 'I told you before, as long as people like me and you live and breathe, the struggle continues.'

'But I can't pay you back, Ray. For any of this.'

The big man studied him for a moment, his grey eyes holding Danny's. 'Look, I'll be straight with you, Danny. You can't stay cooped up here forever, we both know that. And the authorities will never stop looking, we know that too. No, your only hope is a new life, far away from this country.' Ray paused for a moment, then he said: 'The colonies.'

Danny smirked. 'We're not supposed to call them that.'

'Who gives a toss? Canada, Australia, these are places where a man can disappear. I was thinking New Zealand.'

Danny winced at the thought. 'New Zealand?'

Ray stepped closer, his breath reeking of stale coffee and cigars. 'You're not stupid, Danny. You know you'll need more than a latex mask and a new ID to lead a normal life in this country. We can't manufacture a work history, or previous addresses or medical records. But what I can offer you is a chance to get out.'

Danny watched the rain sweep across the patio outside, hammering the window pane. 'With all due respect Ray, how the fuck am I going to get to New Zealand? Even if I did manage to dodge every copper and border agent in the country, what would I do when I got there? I don't know shit about New Zealand.'

Ray held up a hand. 'Slow down, Danny. Come. Sit.' He led Danny back to the couch, then settled opposite him. He poured himself a coffee, took a noisy sip. 'Obviously you can't travel by the normal routes but there is a way, a tried and tested method. There's a place on the Kent coast, a small fishing port, where we have a boat. Nothing fancy, just a fishing boat, but one that can get you out to where you need to be, smack bang in the middle of the international shipping lanes. Busiest in the world, the English Channel. Anyway, every few months a boat comes through, big Norwegian container ship, goes all over the world. The owner's a very good friend of mine, and the crew are all trustworthy, none of that foreign muck. The boat's due to transit the channel just after Christmas. In a couple of months you could be starting a new life in New Zealand.'

Danny was silent for a while, staring at his feet, trying to imagine life on the other side of the world. This was all so sudden, all happening so fast. Eventually he looked up. 'New Zealand's so far away. I don't know anyone there.'

'I have friends in New Zealand, Danny, good friends, powerful friends. Setting you up there will be far easier than here. Not so strict with their controls and regulations, see. As I said, a man could get lost down there. Live a good life. Europe's finished anyway.'

'Yeah,' was all Danny could muster. People always said New Zealand was just like England used to be, even more so now so many had relocated down there. Maybe Ray was right, maybe he could get lost, disappear. There was nothing here for him anyway. Well, almost nothing.

'What about my dad? I can't leave him, Ray.'

'He's been moved to this address in Battersea, a secure hostel,' announced Ray, producing a folded note from his tracksuit pocket. Danny almost snatched the paper from Ray's fingers and tore it open.

'Bastards,' Danny hissed. He looked up. 'Why? He didn't do anything.'

'Why do you think? Just be grateful that they didn't charge him with conspiracy, son. Anyway, the flat's gone, confiscation order…'

'No!'

'…and your dad's under curfew, though it's not a very strict one. Staff there are a bit lax, see. We can get him out, same way as you, but it'll be some time after you've gone. Either way, you and your dad can start all over again, live your lives in peace.'

Danny leaned forward and buried his face in his hands. His dad was innocent, about as non political as anyone could get, and yet he'd lost his home, a place he'd worked long and hard to buy, a place he'd kept spotlessly clean and tidy, a shrine to his long dead mother. And the bastards had taken it, stripped it bare probably, tramping over his life, his memories, piling his possessions into plastic bags and dumping anything that couldn't be sold in the bins at the back of the block. He'd seen them do it before, to the drug dealers and the welfare cheats, carting them off in police vans while the gangs picked over the stuff left behind. Now it was his dad's turn and Danny felt cold fury at the thought of his scumbag neighbours tearing at his dad's stuff like a pack of hyenas, the unwanted things left to rot on the filthy pavements.

It was all his fault of course, all of it. He had to make it up to him somehow, needed to, or he could never look his dad in the eye again. Throughout his life, and despite all his screw ups, his dad had never cursed him, never denied him a thing, always guaranteeing a roof over his head, somewhere to stay, food in his belly. He knew of others on the Longhill, dysfunctional families that tore each other to pieces over the smallest things, the hatred and violence directed at one family member or another, the muffled shouts through the walls and floors, the crash of furniture, the screams of pain and anger. In stark contrast, Danny's dad was always there when he needed him, a smile, a hug, a generous hand in his pocket when Danny was short. In his quest to evade capture, Danny had withdrawn into himself, thinking only of his own future and whatever that might hold. But now his dad was suffering too, his life torn apart, destitute, locked up in some shitty hostel. He had to get him out, make things right. If it was the last thing he did.

'This new life, Ray, for me and my dad. How much is it going to cost?'

Ray toyed with the Rolex on his wrist. 'It's not a case of money. Besides, you haven't got any. No, the currency I'm trading with you, Danny, is loyalty. Devotion to the cause. Patriotism.'

Danny looked Ray in the eye, his finger prodding his own chest. 'I'm loyal, Ray. Dependable. And I'm a patriot through and through. You know that.'

'I believe you, son, I really do, but a man should be judged by his actions, not his words.' Ray paused a moment, his hard grey eyes searching Danny's. 'The time for talking is over. It's action that's required now.'

Danny squared his shoulders and held out his hand. 'You can count on me, Ray. Whatever you need, I'll do it.'

Ray gripped Danny's hand, his tanned face breaking into a bright, beaming smile. 'Thanks, Danny. I was hoping you'd say that.'

✧ ✧ ✧

Cairo

'Come on, Gabe, up you get. The show's about to begin.'

Bryce peered over the edge of the covers at Sully. The Turk was stood in the doorway, a wide smile plastered across his stubble covered face. Bryce rolled over in his bed, tugging the thin quilt up beneath his chin.

'What show?'

'A TV show. You'll see.'

'I'm not coming.'

Sully feigned disappointment, tutting loudly. He pushed the heavily padded steel door wide open and marched towards the bed. He was dressed like a facility orderly, his white tunic and trousers crisply starched, bulging arms hanging beneath short sleeves. In his hand he carried an extendable baton. Bryce winced as Sully racked the weapon out with a loud *crack!* then lifted the quilt around his feet with the tip. Bryce brought his knees up to his chest.

'Get up, Gabe. It's not bedtime yet.' He tapped the baton on the bed covers, very close to Bryce's legs. His scarred, fragile legs. Bryce heaved himself up onto his elbows and threw off the quilt, rubbing his eyes.

'I'm tired. Don't want to watch TV,' he lied. Inside his stomach churned with excitement. Finally, contact with the outside world! Yet despite the urge to leap out of bed he remained immobile, staring at his feet.

Sully leaned over and collapsed the baton on the floor, placing it back in its holder beneath his tunic. 'We all have to do things we don't want to Gabe. I don't want to drive down here twice a week to do your assessment, but orders are orders. So now I'm giving *you* one. Get up.'

Bryce could see the resentment in Sully's eyes, hear the impatience in his voice. He kept up the pretence a moment longer then swung his legs onto the cold floor.

'That's a good boy. Now, get yourself cleaned up. Ring the buzzer when you're done.'

Sully left the room, leaving the door open. Bryce could hear him whistling along the corridor, his sneakers squeaking on the grey linoleum, then a jangle of keys and the loud crash of the security gate. He was gone. At least Bryce had a little privacy now. He stood up and stretched, his bones cracking with the effort, then stepped into his slippers. He attempted a few gentle twists and stretches, working out the kinks and getting the blood pumping through his veins. It wasn't the most demanding workout in the world but it was the only way that Bryce could judge his physical recovery and maintain a modicum of fitness. Later, after Sully had retired for the night, he would march up and down the corridor for an hour, gradually increasing the pace between the far wall of his room and the security gate, until his lungs heaved and his body ran with sweat. If Sully found out he'd be in serious trouble, because Bryce was convinced Sully didn't want him to get well.

He thought back to the night he'd arrived, abandoned on the trolley, believing he was the victim of an elaborate kidnap plot. The next morning he'd been wheeled up to his room on a deserted, top floor wing. Your own private suite, Sully had joked, releasing the restraining straps and leaving him on the trolley once again. Nobody came to see him that first day. Gradually the drug they'd used to paralyse him wore off, but not before Bryce had soiled his clothes and blankets. He'd lain there in his own filth, trying to shout and failing, feebly raising his arm towards the lifeless camera high up in the corner of his new accommodations. He'd felt fear before, in the rubble of Downing Street, but this was different. This was something darker, more terrifying.

The room he occupied was as far removed from the King Edward as anyone could imagine. It was a large, high ceilinged space with room enough for several patients but only Bryce's single iron posted bed occupied the cold room. Next to his bed was a wooden night stand, his few books stacked neatly on a shelf underneath, a reading lamp on top. A large wooden locker stood against the far wall, his hospital clothes hung neatly inside, next to a writing table and a single metal chair. All four walls were padded up to a height of maybe eight feet, the stuffing bursting from worn seams in many places, the once white material now grey and stained with substances that Bryce didn't want to speculate on. He imagined the darker stuff was blood. Above the padding the walls and ceiling were washed in a fading pale blue, the paintwork cracked and blown in a multitude of places, and a row of strip lights behind wire mesh cages ran across the ceiling. The only ones that worked were the twin pair directly above Bryce's bed. Sometimes Sully left those on overnight.

The room was always cold, the huge radiators beneath the barred windows barely giving off enough heat to warm the clothes he left draped across them overnight. The windows themselves were huge, four of them, ten feet high at least, sealed from the inside and obscured by rusted steel bars on the outside. Small air vents cut into the topmost panes circled lazily on still days, spinning with a low hum when the wind picked up. Beyond the bars the windows overlooked an area of open grass, the double chain link fence with its impressive coils of razor wire, then the woods beyond that shielded the facility from the outside world. Sometimes he'd pull up the battered metal chair and sit at the window for hours, watching the clouds drift across the sky, the trees bending in the wind, the first flurries of early winter snow driving across the grounds. Lately he'd changed the chair's angle, ignoring the world beyond the fence and instead concentrating on the comings and goings at the main gate. He was in Hampshire, near the town of Alton, of that he was almost certain because many of the delivery vans had the name of that town emblazoned on the side panels. Pedestrians came and went by a fenced in chain-link corridor adjacent to the security hut. It wasn't a large facility, just three main buildings including the one he was in, but it was certainly secure. After those first few days he realised that his earlier fears of kidnap were unfounded. There were no demands, no talk of a ransom, no hope of a manhunt or investigation. He was simply a prisoner. Security, Sully often repeated, it was all in the name of security.

Outside his room, past the padded steel door, was a short corridor, a large washroom room and toilets on the right hand side. There were two empty utility rooms opposite, one of which Sully occasionally used to say prayers, a large felt arrow mark on the wall indicating the *Qibla*. At the end of the corridor was a steel mesh gate, always locked, and beyond that another world, a world of tortured screams and unintelligible shouts, a nightmare world that Bryce couldn't shut out with the pillow over his head or the pills they forced him to swallow every morning.

The Turk was his only visitor now, just him and the nurse, Orla, although he only saw her at breakfast and supper for his medication. Physically his body had healed well, still fragile but stronger, however it was his state of mind that he was more concerned with now. The reality of his existence here was solitary confinement, the prescription of unknown drugs that induced a frightening cocktail of vivid nightmares and varying states of torpor. There was a deliberate lack of exercise facilities, physiotherapy or even fresh air. Bryce had demanded to see the hospital administrator but Sully had refused his request, like he'd refused his requests for visitors, for phone calls, for internet access or newspapers, his desire to see Hooper and Saeed, anyone in authority. During bouts of livid anger Bryce accused Sully of torture and false imprisonment, promising to have him locked up the moment he got out. The Turk simply laughed, calling Bryce delusional and paranoid, threatened to have him moved to one of the occupied wards with the real nut jobs. Security, Sully repeated again and again. Bryce believed it was Sully who was not quite right, clearly enjoying the increasingly poor treatment he inflicted on his patient.

So when Sully was around Bryce stayed quiet, acted dumb, sometimes forgetful, popped his medication, and usually did as he was told. He'd stopped asking questions, making demands, allowed his physical appearance to deteriorate. As far as Sully was concerned the enforced confinement was working. He was no bother, a danger to no-one, just another ghost in a facility full of them. Outside the world turned, life went on, and Gabriel Bryce faded from view.

He pulled on a threadbare navy blue dressing gown and shuffled down the corridor to the bathroom. He stood over the sink and stared at his reflection in the mirror, its metal frame rusted and spotted with tiny patches of green mildew. How he'd changed since coming here. The thick grey hair was gone, regularly shaved by Sully into a tight crop, the jagged scar on his head pale and prominent. The lines around his eyes had deepened and his broken nose remained uncorrected, the bridge raised and twisted, the nostrils slightly flattened. Grey stubble bristled around his chin and hollowed cheeks but Sully had forbidden regular shaving, allowing it occasionally and only in his presence. He took his pyjama top off and saw the scars on his body, his ever decreasing waistline a testament to the standard of food and its increasing irregularity. He'd lost at least thirty pounds and aged ten years. In a recent act of degradation Sully had forced him to strip naked, ordering him to crouch in the corner of his room while he took several photographs. Bryce did as he was told, the shame and anger boiling inside him. As the camera flashed he kept his mouth shut, dutifully adopting the poses that Sully ordered, staring blankly at the lens as his mind wrestled for reasons behind his forced humiliation. His only consolation was knowing that Sully continued to be fooled by his act.

He splashed tepid water around his face and neck, shivering in the chill of the washroom. Normally he'd shower but with Sully here the order of the day was the dishevelled, vacant look. He towelled himself dry, again wondering if it would've been better to have perished in the blast itself. He tried not to focus on what might have been but, trapped in this facility, he couldn't help himself. Death by explosion; a quick but messy way to go, limbs torn off, body burned and punctured in a thousand places. A state funeral, eulogies from European and world leaders, the masses filing silently by his casket, tearful and distraught at the loss of their leader. Well, perhaps not the last bit. The British public normally saved their collective grief only for royalty. When Queen Elizabeth had finally died there wasn't a dry eye in the house and the nation had mourned for weeks. Some grieved for the passing of an iconic royal personality, others - realists as Bryce liked to think of them - mourned the end of an era, the final death throes of a nation state and the barely-noticed transition to European federalism. The royalists, the sentimentalists, they'd never realised that it was the old girl herself who'd signed the original treaties that sealed Britain's political fate. Would they have mourned her passing so pitifully then? Perhaps, perhaps not. More importantly, was anyone out there mourning Gabriel Bryce's continued absence from public life? Was anyone asking questions in the House, demanding updates on his progress? Maybe today he would find out.

His pulse quickened as he pushed the buzzer and stood waiting. An impatient Sully showed up a minute later, quickly unlocking the security gate.

'Let's go.'

Bryce did as he was told, elated to be off the deserted wing for the first time since he'd arrived. He shuffled behind Sully, head down, concentrating hard on masking his emotions. His eyes roamed the deserted corridors, the empty stairwells, taking in the signs on the walls that pointed to all points of the compass; Cowan Ward, Guthrie Ward, Toilets, Administration, Staff Only. Everything smelt of antiseptic, of stale food and urine. The floors were stained, the linoleum cracked and missing in places, yet in his mind Bryce danced along the corridors, twirling with delight at his new found freedom. The opportunity to reconnect with the world outside was a palpable thing, his thirst for information as acute as a man without water staggering across a wide desert. But instead he stayed silent, trailing obediently behind his minder. Eventually Bryce asked: 'Where is everybody?'

'Watching TV,' Sully replied over his shoulder. 'Whole country will be glued to it tonight.'

Bryce was confused but said nothing, maintaining his vacant act. They passed through three more security gates without seeing a single person, then dropped down another stairwell to a wide landing. A heavy wood panelled door bore the legend 'TV LOUNGE'. Bryce's heart quickened as Sully gripped the handle. Before he opened the door he turned to Bryce.

'Behave yourself tonight and I might consider more TV privileges in the future. How does that sound?' Bryce yawned, nodding dumbly. He followed Sully into the room. Like the rest of the building the paint was peeling off the walls and everything smelled of damp. There were a dozen easy chairs arranged in a loose semi-circle in front of a large TV screen which was flanked by two barred windows. Against the far wall was a long wooden sideboard with plastic cups and empty beakers of water. A bowl of fruit stood alongside the water, the bananas black, the apples brown and shrivelled. A movement caught his eye and it was then that Bryce noticed three of the chairs were occupied. Sully's arm pulled him back behind the door.

'You lot. Out,' Sully commanded. Bryce peered through the gap, saw three men in navy blue sweat shirts and pants get to their feet and shuffle across the room to another door. Their appearance was as dishevelled as Bryce's, heads shaved, skin bleached by a poor diet and a lack of sunlight, clothing hanging off their undernourished frames. And Bryce noticed the eyes too, the dark circles, the haunted expressions. They reminded him of death camp survivors from the Second World War and he felt an overwhelming sense of sadness for them, their broken minds, their shattered lives. The last of the NATO-led ISAF forces had left

Afghanistan years ago, their defeat as resounding as that of any who had ventured into that God-forsaken country over the past two centuries. At the time Bryce had campaigned heavily for the negotiations that ended the bitter war, a conflict that had claimed thousands of lives and trillions of Euros. Ultimately military force had failed, where dialogue and cultural respect, diplomatic strategies that Bryce had always championed, had won the day. Yet Britain still supplied troops and equipment to the UN peace-keeping mission in Afghanistan, a mission that continued to destroy lives, like the poor souls now scuttling from the TV room. He watched the door close behind the last man, banished to their own miserable accommodations.

'Sit here,' Sully ordered, pointing to a chair at the front. 'Tonight's a big night.

'Is it?' Bryce muttered the words, feigning disinterest as he flopped into the chair. Yellow foam stuffing squeezed out of a tear between his legs.

'You'll see.' Sully picked up the remote and settled into the chair next to Bryce, his legs kicked out before him. He started flicking through the channels then settled on the BBC, the screen filled by a low angled aerial shot, slowly panning across a flat landscape of palm trees and ancient monuments, where dazzling lights and piercing laser beams lit up the evening sky in a myriad of colours, where a heaving multitude thronged before a giant, red carpeted stage that was filled with suited and robed dignitaries. Bryce fought hard to keep his expression neutral as he stared at the TV, the camera flashes that lit up the night like a cosmic storm, the long line of limousines, the smart ranks of ceremonial troops, the camera zooming in towards the historic document that rested on its purpose built plinth, waiting to be signed.

Bryce's heart sank as he watched the TV. The world, and his place in it, had indeed passed him by.

Cairo had begun.

The ceremony was held in the shadows of the Great Pyramids of Giza. The sun had already set when the first European leaders arrived, their air-conditioned limousines whisking the dignitaries a short distance from the exclusive and heavily guarded Mena House Hotel to the giant stage erected beneath the towering Pyramid of Cheops.

Saeed's limousine was one of the last to arrive and it deposited him at the bottom of a flight of red carpeted stairs. He stepped out of the vehicle into a storm of camera flashes, the dazzling lights reflecting the gold embroidery of his knee-length black Sherwani jacket and silk trousers. Dozens more cameras tracked his graceful passage up the stairs and across the carpet where he received a standing ovation from the other EU leaders and the hundreds of European politicians and legislators seated before the stage. Saeed took his place in the front row, absorbing the atmosphere of a momentous spectacle about to unfold.

'Impressive, isn't it?' remarked the German Chancellor seated alongside him.

'Indeed,' smiled Saeed. The elevated stage was dressed like a movie set, two terraced rows of luxury seats fashioned like the thrones of the early Pharaohs. Forming the backdrop was a stand of massive columns resembling those at the ancient site of Karnak, decorated with intricate hieroglyphics and flanked by two huge sphinx-like statues with flaming torches set between their massive paws. The Pyramid of Cheops towered behind, a man-made mountain of stone bathed in a magnificent display of lighting that changed colour constantly as the sky darkened and the gentle strains of the Berlin Philharmonic Orchestra drifted on the sultry air, adding to the sense of occasion. The Egyptians had outdone themselves, Saeed decided. Hooper, bowing and fawning before President Vargas in Washington, would secretly kick himself for missing this.

He raised his eyes above the minions seated in front of the stage and out across the desert where an estimated one million people stood behind temporary barriers under the watchful eye of the Egyptian army, an endless sea of bobbing and swaying heads, a forest of arms above them, cameras flashing. Saeed had never been so close to such a crowd before, as if the whole of Cairo had turned out for what was to be an historic night. It reminded him of a scene from ancient history, an army stretched out across the desert, like Saladin's perhaps, awaiting the horns that would signal the start of battle. It was a magnificent sight, and faintly unsettling. He smiled, wondering how many already had their bags packed.

A red light pulsed in the dark sky and Saeed watched an unmanned media blimp drift silently overhead, its multiple camera platforms recording every moment and beaming the broadcast to a waiting continent. A continent about to change forever.

'The gown,' observed the Chancellor, smiling, 'a nice touch. And so representative of modern Britain.'

Saeed smiled alongside the German. Actually the man was a Turk, he reminded himself, born in Hamburg, yet the blood that coursed through his veins was pure Ottoman.

'Thank you, brother.'

'A little overdone perhaps?' ventured the Chancellor, smoothing the expensive material of his own navy blue lounge suit.

'A gift from the Egyptian ambassador. It would have been insulting to our guests not to have worn it.'

'Perfect,' the Chancellor chuckled. After a moment, he said: 'I see things have settled down at home.'

Saeed nodded. 'The new administration in Britain has provided the stability the country so clearly craves. The west abhors chaos.'

'And how is the Prime Minister?'

Saeed pulled a linen handkerchief from his pocket and pretended to blow his nose, discreetly covering his mouth. 'Hooper is a child,' he sneered, 'and easily manipulated. The timing of his trip to America is a measure of the man's naivety.'

'In any case, you did well to encourage it.'

'You've seen the news. The trip goes badly for him. His allies in Cabinet were initially emboldened by the man's unexpected promotion but now they're sensing blood in the water. The opportunity to move against him may present itself sooner than planned.'

'It has to be done subtly, Tariq. Many eyes are watching you now.'

'They shouldn't be concerned.'

The Chancellor leaned over, the beginnings of a scowl creasing his face, his lips barely moving. 'Then do it. Hooper cannot be allowed to stand in our way.'

'It will be done,' Saeed promised, settling back into his chair. An aide approached, one of the Turkish President's entourage Saeed realised, and handed the German Chancellor a slip of paper. He read it, then placed it in his pocket. He sat a little more erect and adjusted the cuffs of his crisp white shirt.

Saeed raised an eyebrow. 'All is well, I trust?'

'They're on their way.'

Sully elbowed Bryce painfully in the arm. 'I'm sure you recognise a few of your old mates there.'

Bryce shrugged, noting the discreet exchange between the exotically dressed Tariq and the German Chancellor, the flunkey who bowed and scuttled back behind the Turkish President across the stage. Where was Hooper? The commentary hadn't even mentioned him yet, focussing instead on who *was* there. Bryce recognised many faces, including representatives from the United Nations, seated just below the Organisation of the Islamic Conference members. It was common knowledge that the OIC was the real power in the UN and the seating plan clearly reflected that hierarchy. In fact, watching the camera pan slowly along the faces of the European leaders, Bryce realised that much thought had gone into every aspect of the seating.

Saeed and the German Chancellor, both major signatories, were in the front row, along with the Turkish President and the French, Dutch and Belgian Prime Ministers. Significantly the Irish and Danish luminaries were seated further back and at opposite ends of the stage, clear punishment for sharing doubts about the treaty similar to Bryce's. Behind the front row was the President of Bosnia Herzegovina, a significant promotion in international terms, Bryce realised. Next to the Bosnian he noticed a diminutive figure wearing a white fez and sporting a grey beard. It took a moment before Bryce recognised the Grand Mufti of Sarajevo, the only religious leader he could see on the stage. How had the Bosnians managed that concession?

In fact, the more he studied the screen, the more he realised the significance of the occasion. He was suddenly reminded of a confrontation in the House of Commons, long before he became Prime Minister, with a young MP from an obscure British independence party. It was late and the man was drunk, obstructing Bryce as he'd tried to leave the lavatory.

'They want it back, you know,' the man had said, jabbing his finger in the direction of Bryce's chest, 'and you'll give it to them.'

'Give who, what?' Bryce had asked. He remembered being annoyed, impatient.

'Europe,' the man had spluttered. 'Don't you get it? Don't any of you lot see? You're being used. They're laughing at us, behind closed doors, in the mosques and madrassas, all over Britain, all across Europe.' The man had raised a finger to his lips, swaying drunkenly on his feet. 'It's their secret, their black manifesto. We're being duped, drugged, lulled into a false sense of security. I know. I can seeee...'

The man had hissed the word like a snake, his amateur dramatics interrupted by an awkward stumble against the wall, giving Bryce the opportunity to leave the lavatory and have the man arrested. Now, watching events in Cairo unfold, Bryce recalled those bitter words, applying their offensive logic to what he could see on the screen before him. The ranks of Europe's elite were heavily sprinkled with prominent Muslims, united, powerful, ready smiles and warm handshakes in abundance, waiting patiently to sign a document that will change the face of Europe forever.

No, he chastised himself, it was a ridiculous chain of thought.

On the screen the live feed cut to an aerial shot of a convoy moving swiftly through the suburbs of Giza. The palm-lined highway was swept clear of traffic, police outriders shadowing the fleet of black Mercedes limousines in a dance of blue lights.

'Here they come,' Sully announced brightly. 'The show's about to begin.'

A ripple of applause reached Saeed's ears, growing louder with each second like an approaching rainstorm. The multitudes were clapping and cheering, the sound rolling across the desert floor in steady waves and crashing against the strings of the orchestra that fought to compete. In the distance a procession of limousines snaked their way towards the pyramids, headlights gliding along the blacktop. Off-stage, men and women sporting headsets and microphones flew into a whirlwind of self-important activity as the convoy drew closer. The stage lighting suddenly increased in intensity as the orchestra shifted gear from the exquisite delicacy of Handel to Beethoven's rousing Symphony number Nine, the conductor whipping the air with his baton and drawing an energetic response from his musicians.

Impressive, Saeed mused, very impressive. The gathered heads of state stood as one as the Egyptian ceremonial troops surrounding the stage came to attention as one, their weapons held stiffly before them. The symphony built towards its thunderous climax, the applause of the multitudes rising like the sound of the ocean into the Egyptian night.

The Presidents of Europe and Egypt, their limousines drawing up at the bottom of the steps in perfect synchronisation, had arrived.

Danny Whelan dragged a chair across the bedroom and sat on the small balcony as darkness settled across the Hertfordshire countryside. It had become something of a ritual at the end of the day, enjoying a cup of tea as he watched the shadows stretch across the fields behind the house, the crisp air punctuated by the call of evening birdsong, the cautious appearance of white-tailed rabbits and other wildlife as an occasional moon bathed the earth in its cold, clear light. As he sipped his brew Danny saw a firework explode somewhere over the rolling hills towards Watford. He took a deep breath and sighed, recognising the perfect moment to spark up a fat boy and get quietly wasted. But smoking was forbidden in the house and besides, he had no gear anyway. In fact he hadn't had a smoke since he'd arrived and he felt better for it, although the withdrawal symptoms were a bitch sometimes. Keep busy, that's what Ray recommended. He was right, as usual.

Another firework bloomed in the distant sky. Everyone'll be getting pissed tonight, and Danny briefly wondered what was going on back at the Kings Head. There was probably some sort of drink-up in progress, seeing as the whole country was officially in party mode, though whether the stupid bastards realised they were celebrating yet another inevitable tax burden was anyone's guess. He was glad to be away from that shithole anyway. The law might still be hunting him but here, behind the walls of the estate, he felt safe. And he was well looked after too. Three hot squares a day, a comfortable apartment, work around the estate; for the first time in many years Danny felt useful and a whole lot healthier too.

He heard the TV on the sitting room wall hum into life and Ray's gruff voice rasping from the speakers. 'Danny? You there?' Danny hurried into the sitting room and reached for the remote control, activating the TV's inbuilt camera. 'Ah, there you are. Come and join the party, son.'

Behind Ray's tanned head Danny could see a group of people gathered in one of the reception rooms of the main house. He could hear music, the buzz of conversation and the odd peal of laughter. Danny hesitated. 'Are you sure, Ray? I mean, I'm supposed to be in hiding and all that.'

Ray's pearl-white smile beamed across the screen. 'Don't worry, son, it's an informal gathering. Old friends, senior members of the Movement, all highly trusted individuals. You couldn't be in safer company.'

Twenty minutes later Danny let himself in through the kitchen door wearing a pair of beige chinos and a freshly pressed white polo shirt. Once again he checked his appearance, this time in the hallway mirror, realising how different he looked from the old custody shots the media were circulating. His hair was still short but had grown a fraction, allowing Tess to tidy it and sweep in a side parting. The beard was neatly trimmed and his complexion had that healthy outdoors look. All in all he felt no-one would recognise him from his mug shot and that gave him a little more confidence. In truth, the thought of meeting Ray's friends was a little intimidating.

'Very handsome.' Danny turned and saw Ray in the doorway of the main reception room. 'Come on, son. Everyone's waiting.'

The wood panelled room was lit by strategically placed candle clusters and a couple of small table lamps that glowed on either side of the large windows. A TV mounted on a trolley next to the door droned quietly, barely cutting through the chatter. The atmosphere seemed relaxed enough and Danny counted maybe twenty people scattered around the room, some well dressed and clearly moneyed, others a bit more down market. The ladies, most wearing party dresses and sparkling jewellery, gathered on the numerous sofas while the men stood in quiet groups. No one noticed

Danny until Ray swept a meaty arm around his shoulders and led him into the centre of the room.

'Can I have everyone's attention for a moment, please.' The chatter died away and Danny's cheeks reddened as the small crowd studied him, curious expressions on their faces. He saw one woman on the sofa whisper something to a heavily made up blond next to her and both women giggled softly, ramping up Danny's embarrassment. Some edged closer to him while others lingered around the walls, their faces lost in the shadows. Danny felt like a specimen in a glass box. Ray's strong fingers squeezed his shoulder.

'Friends, I'd like you to meet Danny Whelan. As most of you know, Danny has been a guest of mine for a while now and I'd like to think in that time we've become friends, right Danny?'

Danny's cheeks burned a deep crimson. Thank God for the beard. 'Er, yeah, of course Ray.'

Laughter cackled around the room and Danny felt a flash of anger for being the focus of their amusement. Ray gave Danny another squeeze and continued. 'When Danny went on the run he used his wits to evade capture, to keep himself fed and dry. He used guile and ingenuity at every turn, hiding by day, moving like a fox through the night, his one aim to make it here, to my door, unmolested. And more importantly, undetected.' Ray let his arm slip but Danny didn't really notice. He was too busy enjoying the quiet respect that Ray's guests were suddenly giving him. Tess appeared next to Ray and silently handed him a champagne flute. 'You've all read Danny's story,' he reminded them, 'you've all read the lies, the distortions, the snarly pictures beamed across the country. The Danny Whelan I know is nothing like that. He's intelligent, loyal, patriotic, has a strong bond with his poor father, and, like all of us here tonight, cares passionately about the future of this country. If anyone encapsulates what it means to be a patriot today, it's this man here. Ladies and gentlemen, I give you Danny Whelan.'

'Danny Whelan,' the guests murmured in unison, raising their glasses. Danny choked up at the mention of his father, at Ray's kind words. In the silence he struggled with his emotions.

Ray emptied the contents of his glass down his throat and smacked his lips loudly. 'Now, all of you go and get pissed!' As the room laughed and clapped, Ray steered a grateful Danny towards the buffet tables set against the wall. The white linen tablecloths were decorated with champagne buckets, neat rows of tall crystal flutes, and an impressive feast of hot and cold foods. Ray studied Danny's face as he set his glass down. 'Don't worry,' he laughed, 'they won't bite.'

Danny stared at the carpet. 'Ray, what you said, those words, I don't know what - '

'Look at me,' Ray ordered. Danny raised his eyes. 'I meant every word of it. You're something of a legend, Danny. You're a symbol of hope to all of us.' Ray leaned over the table, selected a large prawn from a carefully arranged display and popped it into his mouth. 'Every day you wake up a free man, every minute you evade the clutches of the state, that's another small victory for the patriots of this country. You're important to us, Danny. Even more so, now that bastard treaty is being forced upon us.' Ray sucked his fingers clean, picked up another glass of champagne and chugged it back. He handed a full one to Danny.

'Cheers, Ray.' He took a careful sip, enjoying the cold crispness on his tongue. 'Can I ask you something?'

'Course,' his host invited, chomping on another prawn.

'If the treaty's so bad, why have a party?'

Ray burped softly, fish breath wafting across Danny's face. He tapped the side of his head with a greasy finger. 'It's all about mental attitude, son. Every setback must be viewed as an opportunity to do things differently, to reassess one's strategy. The Movement is threatened? Shut down the Movement and go in a different direction. You thought it was dead, right? Take a look around you.'

He pointed a thick finger at the TV screen, where Jacob Hooper's face filled the giant video screens around the stage in Cairo, his transatlantic apology and message of support barely audible over the abuse and hoots of derision around the room.

'It's on us now,' Ray went on, 'nothing we can do about it. By midnight tonight the Treaty of Cairo will be signed into European law without a single referendum in any EU country. That's a major setback, right?' Danny nodded his head. 'Of course it is. In fact I'll go one further – I'd say it's the end of Europe as we know it.'

Danny took another sip of champagne, tiny bubbles exploding inside his nostrils. 'Really?'

'Think about it, son. All someone has to do is find their way to Egypt and claim asylum under European law. And what happens once they're granted leave to stay? You think they'll wait around in that fly-blown shithole until the Egyptians pull their finger out of their arses? No chance. They'll be winging their way westward, into old Europe, where Muslim enclaves spread like weeds, filling the cracks, expanding. A new mosque here, a faith school there, and all the while we've got hospital maternity wings bursting at the seams with foreign litters and governments bending over backwards to fill the begging bowls. And there's nothing to stop these newcomers, no rules, no restrictions, no borders, nothing. The relocation program was the start of all this. I mean, does anyone seriously believe that those bloody refugees will up sticks and relocate back to Pakistan once the war ends? Turn their backs on free health care, central heating, internal plumbing, wide screen TV's, welfare credits? Who in their right mind would do that?'

Ray selected a dainty pastry morsel that Danny couldn't identify and popped it into his mouth whole. He washed it down with half a flute of champagne then wiped his mouth with a linen napkin. When he started speaking again Danny noticed he'd dialled down the volume, yet his voice and words were laced with a bitterness that made Danny feel decidedly uncomfortable.

'We're under attack son, have been for centuries. It's all planned, all been worked out. They can smell the stench of our weakness. Turkey joining the EU, the relocation program and now Cairo - you think they're unrelated events? Think again, son. Europe may be partying tonight but the hangover's going to be like a bucket of ice water in the face. Of course the media will paint a pretty picture at first, smiling families clutching EU passports, deluded liberals regurgitating the same old mantra about the need for millions of immigrants otherwise our feeble little countries will fall into ruin. I give it ten years, maybe less, then a tipping point will be reached. When that happens, they won't bother to hide it anymore. There'll have won and a conquered Europe will sink slowly into anarchy. Ethnic violence, religious bloodletting, cities in flames, you name it. It'll be the end of everything.'

As Ray stared into the middle distance, Danny seized the moment to belt back a mouthful of champagne.

He felt thoroughly depressed by Ray's bleak vision of the future, and as he watched his host he realised the man felt the same way too. Still, he consoled himself, by then him and dad would be half a world away, living a decent life in New Zealand and watching Europe's downfall on the news. They'd miss home of course, but life wouldn't be that bad.

'Evening, gents.'

Danny turned, saw the fat bloke, Marcus, sidling up next to Ray. 'Lovely spread as usual, Mister Chairman.'

The interruption seemed to snap Ray out of his sombre trance. He waved a hand across the food laden tables. 'Help yourself, Marcus.'

'Way ahead of you, Raymondo.' Marcus laughed, patting his pot belly. His fingers moved to the breast pocket of his black shirt, a huge tent-like affair that gathered in scruffy folds at the ends of his wrists. 'Got something for you, Danny. A present.'

'Not here,' snapped Ray. He led them out of the room to a quiet, book lined study across the hallway, closing the door firmly behind them.

'I thought they were your friends,' Danny said, cocking a thumb over his shoulder.

'They are, but anonymity is one of our more formidable weapons,' Ray explained. 'Take Marcus here for example. Only a few of us know he works for the government. Compartmentalisation, that's the key to good security.' He turned to the fat man and held out his hand. 'Let's see it, then.' Ray took the ID card and gripped it between thumb and forefinger, inspecting its detail. He pulled a pair of reading glasses from his pocket and slipped them on, holding the card up to the light. He was silent for a moment, then he said: 'Beautiful. A masterpiece.'

'It's the real deal,' beamed Marcus, 'and so's the national insurance number. The upside of Cairo means the Ministry has to generate hundreds of thousands of new numbers to satisfy the expected waves of migrant workers.'

'Leeches,' Ray spat.

'Did Tom come through with the latex mask?'

'He's putting the final touches to it. Should be here next week.'

Ray handed the ID card to Danny who found himself staring at his own image, complete with expertly applied latex makeup. He barely recognised himself. The name on the bio-metric card read "JOHN D. STEPHENSON". Danny turned the plastic over in his hand. It certainly felt like the real thing, even down to the high-tech hologram and the EMV chip. His inspection of the card was interrupted by the silence around him. He looked up to see Ray and Marcus staring at him.

'Well, what d'you think, son?'

'It's perfect, Ray. Mint.'

'All legal and above board. Airtight,' Marcus assured him.

Danny turned it over in his fingers. 'Thing is, if I'm leaving the country on the quiet, why do I need this?'

Ray took the card from Danny and slipped it into his pocket. 'Remember what I said earlier, about setbacks and opportunities?' Danny nodded. 'Good, because an opportunity has presented itself to us, something that will upset the party mood in Brussels.'

Marcus folded his stubby arms and nodded silently. Danny's throat suddenly felt very dry.

'Really? What's that then?'

Ray didn't reply, just turned away and opened the door to the room. The sound of laughter drifted across the hallway. 'Soon, Danny boy. Now, let's get back to the party, shall we?'

Marcus smiled and winked. He clapped Danny on the back and ushered him from the room.

Deputy Prime Minister Saeed flicked the embroidered vents of his tunic and gratefully re-took his seat, easing himself into the deep red cushion. It was the twelfth standing ovation since the ceremony had begun and his legs were beginning to tire. A short distance away, President Dupont stood behind a bloom of microphones as he delivered a carefully worded address that spoke of peace and unity, of economic progress and the free movement of peoples that would sweep away borders and barricades, both seen and unseen, from the face of Europe. If only he knew, if only *any* of the Infidel leaders realised the gravity of the mistake they were making.

Saeed looked around him, at the Europeans who clapped and cheered their own demise, and felt nothing but contempt for them. At the podium the President concluded his speech to thunderous applause, the multitudes across the desert lending their voices to the ovation. One by one, the heads of government stepped forward and signed the Treaty of Cairo, the line of suited dignitaries winding across the red carpeted stage as the orchestra played softly in the background. As the minutes went by the signatories each stood in front of the marble plinth and made their mark on the treaty then gathered at the side of the stage. Congratulations were exchanged, hands shaken, backs slapped and cheeks kissed as the signatures on the treaty slowly filled the page. History was being made, and they were all part of it.

Saeed's turn finally came. He stepped forward as a million camera flashes lit up the night, twinkling like stars across the desert. He approached the plinth and stood behind it for a moment, admiring the rich texture of the treaty document, the rows of swirling signatures, the declaration at its head that would mark a new stage in Europe's long and bloody history. An aide waited, the uniquely crafted Mont Blanc pen held in an outstretched hand. Saeed took it, then swirled his signature across the page next to his printed name. He straightened up and shook the waiting President's hand as the world's media recorded every moment.

'Congratulations,' beamed President Dupont.

'Allahu Akbar,' Saeed murmured in reply. He saw the President's smile slip just for a moment, the eyebrows coming fractionally together as the words registered in the Frenchman's consciousness. Any reply, if one was forthcoming, was lost as fireworks exploded across the horizon, lighting up the ancient stones of the pyramids and the night sky above in a thunderous storm of noise and colour. The dignitaries and officials seated in front of the stage sprang to their feet, cheering and clapping their joy. Car horns across Cairo joined the clamour, and unofficial fireworks whizzed skyward from thousands of rooftops across the city.

It was a sight like no other. Saeed's senses drank in the celebrations and the smile that creased his face was a genuine one, a triumphant one. The years of hard work, the political manoeuvring, the deal brokering, the unwitting sacrifices of his brothers and sisters in Luton and London, had all amounted to this night. President Dupont was the first to leave, gliding back towards the air-conditioned comfort of the Egyptian premiere's palace in his black Mercedes limousine. Saeed joined the other leaders as they filed slowly towards the steps at the side of the stage, pressing flesh with many of his colleagues on the way, the words of congratulation sincere for the most part. At the top of the carpeted staircase he waved to the world's media and the ecstatic crowds beyond, his memory recording the scene for future recollection. It was truly an amazing sight.

It was at that moment, just before he turned to step down, that he noticed two things. The first was the Irish and Danish premiers, standing in line behind him as they waited to board their respective limousines. While they shook hands warmly with their colleagues around them, their expressions said something else entirely. The smiles were clearly strained, their words lacking conviction, but it was the eyes that told Saeed the rest; doubt, certainly, fear, he hoped - for the opponents of Cairo there would be much to fear.

The second event made his heart beat faster, a warm glow spreading across his chest, the adrenaline pumping through his body. Beyond the pillars and columns of the magnificent stage, the flags of every European Union state hung limply from a forest of flagpoles, teased into occasional life by a sluggish night breeze. It was lost in the darkness, briefly lit by the last of the fireworks and the sophisticated lasers, but Saeed's eye caught it none the less. It wasn't there earlier and Saeed assumed that it wouldn't be there much longer, but to those that recognised it the point had been made.

The wind picked up then and the flag unfurled, snapping open to reveal the white *Shahada* inscription emblazoned across a black background. For that briefest of moments, the flag of the Khilafah, the global Islamic state, flew above the unwitting heads of Europe's elite.

Saeed descended the stairs and climbed into his waiting limousine, the smile on his face a little wider.

'Well Gabe, what did you think of that?' Sully got to his feet, stretching his muscular frame. 'Not a bad show, huh? Minister Saeed did the country proud, don't you think? A true statesmen.'

Bryce shrugged his shoulders, studying his fingernails. Inside his mind was a whirlwind. Hooper in Washington, Tariq in Cairo, the treaty now written into European law. Things were happening so fast Bryce found it hard to cope with the deluge of information. He kept one eye on the scrolling ticker at the bottom of the screen. The City had clearly welcomed the treaty, the global markets responding positively to the formalisation of the energy and trade deals that the treaty had cemented. On the screen the streets of Cairo were mobbed, hundreds of thousands dancing in the streets while cars inched their way through the crowds, horns blaring and EU flags waving. The scene was the same across Europe; London, Paris, Berlin, Rome, every major city witnessed spectacular fireworks and celebrations on a scale that Bryce thought breathtaking. In a few weeks Britain had been transformed from a land plagued by creeping social division and economic uncertainty to a nation filled with hope and a new found confidence, where people danced in the streets and new deals struck with new partners promised a future of prosperity for the continent.

No wonder Bryce was yesterday's man. He was a forgotten figure, a symbol of Britain's bleak past. He'd been banished, in every possible –

'*...that Gabriel Bryce couldn't be here tonight.*'

Bryce stiffened, his eyes flicking toward the screen. A studio panel in London, well known political commentators grouped around a huge circular table, a giant screen behind them, the fireworks that rippled across the night sky throwing the Houses of Parliament into deep shadow.

'*At least Bryce has an excuse. Jacob Hooper chose the Afghan talks and a state memorial service in Washington over one of the most important nights in Europe's history.*'

'*What about his live link address?*'

'*Well, I think that did more to highlight the torrid time he's had in America, rather than show support to the treaty itself. Perhaps not the best display of political judgement.*'

'*Another British Prime Minister potentially undone by Cairo?*' questioned the well-known newsreader chairing the event. The laughter around the table made Bryce bunch his fists in anger. He took a deep breath and relaxed, aware that Sully was studying his reaction. On the TV the debate continued.

'*It's now generally accepted that Gabriel Bryce was going to announce his retirement prior to the Downing Street bomb. His continued opposition to Cairo had made him deeply unpopular in the party...*'

'Not something a politician likes to hear,' Sully tutted, shaking his head. Bryce was about to offer a vague answer when a voice on the TV said:

'*...temper our criticism because of Bryce's recent stroke. Although the security around him remains tight, the reports coming out of Millbank are suggesting considerable mental deterioration.*'

'*That's right, John. His weekly blog had become increasingly rambling. There's been some concern, most recently expressed by various mental health charities, over its continued publication.*'

Bryce stared at the pundits around the table, the expressions of regret, the shaking heads. What bloody blog?

'*Yes, it's all quite tragic. Our thoughts and prayers are with him tonight. Now, if we can shift focus back to Cairo, our viewers have been voting throughout the evening on the treaty and Deputy Prime Minister Saeed's performance in Cairo, both given seemingly overwhelming approval. We'll be sharing those results and getting his own reaction to tonight's historic events from the Secretary of State himself, who'll be joining us live from the British Embassy in the next hour...'*

The words no longer registered in Bryce's consciousness. The pieces were finally falling into place, a sudden flash of light that banished the shadows of deception in his mind. Now he knew, now he realised, the pieces swept from the board until only one remained.

Tariq.

Tonight he'd witnessed a coronation in all but name, his former colleague and political fixer sitting as an equal amongst the other heads of state, relaxed, confident, his place in history assured. His one time friend and ally, the man who'd fortuitously escaped the Downing Street blast, who'd become Jacob Hooper's deputy, who'd assigned Sully to be his minder, the same man who'd never visited him, who'd denied Bryce all contact with the outside world in the name of security, who'd allowed him to rot in this God forsaken facility until -

The TV blinked off. Bryce was rooted to his seat, his legs numb, his eyes fixed to the black screen. He saw his reflection there, a small, frail figure he barely recognised. Sully's dark silhouette stood close by, looming over him like an angel of death.

Of course. Death. That's what Sully represented, what this place had in store for him. He could see it all now, as if a map had been rolled out across a table before him. It all seemed so clear, so obvious, that Bryce felt like slapping his forehead in realisation. But he didn't. Instead he took a deep breath, his eyes fixed on the lifeless screen. He let the muscles in his face relax, his jaw slacken.

'Gabe?'

Bryce turned his head slowly. 'Did they say my name?'

'Yes.' Sully studied him hard. 'You had a stroke, Gabe. The first night. Remember?'

Bryce frowned. He nodded slowly. 'I think so. I couldn't move.'

'That's it.' Sully patted him on the arm. 'We're going to get you more pills, Gabe. Better ones. Make you feel better.'

'A stroke,' Bryce mumbled.

'A bad one. Come on, on your feet.' He felt Sully's strong fingers snake beneath his armpit and lift him out of the chair. He followed him out of the room and up the stairs. Through the barred windows the night was black and a fine mist of rain swept through the security lights outside. The corridors were empty, only the odd shout from a troubled inmate breaking the silence of the facility. Bryce shuffled along the grim hallways, his hands thrust into the pockets of his dressing gown, slippered feet slapping against the cold linoleum. Sully walked ahead, chain looping from his belt, keys jangling in his hand as he whistled tunelessly. Dead man walking - the phrase came to Bryce then, the realisation that he would never again see the outside of these stark, depressing walls. He knew he was a prisoner but now his isolated ward was to become death row. A debilitating stroke followed by significant mental deterioration – they were setting the scene, softening the public blow when the news was finally announced; *Gabriel Bryce, former Prime Minister, died this morning as a result of a second, massive stroke...*

He cupped a hand over his mouth as the bile bubbled up his throat. Sully turned, then ushered him quickly into a nearby utility room. He shoved him past the shelves and in front of a deep sink where Bryce folded over its edge, retching across the scratched and worn enamel. He turned the long handled tap, rinsing his mouth as another wave of nausea gripped his stomach and he vomited loudly.

'Damn, Gabe.' Sully turned away, disgusted. He took a few paces out into the corridor, pulled his cell from his tunic and studied the screen. Bryce came up for breath. As he leaned on the sink his eyes roamed the shelves nearby, stacked high with boxes of medical supplies. The brown cartons were clearly labelled; latex gloves, antiseptic wipes, wound dressings. Then he noticed the lettering on a nearby box and without a second thought, thrust his hand inside, his heart beating rapidly as he secreted the item in the pocket of his dressing gown. He bent over the sink and forced himself to retch again, watching Sully through tear-filled eyes, the Turk's wide shoulders filling the doorway, his back turned away from Bryce's noisy convulsions. His stomach finally emptied, Bryce splashed his face with cold water and straightened up. The panic had subsided, the fear kept at bay, replaced by a clarity that Bryce hadn't experienced in a while. A coup had taken place, a coup so obvious that the public were simply blind to it.

'You all right?'

'Something I ate,' Bryce replied, rubbing a damp hand around his neck. 'I feel tired.'

'Then let's go.' Sully led him back through the corridors and past the steel gate of his empty ward. He slammed it behind Bryce and spoke to him through the rusted mesh. 'Get yourself bedded down, Gabe. Nurse will get you started on that new medicine tomorrow, o.k.?'

Bryce nodded without turning and headed towards his room. He heard doors slamming behind him as Sully disappeared into the night. He made straight for his bed, draping the dressing gown over the thin quilt and burying himself beneath the covers. The room was cold but Bryce didn't really feel it. He didn't have long, that much he knew. His deterioration was now public knowledge, the chances of any recovery about as remote as those poor bastards orbiting Jupiter ever returning to earth. Soon the order would be given and Sully would come for him. The how's or why's didn't matter, only that his life would probably end in this soulless, miserable room. His body would be shipped to a coroner's office somewhere, a certificate of death issued, arrangements made for a private funeral. All above board, all the loose ends taken care of. Despite the public's misplaced faith in the probity of its politicians, the political elite had done it before, removing people who threatened covert agendas. Government scientists killed in Oxfordshire woods, or RAF Chinooks crashing into Scottish hillsides, the end result was always the same. Nothing could be proved, a liberal use of the word 'conspiracy' effectively discrediting any meaningful investigation by concerned parties. The dead were mourned and the world moved on.

And who would mourn for Gabriel Bryce? Not Charlotte, the sister he hadn't seen or heard from in years, married to a Swiss socialite in Geneva. His parents were long dead, his wife too, and there were no children to stand tearfully in the front pew. The flowers on his grave would wilt and die and the moss would creep steadily across the stone to eventually obscure his name. He would be quickly forgotten, a page in history, his legacy one of failure.

Now he felt the hand of Tariq on his back, pushing him towards his impending doom. No doubt Hooper had been manipulated too, his trip to Washington a political embarrassment according to the pundits on the TV. The reality of the conspiracy was almost impossible to accept yet the wheels of state would grind on, the lives crushed beneath its giant cogs of no concern to a population disconnected from the stark realities of modern politics.

With Hooper discredited it was only a matter of time before Tariq made a move for the premiership, of that Bryce was certain. Before then the field of play would have to be cleared. Sometime soon a call would be made, an order given. He'd hear the security gate open for the final time, Sully's footsteps along the corridor, the angel of death standing at the foot of his bed. Bryce felt a mixture of emotions; fear initially, despair and finally anger, cold and calculating. He wouldn't make it easy for them, wouldn't allow them to dictate the time and place of his own demise. If it were to be his final act then at least he would have control over its execution.

Under the covers of his bedding Bryce eased the hypodermic needle and syringe from its shrink wrapped packaging and secreted them inside the frayed lining of his mattress.

London

The Gulfstream Skybird descended rapidly, dipping below the last of the low cloud to reveal a miserable landscape of steel grey seas and dark, oppressive skies. The executive jet tilted into a steep turn, its silver wingtip slicing through the air as white horses galloped across the surface of the sea below.

Tariq Saeed watched from the window as the plane levelled out, effortlessly gliding along its priority landing path towards London International airport. He never failed to be impressed by the feat of engineering that straddled the Thames Estuary, its galaxy of lights sprinkled across the cold waters of the north sea like stars in the sky. He pulled his seat belt a little tighter, settling into the soft leather of the wide seat, careful not to crease his shirt. He was dressed more conservatively than recent appearances in Egypt, a charcoal grey suit, white shirt and a dark blue tie. Serious, sober, assured – that was the impression he chose to convey today, once his meeting with Hooper was over and the media went into overdrive.

Beneath him he felt the landing gear lock into place with a reassuring thump, the whisper-quiet engines change pitch slightly, and he looked down to see rolling waves smash themselves to fine spray against the giant rocks of the outer breakwater. He closed his eyes for a moment, his pulse quickening as he contemplated the morning ahead.

Although he'd enjoyed three days of the most lavish hospitality that Cairo had to offer, there was work to be done. Behind a smokescreen of diplomacy and trade talks, Saeed had delayed his return to the UK by a further three days, forcing Jacob Hooper to weather the storm of his disastrous transatlantic trip alone. Hooper's advisors had all but deserted him, his Chief Press Officer resigning for 'personal reasons', his handpicked team of sycophants and would-be attack dogs too inexperienced to cope with the pressure the media, now camped permanently outside Millbank, were applying. Hooper had called Saeed in Cairo, at first demanding, then practically begging him to come home, but Saeed had declined. The tactic had worked, his network of informants reporting a series of bad tempered meetings, of expletive-filled phone calls and hurled objects. Hooper was losing it, cracking under the pressure. And while the man who would be king paced the floor of his office in Millbank, Hooper's wife was under siege at Chequers, hurling abuse at the camera crews that blocked the surrounding country lanes. Saeed would have laughed were it not for the contempt he felt for their vanity and lust for power. It was all coming apart so graphically, so predictably. The Hooper's had been elevated far above their station but now they'd served their purpose. It was time to bring them crashing down.

The Gulfstream returned to earth with a gentle bump, rolling along the slick black tarmac and taxiing to a halt outside the glass and steel VIP terminal building that glowed in the half light of a cold December morning. Two BMW limousines waited at the bottom of the steps, flanked by several vehicles, black Range Rovers and marked police cars, and a ring of armed officers. Saeed thanked the captain of the Gulfstream and buttoned his jacket in the doorway, the memory of Cairo's balmy climate snatched away by a stiff north-westerly. He trotted down the steps, shivering as the biting wind cut across the tarmac and bringing with it the roar of an Emirates Airbus taking off from a nearby runway. Saeed paused for a moment, watching the double-decked airliner thunder towards the sea in a cloud of spray then tilt skywards, clawing its way up towards the grey ceiling above, heading for somewhere warm no doubt. Saeed felt a pang of envy.

Fazal, his driver, stood by the BMW, the door held open. Saeed despatched his entourage into the other vehicles then ducked inside the warmth of the soundproofed interior. A few moments later the convoy was headed at speed towards the causeway road and the distant Kentish shoreline. Saeed pressed the intercom button.

'How long?'

'Forty minutes,' Fazal replied, 'maybe longer. Even with the escort the rush hour traffic looks particularly bad this morning.'

Saeed followed Fazal's finger to the SatNav system and the angry red lines that glowed across the screen. 'Take your time.' He glanced out of the window as the convoy hummed along the wide causeway, blue lights clearing a path through the early morning traffic. Beyond the guardrail the sea pounded itself against the giant black rocks of the breakwater and sea birds wheeled in the sky above. A miserable day, Saeed mused, depressing even, for Hooper at least. And for him it was about to get a lot worse.

The journey by car was designed to increase the Prime Minister's frustration, his sense of isolation. Saeed checked his cell, monitoring the tweets from one of his informers on the twenty sixth floor. Already Hooper had erupted behind the heavy wooden doors of his office, the muffled shouts barely distinguishable, the crash of an innocent item of furniture hitting the wall. The press weren't letting up in their campaign against the Prime Minister either, the scathing editorials, the relentless news items all heaping further pressure on his shoulders. He was cut off from his beloved Chequers, at the beck and call of European ministers unhappy with his absence from Cairo. Dupont himself had publicly chastised him, undermining his position and, more importantly, badly bruising his ego, something that Hooper would find particularly hard to endure. The psychological evaluations that had resulted in the former Defence Minister's selection for his role were proving to be uncannily accurate.

Saeed felt his cell vibrate in his hand, saw the new message. An argument with his wife now, a full blown row heard by several staff outside his office. Excellent news. Suddenly the phone rang, and Saeed saw it was Hooper himself. He let the call ring out, and the two subsequent calls, knowing it would send the man's blood pressure sky rocketing. Saeed then made several calls himself, to the Privy Council, the Supreme Court, the Attorney General's office and others, confirming legal and constitutional positions, cementing loyalties. Everything was prepared.

Rain drummed on the roof of the BMW as the convoy hissed along the Whitechapel Road. Brake lights glowed red as they carved through the mounting traffic, sirens wailing a noisy path towards the city. Curious faces lined the route, early morning commuters, market vendors and shop keepers, all staring as they gathered in doorways or sheltered beneath umbrellas. From behind the tinted bullet proof glass Saeed stared back and realised that, were it not for the miserable weather, he could still be back in Cairo. The faces he saw were all brown, the shops a colourful mixture of food markets and takeaways, electronic goods stores and clothing emporiums, the signs in Bengali, Urdu and Arabic. Bunting criss-crossed the street, a leftover from the celebrations of last week. The flags were varied, the drab stars of the EU standard easily outnumbered by Egyptian, Pakistani and Bangladeshi pennants. Nowhere did he see a Union Jack, not once. Like the Jews many years before them, the Europeans had been driven out from this part of the city.

Down a dark side street Saeed caught a glint of the new dome above the distant East London mosque. He craned his neck, catching it again as they slowed for a busy intersection. He thought it looked splendid, the burnished gold metal reflecting ambient light even on such a grey day, and the rebuilt minarets were much higher than before, dominating the local skyline. As they should, smiled Saeed.

Soon the suburbs were left behind, the convoy snaking through the city and approaching Trafalgar Square in less than fifteen minutes. The vehicles weaved carefully through the giant concrete vehicle traps at the junction of Whitehall then accelerated south. The pavements were almost deserted, the public barred from Whitehall itself as part of a raft of sweeping security directives designed to protect the fledgling administration from further attack. Now only government employees could access the famous street, yet there were few to be seen as the building works continued and the rain pummelled the pavements, urged on by a strengthening wind. Saeed recalled a recent speech in the House, one in which the leader of the Opposition had referred to the damage caused by the Downing Street bomb. The woman had referred to it as 'jarring to the eye, almost offensive.' Saeed begged to differ.

Through the left hand window, the facade of the Ministry of Defence building was cloaked in white plastic sheets that snapped and rippled in the wind, briefly exposing the workmen behind who toiled away as the bomb damaged building was slowly restored. But it was the opposite view that gave Saeed the most satisfaction. The whole site was sealed off behind temporary fences adorned with hazard signs and demolition company logos, where men in yellow helmets trudged across the muddy ground, backs bent against the wind and rain. What little remained of Downing Street was held upright by an intricate mesh of scaffold tubes covered with plastic sheeting, the fractured brickwork exposed, fragile, like a sick patient wrapped in bandages. The surrounding Cabinet and Foreign Ministry buildings had been partially demolished too, providing unobstructed views across St. James Park. Some said the bomb had ripped the very heart out of London. Saeed preferred to think of it as surgery, intrusive and painful, yet ultimately necessary.

The convoy continued south, passing through the security checkpoints outside the Houses of Parliament and Lambeth Bridge before arriving at Millbank a minute or so later. The BMW glided to a halt and the door opened. Assistants and advisors converged around Saeed's car, umbrellas braced against the wind and rain. The Deputy Prime Minister climbed out and they moved en-masse towards the building, crossing the lobby in a damp procession, the policemen on guard standing a little straighter, the elevator doors sweeping open. Saeed headed straight to his office on the twenty-fifth floor and closed the door. He ordered coffee and a Danish, flicking through the TV channels until he settled on the BBC's Middle East roundup. He'd been watching for less than three minutes when the phone interrupted his thoughts, warbling with the soft tone of the intercom facility. Saeed smiled, muting the TV.

'Yes?'

'Secretary of State, I have the Prime Minister on line one.'

'Put him through.'

A click, then Hooper's voice, sharp, edgy. 'Tariq?'

'Prime Minister. Good morning.'

'I need you up here. Now.'

'On my way.'

Hooper disconnected the call abruptly. Saeed leaned back in his chair, crossing his legs and savouring the rich aroma and smoky flavour of the Cuban Turquino. Five minutes soon became ten, then fifteen. His phone rang again but Saeed ignored it. Instead he used a key to open his desk drawer and extracted the folder that had been placed there while he was in Cairo. He flicked through its contents, satisfied that everything was in order. It was time.

The elevator doors opened on the twenty sixth floor and for a moment Saeed had to check he was in the right place. The first desks he saw were empty, papers scattered in disarray across them, the phones pulsing and warbling, the calls unanswered. He stepped out of the elevator, curious. Only one or two of the Prime Minister's personal staff were at their desks, their faces drawn with fatigue, phones clamped to their ears, talking in hushed tones. He turned to the left, towards the kitchen, where a small group of men and women huddled together behind the glass wall, seemingly locked in fierce debate. Saeed recognised several of them, key advisors from Domestic Policy, Communications, and the European Secretariat. One of them saw Saeed and the others turned, their expressions startled, embarrassed, scattering from the kitchen like exposed mice. There was a sense of panic in the air, of desperation. Saeed likened it to the last days of the Third Reich, the rats buried in their hole, nervously awaiting the end.

He headed across the floor to the south side of the building. Hooper's secretary stood behind her desk in the outer office, chattering on a phone. Behind her he could hear Hooper's muffled voice through the thick mahogany doors of his private office. On seeing Saeed the secretary quickly ended her call, smoothing her skirt and blouse as he approached. She stood smiling in front of him, hands clasped together. Saeed thought she was on the verge of bowing.

'Secretary of State. Welcome back, sir.'

'Thank you, Polly.'

'I'd like to congratulate you on your trip to Cairo,' she gushed, chestnut ringlets bobbing like springs around her face. 'A truly inspiring performance. And a wonderful ceremony.'

'A great day for Europe.'

'Yes. Indeed.'

There was an awkward silence as Saeed held her gaze, his piercing blue eyes rooting the woman to the spot. There was so much more she wanted to say yet clearly she didn't have the nerve. Saeed decided to encourage her. 'And how is the Prime Minister?'

Polly's frown creased her tired but reasonably pretty face. 'It's been a bad week. He's having trouble focussing. President Dupont's office has been ringing all morning, demanding a statement on Cairo, but Jacob – sorry, I mean the Prime Minister - won't take the calls. He's been trying to contact you since you landed.' Her eyes flicked towards the double doors. 'Everyone's been at his throat all week and quite a few of the staff have left or called in sick. I'm worried about him, sir. The Prime Minister has been rather...'

'Yes?'

'Well, tense is probably one way of describing it. He's under a lot of pressure.'

Saeed nodded. 'Don't worry Polly. All this will be sorted out today.'

The secretary beamed, clearly reassured by Saeed's presence. 'I'm glad you're back, Sir. We all are.'

Saeed took a few steps towards the Prime Minister's office then paused. 'Get a message out to the other staff, would you Polly? Tell them that despite the Prime Minister's recent setbacks there's still a job to do, a country to be run. I expect to see people working, not gossiping around the water cooler.'

This time Polly did bow, a very slight one, but a bow none the less. 'Right away, Sir.'

'And no interruptions. At all.' Saeed rapped on the door, twisted one of the brass handles and stepped inside the Prime Minister's office.

And it was a huge office, an executive corner suite with a private bathroom that offered stunning views across an impressive swathe of London skyline. Jacob Hooper stood with his back to the room, staring out through the glass wall where heavy rain clouds scudded across the city and a sharp wind moaned against the glass. His jacket was off, shirt sleeves rolled to the elbows, one hand thrust into a pocket, the other clutching his personal cell. He wore wide spotted braces over a heavily creased blue shirt, the armpits already damp with sweat. He turned his bald dome towards the door and Saeed noted the perspiration on his brow, the tie dragged from the neck, the open shirt collar. The man was a mess.

'Well, well, the prodigal son returns.'

Saeed said nothing, crossing the thick red carpet and taking a seat in front of the Prime Minister's desk. It was an enormous desk too, piled high with papers and folders, forming lazy towers that teetered over the computer pad and the phones. There were sweet wrappers discarded on the floor around Hooper's vacant chair and several dirty coffee cups stood on a sideboard next to the double doors. On the other side of the doors was a sofa, messily decorated with this morning's broadsheets. For Hooper, none of them held good news. A bank of TV screens mounted on an aluminium pole stood in the corner of the room like a high-tech coat stand, each screen tuned to a different news channel. Saeed saw himself in Cairo, signing the treaty, then waving to a jubilant crowd from the balcony of the embassy. He also saw Hooper, puffing up the steps of a British Airways Dreamliner, his wife's face like thunder, not leaving the shores of the United States in glory but rather as fugitives, quickly and quietly, undercover of night. And then he saw Daniel Whelan's face on another, bulldozers clearing the rubble in Luton, long queues at airport security, vehicles being searched by border agents at an obscure British sea port. Saeed smiled to himself. The bank of high definition screens was like a living chess board, all the pieces still in play, manoeuvred into position by the hand of Saeed and others, the game converging towards its predictable conclusion. And of course Saeed would be the last one standing, of that he had no doubt.

'Where the hell have you been?'

Saeed turned away from the screens. 'Jacob. How are you?'

'Cut the bullshit, Tariq. Where have you been?' Hooper crossed the carpet and flopped into the heavy black leather chair behind his desk, the tortured mechanism squealing in protest.

'Cairo,' Saeed answered. He kept his face neutral.

Hooper banged his fist on the desk, threatening to topple the paper towers. 'Don't be bloody facetious, you know what I mean. Why didn't you arrange for the helicopter to pick you up this morning? Why drive in for God's sake? I need you here.' He stabbed the desk with his finger in rapid fire morse code.

'I needed time to think.'

Hooper threw his arms up in the air. 'Think? Really? Well join the bloody club. That's all I've been doing for the past week while you've been basking in glory. Those bastards out there won't leave me alone.' Hooper rubbed his face in exhaustion, breathing heavily through his fingers for several moments. When he finally spoke his voice had lost some of its harshness.

'I'm sorry, Tariq.' He grabbed the edge of the desk and pulled himself in, toppling a stack of papers onto the floor. He didn't seem to notice at all. 'All this shit is getting on top of me. The media are like wolves at the door and I've lost half my team through resignations or sickness, which is bullshit, fucking cowards. I'm like a fucking leper here!' He saw the disdain in Saeed's face and muttered, 'pardon my French.'

The fool couldn't speak a word of that particular language either, Saeed knew. In fact the media had picked up on Hooper's distinct lack of experience for the position he now held, despite the tragic circumstances of his promotion. The country had grieved, buried its dead. Cairo was the turning point, a line in the sand, the moment when the country vowed to move on. Unofficially briefed by Saeed's people, key personnel in the media ran with stories highlighting Hooper's inexperience, the unhelpful mood swings, the lack of progress that the Prime Minister's brief reign symbolised. And the embarrassment his transatlantic trip had caused.

'It's all because of Washington. What a stupid, stupid idea that was. Jesus Christ.' Hooper balled his fists and rubbed his eyes, as if he could physically massage the memory from his mind. 'A monumental fuck up from the moment I got there. I assume you're familiar with the details?' Saeed pulled an uncertain face. 'Well it wasn't pleasant, I can tell you. During the remembrance service they seated me eight rows back, wedged between the Swiss ambassador and some tin pot general from Zambia who spent half the service leering at Millie. Afterwards, at the White House reception, I was introduced as Prime Minister *Hopper*, thanks to the illiterate bloody Master of Ceremonies, and to cap it all Vargas refused a private audience, even after I'd sent the Ambassador to petition him on my behalf. I nearly choked on the humiliation, I can tell you. And Millie – well, the less said the better.'

Again Hooper banged his fist on the desk, sending more papers spilling onto the carpet. 'They're calling me star-struck, arrogant, stuff like that. Now I've got Dupont and half the bloody Commission on my back, demanding answers, talking about souring Euro-US relations. It's a fucking nightmare.'

Hooper placed his elbows on the desk and closed his eyes, massaging his temples with thick fingers. 'I should've concentrated on Cairo, made that my focus. Why did I bother with Washington? Why?'

Because you're an idiot, Saeed didn't say. Hooper's eyes snapped open and he cocked his chin towards his deputy. 'I mean, look at you, Tariq. The media are kissing your arse, singing your praises from the rooftops while I'm made to look like a rank amateur. Things have got to change.'

The Prime Minister pushed his chair back and crossed to the window. He stood there for several moments watching rain flurries lash against the glass. Saeed waited, his fingers tracing the edge of the folder balanced carefully in his lap.

'I've been thinking about Cairo, its success,' Hooper said eventually. 'I want to tap into that success, allow a little of the glory to rub off, exercise a bit of damage limitation. I've still got contacts, some friends in the media.' He turned around. 'There's work to do on the trade talks, yes?'

'Some,' confirmed Saeed, 'although it's very low level stuff.'

Hooper waved the concern away. 'It doesn't matter. I want to announce a trip to Cairo, to help finalise the talks, so to speak. We'll need to arrange something with Bakari, throw in a speech or two, photo-ops around the pyramids, greeting the people. You know the drill.'

Saeed almost laughed; the naivety of the man was breathtaking. 'That's a bad idea, Jacob. Cairo has passed, the stage dismantled. The city has moved on. Besides, President Bakari is embarking on a tour of the Gulf region next week. There'll be no one at home.'

'Shit!' Hooper spat, thumping the glass with his fist. 'Fine. Then we'll organise something else, a state dinner perhaps, right here in London. Egyptian Ambassador, EU delegates, all the players. You can open with a few remarks about Cairo, its obvious success, then lead into my own role in its ratification. I want you to emphasise my contribution, Tariq, from the initial talks to the ceremony itself. I know you did a lot of the leg work, but that was your job, right?' Saeed said nothing, allowing Hooper to immerse himself in his fantasies, his bulging eyes staring into space somewhere over Saeed's head. 'Yes, that's it. I'll start with a few words about Washington, about the recognition of bravery and human endeavour, man's quest for the stars, that sort of rubbish. Give the trip a human feel, gloss over the diplomatic fuck ups. I want to get it across that I didn't go for my own interests, that I spoke to you every night when you were in Cairo.'

'But you didn't,' Saeed pointed out.

Hooper's eyes narrowed. 'I know that. Play along.'

'Why?'

The wind hummed across the glass, driving the rain before it. Saeed thought he heard the faint murmur of the secretary's voice outside the room. It sounded troubled.

'Why?' Hooper's large frame stood silhouetted against the window, his thumbs hooked around the straps of his braces, his legs apart. It was supposed to be an intimidating gesture, Saeed knew, but instead he thought Hooper looked ridiculous, like a West End player, about to break into an absurd dance routine. There was a look of disbelief on his face too, as if he hadn't heard properly and what he thought he'd heard just couldn't be true.

'Why?' Hooper repeated. He marched across the room towards the sofa, snatching up a newspaper in his large hands. He spread it wide so Saeed could read the headline: *Dupont Demands Answers as PM Stalls.* 'No? Still not getting it?' Hooper flung the paper away, its sheets scattering across the carpet. 'How about this one?' *Hooper Implicated in Remembrance Day Cuts,* the headline screamed. 'How the fuck did they get hold of that story?'

Saeed had already seen it, the leaked memos, the subsequent scaling down of the Remembrance Day parade, rubber stamped by Hooper and his Ministers, his unguarded comments about 'stiff-limbed veterans, noisy bands and pointless fly-bys harming Britain's reputation with her European partners' causing particular offence amongst veteran's groups. Saeed swivelled his chair, crossing his legs. 'Actually it was me who leaked that particular piece.'

Saeed heard the secretary's voice again, louder this time, more insistent, competing with the wind and rain. The pressure was building all around, symbolised by Hooper's reddening face. The man looked fit to burst.

'You did what?' There was a menace to his voice, a quality that others might have found threatening. Saeed knew better.

'Are you deaf? It was me that leaked that story. And there'll be others too, unless you do the right thing.'

Saeed flipped open the folder on his lap and produced a cream coloured envelope. He held it aloft for a moment then placed it on Hooper's desk. Hooper flung the newspaper to one side and marched across the room, his eyes locked on Saeed's. He moved behind his desk, scooped up the sealed envelope and turned it over, eyeing it warily. It was blank.

'What's this?'

'Your resignation. Please read and sign at the pencil mark.'

Hooper didn't speak for several seconds, his eyes flicking between Saeed and the envelope. Then he tore it open, scanning the contents quickly. He peered over the top of the page.

'Is this some sort of joke?'

'No joke,' confirmed Saeed. 'Please sign where indicated.'

He watched Hooper re-read the letter, the carefully worded text on rich cream paper bearing the Prime Minister's seal, his full title clearly displayed below the small pencil cross. The letter gave no specific reasons for the resignation, only that the decision hadn't been taken lightly and was to be effective immediately.

Hooper dropped the letter on his desk as if it was coated in poison.

'You're out of your tiny mind, Tariq.'

'This isn't up for discussion, Jacob. Sign it and go now, today. It's in your own interests. And in the interests of the country, of course.'

Hooper placed his hands on the desk and leaned forwards. Saeed noted the thick, hairy forearms, the huge dome of a head, the hair spilling out of the collar of his shirt. He was like an ape, Saeed realised, a sweaty, uneducated ape. He caught the odour of stale coffee as Hooper barked at him across the desk.

'Who the hell do you think you are, Tariq? You think your little song and dance in Cairo has given you the balls to challenge my position? How fucking dare you.'

'You're out of your depth, Jacob. You're not up to the task. Everyone knows it except you. Go now and you'll get to keep your pension, walk away with some dignity. Fight me on this and you'll be making a very big mistake.'

'Fuck you!' Hooper swept the desk clear with his forearm, scattering phones and papers and sending his computer pad tumbling across the carpet. Saeed turned towards the door, towards the frosted glass where the opaque circle of the secretary's face was frozen outside the room.

'I suggest you calm down, Jacob.'

Hooper scooped up the resignation letter and stuffed it back into its envelope. He skimmed it into Saeed's chest where it flapped to the carpet. 'Change of plan. I want your resignation, you jumped up little shit.'

Saeed took a deep breath and sighed. He'd been expecting this, the anger, the desperation. He knew

Hooper wouldn't go willingly so now it was time to up the ante. He got to his feet, extracting several documents from the folder, and laid them carefully across the recently cleared space on Hooper's desk. The Prime Minister frowned, the boiling anger suddenly tempered by confusion.

'What's this?' he growled.

Saeed laid the last item down, a thick padded envelope, then spread his hands across the table, like a magician presenting his opening illusion. 'It's a road map, a route you will travel if you refuse to go quietly.' Hooper snatched up the first document as Saeed continued. 'That one is the order to have Gabriel Bryce removed to a NHS psychiatric facility, signed and dated by you. Attached is a printout of the confidential email ordering me to begin the process.' Saeed's finger traced over the documents along the desk. 'This is a printout of the visitor's log at Chequers, recording Duncan Parry's stay.'

'Duncan?'

'That's right. He's signed an affidavit, stating that you forced him to circumvent admission procedures and accept Bryce as a patient in the name of national security. I've done the same, expressing my deep disquiet as to your motives and my concern for Gabriel Bryce's health. These documents were drafted and lodged with the Attorney General's office at the time. They will remain in her possession, sealed, as long as you announce your resignation today.'

Hooper's face had turned from puce to ash white in less than a minute. He picked up the papers one by one, his disbelieving eyes scanning their contents, turning them over in his sweaty hands as if careful scrutiny would reveal them to be forgeries. Finally he dropped them back on the table, his shoulders sagging just a little. 'All this was all your idea, Tariq. The only way to guarantee Cairo, you said. Take the country forward.'

'I think you'll find that you were more concerned about Washington than Cairo, right Jacob? Which is why a message was conveyed to President Vargas before your visit to –

'What?' Hooper stormed.

'That's correct. It was felt that the White House should be given the opportunity to distance itself from you and any potential scandal. Your humiliation in Washington is proof that they took that opportunity.'

Hooper's face boiled. 'You fucking snake,' he hissed, his lip curled into a sneer. 'You back stabbing little shit. You think I'll just bend over, let you fuck me up the arse with this? I'll bring you down too, smear you with enough dirt to screw up your own - '

He stopped suddenly, the words hanging in the air. Then the sneer morphed slowly into a knowing smile. 'Oh yes, I get it now. Prime Minister Saeed, eh? You think that's got a nice ring to it? You like the look of this office?' He jabbed a finger towards Saeed's chest. 'The bright lights of Cairo have fried your brain, Minister. You think I'm going to make way for you? Think again.'

Saeed took a step back and sat down. There was only two ways this would go and clearly Hooper wasn't going to take the easy route. 'I'm sorry you feel like that, Jacob, truly I am. This country has suffered a lot of turmoil since the terror attacks and Cairo has given us all much hope for the future. You don't figure in that future, Jacob. Your reputation is in the toilet, you've lost the confidence of the party and the people. Even your own staff are jumping ship.'

Saeed shifted in his seat and crossed his legs, brushing a speck of imaginary dust from his trousers.

'Consultations with the Palace, the Privy Council's office and the Parliamentary Party are complete and unequivocal – Jacob Hooper is a political liability and must be replaced. This afternoon I will issue a statement in the House calling for a vote of no confidence. And I'll get it Jacob, because the deep disquiet felt by many in regard to your stewardship will not go away. The country has lost faith in your abilities to carry it forward and many European leaders have expressed a reluctance to work with you. And abroad? Well, I think your international reputation speaks for itself. But there's more.'

Hooper remained rooted to the spot, his eyes darting between Saeed and the evidence laid out before him. Saeed waved a hand towards the buff coloured padded envelope on Hooper's desk.

'That last envelope contains further evidence against you, Jacob, evidence of more nefarious activities carried out in your name. Open it.'

Hooper snatched it up and tore it open, the contents spilling out over the desk. There were more documents and photographs this time, glossy black and white ten by eights, with stark, disturbing images. He saw Hooper lift them up to his face, his eyes narrowing at first, then widening as he finally grasped what he was looking at.

'Jesus Christ, is that - ?'

'Gabriel Bryce, yes. Evidence of the treatment you condemned him to, his graphic deterioration in that awful facility. It's all there, all engineered by you, your orders.'

Hooper let the photographs slip from his fingers, skimming across the smooth surface of the desk onto the floor. One of them landed by the heel of Saeed's immaculately polished brogue, a disturbing image of Gabriel Bryce, stripped naked and crouched in the dark corner of a padded room, bony arms wrapped around his knees, his eyes pleading, haunted. Even Saeed was shocked when he first saw it.

'Jesus Christ,' Hooper repeated quietly, 'what sort of animal are you?'

'There's something else.' Saeed leaned over and pushed another photograph across the desk with his finger. Hooper stared at it.

'You remember this occasion?'

Hooper frowned, then nodded. 'My last tour of Afghanistan.' He picked it up, studying it hard.

'Correct, taken twelve years ago, just before you resigned your commission and became MP for Bolsover. An interesting composition, don't you think?'

On the surface the photograph was unremarkable as military photographs went, a dozen soldiers in desert fatigues and UN berets grouped in front of a large truck, smiling faces, eyes squinting in the harsh Afghan sunlight. Hooper was at the front, overweight even then, arms clasped stiffly behind his back, puffy red face sweating in the heat.

'Where did you get this?'

'Chequers.'

Hooper's eyes narrowed. 'Excuse me?'

'Your personal data drives, actually. Millie has been most co-operative. I think she's suffered more from the Washington fiasco than you, actually. She's a very defensive woman, very bitter. And she blames you, of course. I have it on good authority that she's been in contact with a very reputable firm in Lincoln's Inn that specialises in divorce.'

Hooper reacted like he'd been punched, grabbing the edge of the desk. 'She what?'

'Don't be naive, Jacob,' chuckled Saeed. 'We both know your ambition is easily surpassed by your wife's.

In fact her abuse of the system is becoming quite legendary. I'm told she requisitioned the helicopter for personal use on at least two occasions, no doubt with your knowledge.'

'Stupid bitch,' Hooper muttered under his breath. He looked at the colour image again. 'So she gave you a photo, so what?'

Saeed pushed the glossy paper back across the desk and tapped it with his finger. 'As I said, an interesting composition. The man at the back, fourth from the left. You recognise him?' He watched Hooper lower his head, his eyes squinting.

'No. Should I?'

'Yes, you should. That's Daniel Whelan.'

Hooper's mouth dropped open, a thin bar of saliva bridging his lips. 'Bloody hell, so it is. I'll be damned.'

Saeed smiled. 'An accurate assessment, Jacob.'

'What?'

'The photograph *is* damning. It connects you to Whelan, to Luton and Downing Street.'

'What? Don't be ridiculous,' Hooper snorted.

Saeed noted the incredulous look, the mirthless chuckle. 'Hard to believe, I know, but let's look at the facts. You both served in Afghanistan at the same time.'

'So what?' exploded Hooper, waving the photograph in the air. 'This was taken at Kandahar. There were thousands of troops there, how the hell am I supposed to remember every man under my command. Especially a fucking private!'

' - and some years later your careers in Whitehall overlapped too,' Saeed continued. 'In fact, at one point you both worked in the same building. You see the link now? Whelan committed the Luton atrocity and is by default connected to the Downing Street bomb. Somehow access was gained to the government vehicle used in the attack for an extended period of time, which proves Whelan had an accomplice with significant security clearance. The explosive material was military grade, and you have extensive contacts throughout the armed forces in your previous roles as Defence Minister and your service in the Logistics Corps. You avoided the blast itself - '

'Because you called me!'

' – and immediately assumed authority. Since then the hunt for the bombers has stalled and Whelan remains at large. A dossier has been compiled. There are grounds for investigation.'

Hooper swayed on his feet, then dropped heavily into his chair. He looked shell shocked, defeated. 'This is an outrage,' he whispered, 'all a complete pack of lies. You can't prove a thing.'

Saeed laughed. 'What's the quote, Jacob? *A lie can travel the world while the truth is still tying its shoes?* The truth doesn't matter. Proof doesn't matter. Your reputation is already holed below the waterline and if this goes public you'll sink without trace. I have it on good authority that the police will be forced to interview you formally, under caution. With your name already in tatters, the stain of suspicion would be hard to erase, whatever the real truth may be.'

Hooper buried his face in his hands, his breath coming in small gasps. At first Saeed thought he was crying, then changed his assessment to panic. The fight had certainly left him, he could see that now. Still, it wouldn't hurt to turn the screw a little more, just to be sure.

'But it's not just about you, is it Jacob? There are your two young sons to consider, both nicely settled in their new school. Charterhouse, is that right? An outstanding school, certainly one of the best, however the board will frown upon their association with the Hooper family name and the stench of failure and disgrace. Not a good example for the rest of their young charges, and I'm sure the other parents will have something to say too. A shame really, all because their father refused to co-operate for the good of the country.'

Saeed reached down and picked up the resignation letter at his feet. He smoothed it out and leaned over, sliding it across the desk. 'It doesn't have to be this way, Jacob. Sign that and leave now, today. Arrangements will be made. You'll be comfortable, nothing extravagant, but comfortable, a decent pension.'

'What about my boys?'

'They'll stay at Charterhouse, as long as you do as you're told. After all, why should the sons be punished for the sins of the father? Unless of course the father decides to open his mouth, in which case their little feet won't touch the ground.'

Hooper slumped further down his chair, like a boxer on his corner stool, bloodied, beaten, unable to continue the fight. His face was a sickly grey colour, his eyes fixed on the landscape beyond the window. Confusion, disbelief, anger, denial, acceptance – Saeed had seen them all today and in a relatively short space of time. Hooper was a predictable animal and he'd played his role perfectly, but now it was time for the principle to leave the stage. Saeed slipped his cell from his pocket and punched a number. 'Come up now,' he ordered, then ended the call.

Hooper lifted his head. 'Who are you calling?'

'I have a small team waiting downstairs. Time is of the essence, Jacob, the continuity of government paramount. The office of the Prime Minister is to be reorganised.'

'What happens now?'

'You'll sign the letter, then a car will take you to Chequers. You have three days to vacate the premises, after which I suggest a long holiday, somewhere private. Perhaps you'll be able to save your marriage, perhaps not, but you'll talk to no-one. A security team will be assigned to you and there'll be no contact with the media. In a few months you'll be assessed, then we'll figure out a position for you somewhere, possibly Europe. It'll be very low key but you'll get used to it. The alternative will be much worse for you and your family.'

Saeed got to his feet and gathered his documents together, slipping the photographs back inside the folder. Through the frosted panels he saw a group of people enter the outer office. As he reached for the door handle, Hooper said, 'Why, Tariq?'

'Excuse me?'

Hooper remained slumped in his chair, his eyes fixed on the view beyond the window, his voice almost a whisper. 'Why? Why set me up, threaten me, threaten my children? What did I ever do to you?'

Saeed walked towards the desk. He kept his voice low too, conscious of the bodies outside the door. 'Look at me, Jacob.' Hooper turned his head. 'Would you have gone if I'd have just asked nicely? Of course not. For you the premiership represents nothing more than power and prestige, the status to be savoured and enjoyed like exquisite food or vintage wines. You're right, I *do* want this job but for entirely different reasons than your own.' Saeed glanced towards the door, then leaned over the desk, the whisper barely audible. 'You see, the country is heading in a new direction, one that you could never contemplate steering towards nor comprehend why. I, however, do understand, as do others in Europe and elsewhere. The vision is a clear one, the goal now achievable. The task will take decades but the groundwork has now been laid. This office and the responsibility it brings is nothing more than a tool to be used in the construction of something magnificent, a historical vision that has fired the imaginations of men for centuries. You think I care about country mansions and helicopters? I couldn't care less.'

Saeed straightened up and shook his head. 'You are a stupid man, Jacob Hooper, stupid and arrogant. I think the media have you pegged rather well at the moment. And later today the headlines will add 'finished' to their growing list of superlatives.' He tapped the resignation letter on the desk. 'Sign it. People are waiting.'

Hooper hung his head, chin on his chest, legs splayed out before him, arms dangling over the rests of his chair. If he was beaten before, he was well and truly crushed now, Saeed realised. He'd get no more trouble from him.

Hooper raised his tired, bloodshot eyes. 'Give me a couple of minutes, would you Tariq? Allow me to compose myself?'

Saeed glanced at his watch and nodded. 'You've got five.'

There were a dozen people waiting in the outer office, handpicked to take over the running of the Prime Minister's office. Most were communications staff, ready to begin the task of informing the media of Hooper's resignation to a waiting world. The news would not come as a shock, Saeed knew, because Hooper had performed so badly, and with the Christian festival of Christmas around the corner, the people would be keen to see a steady hand on the tiller as quickly as possible. And that would be Saeed's hand, of course.

'Is the Prime Minister all right, sir?' Every head in the outer office turned towards Polly.

'Yes,' Saeed smiled, 'although he will be leaving us shortly.'

'Leaving?' Polly looked nervous, as if whatever fate was about to befall Hooper would apply to her also. Saeed didn't blame her. Her boss had been under tremendous pressure for the last week, and her job couldn't have been easy. In addition, her office had just been invaded by a large group of people who were under strict instructions to say absolutely nothing to anyone.

'Don't worry, Polly, you're an integral part of the team. I'll be needing you.'

Polly's shoulders sagged with relief. 'Anything I can do to help, Sir.'

For now, Saeed didn't add, just until the fuss died down. Then you'll be moved, quietly, to another department, just one more change in a long list of changes that people were going to start seeing. Now, where the hell was Hooper?

He saw his bulk through the frosted panels beside the door, moving around the room towards the door. Finally.

Everybody in the outer office heard the solid click as the doors were locked from the inside. Puzzled, Saeed stepped forward and twisted the brass door knob. He turned to Polly. 'Get security up here now.'

There were several thumps from inside the room, loud ones that Saeed felt through the soles of his shoes. He rapped the thick wood with his knuckles. 'Jacob, open the door. Jacob!' There was no answer, only several more thumps, each one successively louder. What was this, some sort of last minute tantrum? Whatever dignity Hooper had left was now gone. Saeed had a mental image of him being led out into the street in handcuffs. Or maybe even a restraining jacket, like a mental patient. He must make sure the footage was released to the media at the earliest opportunity.

The loud crash of glass behind the door was like a bucket of water in the face. Several people in the room gasped, and Polly uttered a shrill yelp of fear.

'Everybody out! Clear the room!' Saeed ordered. Just then two government security men appeared, dark suited, with wide shoulders and large hands. Saeed pointed to the thick double doors. 'Break it down.'

The men set about the task with relish, taking turns to aim ferocious kicks against the brass mechanism. Rough hands rattled the door knobs, pummelled on the thick mahogany wood. Within thirty seconds both men were sweating, within a minute panting for breath, their faces twisted in anger. Suddenly the wood beneath the door knobs splintered, cracking like a pistol shot. The younger of the two men took another step back and drove his foot into the area around the lock, sending one of the doors flying inwards and crashing against the frosted panel, shattering it. Saeed bundled in after them.

Everybody froze. Hooper stood by the broken glass wall as a cold wind barrelled around the room, swirling and snatching at discarded newspapers and documents and tossing them into the air. Saeed saw the chair was gone, Hooper's heavy leather chair, no doubt lying in the street below. Hooper's shoes were inches from the edge, his gaze off towards the distant horizon. Saeed turned to the security guards and ordered them to stay back. He took a few paces toward the window and stopped.

'Jacob,' he said quietly.

Hooper turned, just as Saeed heard the shouts, the muffled thump of boots on carpet, the rattle of equipment. He turned and waved his arms furiously, barring entry to the police officers who spilled into the outer office behind him. He raised a finger to his lips, silencing the new arrivals, who backed away from the open door. No one spoke, no one made a move, allowing Saeed to take a pace closer towards Hooper, then another. He studied the Prime Minister carefully; his behaviour was so much more than childish frustration, so unexpected, yet tantalising for its potential. He saw Hooper's face streaked with tears, saw the resignation in those bulbous, bloodshot eyes, the prospect of a life without meaning, without purpose, a life lived at the outer fringes of obscurity. The eyes shifted, locking with Saeed's, searching for hope, for forgiveness, and finding none. Instead Saeed nodded, a tiny, almost imperceptible movement of the head.

Hooper took one more look at Saeed, at the uniforms that filled the room behind him. Shirt soaked by the invading rain, his tie flapping wildly in the wind, Jacob Hooper closed his eyes, took a sharp breath, then stepped over the window ledge.

Hertfordshire

Kneeling on the carpet, Danny traced the green plastic cable along its length, his fingers groping between the prickly needles of the Christmas tree – an imported Norway spruce, according to Ray - until he found the offending bulb. Its tiny filament was burned black, so Danny replaced it with another then reached over to the skirting board and threw the switch. The room was instantly bathed in the soft glow of decorative lights and Danny scrambled to his feet to admire his handiwork. All he had to do now was hang a few baubles, put the fairy on top, then vacuum the million bloody needles that had fallen off while he fixed the stupid lights.

A real tree? A real pain the in arse, more like. Danny recalled a drunken Christmas a few years ago, staggering out of the Kings Head and seeing the van parked outside, crammed with rows of genuine fir Christmas trees. He'd parted with a few Euros then waltzed it across the estate, singing merrily. The lift in his block was busted of course and by the time he reached Dad's flat he realised the tree was almost naked, a trail of dead needles leading from the front door back down the stairs. He remembered his Dad laughing as he fetched the broom, the valiant attempt they both made to decorate the sorry looking tree as it stood virtually naked in the living room. Danny tried to remember exactly when that was but failed. The festive celebrations he'd experienced over the years had jumbled into a confusing mix of fleeting memories, most of them spent stoned and pissed in the Kings Head. But this year would be different, he was sure of that.

He delicately positioned the last golden bauble then turned off the main light, the mood of the drawing room changing instantly. *Now* it felt like Christmas. The air was sweetly scented with balsam and a fire crackled in the grate, filling the room with what Danny could only describe as Christmas cheer. For a moment he felt like a kid again.

Satisfied with his efforts, he picked up a dustpan and brush and dropped to his knees, beginning the painstaking task of needle removal. Behind him, the door swung open and Tess poked her head around the frame.

'Danny love, can you – oh wow!'

She swished into the room, bundled up inside a green North Face parka and white roll-neck sweater. Her cheeks were flushed red by the central heating, her eyes fixed on the glowing, sparkling evergreen that reached majestically towards the high ceiling. 'Oh Danny, that's beautiful. Really lovely. You've done a wonderful job.'

He got to his feet, smiling. 'Cheers, Tess.'

'Ray's useless at that sort of thing,' she told him, her fingers making her own delicate adjustments to the ribbons of light and shimmering tinsel. 'You've got a real eye for it though.'

'Took me ages,' Danny confessed, warming to the appreciation. 'To tell you the truth I had a spot of bother with - '

'Make sure you get rid of all them needles, won't you?' Tess tutted, clicking her tongue loudly. 'Look at them, all over my good carpet.'

Danny forced a smile. 'No worries, Tess. I'll sort it.'

'Good. When you've done that, the pickup needs unloading.'

Outside, the light was fading fast and the freezing rain threatened to turn to sleet. The rear of the Nissan was filled with cardboard boxes and plastic carrier bags bulging with groceries. Despite the cold Danny was sweating by his third trip, trudging around the side of the house where he piled the supplies up just inside the kitchen door. It took several more trips before the task was complete, then Danny slipped his wellington boots off outside and padded around the kitchen in white socks, his feet making sweaty footprints on the highly polished floor tiles as he marched back and forth between the back door and the kitchen's impressive centre island. He hefted the last bag onto the flecked black marble surface and let out a sigh of relief.

'There you go,' he puffed, 'last one.'

'Thanks,' Tess mumbled, tapping away at her cell phone. 'Put the meat away, would you, love? Took me an age to find non-Halal chicken in Watford.'

'Right-ho.' He rummaged through the bags, found several packs of chicken breast, and carried them over to the American-style refrigerator. 'Fridge or freezer?'

'Mmm?' Tess turned around. 'Oh, freezer please, Danny. We won't need it straight away. Ray's organised a couple of turkeys for Christmas Day.'

Danny stacked the shrink wrapped packs of chicken neatly inside the icy compartment and closed the door. 'You expecting many this year?'

Tess shook herself out of her parka and pulled the hem of the roll neck jumper over the wide expanse of her bottom, her wrists jangling with trademark jewellery as she stowed groceries in various cupboards.

'There'll be eight of us on Christmas Day and about twenty for the party on Boxing day.'

'Nice,' Danny smiled, leaning against the centre island. 'My dad usually does Christmas dinner but he's not the best cook in the world. To tell you the truth it gets a bit boring, and dad usually sleeps all afternoon anyway, so I'm sort of on me own. It'll be different this year. I'm really looking forward to it.'

Tess's hand froze momentarily as she stacked tins of pineapple rings away in an overhead cupboard. She positioned the last can carefully and closed the door.

'I'm sorry, love. I don't think you'll be joining us.'

Danny swallowed hard, his cheeks burning bright red. 'Oh,' was all he could manage to say.

The security light over the kitchen door blazed into life and Ray peered in through the glass. He pushed the door open and stepped inside, his Barbour jacket and wide-brimmed Bushman hat spotted with water droplets.

'Bloody rain. Freezing out there.' He slammed the door behind him and crossed the kitchen, his footprints leaving a damp trail across the floor. 'You get everything?'

Tess nodded. 'Pretty much. Had a real job finding proper chicken. In the end I went to the one on Upton Road. Butcher there says it won't be long before he's forced to stock just Halal.'

'It's happening everywhere,' Ray grumbled. He pointed to the TV on the wall, where Prime Minister Saeed was giving his first speech to the European Parliament. 'What do you expect with him in charge. It's only going to get worse, am I right Danny?'

'I told Danny about Christmas,' Tess said, emptying the contents of another carrier bag on the counter. Danny caught the look between them and felt instantly uneasy. Ray motioned him towards the door.

'That's alright, my love. I think it's time me and Danny had that little chat anyway. Would you give Joe a buzz, ask him to join us in the barn?'

Outside, Danny pulled his boots back on and followed Ray around the house, snapping the collar of his waterproof jacket up as another belt of rain swept overhead, lashing the driveway in cold sheets. He felt nervous, apprehensive. A little chat. People only said that when they had bad news. Was Ray going to ask him to leave? One thing was for sure, he wouldn't be having Christmas dinner in the main house. Maybe that's what Tess meant. Maybe he'll still be here, but confined to his little flat above the garage. If that was the case then great, he could hack that, but what if it was something else? His heart thumped loudly as he followed Ray beyond the garage and past a row of tall conifers that swayed and hissed in the wind.

The barn was tucked behind the trees, a single storey construction with a curved, sheet metal roof streaked with rusty stripes. Despite the obvious assault from the weather Danny thought the barn looked fairly new. Ray took a key from his pocket and unlocked an industrial-sized padlock, sweeping aside the large concertina door. He crossed the threshold and ducked to his left as an urgent beeping echoed around the darkness. Danny stepped out of the rain and watched Ray disable the alarm, the lights of the control panel glowing brightly. Despite the gloom, Danny could see the outline of a car under a thick tarpaulin in the centre of the concrete floor.

'That's a Vauxhall under there,' Ray explained, 'one of the last to roll off the production line. We'll get to that in a minute.'

A figure loomed in the doorway and Joe appeared, wet hair plastered to his head, dressed in an old combat jacket and jeans, the Mossberg hanging from his shoulder. Danny noticed the barrel was pointed down, to avoid the rain that drummed noisily on the metal roof. Old habits died hard for soldiers.

'Ah, Joe. Get the door please.' Ray threw a light switch and fluorescent tubes, suspended from a metal grid overhead, buzzed loudly then blinked into life. Danny had a good look around. From the cinderblock walls hung an impressive array of engineering tools and the workbench that ran the length of the far wall was covered in battered technical manuals, sprays and lubricants and piles of oily rags. Scattered around the other walls were Jerry cans, oil drums, agricultural equipment and various motor spares.

'All part of the deception,' chuckled Ray, waving his hands around the barn. He approached the workbench and slapped his hat down on the surface. He stood near the centre, gripping a section of the bench while he fingered something beneath the oil-stained wood. There was an audible click, then Ray pulled a part of unit away from the wall. He ducked behind the gap, sliding out a cleverly-disguised drawer, and produced two items that he placed on the soiled wooden surface. The first was clearly a pistol, its undeniable shape wrapped in a faded green cloth. The second was a black plastic shockproof case which he laid gently on the workbench. He brushed his hands on the legs of his corduroy trousers.

'This is it, Danny. This is what it's all been about.'

Danny stared at the cloth, bewildered. 'What's the gun for, Ray?'

'Self-defence, son. For you. And us.'

'I don't get it.'

'Course you don't. Let me explain.'

He strode towards the vehicle in the centre of the barn and dragged the tarpaulin off its smooth lines. It was a Vauxhall as Ray had declared, a modest four door hatch-back saloon, dark blue in colour, the type used by families with small children.

'As I said, one of the last off the production line,' Ray explained, slapping his hand on the roof. 'And because Vauxhall were going out of business there were quite a few problems with this particular model. With the Tracker units in fact. They were all recalled and the problem rectified. Well, most of them anyway.'

Danny looked confused. 'What problem?'

'A design flaw in the Tracker unit hardcode. Made in China of course, so the rumour was some sort of industrial sabotage. Probably was, knowing the bloody Chinks.' Ray winked at Joe and the ex-soldier laughed. It didn't look right. 'The thing is, the maintenance interface of this unit is completely programmable,' Ray explained. 'For our immediate purposes it's been uploaded with a bogus journey history, toll road payments, even a fictitious owner.' He fumbled in the pocket of his Barbour. 'Here, you might as well take this now, get familiar with your new persona.'

Danny took the ID card from Ray's outstretched hand, studying his photograph, the personal details. 'I still don't get it,' he muttered.

'Remember when I spoke about action, not words? Well, that time is now.' Ray rummaged in the hidden drawer and produced an old IPad. His fingers danced across the touch screen and then he passed it to Danny. A slideshow of high-resolution images scrolled across the display.

'What you're looking at is the Muslim Council of Regional Representatives' building in Birmingham, a huge concrete monstrosity built with tax payer's money. In their ongoing efforts to integrate with British society, the Council has decided to forgo the Christmas holidays and hold their annual General Meeting in the building on Christmas Day. Keep scrolling through the pictures, Danny.'

He did as he was told, the images changing from external shots to well-lit interiors, long carpeted hallways with potted plants and exotic artwork lining the walls. There were other shots of ceiling vents and pipe works, of maintenance covers and plant rooms. Ray's gravelly voice echoed around the barn.

'On Christmas Eve you'll travel up to Birmingham in the Vauxhall. You'll go to the Council building after nine p.m., when the recently employed security guard will be on shift. This bloke is brand new, a complete muppet by all accounts. In any case, you'll be posing as an air-con engineer attending a call-out. Don't worry, I've got all the paperwork. Once you're in, you'll head to the plant room on the top floor, where you'll find an access hatch near the main condenser. All the plans are right there on the IPad.'

Danny's eyes flicked between Ray and the images on the screen. 'And do what, a bit of vandalism? Flood the building or something? Sure, I can do that,' he blurted, hoping, praying it was nothing more.

'Vandalism?' Ray glanced at Joe. 'What's he like, eh?' He slapped Danny on the back, then the smile slipped from his face like melted wax. 'You think I'd go to all this trouble just to break a couple of fucking windows? I could get kids to do that. No, this is bigger, Danny, much bigger. More your style. Here, look at this.' He snapped open the black case on the workbench. Inside was a white plastic container nestled in purpose cut grey foam. On its uppermost surface, fixed into position with blue electrical tape, was a small digital timer. Danny took a step back, his bearded face draining of colour.

'Jesus.'

'It's not armed.'

'Is that what I think it is?'

'Not quite,' Ray assured him. 'It does possess some small explosive properties but essentially it's just a plastic container. It's what's inside it that matters.'

'Inside?'

'The ingredients, Danny. The cocktail.'

Danny's face was a blank canvas. 'What?'

'Bloody hell, I thought you'd be used to all this,' Ray bristled. 'I'll spell it out for you, son. It's a bio-weapon.' Danny said nothing, just stared at the blank timing mechanism, the white powder inside the plastic container, as his mind struggled to process what he was hearing. 'Technically it's an organophosphate pesticide derivative,' Ray continued, 'but you don't need to worry about the details. All you need to do is place the device behind the correct inspection hatch, remove a few filters, then set the timer for seventy two hours. On the third day of the Council's unholy meeting this little baby will go off with a quiet pop and start working her magic. The air con system will do the rest. I'm told that the nerve agent will be fully dispersed around the main conference chamber within thirty minutes. With luck, if it doesn't dilute too quickly, it'll claim a few more lives around the rest of the building. We're talking about a hundred casualties, maybe a hundred and fifty.'

Danny stood in silence for a long time, his eyes wide in disbelief. Several times his mouth moved to form words but no sound made it passed his bloodless lips.

'Now I don't want you to worry,' Ray urged, easing the IPad from Danny's frozen fingers. 'We're going to spend the next couple of days going over the details, rehearsing the route, your interaction with the geezer on the gate, that sort of thing. I've rigged up a dummy inspection hatch too, so you can familiarise yourself with the positioning of the weapon. Just remember, you'll have a kosher ID, all the right documentation and an untraceable car. Couldn't be easier, right? And you'll have the gun of course, as a last resort.'

'Nerve agent?' Danny finally managed to say.

Ray smiled. 'Now you're getting it. Improvised but very effective. Within twelve hours of getting a lungful of this, those heathen bastards will start to suffer, am I right Joe?'

The ex-soldier nodded enthusiastically. 'That's right, Ray,' he confirmed in his west country drawl. 'Early symptoms are breathlessness, fatigue, bronchial problems. Later they'll begin vomiting, then bleeding from every fucking orifice in their bodies. It's a slow, nasty way to die.'

Danny had never seen Joe so animated. His eyes burned brightly, his cheeks flushed with hatred. Danny glanced at Ray, who smiled along with Joe like some sick father and son double act.

'Amen to that,' Ray added, snapping the case shut. He patted its closed lid gently. 'This is it, Danny, the first blow.' He picked up the cloth-covered pistol and unwrapped it, handing the firearm to Danny who took it without thinking. 'That's an Accu-Tek semi automatic. Go on, get a feel for it, son. Joe will take you in the woods tomorrow, get you properly acquainted.'

'Point three-two calibre, twelve round mag,' Joe explained. 'Designed more for concealment than pure firepower but it'll do the job if you run into trouble.'

'Ideally, you'll come back with all twelve rounds,' Ray said. 'Keep it with you from now on, alright?'

As Danny stared at the pistol in his hand, Ray threw an arm around his shoulders and squeezed. 'Look at him. Cool as a bloody cucumber this one, eh Joe?' His eyes bored into Danny's, his fingers digging painfully through the material of his jacket. When he spoke it was with a passion that Danny found distinctly unnerving.

'There'll be other jobs after this one, son. The country's in turmoil right now, what with Hooper offing himself and that Paki bastard stepping into his shoes.' Ray made a face at Joe. 'Tariq Saeed – what a name for a British Prime Minister, eh?'

'Fucking disgrace,' Joe grumbled.

'All the pieces are in place now, the money, the technical support, the weapons. This country is about to witness a campaign of terror the like of which has never been seen before.'

'What do you mean?' Danny stuttered.

'I mean violence, Danny. Riots, street battles. The fight back I've planned will pitch community against community, igniting the tensions everyone pretends don't exist; Muslim and Hindu, Tutsi and Hutu, Turk and Kurd, black and white. By the time I've finished they'll all be at each other's throats. Cities will burn and the streets will run with blood.'

Ray took a moment, clearly savouring the images of violence in his mind. Danny glanced at Joe, who watched Ray with a look of pure admiration. Ray spread his arms wide. 'Then, like a phoenix from the ashes, Raymond Carver will step into the light, leading a new party, with a new ideology, one that will banish Britain's multicultural experiment to the dustbin of history, promising a new period of peace and prosperity, of British power and influence, free from the shackles of political correctness, from the iron grip of Brussels. And people will flock to us, yes they will, because they'll want to see an end to the violence, to the unbridled immigration and the rape of our laws and customs. The people of this land deserve something better, a new start, in a country that has had a gut full of multiculturalism.'

Ray gripped Danny by the arms, his grey eyes bright with excitement. 'And you,' he whispered, 'you'll be my secret weapon, the catalyst from which the violence will spring. You'll be like a ghost, a different ID, different disguise, for every mission you undertake. A shooting here, a well-placed bomb there, each incident ramping up the tension, each side blaming the other.'

Ray grasped Danny's hand in both of his and squeezed. 'I can't tell you how proud we all are of you, son. For Luton, for Downing Street. For what has gone before and for what will be. You're doing God's work, Danny Whelan. What we're embarking on is a Crusade, and the Lord has looked down from on high and sent me a true Christian soldier.'

The rain pummelled the roof, the wind rattling the concertina doors, whistling through the cracks and gaps. Danny looked at the shockproof case, at the gun in his hand, at Joe's cruel grin. Finally he looked at Ray. 'But you don't even go to church,' he mumbled.

The big man chuckled for a moment, then let go of Danny's hand. He looked confused. 'What's that got to do with anything?'

Danny began to shake his head. 'Listen, you got it all wrong, Ray. I had nothing to do with Luton, or Downing Street.'

Ray laughed, waving a dismissive hand. 'It's alright, son, you can drop the bullshit. I told you from day one, you're amongst friends here.'

'You're not listening to me, Ray.'

The older man took a step closer, his cold eyes searching Danny's. 'Yes I am. I hear what you're saying, son. Trust takes a long time to nurture before it can really take root. You came here, to me, when your

300

friends were arrested, when your support network crumbled in the wake of the bombs. You trusted me to keep you out of harm's way, to feed you, put clothes on your back. I saw that as a test, Danny, a test of my own resolve, my own commitment to the cause. I've never once asked you about Luton or Downing Street, because I wasn't privy to the details of those operations, played no part in their execution. Who was it, by the way? Who were the principles?'

'The what?'

'The key players. Who organised those jobs, funded them? Was it Kevin Brady from the Defence League? Sean Turner?'

'Who?'

Ray looked away, stroking his face. 'I had a feeling they'd be involved. Good boys the both of them, committed, intelligent. Fucking shame about their arrests. Still, at least they've not been stitched with terrorist charges. Well, not yet anyway.' He turned back to Danny. 'They'd be proud of you, son, keeping your mouth shut like this, keeping up the pretence of ignorance, but you can relax now. It's time to move on, continue the struggle that they started.'

Danny took another step back. 'Ray,' he said slowly, quietly, 'I don't know what you're talking about. I was fitted up over Luton. I thought I was delivering a fridge, that's all. I got paid too, a thousand Euros. I never knew it was a bomb Ray, not in a million years, and if I did I'd have run a mile.' Danny pointed over Ray's shoulder, to the shockproof case. 'What you're asking, I can't do it. I don't care whether they're Muslims or fucking Moonies, I'm not a murderer, Ray. I'm just a normal geezer.'

Ray stood completely immobile, his tanned face a mask of confusion. After a moment he began to shake his head. 'No, that's not right. I knew everything about you long before you even got here. I've had my people check you out, your background, your story. I'm not wrong, no way.'

'You are!' Danny insisted. 'I thought that's why you let me stay here, because I *was* innocent, because I *was* a member of the Movement. Because you hate the government like I do, for the lies, the bullshit, especially the stuff they're saying about me.' Danny took a step towards Ray, the emotion almost choking his words, his eyes filling with tears. 'Don't you understand? All I want is to stay here, Ray, just stay here and get my head down, keep out of the way. You and Tess, you're the only friends I've got. I'll do anything, you know that. Help around the estate, like I've been doing, shopping - '

'Shut up!' barked Ray, shaking off Danny's outstretched hand. The rain had intensified, hammering the metal roof in noisy waves. All three men stood in silence, water dripping from their coats and forming oily pools on the ground. Ray stared at Danny for a long time.

'No,' he finally decided, poking a finger at Danny, 'you did it. You've got contacts in the military. They found plans for the mosque hidden in your flat.'

'It was all planted!' Danny protested. 'What the fuck do I know about architect drawings? Or making bombs? I'm nothing Ray, a nobody.'

Ray didn't say anything. He stared at his shoes, breathing heavily, like he'd just walked up a long flight of steps. Joe stood off to one side, the Mossberg now cradled in his arms. He was like a faithful pet, Danny realised, his cold eyes flicking between Ray and himself, between master and trespasser. Danny ignored him, hoping, willing Ray to believe his story.

Eventually Ray looked up and said, 'Let me get this straight, Danny. You *didn't* carry out the Luton operation?'

'Operation?' Danny scoffed. 'Of course not.'

'But you - ' Ray stopped himself.

'I didn't do it,' Danny said quietly. He studied the man in front of him, saw the confusion and disappointment on his reddening face. Danny felt bad for Ray, as if somehow he'd betrayed him. 'Looks like we've both made a mistake, Ray.'

'Don't be a fucking smart mouth!' Ray hissed. He poked Danny hard in the chest, his finger stabbing the air in front of his face. 'You don't know anything.'

'You're right, I don't.' Danny admitted, holding his hands up. He didn't like the look on Ray's face, nor the way Joe had changed his grip on the shotgun, the barrel slowly turning in his direction. Just keep your mouth shut, Danny. But the words were out before he had time to think.

'I know Tess wouldn't like you doing all this.'

Ray's eyes flashed with anger. His arm snaked out before Danny could react and the open handed slap caught him full on the cheek, sending him staggering against the car. The gun left his hand, skidding across the concrete. Ray moved in quickly, pulling Danny towards him, his fists bunching the coat beneath his chin. Danny could feel the strength in Ray's arms, the hatred in his words.

'Remember seven seven, you little prick? Tess was there when that fucker detonated his bomb at Aldgate tube. Lost half her lower intestine, womb destroyed. Killed the baby she was carrying, a little boy. My boy. Don't ever mention my wife's name again.' He shoved Danny hard against the car. 'I could've turned away, thrown you to the wolves, but no. I took you in, treated you like one of my own, all the time believing that you were a fighter, a true patriot.'

'I am,' Danny protested, 'I just can't do what you- '

'We're at war!' Ray bellowed, his voice booming around the barn. Danny flinched as a crack of thunder split the air overhead, rattling the roof of the barn. 'Don't you get it, you ignorant fuck? I need people like the ones who did Luton and Downing Street, soldiers, willing to go the whole nine yards, to do what has to be done.' He looked Danny up and down, his mouth twisting into a vicious sneer. 'What I *don't* need is white trash cowards like you, coming into my home, abusing my hospitality, taking the fucking piss.'

'No!' Danny pleaded, 'for Christ's sake it's not like that!'

Ray spun away, his hands covering his mouth. 'Jesus Christ, what a mug I've been. A complete and utter mug. Why didn't I see it. Why?' he turned back to Danny. 'The arse kissing, the little boy lost routine, I thought that was all part of the act, some sort of test. But it's wasn't, was it? You really are innocent in all this.'

Danny pushed himself off the bonnet of the Vauxhall. He felt the toe of his boot make contact with the pistol, heard the scrape of metal on concrete. 'That's right, Ray. I swear I didn't do anything. I just want to disappear, maybe to New Zealand like you said.'

Ray shook his head. 'There is no New Zealand, Danny, never was. Container ships stopping in the English channel? Are you fucking nuts?'

Danny saw Joe take a step forward, his face devoid of emotion, his white-knuckled hands gripping the Mossberg. He spoke to Ray but his dead eyes never left Danny.

'Why don't you let me take Danny for a walk, Ray? Let things cool down.'

Ray's eyes flicked from Joe to Danny then back again. 'A walk. Yeah, good idea. Give me time to think things through.'

Joe arched an eyebrow. 'We'll have a wander down to the lower wood, check the traps, yeah?'

The woods, the hole in the ground...

'The lower wood,' Ray echoed. He was silent for a moment, his brow furrowed as if locked in some internal debate. Finally he let out a long sigh. 'A shame,' he muttered to himself, 'a real fucking shame. O.k.,' he said to Joe, 'you take Danny down there with you. You've got your radio?'

Joe shifted the shotgun over to his left hand and reached into the pocket of his combat jacket. In one swift movement Danny knelt down, cocked the pistol and pulled the trigger. The back of Joe's skull exploded in a puff of red mist and his body folded to the ground, the Mossberg clattering beside him. Ray screamed and charged forward and the pistol barked again. Ray hit Danny at full speed and their bodies crashed into the Vauxhall, Ray's hands flailing at Danny's face, strong fingers searching for his eyes, his mouth. Danny twisted his head violently and the pistol barked again. Suddenly Ray's hands went limp and Danny rolled across the dented hood of the car and out of Ray's grip. He stumbled away, body shaking, ears ringing from the deafening gunshots. Thin wisps of cordite lingered in the air. Overhead the storm rumbled on.

Ray slithered down the bonnet and flopped onto the cold floor. His hands shook violently and Danny saw a dark streak had followed him down the paintwork of the car. Ray swore, pushing himself up onto his knees and fumbling with the zip of his Barbour. He felt inside his coat then winced, pulling his hand away and holding it up in the air. It was bright crimson.

'Oh Jesus, look what you've done,' he rasped, his eyes wide with fear.

Danny took a step towards him. 'I know about the woods, Ray. About the hole in the ground. I seen it myself.'

'That was a precaution,' Ray gasped, 'just in case you fucked things up.'

'Ray, I - '

The big man held out a bloody hand. 'Help me up, son. C'mon.'

Danny shoved the pistol into the waistband of his jeans and went to Ray's side, hefting him up under the armpits of his Barbour. As Ray straightened up, Danny saw his corduroy trousers were soaked with blood.

'Oh God, oh God - look what you - you've gone and done.' Ray trembled violently, one hand clutching his bloodied belly, the other arm draped around Danny's shoulders. 'Get me to the house, son. Tess'll know what to do.'

They shuffled awkwardly towards the sliding door, Danny struggling under Ray's bulk. He glanced over his shoulder, where a dark trail of blood smeared across the floor behind them. So much blood. Ray stopped suddenly.

'Take a - a breather,' he gasped. 'Hurts.'

Danny lowered him to the ground and dragged him towards the wall, resting his back against the cold cinderblock. His face was now deathly white, his skin beaded with perspiration. His jaw hung open, a thin stream of saliva dangling from his lip.

'Wait there, Ray. I'm going to run to the house, call an ambulance.'

'No,' Ray croaked, his blood-soaked hand groping for Danny's wrist. 'No outsiders. There's a doctor in the – in the village. Tess knows.'

Danny took two paces towards the barn door when Ray scraped sideways down the wall, his arms flopping uselessly beside him. He lay on the ground, his blood shot eyes rolling in their sockets, his mouth moving faintly. Danny leaned in close, loosening his collar. It was the only first aid he knew. His fingers brushed Ray's neck, the skin cold and damp.

'Where's Tess?' Ray whispered, 'Where's my baby? Oh, there you are...'

Ray's throat rattled, an unnatural sound that frightened Danny. Ray took another breath, more like a short gasp, then his eyes glazed over as the life ran out of him across the floor of the barn.

Danny scrambled away from the body and stood up, his hands and clothes smeared with blood. Two men dead, killed by Danny's own hand. And Ray's corpse bothered him. The man had been good to him, showered him with hospitality, given him the chance of a new life, yet the end result was always the same for Danny. Every time something in his life went right, fate was waiting around the corner to fuck it all up. Ray Carver; decent, respectable, wealthy - Danny's saviour and benefactor – a complete lunatic. He should've seen this coming, but he was too blind, too stupid.

He snapped himself out of his self-pity and turned back to the Vauxhall. He flung open the door and peered inside. The ignition code was taped to the keypad. He started the vehicle up, extinguished the lights and pulled back the concertina door. He grabbed Joe's body by the feet and dragged it out of the way, leaving a long dark streak of blood and brain matter across the floor. Five minutes later he pulled the car around the front of the main house, steering towards the deep shadows beneath the cedars. On the seat next to him were all his personal possessions, stuffed into a backpack. He headed around the side of the house, not bothering to take his boots off as he crossed the kitchen floor. He started with the fridge, grabbing cartons of orange juice and bottled water and stuffing them into a couple of Tess's large shopping bags. Canned goods were next, his hands fumbling with tins of beans, spaghetti, macaroni -

'Danny? What the hell do you think you're doing?'

Tess stood in the doorway of the kitchen, a pair of oven mitts tucked beneath her arm. It was only then that Danny noticed the joint in the oven, the smell of the roasting meat dispelling the acrid stench of cordite that had plugged his nostrils.

'Tess, I - '

'Bloody hell, Danny! Look at my floor!' Tess marched across the kitchen, grabbing a roll of kitchen towel from the marble worktop. She started unravelling it across the trail of wet footprints. 'You know better than to come in here with filthy shoes,' she puffed, working away at the dirt on hands and knees. Then she stopped. She sat back on her haunches, her eyes taking in the shopping bags, the food spilling over the top, the open cupboards. Finally she stared at Danny. 'What are you doing in here anyway?'

Danny dragged the bulging bags from the counter and stood there, one in each hand. He'd never felt more ashamed, more guilty than he did right now. He must look like some sort of sneak thief, a criminal.

Tess got to her feet 'What's that on your clothes, Danny?' She took a few paces towards him. 'Is that blood on your face?' Her eyes suddenly widened. 'Where's Ray?'

Danny bit his lip, unwilling to meet Tess's gaze. 'There's been a terrible accident, Tess. It wasn't my fault, I - '

Tess closed the space between them, gripping his arms with her chubby fingers. 'What accident, Danny? Is Ray alright?'

Danny dropped his eyes, his voice shaking. 'I didn't want to hurt anyone - '

Tess shook him, her eyes watery, pleading. 'Danny, what are you talking about? For God's sake, where's Ray?'

'He's in the barn, Tess. I'm sorry.'

She searched Danny's face, her wide eyes blinking away the tears, her own face a mask of dread. She spun on her heels and headed for the kitchen door, wrenching it open. A cold wind funnelled through the house as she disappeared into the darkness, the familiar jingle of her bracelets drowned by the rain and the rumble of thunder.

Danny moved quickly, out to the waiting Vauxhall. He selected drive and floored the accelerator, raindrops lancing through the headlight beams, wipers thrashing the windscreen. As he neared the main gates he stamped on the brakes and leapt out, leaving the engine running as he ducked into the bushes and located the control box. He shivered as wet leaves dripped cold rain on his face and neck, as his blood-stained fingers fumbled in the dark. Then the gates hummed into life, swinging inwards, painfully slow.

Danny was about to climb back into the Vauxhall when he heard it. He froze, one foot inside the vehicle, his hand on the doorframe. Heart pounding, sick to his stomach, he clambered inside, slammed the door shut then roared out into the Hertfordshire night.

Behind him, Tess's pitiful scream echoed across the dark estate.

✧ ✧ ✧

Alton Grange

It was the rattling of the key in the security gate that woke Bryce.

He opened his eyes, the blistered paintwork on the ceiling above swimming into view. The room was still in shadow, the sky outside the barred windows a deep blue that paled to the east, the sun not yet risen above the surrounding woods. Denied a watch, bedside clock, radio or TV, Bryce had become used to measuring time in other ways. The sun was the simplest method, as it always had been for mankind, its predictable arc across the sky as accurate as a mechanical timepiece once you got used to its pattern. But the earth was now officially locked in a climatic cooling cycle and even Bryce, a prisoner inside this depressing wing, realised that the country was experiencing a particularly wet winter. However, in the absence of the sun there were other ways to mark time. The main gate for example, the comings and goings, the guardhouse shift changes, the ebb and flow of vans and cars, staff and visitors, those were his timepieces. And by any measurement, today's wakeup call was earlier than usual.

He heard nurse Orla's clunky footsteps along the corridor, then the lights blinked and buzzed into life overhead. Bryce's heart began to beat loudly in his ears as the nurse swept into the room, thick winter coat wrapped tightly around her ample frame, a red knitted hat pulled down over her ears. She sniffed loudly as she approached Bryce's bed, wiping her nose with the tissue balled in her hand.

'Time to get up,' she announced, the soft Irish tones jarred by her blocked nasal passages. 'Jesus, it's cold in here.'

Bryce didn't move, cocooned like a larva inside his thin duvet. 'It's early.'

'Don't I know it,' complained Orla, setting her bag down on the end of the bed and rummaging inside. She produced a blister pack of tablets, fat, dark spheres of God knew what. 'There's been an outbreak, MRSA, two patients in the ward below,' she announced. 'so all bedding in this wing is being destroyed. I need you up and out of that bed in the next five minutes. Leave the mattress at the gate for Sully to take care of.'

Bryce peered from between the folds of his duvet. 'Can't I do it later?'

'No, you can't,' Orla shot back, popping two of the pills into her hand and placing them on Bryce's nightstand next to the bed. 'There, those are for you. I don't want you taking them now though, not before you've moved that bloody mattress. Sure, I'm not getting my hands dirty today. I've got a Christmas lunch to go to later.'

'Christmas?'

'Winter festival, then,' Orla corrected herself, a sheepish look on her face. 'I know some find it offensive but I can't get used to calling it that. I was a good catholic girl once.'

Despite the act, Bryce already knew that the holiday period was just around the corner. Public institutions were prohibited from displaying any specific Christian references to the upcoming festivities, but the guards had strung up a banner of coloured lights in the gatehouse and some of the delivery vans had tinsel wrapped around their wing mirrors or framing the inside of their windscreens. Cairo had been signed in the last week of November and since then Bryce had scratched the days away on the wall behind his bedside table, wondering if each notch would signal his last, if

Sully would appear in the doorway without his breakfast tray, instead pushing the trolley that would take his body to the mortuary.

'Where's Sully?'

'He'll be here soon,' Orla warned, 'so make sure that mattress is moved and you've taken your medication before he turns up. You don't want to get him mad, not today.'

'Why? What's so special about today?' Bryce searched the woman's face for a tell, a clue, anything.

'Nothing. Come on, out of bed.'

Bryce threw off the duvet and reached for his dressing gown. On the surface he kept up his sluggish pretence but inside his stomach bubbled with acid and his nerves jangled. Was this it, the day they came for him? Had the call been made, the order given? He stood up, faking a loud yawn and stretching his arms over his head. He stepped into his slippers and slowly began pulling the covers off the mattress, keeping his back to the nurse.

'Here, let me help,' she said, snapping on a pair of latex gloves.

'I've got it,' Bryce assured her.

'I told you, I haven't got all day.' She elbowed Bryce aside and hurled the rest of the sheets onto the floor. 'Fold that lot up and leave them by the gate. I'll take care of the mattress.'

'I said I've got it.' Bryce gripped the handles on one side of the mattress and tried to stand it up. Orla grabbed it anyway, pulling it off the bed and heaving it upright. Something hit the floor. Bryce froze, the objects caught it in his peripheral vision, not one, but two, three, four, rolling across the cracked linoleum. Orla let the mattress fall back onto the bed. She bent down, picking up one of the tablets that had come to a stop between her sturdy shoes. She examined it for a moment then turned on Bryce, her face flushed with anger.

'What the hell's this?' she demanded. 'You've not been taking your medication? Is that it?'

Before Bryce could answer Orla shoved him aside and started inspecting the seam of the mattress with a practised eye. She found the tear in a matter of moments and stuffed her hand inside, pulling out dozens more tablets that spilled to the floor. Then she found the hypodermic syringe, a green plastic safety cap shielding its needle.

'You crafty bastard,' she breathed, holding the syringe up to the light. She shook it, inspecting the clear liquid inside. 'Do you realise how much trouble you're - '

Bryce's bony fist caught Orla full in the face, sending her staggering backwards. She lost her footing and hit the ground hard, her head cannoning off a thick radiator pipe with an audible crack. Bryce winced. He stumbled after her but Orla lay still, her legs splayed out before her, arms spread wide, a pool of dark blood already spreading across the floor. Bryce grabbed a sheet and knelt beside her, balling the material up and placing it behind her head. His mind raced, uncertain what to do except stem the flow of blood. Already the warm liquid had reached his knees, staining his pyjamas. Then her eyes suddenly opened, frightened, pleading and accusing all at once. She moaned softly, her bloodless lips mouthing unintelligible words. Bryce swept a few strands of auburn hair away from her face.

'What shall I do, Orla? Tell me what to do!'

Her lips moved again and he leaned close, straining to hear the words. Her breathing was laboured, short gasps that rattled between her bloodied teeth. Bryce stood up. His first instinct was to get the poor woman some help but that would surely hasten his own demise. He perched himself on the corner of the bed, his head swimming. Despite his clandestine fitness regime he was woefully out of shape. His legs and arms felt like water and his hands shook badly, but that was nothing compared to the sickness in the pit of his stomach, the mixture of fear and adrenaline that meant he was now fully committed. Do or die, those were his only choices. If Sully walked in now, saw nurse Orla, the blood on his pyjamas, he wouldn't live to see the day's end, of that he was certain.

He stood, eyes roaming the floor. The syringe had come to rest against the wall, thankfully still intact, and he slipped it inside the pocket of his dressing gown. He got down on all fours, herding the tablets together with his hands and scooping them into a pillowcase which he stuffed inside the drawer of his night stand.

Orla moaned again. Bryce tried to ignore her, found her bag on the floor, and rummaged inside until he located the blister pack of tablets. He studied the label; Flunitrazepam. Bryce had never heard of it but whatever it was it was a powerful sedative. Thankfully, Sully and Orla had become complacent during his incarceration, the rudimentary check of his open mouth never discovering the pill wedged up inside the gap between his back teeth, or the torn seam in his mattress where they'd been hidden, hoping somehow he would have the courage and opportunity to make use of them by –

The security gate opened with its familiar metallic screech. Bryce froze, eyes wide, heart pounding, the sound of Sully's tuneless whistle echoing down the corridor. The gate slammed with a loud rattle, his trainers rasping on the linoleum, getting closer. Bryce scuttled behind the padded door, his heart threatening to burst from his chest, the blood rushing in his ears. He'd only get one shot and it had better be right or Sully would kill him with his bare hands. He lifted the syringe from his pocket and pinched the safety cap with his thumb and forefinger.

It didn't move.

A flash of white passed the crack in the door, the uniform, Sully's familiar shape. 'Orla, I told you to have the mattress ready,' he complained loudly as he entered the room. 'Where's - '

Then he stopped and Bryce flinched as he heard Sully rack his baton out. He gripped the safety cap again, tugging with all his might, his fingers burning with pain. Then it snapped off with an audible click. The door swung open and Sully stood there, half shielded by the thick padding, the baton raised in his right hand.

'Don't move!' he yelled, his eyes noting Bryce's blood soaked pyjama legs. Bryce shrunk away, expecting the ugly black baton to come whipping down on his head and body. He crouched in a defensive ball, his hands shielding his face.

'It was an accident,' he blurted, 'I swear to God!'

Sully eyed him for a long moment before lowering the baton, letting it dangle by his leg. Then he took a step back. Bryce was relieved, then unsettled, to see a smile on his dark face, almost a look of amusement. 'I can't leave you two alone for a minute, can I?' Bryce didn't answer and Sully motioned with the baton. 'Move. On the bed.'

He did as he was told, giving Sully a wide berth and shuffling across the room. He acted as he always did around his keepers, lifeless eyes and listless limbs, but his heart hammered like a pneumatic drill inside his chest. By some miracle Sully had failed to spot the syringe cupped in the palm of his hand, the needle poking between his fingers.

'Good boy. Sit.'

Bryce plopped himself on the mattress. Sully tucked the baton under his arm and gave Orla the once over, careful to avoid the large pool of blood spreading across the floor. He bent over her and cocked his head, listening for the sound of her breath, feeling her neck for a pulse. Finally he pulled off her hat and inspected the wound at the back of her skull. Even Sully winced.

'Not good. Not good at all.' He straightened up. 'What happened?'

'I just wanted some fresh air,' Bryce explained, his head held low, eyes on his slippers. He heard the squeak of Sully's shoes, the toes of his trainers nosing into view. 'We argued, she tried to hit me. She slipped, banged her head.'

'Bullshit,' Sully shot back, 'that's not her style.'

Bryce saw the hands move, the baton retracted and slipped into its holster on Sully's belt. 'It's the truth,' he said quietly, acting like an admonished schoolboy.

'Sure it is,' Sully laughed. He took a deep breath and folded his arms. 'Well, it seems we have ourselves a bit of a predicament.'

Bryce looked up, wearing what he hoped was a truly pathetic countenance. Sully was lost in thought, his hand stroking the dark stubble of his chin, his thick eyebrows knotted together. He stood that way for several moments, then he said, 'Stay there. Don't move.'

He picked up a pillow case and quickly tore it into strips as he approached Orla's still form, then knelt down beside her. His hands were doing something around her face, his shoulders hunched with effort.

Bryce couldn't quite see what was happening so he stood up and took a few steps towards them. He froze, horror numbing his mind - Sully was stuffing the torn material into nurse Orla's open mouth. The words were out before he could stop them.

'Jesus Christ, Sully, stop that!'

'Back on the bed!' Sully roared. He forced more ripped sheeting into Orla's mouth, packing it in tightly. Bryce watched Orla's fingers twitch violently. He held his face in his hands, not wanting to look but unable to stop himself. 'For God's sake, you're killing her!'

Sully leaned over the nurse, grunting with the effort of suffocation, then finally sat back on his haunches and inspected his handiwork. 'That should do it.'

Bryce turned away, sickened, his hands groping for the bed, his legs like water. 'Why? Why did you do that?' he whispered.

Sully climbed to his feet, brushing the dust from his knees. 'Why prolong the inevitable?' he answered. 'Besides, I just finished what you started.'

Orla's fingers had stopped twitching. 'I wasn't trying to kill her, you bloody animal!'

Sully sprang to his feet and marched towards the bed. He grabbed Bryce by the face, squeezing his cheeks together, his nose an inch from Bryce's. He stared into Bryce's eyes, searching them, then pushed him back onto the mattress. 'Not taking your meds, eh Gabe? Is that what you argued about?' Sully's voice was so quiet, so laden with menace that Bryce believed the end was moments away. He twisted his head free from Sully's painful grip and pushed himself away.

Sully smirked. 'Yeah, you'd better be scared.' He cocked his head towards Orla's corpse. 'This is messy, Gabe. I don't like mess.'

'It was an accident,' Bryce repeated.

'The thing is, she was being retired after this anyway. A fatal car crash maybe, a slip in front of a train, a brutal mugging gone wrong – the details hadn't been worked out. I can tell you one thing though, it wasn't supposed to be here, like this.' Sully glanced over his shoulder then turned back to Bryce and smiled. 'Attacked by a deranged inmate. Yeah, that would work.'

Bryce shook his head. 'I didn't kill her. You did.'

'Whatever,' Sully shrugged. 'Calls will have to be made. The Prime Minister told.'

'Yes, do that,' urged Bryce. 'Jacob should know what's going on here.'

'Hooper?' Amusement played behind Sully's eyes. 'You've not heard? Jacob Hooper is dead.'

Bryce felt the wind punched from his lungs. 'Dead?' he repeated after a moment. 'How?'

'Took a swan dive out of his office window at Millbank. Things weren't going well for him, pressures of the job, troubles at home. I heard they were scraping him off the walls for days. A real tub of guts.'

'Jesus Christ,' Bryce breathed. 'Then who is - ?' He stopped suddenly, realising the answer to his own question. How far Tariq had risen in a couple of months, from a minister on the verge of disgrace to leader of the country. And how Bryce had underestimated him.

'You've got it,' Sully smiled, reading Bryce's face. 'Anyway, Hooper's funeral was a few days ago. A family affair, very quiet. No press. '

'Poor Jacob,' Bryce whispered.

Sully laughed. 'It was poor Jacob that had you transferred here.'

'No,' Bryce said emphatically, 'we both know this is Tariq's work.'

Sully waved an admonishing finger. 'Show some respect, Gabe. It's Prime Minister Saeed to the likes of you and I. Anyway, it was Hooper's signature on everything, so he'll take the fall. Literally, as it turns out.' Sully chuckled at his own joke, then he said: 'It's all working out nicely too. There's barely a mention of you these days. No one wants to hear about sick people, Gabe, not even ex-Prime Ministers. The world has moved on. You're just a news flash waiting to happen.'

Bryce searched those cold, hard eyes as Sully's cruel laughter rang in his ears. With Jacob gone, his own demise was surely just around the corner. He found it almost impossible to believe that a couple of months ago he was safely ensconced in Downing Street, the leader of the nation. Now it seemed like another world, someone else's life. He shivered, pulling his dressing gown tightly around him, his hands tucked beneath his armpits.

'Someone will find out about all this,' he warned. 'People have died. It'll get out, sooner or later.'

Sully came and sat on the bed next to him. He spoke softly but his eyes bored into Bryce's. 'Really? And who's going to tell them? You? If you walked out of here today who would believe you? Your reputation is shredded and everyone thinks you're a basket case. All you'd be is a mentally disturbed ex-politician wailing about a conspiracy, that's the story that would hit the headlines, that and your wild-eyed picture. Bottom line is you'd end up back here. With me.' Sully patted Bryce's leg and chuckled darkly. 'And to cap it all you're a murderer now. I mean, look at what you've done to poor nurse Orla. Who'd ever believe a deranged murderer?' He turned away from Bryce, his eyes drawn to the body by the wall. 'Anyway, I can't sit here chatting all day. This mess needs to be cleaned up.'

As Sully stood up, Bryce grabbed his tunic and sunk the needle into his backside, depressing the plunger in one swift movement. Sully yelped, his body arching and his arm swinging viciously at Bryce's head as he twisted away. The blow caught Bryce on the shoulder and he tumbled backwards across the bed. Sully winced, clenching his teeth as he yanked the syringe from his right buttock. Bryce dropped to the other side of the bed, keeping it between them. He watched Sully as he studied the syringe with disbelieving eyes. An empty syringe.

He hurled it at Bryce's head, missing him by a fraction. 'What was it?' he screamed, reaching for the baton beneath his tunic. He racked it out, his eyes blazing with a fury that terrified Bryce. He pushed the bed towards the enraged orderly and ran for the door as Sully staggered after him.

'Bastard!' The baton swished through the air inches behind Bryce's head. He ducked into the corridor, yanking the door closed behind him, his hand shooting up for the heavy dead bolt and slamming it home. He backed away from the door as it shook under the force of Sully's assault, his desperate thumping muffled by the thick padding. The handle rattled violently, the shouts and curses promising a world of violence. Sully was like a wild animal suddenly caged, vicious, deadly, desperate. Bryce held his breath, willing Sully to shut up, terrified the syringe had failed to do its job, that the drug inside had somehow lost its potency.

But slowly the blows on the door weakened. The handle stopped rattling. He heard his name and crept towards the door.

'Gabe,' the muffled voice rasped. 'Can't breathe. Get…get some help'

It didn't sound like Sully, the usually deep, confident tone replaced by a choking, high pitched pleading. There was another thump on the door, softer this time, like a child's. He looked down, where the pale dawn light inched beneath the door. He saw shadows, Sully's feet, moving, shifting balance. Then the light was extinguished as the sound of a body hitting the floor reached Bryce's ear. He thought he heard the baton clatter across the linoleum.

He got down on his hands and knees and peered under the gap. Something white was pressed up against the door on the other side. Sully. Faking it or out cold? Bryce decided to wait.

He went into the washroom and splashed cold water on his face. He inspected himself in the mirror, his face pale, glistening droplets clinging to the stubble of his face and head. A small vein throbbed in his neck and he gripped the edge of the sink to stop his hands from shaking. If this was going to work he'd have to shape up, pull himself together. He began to breathe deeply, filling his lungs and exhaling slowly. Eventually his heart rate slowed, his hands stopped shaking.

He stayed in the washroom for a while, perched on a lavatory seat, listening for movement from the bolted room, from the rest of the wing. It was quiet, only the sound of dripping water, the distant toot of a vehicle at the main gate, the disturbed wail of a patient from somewhere within the facility. Business as usual.

Fifteen minutes had passed, maybe twenty, when Bryce poked his head out into the corridor. The light under the door was still blocked out, the room ominously silent. On hands and knees Bryce peeked under the door again. Sully's body appeared not to have moved, a crush of white material filling the gap. Perhaps it was all a sham, Sully lying with his back to the door, his eyes open, a cruel smile on his face as Bryce released the bolt and pushed open the door. How long could he wait like that? Hours maybe.

The question was, how long could Bryce afford to wait? Would anyone come looking for Sully? For nurse Orla? She was Bryce's full time carer whereas Sully oversaw the whole thing, monitoring, reporting – goading - always making sure Bryce remained isolated, confined to his wing, that the windows and locks were not interfered with. And now his gaolers lay on the other side of the door, one certainly dead, the other out cold. Probably.

Another hour passed, then another, but Sully never moved. Bryce watched from the utility room window as the grocery truck honked a greeting at the main gate, the red and white barrier lifted, the driver waving to the guard from his window. That truck usually arrived long after the staff did, around ten o'clock Bryce calculated. That meant fresh fruit and veg for lunch and dinner, not that Bryce ever saw much of it. His meals were usually a mixture of watery potatoes and overcooked vegetables, the meat barely identifiable, the same pallid looking flesh appearing in next day's curry or stew. So, it was mid morning then. Soon it would be lunchtime and the ebb and flow of traffic would begin again, funnelling through the main gate with predictable regularity. Bryce took a deep breath, knowing the moment had finally arrived, knowing that further inaction and delay would result in his own fate being swiftly sealed.

He checked beneath the door, his eye finding the crease in Sully's uniform just below the rusted screw of the door's footplate. The crease was still there, unmoved, which meant Sully had lain completely immobile on the floor for more than three hours. If he was faking it then he was good, but now he had no choice. The longer he waited, the more chance Sully would start to revive and Bryce couldn't risk that. He reached up and dropped the bolt, pushing the door open against the weight of Sully's body. He peered around the jamb. Sully lay curled at his feet, immobile, his mouth and eyes wide open, his dark features now a sickly grey. The baton had skittered across the floor and lay at the foot of the bed. Without thinking Bryce hopped over Sully and raced towards the weapon, scooping it up and spinning around to face the Turk.

Nothing. Sully remained on the floor, his knees drawn up into a foetal position. Bryce advanced slowly, poked Sully's trainers with the baton. He moved closer, navigating the tip towards Sully's genitals. Sully didn't flinch, not even when Bryce prodded the hardened plastic tip deep into Sully's crotch. The Turk's eyes stared into space, a pool of saliva beneath his chin staining the linoleum. Bryce waved the baton near his face just to be sure and Sully's eyes remained open, unblinking. Bryce tucked the baton under his arm and grabbed Sully's legs, straining with the effort as he pulled him clear and out into the middle of the room. He removed his white tunic and trousers and folded them carefully over the back of the chair. He began to undress, his back to Sully, unable to meet those accusing, lifeless eyes. How much of an unidentified drug he'd given him Bryce didn't know, but it had killed him. Two tablets a day, the clear fluid inside carefully decanted into the syringe over the last month until it was full. A fatal overdose then, another death on Bryce's increasingly bloody hands. He couldn't bring himself to confront that reality right now, forcing it from his mind. Later, maybe. Not now.

He changed into Sully's uniform, rolling up the legs and cuffs. Still it looked too big, so he pulled on a pair of track bottoms and a couple of sweatshirts to fill himself out and tried again. Better, he thought, looking down at himself. He removed Sully's trainers and slipped them on his feet, wriggling his toes and discovering they were a size too big. It didn't matter, he had no intention of running anywhere.

He relieved Orla of her money, her cell phone, travel smart card, access keys and security swipe. Finally he scooped up Sully's identification card and placed the lanyard around his neck. From the window he saw the hospital was operating normally, the guards safely ensconced inside the gatehouse as a fine mist of rain painted the roofs and roads with a wet sheen. Just another day in paradise. He left the room without looking back, bolting the door from the outside.

In the washroom Bryce shaved carefully, removing his stubble and tidying up his sideburns. He used a pair of nail scissors from Orla's handbag to trim his unkempt ears and eyebrows then washed his face vigorously with soap and water, scrubbing a healthier complexion back into his pallid skin. He towelled himself dry and studied his efforts. Shaved, trimmed, an official uniform, an ID lanyard hanging around his neck. All in all, not too shabby. He might pass a cursory glance but any serious study would reveal what Bryce believed were screaming inconsistencies. No matter, he had to keep moving now.

He placed Orla's items in his right pocket, Sully's in his left. The trademark keychain hung from his belt in a jangling loop. Bryce used it to open the security gate, as he'd seen Sully do countless times before. He locked it behind him, then pushed open the unlocked double doors. Opposite was another set of doors, an occupied ward beyond. To his right a staircase. He made his way down to the next landing, then the next. More double doors, more wards. He kept moving until he reached another steel mesh gate at the bottom of the stairs. Through the intricate metal pattern he could see a long corridor that led towards another door at the far end. Beyond that, daylight beckoned, like light at the end of a tunnel. The lack of CCTV and the signs on the wall told Bryce all he needed to know; Visitor Waiting Room, Kitchen, Storeroom – this was a non-secure area. Further along the corridor a cleaner wiped a lazy mop across the floor, a yellow warning triangle blinking in the gloom. Sully's key slipped into the lock and it opened on well-oiled hinges. Bryce saw a notice board to his left, some sort of timetable pinned to it. He snatched it off the board and pretended to study it as he walked along the corridor. The visitor room was empty, and Bryce glimpsed a low table littered with magazines, several easy chairs and a battered vending machine. The kitchen was nothing more than a narrow room with a kettle and a microwave.

The cleaner eyed him as Bryce approached, the mop swishing across the floor in a damp figure of eight. He was African, Bryce judged, his ebony cheeks scarred with tribal markings. Bryce stopped short of the wet floor, leafing through the papers in his hand. He gave the man a friendly nod, betting his white uniform trumped the light blue fatigues of the cleaner.

'Hi. Can you tell me where the staff locker room is? I'm new and I've lost my bearings.'

'Nursing or auxiliary, Boss?' The cleaner spoke in strongly accented English. He eyed Bryce up and down, clearly expecting him to say nursing.

'The nearest one,' Bryce answered. He waved the papers in his hand. 'MRSA check. I'm taking swabs, recording levels.' *Keep it simple.*

'Oh,' the cleaner said. He pointed along the corridor. 'Blue door, as you come in. Take de stairs to basement. The locker room is there.'

'Down here?' Bryce pointed, already moving away.

'Yes, boss.'

Bryce went through the door and descended the stairs. He found the locker room easily enough, the stale air inside tinged with sweat. Thankfully it was unoccupied, just several rows of grey lockers and a few wooden benches in between. Off to the right was a washroom, toilets, and two shower cubicles marked male and female. From the full rubbish bins, the discarded clothes and wet towels on the floor, Bryce guessed that this was the auxiliary workers changing room. He took the opportunity to nose around, carefully checking the lockers. Some were secured by small padlocks but many weren't. With one ear open for the door, Bryce went through them quickly, finding what he was looking for in a matter of minutes. The blue puffer jacket with a cheap branded logo on the breast pocket fit snugly over the bulk of Bryce's uniform and sweatshirts, the beanie hat with the initials 'NY' an added bonus. Then he saw the clock on the wall.

A long time had passed since Bryce had seen any sort of timepiece. Sully and Orla had never worn watches in Bryce's presence, no doubt to add to his sense of disorientation. He paused for a moment, watching the red second hand moving around the dial, the larger hands working their way up towards the hour. Part of him felt like some sort of prehistoric cave dweller encountering this wondrous instrument for the first time, and he watched it for several moments. The clock read eleven forty two. By Bryce's estimation the lunchtime period began at twelve. That was when the main gate got busy, when foot traffic flowed through the cage alongside the gatehouse. A voice inside screamed at him to go now, run, but Bryce fought the impulse and instead locked himself inside the male shower room. He sat on the small wooden bench and waited, willing the minutes to pass. He arranged the items around his pockets, selecting one or two for easy access. Someone entered the locker room outside and Bryce heard a muffled conversation and a peal of laughter. Locker doors slammed, then the room was quiet again. Bryce waited a while longer then stood up and pulled on the beanie hat, tugging it over his shorn head and covering his ears. He stepped outside, walking briskly towards the locker room door. The clock on the wall read 12:04. He hoped, prayed, that he didn't bump into the owner of the hat and jacket in the next five minutes.

At the top of the stairs daylight beckoned outside the security door. Bryce waited in the stairwell, studying the door itself. There was no obvious lock, just a swipe card reader and a hand plate. The windows on the door were impregnated with wire but that was the extent of the security measures. He climbed the last step, turned to his left and fished for the swipe in his pocket. It was nurse Orla's. A buzzer sounded and Bryce pushed the door open and stepped outside the building for the first time since he'd arrived. As he walked he filled his lungs with fresh air, tilting his chin towards the sky as a fine drizzle cooled his face. It was a wonderful feeling, to be free from the prison behind him, to feel the cleansing elements of nature, the rain on his skin, the cold air that cleared his head and fogged his breath. The urge to run was almost overwhelming but he kept his pace deliberately casual, following the path towards the main gate. He noticed others around him, medical staff and hospital workers wrapped up against the weather, all converging towards the main entrance.

He saw other uniforms around him, white, blue, green, bundled up in coats or shielded beneath umbrellas. A jam of cars inched towards the gatehouse, brake lights pulsing, the red and white barrier raised and lowered as they passed out of the facility. He joined a queue that shuffled towards the cage, a short corridor of steel fencing that ran alongside the gatehouse. He watched the people in front of him carefully, using their swipes on the reader one at a time, entering the cage and swiping the other reader to exit the facility. The man in front, a large, shaven headed orderly, swiped his access card and pushed the gate as it buzzed. Bryce held nurse Orla's swipe in his hand as his eyes flicked towards the gatehouse, to the computer screen that glowed behind the smoke glassed windows. He saw the orderly's face flash up on the screen, his name and personal details. Bryce's heart hammered as he quickly dropped Orla's swipe back into his pocket and fished inside his coat for Sully's. He found the cell first and pulled it out.

'Come on, come on,' muttered an impatient voice behind him. Then his fingers found the card and he swiped the reader. The inner gate buzzed loudly and then Bryce was inside the cage, his head turned away from the control room, nodding as he faked a conversation on the cell. He swiped again and the outer gate unlocked. He pushed it open then walked through, out onto the grass lined footpath that led to the main road. The hairs on his neck stood on end as he felt every eye on the facility watching him, the confused look of the guard inside the gatehouse, his hand poised above the large red button that would trigger the wail of the sirens and send the facility into lockdown. But nothing happened. Cars passed him in a steady procession, pausing at the junction ahead and turning out into the country lane.

Across the road a bus waited in a cut away, the destination glowing digitally above the driver's window: BAGSHOT. Bryce followed those ahead of him, crowding onto the bus. He used Orla's travel card and wedged himself in by the window. After a minute or so the doors hissed closed and the bus moved off. *Alton Grange,* the illuminated sign announced. Bryce had never heard of the facility, at the same time realising he would never forget it. He watched the gatehouse slip by, the bus accelerating past the wire topped fences that ran along the tree line until they disappeared and all he could see were grey slate roofs in the distance. After a while they were gone too, swallowed up by the mist. He'd made it.

His legs began to shake and he found a seat by the window, his face pressed against the glass. The mixture of diesel fumes and damp clothes made Bryce feel ill but he daren't reach up for the sliding window. Instead he took several deep breaths and concentrated on the world outside, the passing fields, the trees and hedgerows. Escaping the facility was just the first hurdle; *don't pat yourself on the back just yet, Gabriel.* There was still a long way to go, a leap into the unknown that could end with him being back behind bars before the day's end. Or worse.

Looming ahead through the windshield and the rhythmic swish of the wipers, Bryce saw the neon glow of a hypermarket. People got out of their seats and joined the throng at the doors as the bus slowed, then drew to a stop. Bryce kept his head down as he allowed himself to be swept along by the crowd and onto the pavement. He moved with them towards the hypermarket, lost inside their protective cordon, sheltered from the fine rain by a covered walkway that led to the store's wide entrance. He slowed his pace, allowing the others to pass, then turned and watched the bus disappear to the north, heading towards its final destination at Bagshot, the cell phones, swipes and travel card stuffed in the crack of the seat. He would be untraceable now, the eventual manhunt hopefully focussed in the wrong direction. He was kidding himself of course; once they discovered his escape no stone would be left unturned until Bryce was back in protective custody. No, killed while escaping, that was a more likely outcome. So Bryce had to think out of the box.

Inside the hypermarket he found the DIY section and purchased a pair of cheap navy overalls with some of Orla's Euros, spending a few more on a pre-paid cell phone and a local ordinance survey map. He used the public toilets to change, stuffing Sully's white uniform into the waste bin and covering it with wet paper towels. Then he left the store, heading south to the other side of the town.

He found a coffee shop with *Season's Greetings* sprayed in fake snow across the windows and wandered in, taking a seat near the counter. There were several patrons, women with toddlers and small groups of labourers and Bryce relaxed, knowing he didn't look out of place in his overalls, winter hat and coat. No-one would recognise him either, not forty pounds lighter with a broken nose and shaven head. Feeling reasonably relaxed, he ordered a roast chicken salad sandwich – made with fresh farm produce, the menu promised - and a glass of freshly squeezed orange juice. He picked up the media tablet from its receptacle and flicked through the news items with his finger. Sully was right, the world had indeed moved on. There was no mention of him and he daren't use the search option, knowing that all public searches were tracked and logged. Instead he read about the tensions on the

Iran-Iraq border and the peace march held in London by Sunni Muslim groups that ended with the firebombing of the Iranian embassy. A Catholic priest had been arrested in Leicester for displaying a nativity scene outside his church and a car bomb had been detonated outside Glasgow Rangers' Ibrox stadium prior to their British Premiership fixture against Celtic. Fourteen people had been killed. Bryce clicked the depressing tablet back into its base unit.

The food arrived, the middle aged waitress all smiles as she proudly laid the plate before him. Bryce thanked her and ate, the sandwich probably the finest he'd ever tasted in his life. He wasted not a single crumb, savouring every delicious mouthful and washing it down with the orange juice. He couldn't remember the last time he felt so satisfied after such a simple meal, and he sipped at a coffee while he digested his food and pondered his next move. He needed to get far away from Alton but it was too early, too light, to start trudging along the side of a busy main road. He needed somewhere to hole up for a while, somewhere where he could idle away a couple of hours before he made the call. Then he would know, either way, how all this would turn out. He bought another sandwich and a small bottle of water to go, stuffing them into his pockets.

The pub was called *The Windmill* and was set back off the road a few hundred yards south of the coffee shop, an old building with a thick thatched roof, a Tudor frontage and small framed windows behind which a warm glow beckoned. The building marked the southern boundary of Alton, the road beyond carving through green fields and gently sloping hillsides. Still the rain fell, vehicles hissing past, headlights on, wipers frantic. Bryce cut across the empty car park and ducked inside the pub. It was dark and cosy, with low beamed ceilings, and a fire burned in the open hearth opposite the small bar. It wasn't busy, just a few locals scattered around the tables, all in working clothes. Again, Bryce congratulated himself on his choice of attire. He strode confidently across the red patterned carpet to the bar.

'Orange juice, please.' The barman, a spotty youth with shoulder length hair, cracked open a bottle and dumped it in a glass over ice. Bryce handed over four Euros and found a table in a dark corner near the fire. He slipped out of his coat and settled down, stretching his legs out before him. The clock above the bar read three fifteen and the world outside had turned a darker shade of grey. He wondered if they'd found the bodies yet but thought it unlikely. No-one ever came up to his ward except Sully and Orla. But still, Bryce kept a wary eye on the road outside, watching for police cars or any other unusual traffic, listening for the wail of distant sirens. So far there was nothing to worry him unduly but that wouldn't last. He spent the next hour carefully studying the local map until the streetlight across the road blinked into life. He got to his feet, pulling on his coat. It was time.

He approached the bar, making a show of patting his pockets. 'Is there a phone I can use?' he explained to the barman, 'I think I've left mine on the job.'

Without looking up from the game on his phone, the youth pointed to a dark corridor that led towards the toilets. 'There's a web terminal down there. Takes pre-pay cards. You want one?'

'Please.'

'Five, ten or twenty Euros?'

Bryce fingered the slim wad of notes in his pocket. 'Five will do.'

Bryce took the card and headed along the corridor. The booth was on the left just before the men's toilet and Bryce slid the door open and settled down on the seat inside. It was snug, almost soundproofed, a single touch screen terminal shielded from prying eyes by the frosted glass of the booth. Bryce searched inside his coat and produced the card, now worn and dog eared, but still readable. He pulled the pre-paid cell from his pocket and dialled the mobile number on the card. His heart began to beat faster as the calling tone reverberated in his ears. Then a click on the line, the connection successfully made.

'Hello.'

The voice was the same, that confident tone that Bryce remembered so well. He closed his eyes, the memories flooding back, the heat of the flames, the strong hands that never stopped working, tearing at the timbers that held him, setting him free.

'It's good to hear your voice again,' Bryce began, hoping, praying, Mac would recognise his own.

There was a pause on the line, then: 'Excuse me?'

Bryce willed himself to think and act carefully. He knew the level of sophistication of the government's monitoring programs, the constantly shifting flag words that initiated remote recording, the men and women who worked in the shadows, listening, tracing...

'I was hoping you might remember me. You helped me out a while back in London. I was trapped. My leg was injured. You sent me a book, in hospital.' *Come on, Mac, think!*

'A book? I don't - ' Then he stopped talking. Bryce could hear other voices in the background, men's voices, laughter echoing in a large empty space. 'Is that you, Prime - ?'

'Yes,' Bryce confirmed, cutting Mac off. He closed his eyes briefly, the phone clamped to his chest, relief flooding through him. 'Yes, it's me. Contrary to popular belief, I'm still in reasonable shape.'

'I don't understand,' Mac whispered. 'I thought you were - '

'Don't speak. Just listen, let me talk for a moment, o.k.?'

In the background someone hammered away at something, the sound echoing down the line. Eventually Mac said: 'Sure.'

Bryce took a deep breath. 'Good. Thank you.' He cleared his throat. 'The truth is, my life is in danger and I need your help. Before you ask, there's no-one else, no-one I can trust. I can't go into any detail, only that I need to disappear for a while.' Bryce paused for a response but all he could hear were voices in the background. 'Hello?'

'I'm still here.'

'I'm sorry, it's a huge ask - '

'Go on.'

Bryce shifted the phone to his other ear and reached into his pocket. 'I have a plan, sort of. Right now I'm in a town called Alton. You know it?'

'Yes.'

'After I end this call I'm going to head south, towards the next town. It's called Four Marks.' He smoothed the carefully folded map out on his thigh. 'There's a bus stop to the south of the town, just after the dual carriageway ends. I'll wait there for, well, I don't know – until midnight. If I don't see you before then, I'll assume you're not coming and move on. Sometime after that I'll probably be dead. I don't know how the story will break but whatever it is it won't be the truth, you can believe that. I'm not ill. There was never any stroke.' Bryce paused for a moment, then said: 'That's it, that's all I can say right now, but I want you to know something. If you decide to have nothing to do with this, I will respect your decision and never contact you again. You have my word.'

Bryce sat in silence, his eyes closed, fingers pressed against his temple. He could hear the chatter in the background, the sounds of industry echoing around those distant walls. In the corridor the toilet door creaked and slammed. A shadow lingered outside the frosted glass, then moved away. Bryce held his breath, the phone clamped to his ear.

'Start walking,' Mac said, 'I'll be there in two hours.'

The line went dead. Bryce sat quietly in the booth for several moments, head in his hands, using the cuff of his sweatshirt to wipe away the tears.

Buckingham Palace, London

The conversation stopped and Saeed turned towards the door as the Prince of Wales strode into the room. His dress was both sober and elegant the Prime Minister noted, a dark grey suit and black tie, the formal shoes polished to a mirror-like sheen. Over the years the Prince had transformed himself from an awkward and stuffy heir to fashionable urbanite, seduced like so many of his parasitical peers by inherited wealth and the glittering lights of celebrity. A stark departure from the previous generation but in many respects far more malleable, Saeed mused. The Prince crossed the thick carpet towards the three men who rose in unison from their chairs to greet him.

'Salaam Alaykum, Gentlemen,' the Prince began, 'my apologies for the delay.'

In the doorway a personal aide loitered inquisitively, no doubt eager to share her observations in whispered tones with the other servants below stairs. Saeed took a few steps, smiled at the royal lackey, then swung the heavy door closed in her face, banishing the eavesdropper to the dimly-lit corridor outside. He turned and watched the Prince greet the bespectacled Somali, Professor Mohamed Handule, the current EU ambassador of the Organisation of the Islamic Conference in Brussels. The Prince shook the smaller man's hand, bowing slightly as he did so and kissing him lightly on both cheeks. Then he turned to the Egyptian Minister of Justice, Galal Sharawi, and finally Saeed. No kisses for them, Saeed observed, which suited the Prime Minister. Personally he wasn't one for awkward physical contact, particularly with those not of the faith, but it was encouraging to see such supplication from the senior member of the

337

Royal Family before a lowly Somali professor, head of the OIC or not. The Prince showed great respect towards Islam, much like his father before him.

The heir to the throne settled into a chair opposite the three men, running a hand across his fast receding but perfectly coiffured blond hair, then smoothing the folds of his tie. Saeed noticed the small emblem of the RAF woven into the silk, the Prince's former service arm of choice. He still flew helicopters to this day, often buzzing from one Palace to another at considerable cost to the tax payer, a luxury that Saeed was prepared to condone. For now.

The room was situated on the second floor of the north wing of the Palace, one that encompassed the Prince's private accommodations and overlooked the darkened grounds beyond. Saeed decided it wasn't as gaudy as other parts of the Palace, those cold, draughty state rooms littered with discerning yet uncomfortable furniture, the walls lined with portraits of long dead, pale skinned Infidels. The sitting room they occupied now was a welcome departure from the rest of the building, with its subtle lighting, under floor heating and warm ambience. The furniture was deep and comfortable, the carpets luxurious, the silver trays of recently delivered refreshments of the highest quality; an intimate and appropriate meeting place for men of power and respect. And the Prince, of course. It was the diminutive Professor Handule who began the discussion.

'The funeral, it went as well as expected?' he asked, one thin leg folded over the other, a china cup of coffee balanced on the knee of his white gown.

The Prince nodded gravely. 'It did, Mohamed, thank you. Terrence was a great friend and a well-respected pilot, and the Cardinal delivered a very touching eulogy, not a dry eye in the house. Such a shame. He was still young, only forty-six.'

'Cancer took both my father and mother,' the overweight Sharawi stated gruffly, his fingers hovering over a perfectly arranged plate of pastries. 'My condolences.'

'Thank you, councillor.'

'You'd served together, is that right?' Saeed prompted.

'Yes, that's right, as part of the RAF Search and Rescue force up in Anglesey.'

Saeed noticed a look pass over the Prince's face, a vague mixture of sadness and a painful smile, no doubt triggered by the sudden recollection of a long forgotten memory. Handule must have noticed it too, clearing his throat loudly and bringing the Prince's focus back into the room.

'Before we begin I'd like to thank you for this private audience, your Highness. Your generosity on such a sad day is to be commended.'

The Prince waved his hand. 'Not at all, it's my pleasure. Tell me, Mohamed, how are things in Brussels?'

'A constant battle,' Handule sighed. 'Islamophobia spreads like a virus, no more so than here in Europe, and our organisation is growing increasingly concerned. We've made it clear to the Commission that much emphasis must be placed on eradicating the discrimination and violence directed at our communities, particulalrly in light of recent events.'

'An unacceptable situation, I agree. However I'm sure we're doing all we can here in the UK to combat this menace, right Tariq?'

Saeed nodded as the Egyptian minister slurped his coffee loudly then placed the cup and saucer on the table between them. 'May I say how grateful the Egyptian people are for your support for the Treaty of Cairo and our membership of the European community. You are held in high regard in our land, your Highness, more so than any other western leader before you. And if I may be so bold, perhaps even your father.'

'Please,' the Prince protested, 'you're too kind.'

'Nonsense,' Sharawi persisted. 'Your father did much to encourage greater understanding of Islam, to highlight its many contributions in the fields of science and exploration, to champion its commitment to peace across the world. It is a great tragedy that he cannot be here today.'

Saeed battled to keep the smirk off his face. The King had been a prolific campaigner for worthy causes, particularly sustainable farming, so the irony was not lost on many when the old man had been trampled by a herd of panicked Friesians on his Gloucestershire estate. Even Saeed, normally above the distractions of frivolity, had recognised the comedic quality of the whole episode. The octogenarian King, now permanently retired from public life, apparently still bore the hoof marks across his back. Saeed massaged the threat of a smile from his lips and concentrated on the business at hand.

'Thank you for those kind words, councillor,' the Prince replied. 'I know my father would have welcomed you all here today. And shared your concerns.'

'Concerns shared not just by us, but the whole of the Muslim world,' Handule pointed out, his thin face narrowing, his high forehead creasing into troubled folds. He leaned forward in his chair, waving an admonishing finger. 'The crimes carried out on your shores, by your citizens, have left a great tear in the hearts of Muslims everywhere. The pain of Luton is felt by us all.'

The Prince nodded sympathetically. 'Believe me Mohamed, many of us who represent Britain on the international stage feel tremendous shame over the events of September. Thankfully my new government, guided by Tariq's measured hand…' - Saeed acknowledged the compliment with a gracious nod – '…has taken great strides towards rebuilding the bridges between our affected communities. In fact the Treaty of Cairo would have been much delayed were it not for Tariq's leadership.'

'True,' the Somali allowed, 'the Prime Minister is indeed a credit to your nation, but he believes, like many of us do, that more needs to be done.'

The Prince looked puzzled, glancing towards Saeed. The Prime Minister said nothing, quietly hoping Handule hadn't gone too far. The Prince had proved to be the most popular member of the Royal for many years, a firm favourite with the media and the wider public. He always drew large crowds at every engagement, glamorous wife in tow, the twin girls looking more like their iconic grandmother at every appearance. The family possessed a celebrity quality, and the Prince was well-versed in both domestic and international affairs. When he spoke, people listened. To have him onside in the coming months would be a huge advantage.

The Prince shifted in his chair. 'I don't doubt that Mohamed, but like I said, as a nation we're going to great lengths to ensure that Britain learns its lesson from the terrible events of September. For example, refugees arriving on these shores no longer have to suffer the indignity of the relocation centre at Heathrow, and we are doing our best to cope with the considerable influx of economic migrants and displaced persons that have entered the UK since Cairo came into force.'

The Prince crossed his legs, folding his hands in his lap. 'Frankly the sheer weight of numbers has surprised us all, yet it's my belief that the UK is responding positively to these continued challenges, more so perhaps than many of our European partners. Wouldn't you agree Tariq?'

Saeed nodded. 'Indeed, and the UK continues to extend a warm welcome to its newest citizens, however, I believe the ambassador is referring to a different issue.'

The Prince swivelled back to Handule. 'Oh? In that case my apologies, Mohamed. Please continue.'

'Thank you,' the bespectacled Professor nodded, a toothy smile carving across his ebony face. 'What you say is true, Britain has done much to heal the wounds of Luton and extend the hand of friendship towards our brothers and sisters from Pakistan and elsewhere. But there is another issue, one that will do more for Britain's moral redemption in the eyes of the Islamic community than previous efforts.'

'Go on.'

'Are you as familiar with the Qur'an as your father once was, your Highness?'

The Prince looked suddenly embarrassed, shaking his sparse dome. 'Sadly not. I've been meaning to get round to it of course, but my schedule has been full and...'

'Permit me to impart a small education then,' the Somali offered, pinching his thumb and forefinger together. His cleared his throat then said in a soft voice: '*And we ordained therein for them: life for life, eye for eye, nose for nose, ear for ear, tooth for tooth and wounds equal for equal.*'

The Prince nodded solemnly. 'The language and cadence of Islam's holy words are truly inspiring,' he fawned, 'but please forgive me Mohamed, I'm not quite sure where you're going with this.'

'Daniel Whelan,' Saeed explained.

The Prince's eyes flicked from Saeed to the Somali and back again, while the Egyptian helped himself to yet another pastry. He held up his hands. 'You've lost me,' he admitted.

The ambassador's face darkened. 'This Whelan creature must be brought to justice,' he growled, his finger pointed righteously at the ceiling.

'And he will,' insisted the Prince. He turned to Saeed. 'No stone is being left unturned, isn't that right, Tariq?'

'Correct.' Saeed privately refused to use the term 'your highness', unwilling to formally recognise the authority of the House of Windsor. In all his dealings with the Prince, he'd never once been corrected. 'The hunt for Whelan goes on,' he continued. 'It's true, he's managed to evade capture so far and this is for two likely reasons: either he's already dead or he's in hiding somewhere. Either way, the truth will soon be known.'

'He could have fled abroad,' the Egyptian speculated, noisily sucking flakes of pastry from the ends of his fingertips.

Saeed shook his head, faintly amused by the look of disdain on the Prince's face. 'Unlikely. According to the intelligence Whelan is a poorly educated, penniless criminal with little or no support network. Travel outside the UK would be far out of his comfort zone. No, he's still here somewhere, hiding like a rat in a hole no doubt.'

And yet Whelan's disappearance was a mystery to everyone, especially Saeed. Generally it was only organised crime syndicates that possessed the money and resources to squirrel away one of their own.

Whelan was at the other end of that scale, a living, breathing definition of the word petty, yet somehow he'd managed to evade the biggest manhunt Britain had ever seen, not to mention a ridiculously large reward. Whelan had been chosen after a long exercise, an exacting filtration process that had finally identified the ex-soldier as *the* perfect candidate. Yet somehow he had outwitted them all. Or fallen down a hole. The Prime Minister's eyes wandered to the window, to the distant lights of the city beyond. He was out there somewhere, perhaps not far...

'Trust me Mohamed, it's only a matter of time before he's caught,' the Prince assured the ambassador.

'Everyone Whelan has ever known is either under surveillance or co-operating with the authorities,' Saeed confirmed. 'It's a case of sooner, rather than later.' He turned towards the Prince. 'The reason we're here tonight is to discuss what happens after he's in custody.'

The Prince shrugged his shoulders. 'Well, he'll be tried and convicted I imagine. Like any other terrorist.'

'Tried here? In a British court? Out of the question!' the ambassador barked, waving away the suggestion with a dismissive flick of his wrist. His voice dripped with disgust. 'The thought of this terrorist languishing in one of your gaols, watching TV, indulging in drugs and pornography, would be a profound insult to Muslims everywhere.'

The Prince, momentarily surprised by the venom of Handule's outburst, tempered his own disquiet. 'To some extent I agree Mohamed, yet Whelan has to be afforded certain rights under European law.'

'Ridiculous.'

'What else would you have us do? Send him to a gaol in Mogadishu?'

The Somali tilted his head and smiled without humour, his dark eyes unblinking behind his spectacles. 'Rest assured, Whelan's sentence would be served in far less comfortable surroundings were this true. But no, there is another way.'

'An informal consensus has been reached,' Saeed announced, 'and the wheels put in motion. The trial will be held at the International Criminal Court.'

The Prince looked puzzled. 'The ICC? Really? As much as it pains me to admit it, Whelan is a British subject, and the crimes took take place on British soil. Does the ICC even have jurisdiction in this case?'

"The terrorist's victims came from a diverse range of ethnic backgrounds,' the Egyptian minister explained, 'many of them from my own country.'

'Yes, I know. What incredible bad luck those poor tourists chose to visit Luton on that day.'

'Tragic,' Sharawi agreed, 'so you see, the repercussions of these crimes are international ones, not just confined to these shores.'

'Yes, but - '

'Justice must be served,' Handule warned. 'Our people demand it.'

The Prince squirmed in his chair, adjusting the knot of his tie with nervous fingers. 'I understand your anger, Mohamed, I really do, but I don't see what any of this has got to do with me. After all, I'm not a politician.'

The Somali leaned forward in his seat. 'That may be so, but you *are* a figurehead, an international statesman who commands great respect. Your words of support during the dark days of September still resonate across the Islamic world.'

'What the ambassador is saying,' Saeed added, 'is that the judicial process must not be questioned. The Attorney General, the Supreme Court here and the European Court of Justice in Luxembourg are all in agreement; an example must be made of Whelan. However, the court of public opinion must also be served. You know yourself that many Europeans still harbour quiet animosity towards Islam and its followers, particularly in light of Egypt's recent accession. They are distrustful of the state in all its forms.'

'It's true,' confirmed Sharawi, eyeing the single remaining wafer on the bone china plate. 'Some of our citizens across Europe have suffered physical attacks since Cairo. There have been reports of beatings, property damage.'

'Disgusting,' breathed the Prince.

'Quite.' Saeed watched the Egyptian scoop up the pastry and take a bite. 'The fact is, Whelan, and many right-wingers like him, loathe the direction Europe is taking. They believe another agenda is being quietly implemented, one designed to destroy their way of life. If these conspiracy theorists convince themselves that the law is being deliberately manipulated to quench the thirst for justice the Muslim community so rightly deserves, well…it could lead to further problems.' Saeed waited a moment, then said: 'Perhaps even a repeat of September. Or worse.'

The monarch paled. 'No, that can't be allowed to happen,' he whispered. 'Everyone has worked too hard to find a way forward.'

'Especially you,' Saeed reminded him. 'The Prince of Wales is admired and respected, especially by traditionalists on the right of the political spectrum. They feel, as many of us do, that the Royal family is woven into the cultural fabric of this country. To them you are the embodiment of living history, a reminder of the glories of Britain's past.' Saeed paused, almost choking on his own bile. 'Your support for the judicial process will go a long way to alleviate any public disquiet amongst those subjects who may have doubts. When the time comes to seal Whelan's fate we must all be of one voice.'

The Prince sat quietly in his chair, lost in thought. After a few moments he said: 'Well, royal endorsement or not, this Whelan character is a mass murderer. Whatever court he's convicted in, I'm sure the vast majority of Europeans will rejoice in his demise. If he disappeared into a very dark hole I don't think many people would shed a tear. Even the little Englanders.'

Saeed and Sharawi shared a look, a smile creeping across the Egyptian's pockmarked cheeks.

'Then we can count on your public support?' Handule asked.

The Prince nodded emphatically. 'Of course, gentlemen. As you rightly pointed out, justice must be served.'

'I'll have a statement drafted,' Saeed offered, 'reflecting the royal family's confidence in European justice, its determination to send a clear message.'

The Prince held up a hand. 'That's fine, Tariq, but I've got some ideas of my own.'

'Yes. Your voice should be heard,' Saeed allowed.

Beside him, Handule nodded enthusiastically. 'Indeed it should. Then perhaps, in return, the Prince may care to address the Islamic summit in Casablanca early next year? As keynote speaker?'

'Really?' The Prince clapped his hands together at the prospect and Saeed silently admired Handule's masterstroke. Infidels were rarely invited to speak to the OIC, and never at the summit which only occurred once every three years. For a man like the Prince the opportunity would be a mouth-watering one.

'That would indeed be an honour,' he grinned. 'Thank you, Mohamed.'

'I shall speak to our Secretariat.'

The Prince sprang to his feet, prompting the others to rise also. 'Rest assured gentlemen, whatever legal process is employed to convict Whelan you'll have the unequivocal support of the Royal Household. Now, I must bid you all goodnight. My equerry will be along shortly to show you out.'

He shook hands with all of them and left the room. The three men retook their seats.

'Nicely done,' said Sharawi, popping the remaining morsel of pastry in his mouth.

Saeed kept his voice low. 'Easier than I thought. His father also enjoyed meddling in politics.'

'The apple rarely falls far from the tree,' Handule observed.

'Many in Britain are still blinded by the glitter of royalty,' Saeed explained. 'The Prince's endorsement will add further legitimacy to Whelan's fate. In the fullness of time it will be seen as the norm.'

The Egyptian snorted, wiping the grease from his lips with an expensive white napkin. 'Things move too slowly,' he complained. 'Our power in Europe grows daily. What do we care what the Infidels think? They will bend to our will either way.'

Saeed held up a cautionary hand. 'Patience, my friend. If we flex our muscles too soon we could provoke a backlash. If anything we must tread more carefully.'

Saeed was aware of the media rumblings, the vague concerns expressed by talking heads, the faint tone of suspicion in normally compliant editorials; a growing Islam-centric government had the potential to undermine existing foreign policy, damage long standing international relationships and sow discord amongst the electorate. The sceptics amongst His Majesty's Opposition, those who couldn't be coerced or threatened, could cause further trouble, perhaps even rebellion. Careful navigation was required, until the sails of Islam could be fully unfurled. ''We must be cautious, embrace our enemies as if they were friends. The Qur'an teaches us this, does it not? A generation must pass before we show our true colours.'

Sharawi looked aghast. 'I'll be in my grave before then.'

'Do not be ungrateful,' the Somali scolded. 'You are here now, a witness to history. This is Allah's will. Surely that is reward enough, my brother.'

Sharawi shook his head and smiled. 'Always the voice of reason,' he sighed, balling up his napkin and tossing it on the solid silver tray.

Handule laid a gentle hand on Saeed's arm. 'By the way, I have a message for you, from our friends in Riyadh. The item you await is almost ready for delivery. It should be with you next week.'

'Really?' Saeed beamed. 'That's wonderful.'

The Egyptian raised an inquisitive eyebrow. 'What's this?'

'You must come to Whitehall,' explained an amused Saeed. 'Then you will see.'

Sharawi's eyes narrowed. 'I'm intrigued. Tell me more.'

The Prime Minister shook his head. 'No, it's better if you see for yourself. You won't be disappointed.'

'It is true,' the Somali added with a mischievous smile. 'I've seen it myself. Very impressive.'

'Then at least give me a clue,' Sharawi persisted. 'I cannot -'

The door swung open and the Prince of Wales' personal equerry appeared, dressed in the immaculate uniform of the Welsh Guards. He introduced himself and invited the group to follow him to their waiting car. A visibly annoyed Sharawi glowered at the retreating soldier, tutted loudly and got to his feet. Suppressing a smile, Saeed followed him from the room and out into the corridor.

The Prince's continued commitment to his father's environmental legacy was evident by the sparsely lit hallway. As they headed for the deeper shadows of the distant lobby, Sharawi tugged on Saeed's sleeve.

'Come, Tariq. Shine some light on this little secret of yours.'

Saeed glanced around, at the empty corridor behind, at the immaculately-dressed Major striding ahead along the thick red carpet.

'A secret?' he shook his head. 'No my friend, it is so much more than that.'

'Well? What is it?' breathed the Egyptian.

Saeed's smile radiated in the gloom, his voice barely a whisper. 'A vision.'

South London

Danny drifted slowly back to consciousness, pale rays of wintry sunlight streaming through the filthy windows and piercing the papery skin of his eyelids. Something had disturbed him, something that filtered through the layers of fatigue to penetrate his dreamless sleep. He lay motionless for several moments, his ears registering three distinct sounds. The first two belonged to a passerby, whistling an unknown tune as shoe leather tapped smartly along the pavement outside. The third was an amplified voice, carried on the wind, urging the faithful to morning prayers. Unlike the passerby, the bloke in the mosque couldn't hold a tune, Danny decided. It was the bloody wailing that had woken him.

He stretched, yawning deeply, then checked his watch. Almost time to start the day. Still, he remained wrapped inside the questionable warmth of a thin blanket, unwilling to move. He stared at the ceiling. There must be a leak somewhere in the roof, he realised. A brown stain had worked its way across the cracked plaster, blistering the paintwork and encircling the bulb-less light fitting above his head. He thought about the previous occupants, a family probably, judging by the faded cartoon murals in one of the empty bedrooms. The rabbit-shaped nameplate on the door read *Rebecca* in faded blue lettering. It was difficult to get any sense of history about the place because everything of any value had been stripped out, right down to the fireplaces and the cornice work. Even the skirting boards were gone. Bloody shame, really.

Danny threw off the blanket. He pulled a roll-neck jumper over his t-shirt, slipped his training shoes on, then waited. A few minutes later a commuter train clattered along the embankment behind the house, shaking the windows and masking his creaking progress down the stairs. In the empty shell that was once a kitchen he used a standpipe to fill a bucket, splashed cold water over his bearded face then brushed his teeth. He was careful not to spill anything on the tiles; even though the front door was boarded up against trespassers, he couldn't afford to leave a single trace of his temporary occupation.

Back upstairs he fished inside the grocery bag and found a banana. He peeled and ate it, washing it down with the last of the orange juice. He put the refuse back into the bag then spent a few minutes cleaning the pistol with a small cloth. He ejected the magazine, worked the action several times when another train rumbled by, then re-loaded the weapon. Satisfied it would work if needed, he slipped it back into the waistband of his jeans and began his vigil.

He glanced at his watch; 8:12 am. From behind the dirt-streaked windows, Danny observed the scruffy hostel building across the street. Most of the rooms were still shrouded in darkness, curtains drawn, but others showed signs of life. There was even one brave soul near the top floor, their window defiantly decorated with a lurid neon manger scene, the colourful characters an inviting target for the local council busybodies who were always on the lookout for so-called offensive religious symbols. That sort of thing normally incensed Danny but right now he couldn't care less. All he wanted to do was get as far away from here as possible.

It had been four days since he'd fled Ray's estate. He'd driven east that night, keeping to the country lanes until he'd found a small hotel outside of the village of Flaunden, coasting quietly into the car park and coming to a halt where the shadows were deepest.

It was too risky to travel the roads at night, the chances of a routine police stop, particularly in rural areas, all the more likely after midnight. So he'd slept fitfully behind the wheel, waking with a start at every call of a night bird or rustle in the undergrowth. When morning came he'd tuned into a news station, fearing the worst but hearing nothing. His name wasn't mentioned, nor the deaths, or news of a manhunt. As he eased the car out into the lane and headed towards the M25 with the morning traffic, Danny kept his speed down and his eyes on the road ahead. The motorway took him past the sprawling relocation camp at Heathrow and Danny forgot his plight momentarily, making sure he followed the other drivers and stuck to the outside lane to avoid the stone throwing kids behind the fences.

He passed two police cars idling in a lay-by just past West Byfleet, the powerful black vehicles squatting like fat insects as their on-board cameras scanned the licence plates of the heavy morning traffic. Danny's heart was in his mouth as he cruised by at a steady sixty-two miles per hour, expecting the scream of sirens to cut through the voices on the radio, his rear view mirror filled with blue and red lights, the metallic commands ordering him to *Stop! Your vehicle is about to be disabled! Stop!* But nothing happened. As Ray had promised him, the car was clean.

The further he travelled, the more convinced he was that Tess hadn't reported the deaths of her husband and Joe. It was also a fair bet that Tess didn't know the details of the car or even if she knew what colour it was. For all of his faults, Ray loved his wife and Danny felt certain he would've kept any incriminating details from her. In any case, Tess would be up to her neck in it too if the police came sniffing around. Instead Danny imagined a night of frantic phone calls, begging loyal friends to clean up the mess, concocting some sort of cover story for Ray's absence. He had a mental image of the fat bloke, Marcus, rolling Ray's body in on top of Joe's in that dark clearing, patting the ground with a shovel, wiping his hands as he led an inconsolable Tess back to the house. If that was the case, and Danny prayed it was, then he had a clear run down to the coast. Clean car, clean ID. He had a chance to start his life again.

Reaching the south London suburb of Battersea by mid-morning, Danny left the Vauxhall in a side street and reconnoitred the hostel. The derelict buildings opposite made a perfect observation post and Danny retrieved his supplies from the car and slipped quietly inside one of the houses after dark. It was on the second morning he saw his father, his heart beating loudly, his throat choking with emotion. He wanted to bang on the filthy glass, call out to him, but he had to be certain he wasn't being watched before he made a move. The old man had shown no signs of random behaviour; a couple of laps around the nearby park and a thermos of tea on a bench overlooking the river was about the strength of it. That was typical of dad, a creature of habit, a man who liked routine. Danny was thankful for it.

For the last couple of days he'd trailed his father from a distance, making sure he wasn't being observed by others, but it was difficult to tell. He was no expert in counter surveillance but he had to take a risk. He needed to see his dad, speak to him, before he left for good.

Danny watched his father emerge from the hostel just before nine, taking time to sweep the pavement outside the weathered front door. That was another of dad's traits, hated mess wherever he was, always willing to help out. Danny studied him from across the street. It had only been a couple of months but already the back seemed a little more curved, the skin a little paler, gathering in loose folds around his neck, the grey hair noticeably thinner. Stress, probably, and worry. His neat home gone, his son branded a mass murderer and still on the run. The guilt made Danny feel physically sick. He watched his dad push the broom wearily, sweep and tap, sweep and tap, his movements precise, the frequent stops to flex the arthritic fingers, the fat electronic tag around his ankle forcing a slight limp. Bastards.

Another hour passed before the old man re-emerged in a faded navy tracksuit and trainers, a small rucksack slung across his shoulders, a pale yellow scarf wrapped around his thin neck to combat the sharp December winds. Danny slipped on his quilted parka as he watched his dad head up the street towards the park. He left the house by the rear garden, squeezing through the side alley that was choked with broken furniture and stinking rubbish, and emerged into bright sunlight. He slapped the dirt from his clothes and stepped out onto the pavement, following his father from a safe distance. There was no rush. He knew where he was headed.

'Oi! You!' Danny glanced over his shoulder without breaking stride. 'Yeah, you!'

He stopped, heart pounding in his chest. Coming up fast behind him was a local roughneck, wearing the black fatigues and high-visibility vest of a Civil Enforcement Officer. Danny sized the man up. He was in his forties, tall and powerfully-built, a shock of bright ginger hair spilling out beneath the band of his black baseball cap. He stopped a few inches away, looming over Danny, his face crimson with latent anger.

'You deaf? When I say stop, you stop. Get me?'

'Sorry, bruv.'

The enforcer studied Danny like an insect, the nostrils of his boxer's nose flaring. Danny lowered his eyes, noticing the fingers that flexed around the handle of a thick black baton dangling from the enforcer's belt. He was sure the man wouldn't need much excuse to use it.

'What were you doing down that alley?' he demanded.

Danny thought quickly. If this idiot wasn't satisfied with his answers, it could get ugly. He shrugged his shoulders and smiled, keeping his demeanour as casual as possible.

'Taking a piss. Got caught short.'

'A piss?' echoed the enforcer, his nose wrinkling in disgust. 'Do that at home, you dirty bastard.' Suddenly the man frowned and took half a step back. 'You're not local, are you? Break out some ID.'

The false ID card was safely tucked inside the pocket of his jeans, the latex face piece and the rest of his gear hidden in the derelict house. Unless he absolutely had no choice, the only time he would use his new identity would be at the ferry port. What he didn't need was a routine check, a street stop, a study of his ID picture, the details logged onto the system. He had to think quick.

'I don't want any trouble, bruv. I'm in a bit of a hurry as it goes.'

'Trouble? I never mentioned any trouble. Got a guilty conscience?' His hand moved towards the radio on his shoulder.

'Alright, I wasn't having a piss,' Danny confessed. He took a step closer, lowered his voice. 'Look, between you and me, I was looking for wiring in them old houses back there. You know, strip out the copper and sell it, yeah?'

The enforcer's hand still hovered near his radio. 'That's trespass and criminal damage. Name?'

Shit. This was going from bad to worse. A car drove by, the occupants staring at them as they cruised past. Across the street, a group of women pushing a brood of wailing brats stopped their buggies to watch. He had to think fast.

'You want the truth? I found a holdall, stashed under the floorboards in one of the rooms upstairs. You know what bearer bonds are?'

The enforcer growled. 'Course I do.'

'The holdall's full of 'em. Each one's got a value of five hundred Euros. We could split the lot, fifty-fifty.' Danny watched the enforcer's eyes dart left and right, his mind clearly debating the offer. Council stooges like this one were paid minimum wage for long hours. They didn't even get free travel. In the distance, above the pale chimney stacks of the derelict power station, a police blimp drifted across the sky. 'Well? What d'you think?'

The enforcer hesitated, glancing up and down the street. He saw the women across the road, watching, and drew his baton. 'Lead the way,' he ordered, jabbing Danny in the chest. They headed back towards the alleyway, clambering over the rubbish and into the rear garden.

'Maybe it fell off a train or something,' Danny ventured, pointing at the steep embankment. Beyond the wire fence a spur line carried commuter trains into the terminus at Victoria. He studied the enforcer carefully, how his eyes roamed the garden that was deep in shadow, overgrown with weeds and bordered by a sagging brick wall that was slowly crumbling under the weight of the railway embankment. The properties on either side were also derelict, silent and empty.

'How'd it get in the house, then?' the enforcer demanded, doubt in his voice.

Danny ducked past him, his legs swishing through the dewy grass. 'Maybe someone found it, stashed it under the boards, who knows? Tell you what I do know – they're worth a fortune to the right person. We could buy our way out to the colonies.'

'Watch your language,' warned the enforcer, following Danny up the narrow staircase.

'You know what I mean. Relocation packages and residency permits cost money, bruv. New Zealand ain't so bad but Australia and Canada is where people are going. Trouble is, they charge the most. Still, it'll be enough to get us out of earshot of them bloody minarets, eh?'

'I told you, I don't want to hear that sort of talk. I won't warn you again.' The enforcer stamped along the gloomy landing, his pace a little quicker, the floorboards creaking under his heavy black boots. The radio clipped to his shoulder hissed continuously, garbled voices trapped within the damp walls. Danny stopped at the threshold to a room and invited the enforcer inside.

'This is it.'

The big man pushed past Danny as his eyes swivelled greedily around the empty bedroom. The filthy window started to rattle as a low rumble filled the room. 'Where is it? Where's the bag?' he snarled, spinning around, the baton gripped in a tight fist.

The pistol was already in Danny's hand. 'Don't move, bruv. Don't make a sound.'

The enforcer paled at the sight of the gun but held his ground. He lowered the baton. 'Just take it easy, mate,' he soothed. 'No one has to get hurt here.'

Danny's mind spun wildly. Now what? 'You're right, no one need get hurt so just do as I say.'

'Yeah, whatever. You're the boss.'

Danny took a step back, his eyes scanning the room. This idiot had to be kept out of sight for at least twenty four hours, maybe more. That would mean tying him up, gagging him. But how? What with? Fucking place was bare. Then he saw the man's utility belt.

'Give me those cuffs,' Danny ordered. He had to raise his voice, the sound of the approaching train reverberating around the walls.

'What d'you want them for?'

'I'm gonna handcuff myself and let you nick me, you fucking idiot. Just give 'em to me.' The man didn't seem scared, his tone casual, almost challenging, and that unnerved Danny. 'Do it! Now!' he snapped.

The enforcer's hand went to his belt, eased the cuffs from their holder. 'Just take it easy, alright mate?'

'Stop telling me to take it easy.' Danny held out his hand. The enforcer stepped forward. Outside, a commuter express thundered past the window, shaking the whole building. Danny reached for the cuffs and the enforcer let go. They clattered to the floorboards. 'Idiot,' Danny cursed and bent down to pick them up. He saw the enforcer's feet move, heard the swish of something slicing through the air. He twisted his head away just as the baton came down, crashing into Danny's shoulder. Both men screamed, Danny in pain, the enforcer in a blind rage. Danny scrambled backwards as the enforcer raised the baton again, fury in his eyes. The shot exploded in the confined space, the bullet punching through the enforcer's neck in a mist of blood and matter. The big man staggered, eyes wide in terror, the baton clattering across the room. His hands reached for his throat, desperate to stem the blood that sprayed between his fingers. He dropped to his knees, spewing a mouthful of dark blood that painted his hands red, soaking the front of his uniform. Then he fell forward, his head thumping onto the floorboards. The panic was gone now, the mechanism of death consuming his body. His eyes bulged, his mouth opening and closing like a beached fish as he gasped his last, futile breaths. Then he lay still.

As the sound of the train receded Danny turned away from the body and thrust the pistol back into the waistband of his trousers. 'Fuck, fuck, fuck,' he whispered. Then his stomach lurched and he threw up over the floorboards, retching until his guts were empty. He dragged himself against the wall and sat there for a moment, panting for breath, a cold sheen of sweat on his bloodless face. Another death on his hands – Jesus Christ, he was turning into a bloody serial killer- and people were going to be looking for this one very soon. As if to emphasise the point, the radio on the enforcer's shoulder burst into life, the words and numbers meaningless to Danny. He leaned over and gingerly disconnected the battery from the man's radio. He had to move, and move fast.

Twenty minutes later he steered the Vauxhall through the gates of Battersea Park and left it next to a row of recycling bins. He strode along the tree-lined avenues, his parka zipped high against the cold, his shoulder throbbing painfully. Litter scraped and tumbled along the paths and the air was tinged with the scent of wood fires, signs of the growing number of homeless refugees camping in London's parks. Everywhere groups of veiled women wandered the pathways, their children furiously pedalling small bikes or chasing squirrels between the horse chestnuts and weeping elms. In open spaces, dark-skinned men flew a multitude of kites, coloured sails swooping and soaring on the gusting winds. Danny kept his head down and trudged around the edge of the lake, forcing himself to walk slowly, to act casual, but fear stalked him through the park. This was a mistake, warned a voice inside him. He should go, leave now, never look back. *Run, Danny, run...*

When he reached the embankment overlooking the Thames his dad was already seated on a park bench, munching on a sandwich as he watched the river drift by. Danny studied him from the shelter of a tree for a few moments, took one last look around, then set off across the open ground. His heart began to beat faster as he closed the distance, circling a muddy football pitch where a group of refugees played a boisterous game of soccer. There was a chorus of shouts and Danny saw the ball skimming across the grass towards him. He kicked it back, receiving a chorus of *thank you's* in heavily accented English.

A few moments later Danny slid onto the end of the bench, digging his hands deep into his pockets. He watched the slow-moving river, glancing at the old man who turned to him briefly then looked away. Then the bovine chewing suddenly ceased. From the corner of his eye Danny saw disbelief, then recognition, slowly register across his father's craggy face. The old man turned to Danny again, his hands trembling, the colour draining from his cheeks.

'Son?' he whispered.

'It's me, pops,' murmured Danny, his lips barely moving. 'You alright?'

The old man's eyes searched his son's face. 'Bearing up. You look different.'

'That's the idea,' he replied, scratching his thick beard. He glanced over his shoulder. The footballers were gone, the pitch suddenly deserted. 'I can't stay long, dad.'

The old man's lower lip started to tremble. 'You shouldn't have come,' he warned, his voice shaking.

Danny frowned. 'You've seen the news, yeah? Heard what they're saying about me?'

'I saw your letter, son. I know you're innocent.'

Across the river a police car wailed along Chelsea Embankment until the siren faded into the distance. 'That's why I've come back dad, to say goodbye. I've got to get out of here, leave the country. I'm heading abroad, Corsica maybe, Greek Islands. Somewhere quiet where I can - '

The words caught in his throat as the uniforms emerged from beneath the surrounding trees in an extended line, moving swiftly towards them, weapons raised. He turned at the sound of roaring engines as several unmarked vehicles carved across the open spaces, tyres spinning rooster tails of mud and grass. In that moment Danny knew the hunt was finally over. He didn't move, didn't reach for the pistol, just in case a stray bullet found his dad.

'They've been waiting for weeks,' the old man confessed in a quivering voice. 'They said you'd come, sooner or later. I prayed you wouldn't.'

Danny winced as he laid a hand on his father's knee and patted it gently. 'Don't worry, pops. It's not your fault.' The cars slewed to a halt around him as the uniforms drew closer, faces hidden behind black ski masks, a dozen red dots swarming across his torso like angry fireflies. He stood up slowly, his hands held wide, palms open. For a moment he forgot the pain in his shoulder. 'Never got anything right, did I? Never been any good.' Fear gripped him then, fear of what was to come. Whatever happened, it was going to end badly. 'I'm sorry, dad. Sorry for everything.'

Beside him, the old man smothered a sob with a bony hand. With the other he reached out and grasped Danny's with a strength that belied his advancing years.

Netley, Hampshire

'We interrupt this program to bring you some breaking news…'

Bryce's hand froze on the tap, the empty kettle held rigidly beneath the running faucet. His eyes flicked to the radio on the kitchen counter.

'At least three US soldiers have been killed in overnight clashes with Mexican security forces in El Paso, Texas, in an escalation of the recent violence that has seen hundreds killed along the volatile southern US border region. In Washington, President Vargas has condemned the violence, blaming right-wing elements in the US military for stoking tensions, and has vowed to crack down on Tea Party Revolutionaries…'

Bryce finally exhaled as his pulse rate began to settle. Still no word on his escape. Although he dreaded the sound of his name being broadcast across the airwaves, the distinct lack of news regarding his violent flight from Alton Grange possessed its own unnerving quality.

He nestled the kettle into its receptacle and snapped the switch on, staring out of the kitchen window as the water began to hiss noisily. It wasn't much of a view. Across the narrow lane was a high stone wall crowned with a mature wisteria, its heavy foliage glistening with silvery beads of rainwater. Beyond the wall was a wood, a dense mixture of oak and beech if Bryce wasn't mistaken. He leaned over the sink and craned his neck. The sky was a dull canvas of grey tones, traversed by darker clouds that drifted above the swaying treetops beyond the wall. A miserable day for sure, but a world away from his recent accommodations.

The cottage was the last of four, nestled at the end of a pea shingle lane close to the village boundary of

Netley. Mac had brought him here five nights ago, under cover of darkness, the car left by the kerb out on the main road. They'd headed up the lane, keeping to the shadows of the high wall, their footsteps sounding to Bryce like a Household Division on the march, the crunch of shingle underfoot shattering the still night air. He'd watched the cottages carefully yet nothing had stirred, no sudden glare of a porch light, no subtle twitch of a bedroom curtain. The cottages were unoccupied, Mac had whispered, sensing Bryce's unease. Holiday lets, full in the summer, empty for the most part during the winter. The last one belonged to Mac's company, private accommodation for visiting boat owners and out of town clients. As Mac unlocked the front door Bryce kept to the shadows, his eyes watching the end of the lane, his ears alert for the noises of men. But the night remained still.

The lights were kept off until every curtain and blind in the cottage had been pulled or lowered, Mac finally snapping on the hall lamp and dimming it to its lowest setting. Even by its pale luminance Bryce could see that the interior was simple yet tastefully furnished; polished floorboards underfoot, cream coloured sofas in the adjacent sitting room, gleaming units and granite worktops in the kitchen. There was a new smell to the place, tinged with a salty mustiness that Bryce found faintly comforting. Anything was better than the antiseptic stench of Alton Grange, a smell that he knew would haunt him for the rest of his life.

Mac had given him a whispered tour of the cottage, pointing out the facilities and settling him into the larger of the two bedrooms. After some brief instructions he was gone, and Bryce was left alone. Despite the long forgotten comforts of a king-sized bed and a fresh duvet, sleep evaded him that first night, his eyes snapping open with every creak of timber, every call of a night bird from the shadowy woods across the lane. Sometime after midnight he'd heard a car pass by along the main road, tyres hissing on the wet tarmac, and he imagined a violent turn of the wheel, the roar of engines in the lane outside, the crash of the door, the thump of heavy feet on the narrow staircase as they came for him. He'd found a small portable radio in a bedside drawer and lay with it under the quilt like a furtive child, listening to the BBC updates, expecting news of his escape to be broadcast across the airwaves but hearing nothing. He re-tuned to a Hampshire station where old ballads jostled for airtime alongside local news and shipping forecasts, the soothing tones finally lulling Bryce into a fitful sleep. Gradually the tension that gripped him eased, and as each night passed he'd slept a little better, managing almost six hours the previous evening. Physically he was recovering but mentally was a different story. Despite fleeing the morbid confines of the psychiatric unit the reality was he remained a prisoner, trapped within another set of walls. And they were closing in.

After five days the media were still silent about his escape, yet Bryce had no doubt the dogs had been let loose, even now desperately seeking his trail. Senior security personnel, as well as carefully selected Commissioners and Chief Constables, would've all been quietly briefed, the available intelligence painting a very different picture of Gabriel Bryce.

As he stared out of the window at the falling rain his mind pondered the exercise, the cover story that was no doubt already in play. The Downing Street bomb had left the Prime Minister mentally scarred, that was the seed already planted in the public consciousness. His mind had been tortured by the horrors of his experience, the security scare at the hospital tipping a dangerously fragile man over the edge. Further intense therapy had failed, as had the cocktail of barbiturates and pain killers that poor Gabriel had become overly dependent on. The former Prime Minister was now a shell of the man he'd once been, and to protect his reputation and remaining dignity he'd been quietly transferred to Alton Grange where post-traumatic stress specialists could take better care of him. But something had gone terribly wrong. Gabriel Bryce had somehow snapped, brutally killing a nurse and an orderly before escaping the prison. He'd fooled them all, the doctors and the nurses, and now he was on the loose, coherent yet criminally unhinged. He wasn't to be approached or spoken to, and should members of the public discover his identity they should be firmly reminded of the need for discretion. The police should be called, the patient returned to another institution, one with higher walls and more guards. A place where Gabriel Bryce would never leave, never see the light of day again.

Or something like that. Whatever story had been cooked up, it would be convincing enough to fool everyone. So he had to remain hidden, behind locked doors and curtained windows.

Unless...

He heard the crunch of footsteps in the lane outside and saw Mac trudging towards the cottage. The rain had turned to a fine sleet and the ex-marine was bent against the weather, hood masking his face, the two bulging carrier bags dangling from his hands brushing damp patches on the legs of his jeans. Bryce unlocked the door and scurried back inside the kitchen. Mac stamped his feet on the mat in the hallway before appearing in the doorway.

'Temperature's dropped out there. That sleet could thicken up.'

'Nasty stuff,' Bryce agreed, stirring the freshly made pot of coffee.

Mac lifted the carrier bags onto the counter and swept the hood from his head. He began unpacking the groceries; shrink-wrapped chicken, tins of soup, earthy potatoes, fresh carrots and courgettes. It was wonderful to be eating nourishing food again and Bryce felt his health had improved markedly since he'd arrived at the cottage. Mac produced a dark bottle from one of the bags.

'Got you some Merlot, Prime – sorry, Gabe.'

Bryce smiled. 'Don't worry Mac, you'll get used to it.'

The ex-marine handed over the wine. 'It's a decent one I'm told. Afraid I'm no expert.'

Bryce took the proffered alcohol and inspected the label. 'Jesus, I haven't had a drink in months. Chilean too, good choice. Who knows, I may finally feel civilised again.' The smile faded as he slid the bottle carefully into the rack on the counter. 'Did you see anything out there? Any police activity? Check points?'

Mac shook his head, wrestling the coat from his shoulders. 'Nothing.'

'Really?' Bryce fretted, taking a seat at the kitchen table.

Mac poured himself a coffee and joined him, sliding into a chair opposite. 'Quiet as the grave.' He brought the mug to his lips, blew gently, and took a sip of coffee. 'So, Gabe. I think it's time you told me what all this is about.'

Bryce dropped his eyes, inspecting the steaming contents of his own mug. Mac had been decent enough not to press him since that night in Four Marks. He'd seen the shock on the younger man's face, when the door had opened and the interior light illuminated Bryce's gaunt features, but the questions had only been about his well-being and comfort, nothing else. In fact it was Bryce who'd asked the questions, about the aftermath of the bomb, whether Mac had made an official statement (he hadn't, thank God – after a brief check-up by the paramedics he'd quietly slipped away, an unsung hero), or if he'd been questioned about the book he'd sent to the hospital. Again, Mac had replied in the negative and as far as they'd both been able to establish, Gabriel Bryce couldn't be linked in any way to the man sat in front of him. He owed him something, that was only right, but just how much of the truth could Bryce afford to reveal?

'I understand your frustration,' Bryce began, 'however it's complicated. It may be better if I don't say anything.'

Mac shook his head. 'That's not good enough. I'm guessing your being here is enough to get me hung anyway. Whatever it is, you can tell me.'

Bryce stared at the former marine for several moments. Despite the casual tone the dark eyes remained suspicious, the stubbled chin lifted a little too challengingly. Mac wasn't going to be fobbed off easily, that was obvious, and he was struggling to disguise his growing impatience. After almost a week holed up in the man's cottage without a single word of explanation, Bryce didn't blame him. But this was different. He had to tread carefully.

'You have a family, Mac. Two young boys, right?'

Mac's eyes narrowed 'So?'

'I told you, that first night, my being here can put you in harm's way.'

'I remember.'

'That means your family too.'

Bryce flinched as Mac slammed a hand on the table. The mugs jumped, coffee slopping across the polished oak surface. He jabbed a finger towards Bryce. 'Right, that's it. No more fucking around. You'd better start telling me what's going on. Now.'

'Like I said, it's complicated,' Bryce muttered, snapping a couple of paper towels from a roll and mopping up the spilt coffee on the table.

Mac's hand snaked out and grabbed his wrist. 'I don't give a shit,' he growled. 'I don't care who you are or where you've been - if my family's in danger then I need to know what sort of threat I'm facing, got it?'

Bryce looked down at the tough, calloused fingers gripping his wrist. 'Alright, Mac.' The younger man released his grip and Bryce rubbed the reddened skin. 'You must understand that I never meant to involve you in any of this. The simple truth is I had no other choice.' Mac said nothing, just stared at Bryce from across the table. 'If I tell you the whole story, what I know, what I think I know – well, that can only increase the danger to you.'

'I get it.'

'Do you, Mac? Because the people we're dealing with are ruthless. They've killed before. Our lives – me, you, your family - are meaningless to them.'

Mac tapped the table with a finger. 'Listen, I don't care what it is, or how deep you're in it. Just give it to me straight. You owe me that much.'

Bryce drained his mug and pushed it across the table. 'Jesus, when I say it out loud it'll sound so ridiculous. And the drugs – I can't remember everything.'

'Try,' ordered Mac.

Bryce inhaled sharply, then said: 'Ok, short version? The bomb in Downing Street had nothing to do with any right-wing conspiracy. Instead it was a deliberate attempt to wipe out the Cabinet and replace it with another - what we politicians like to refer to as regime change. When I inconveniently emerged from the wreckage they kept me hospitalised and heavily sedated, ensuring I was unable to retake the reins of office. Later they had me moved, under the pretext of another bomb scare, to a secure psychiatric facility not far from where you picked me up. There they kept me locked in a decrepit isolation ward, fed me all sorts of powerful drugs, and half-starved me to death. The media reports about my condition were a complete fabrication. There was no stroke, no mental deterioration - apart from my own desperate feelings of hopelessness of course. I was being held prisoner, hidden from public view, until I could be conveniently disposed of, no doubt in a considerably less dramatic fashion than previously planned.'

Bryce hesitated. He lowered his eyes, his voice suddenly quiet. 'But I fooled them, the people who kept me locked away, until the day I escaped. That's when I killed them both.'

For several long moments the only sound in the room was the ticking of the cooling kettle. Mac's face was a mask of disbelief. He stared at Bryce, a hand massaging the grey-flecked stubble of his chin. When he finally spoke his voice was incredulous. 'You did what?'

'Don't make me repeat it, Mac. It's bad enough having to relive it in my head every hour of the bloody day.'

'Ok,' Mac soothed, 'take it easy.' He grabbed the coffee pot from the kitchen counter and brought it back to the table, filling both their mugs. 'Right, forget the short version,' he said, leaning back in his chair and sipping the hot brew carefully. 'Tell me absolutely everything. From the beginning.'

So Bryce told him, about Heathrow, Cairo, about Tariq and Hooper, Sully and Nurse Orla, and every detail in between he could possibly recall. It took almost an hour, during which time Mac interrupted maybe half a dozen times to ask pertinent questions. When Bryce finally finished his monologue he felt a strange sense of calm, as if he'd unburdened himself of some of the guilt that plagued him. But only some of it. He knew at the end of the day, when he lay in his bed, the faces of the dead would emerge from the shadows to taunt him.

For a while Mac sat motionless, his fingers gently drumming the table top. 'Jesus Christ,' he eventually whispered.

'It's true, Mac. All of it.' Bryce thought he looked a little paler than before.

'You weren't joking when you said it was complicated.'

Bryce tried to read the expression on Mac's face. He'd seen it once before, in the glow of the fires of Downing Street. It wasn't outright fear - Mac certainly wasn't the type to scare easily - but it wasn't a million miles away either.

'Why don't you just march into the nearest TV station,' he suggested, 'tell the world you're still alive? You could end all this right now.'

Bryce shook his head. 'Trust me, Mac, it's not as simple as that. You can forget any notion of an objective, independent media coming to my rescue. The people that run the newspapers, the news channels, they consider themselves part of the same intellectual elite as mainstream politicians. They don't see themselves as public servants – they believe they exist to educate the masses, not inform them. I'm on the outside now. The minute I walk into a TV studio I'd be whisked into a nice quiet room out of the way. A call would be made. I'd disappear within the hour.'

Mac scraped his chair back and got to his feet. He leaned against the sink, arms folded across his chest, lost in thought. Then he fixed Bryce with a hard stare. 'Listen, I've helped you this far but this is way over my head. I won't expose my family to this sort of risk. You'll have to find somewhere else, another friend who can help.'

Bryce stood up and joined Mac at the kitchen counter. 'I've given that some thought. I think I might have a plan.'

Mac's frown evaporated. 'You do? That's good.'

'I need to get to Tortola.'

'Tortola? In the Caribbean?'

'The very same. I know someone there, an old friend. I'm certain he'll help me.'

Mac's frown reappeared. 'Really? And how the hell do you plan on getting there? You've got nothing except the clothes on your back.'

Bryce pulled a dog eared, crumpled business card from the pocket of his sweat pants and held it up. 'I know a man, one whose business is carrying out boat deliveries. Worldwide, it says here.'

Mac's eyes flicked to the card then back to Bryce. 'Convenient.'

'Remember what I said when we spoke on the phone, Mac? Well, the same rule still applies. You say the word, I'll walk out that front door. You'll never see me again. And I promise you, when they eventually catch up with me - which they will - I'll do my best never to reveal your name.'

Mac's face darkened. He stared at Bryce for several long, intimidating seconds. 'You bastard,' he breathed, 'you've had this planned all along.'

Bryce stood his ground. 'It was you that sparked the idea, Mac. Look, I'm not superstitious or anything but somehow the gods conspired to bring us together. The first time was in Downing Street, the night of the bomb, when you appeared from nowhere to save me.' Bryce held up the crumpled business card. 'The second time was in the hospital, when I started to feel that something wasn't quite right. That's when this arrived. You see? On some strange, metaphysical level you reached out, threw me a lifeline - '

'Bullshit.'

'Maybe,' Bryce countered gently, 'and yet here we are again, together, with danger closing in.' He placed the worn rectangle of card on the worktop, sliding it across the smooth granite towards Mac with a single finger. 'Whatever the reasons, you are my only option. There's no-one else I can trust. I've no family here to speak of, no real friends I can rely on. You and I can't be connected, we've proved that. And you can offer me a way out. If you want to.'

'Jesus Christ,' Mac fumed, spinning around and bracing his hands on the sink. He stood that way for a while, watching the sleet lancing past the kitchen window. Bryce kept quiet. There was nothing more to say now. His fate would be decided in the next few moments, that was certain. The cottage was silent, broken only by the sound of the wind rustling the wisteria outside the window, the occasional vehicle passing at the bottom of the lane. After a while Mac straightened up and turned to face Bryce with hostile eyes. This is it, Bryce realised - everything hinges on this moment. He held his breath.

'You've really dropped me in the shit, you know that?'

Bryce raised his hands. 'Not intentionally, Mac.'

'Don't bloody lie to me.'

Bryce could see the anger etched across his face, the spidery vein that pulsed on the side of his forehead, the white-knuckled hands that flexed by his side. He'd pushed the ex-marine hard and now guilt consumed Bryce again, stirring the acid in his stomach. 'Think about it, Mac. Think about everything that's happened to me, everything I've told you. What would you have done? In my position?'

Mac swore and turned away. He stayed silent for a while, eyes fixed on the falling sleet as it turned to icy droplets against the window. Eventually he sighed, shook his head and said. 'Same thing probably.' He watched the sleet for a moment longer then turned around and reached for his jacket.

Bryce pushed himself off the counter. 'Where are you going?'

'Where do you think?' Mac zipped up his jacket and tugged the hood over his head. 'If we're going to get you out of here arrangements have to be made.' Bryce closed his eyes as an overwhelming wave of relief swept away the tension that gripped his body. He placed a hand on the counter to steady himself. 'And another thing,' Mac said, 'from now on, what I say goes. No more secrets, no more bullshit, got it?' Bryce nodded. 'Good. Because I swear to Christ if I find out you've kept something back I'll drive you to the nearest nick myself.'

'I've told you everything.'

'Keep it that way,' Mac warned. 'And there's a financial cost involved here too. Money will have to be spent. I'll need to be compensated.'

'It'll be covered,' Bryce promised, 'every penny. Just get me to Tortola.'

Mac grunted and spun on his heel. 'Stay inside,' he called from the hallway.

'When will you be back?'

'Later.' As he slammed the front door behind him the windows rattled.

Bryce went into the sitting room and slumped onto the sofa, flicking the TV on. Instead of dancing with joy he struggled with a deep sense of shame. He'd forced Mac's hand, manipulated him, and by extension threatened his loved ones. What sort of man was he? *A desperate one,* the voice inside him countered. It was true, he was desperate. His life was on the line and he'd deliberately coerced Mac into aiding his escape without divulging the true danger of his complicity. In short, Mac had been screwed. Bryce kicked his feet up on the deep cushions and rubbed his eyes. It wasn't the first time he'd screwed someone for personal gain – he was a politician after all – but not a man like Mac, a decent, hardworking type. Besides, his previous victims had all been fellow politicians and accepted the rules of the game. Mac, on the other hand, was more inclined to break his neck. He lay there for a long time, staring up at the ceiling, until his eyes began to close, the drone of the TV gently lulling him into a welcome sleep…

Bryce lurched upright, fumbling for the remote and shutting off the TV. The car outside rolled along the gravel then crunched to a stop, engine idling. Mac had returned sooner than expected. The last thing he needed to see was Bryce sprawled across his sofa having a mid-morning nap. He quickly plumped the cushions and trotted upstairs. On the landing he paused, listening for the sound of the key in the door.

Nothing. He went into the spare bedroom at the front of the house, towards the window that overlooked the lane. If Mac needed help with something then the least he could do was go down and –

Bryce scrambled backwards at the sight of the police patrol vehicle squatting outside the cottage. He heard the crunch of footfalls on shingle, then three loud bangs on the door. Bryce froze, terrified. His first thought was Mac - had he gone to the police after all? No, he quickly realised, if he did there'd be no polite knock on the door. In fact the door would be lying in the hallway. No, this was something else.

The knocking sounded again, echoing up the stairs, urgent, insistent. He heard another sound, someone else skirting the side of the house, the metallic click of the rear gate latch. Two of them. Bryce held his breath as the other person clumped across the back garden, heard the scrape of boots coming to a halt, the sharp rap of a ring finger on the patio glass echoing downstairs. Bryce pressed himself up against the wall, trapped like a rat.

'Police!' The deep voice boomed up the stairs, reverberating around the walls of the cottage. 'Open the door, now!'

Bryce ducked into the bathroom and quickly ran his head under the tap, splashing water on his face. He kicked off his sweatpants and threw a bathrobe on, tying it around his waist. He padded downstairs in bare feet, heart pounding in his chest. The letterbox was open. A pair of suspicious eyes rooted him to the spot.

'You. Open the door. Now.'

The eyes disappeared and the letterbox slapped shut. There was nowhere to go, nowhere to run to. His fingers shook as he turned the lock and yanked the front door open. The policeman was tall, filling

378

the porch with black body armour, a heavy-looking pistol strapped to his thigh. He was hatless, his sandy blond hair cut into a severe short back and sides. Behind him was a large Toyota four by four with a blue and yellow checked band running down the side, silver paintwork gleaming in the rain. A cold wind invaded the hallway and Bryce pulled the bathrobe tightly around him. The policeman attempted a smile and failed miserably.

'Morning, sir.'

'Morning,' Bryce croaked. 'Is there a problem, officer?'

The policeman rooted Bryce to the spot with a penetrating stare. Bryce swallowed hard, his cheeks reddening. The suspicious eyes flicked over his shoulder, probing the gloom of the hallway, peering up the staircase. 'Can I ask what you're doing here?'

Bryce's mind raced, his thoughts a jumbled confusion of fear and panic. 'What? What I'm doing here?'

'It's a simple question.'

Just then the other policeman appeared, similarly dressed but shorter, wider, his impossibly young face flushed pink by the cold, his hands tucked beneath the armpits of his black body armour. He took up position behind his older partner, watching Bryce intently. Sleet settled on their heads, on their wide shoulders.

'Why don't you come in,' Bryce offered, 'get out of this miserable weather.'

The older policeman nodded. 'Fine.' They moved past Bryce into the hallway, forcing him up against the wall, the scrape of nylon and the stale odour of sweat leaking from their uniforms as they brushed past. The younger one peeled off into the sitting room. Bryce followed the older one into the kitchen.

'Nice place,' he said admiringly, his eyes cataloguing the expensive units, the subtle lighting, the limestone tiles.

Bryce's heart leapt as he noticed Mac's business card on the kitchen counter. He strode towards the cupboards, flinging them open. 'Can I make you both a coffee?' The voice inside screamed *you bloody fool!* but it seemed, normal, natural. He scooped up the card and thrust it into the pocket of his dressing gown, at the same time reaching for two mugs. 'Milk? Sugar?'

'No,' the policeman said, slowly circling the kitchen table. Bryce saw the other one head upstairs without being invited. 'I'll ask you again, sir. What are you doing here?'

Bryce snapped the kettle on, dumped a spoonful of coffee into a fresh mug. 'Not an offence to visit the coast, is it?'

'Don't get smart,' the cop warned, his mouth twisting into a sneer. 'These places are normally empty during the winter, so we give 'em the occasional once-over. Saw your kitchen light on.'

'Of course, officer. I wasn't implying anything - '

'It might look nice and quiet around here but you get a fair bit of crime spilling over from Southampton. We've had break-ins over the years, squatters, travellers...illegal immigrants.' He almost spat the words, Bryce observed. 'So, what are you doing here?'

The kettle began to bubble noisily. 'Ah, nearly there,' Bryce said, grabbing the handle. He watched the steam rise from the spout, tiny droplets of boiling water leaping into the air. He felt the walls moving in again, the air getting heavy, thickening in his lungs. His mind raced. He was trapped. His skin prickled and his heart rate accelerated, preparing the body for flight...

He spun around, dashing the scalding water in the policeman's face. The man screamed, staggering backwards and crashing to the floor, his sickening wail bringing the other one charging back down the stairs. Bryce fumbled for the gun on the wounded man's thigh, wrestling it out of its holster as the young one skidded into the kitchen. Bryce raised the heavy black pistol and pulled the trigger, the gunshot deafening in the confined space…

'What happened there?' the policeman said.

Bryce shook his head, the words slicing through his dark thoughts. 'I'm sorry?'

'The scar.' The policeman tapped his own close cropped skull. 'That's quite a war wound.'

Bryce touched the long welt on his head, the white line where the hair didn't grow anymore. He took a deep breath. 'That was the bomb. The one in Downing Street.'

The policeman's eyes narrowed. 'Say again?'

Heavy footsteps on the stairs signalled the return of the younger policeman. 'Clear,' he reported as he entered the kitchen. His partner nodded and turned back to Bryce. 'You were saying?'

Bryce took a seat at the table. He rubbed his face, running his hands through the stubble on his head. 'I was travelling on a bus along Whitehall when the bomb went off,' he began. 'I was making my way home from work, you know, just another day at the office. Then, as we passed Downing Street, there was a tremendous bang. The bus was literally picked up off the road, flipped through the air.' Bryce closed his eyes, remembering the double-decker bus in Whitehall, the inferno beyond the shattered windows, the charred corpses melted into their seats. 'I was thrown from the bus,' he continued, 'woke up on the road. There was nothing but silence, an awful, ghastly silence. And the dead were everywhere, in every direction, some in pieces, some bizarrely unmarked but just as dead. A terrible sight,' he whispered in conclusion, 'I'll never forget it.'

He rubbed his eyes and glanced up. Both policemen were watching him silently, clearly enjoying every gory detail. 'Since then I've had some mental health issues,' he admitted, 'nightmares, panic attacks. My GP thought I should have a change of scenery. I saw an ad for this place on-line.'

'I see,' replied the older cop. He studied Bryce a moment longer, his experienced eye clearly reappraising the man before him, noting the scar, the shorn scalp, the gaunt features. 'Must've been terrible,' he admitted, sympathy leaking into his voice.

Bryce nodded, then covered his face with his hands. 'It's really taken its toll. My partner back in London – ex, I should say - well, he couldn't cope with it at all. In fact I'm still having trouble sleeping. If you want to know the truth I was having a nap when you arrived.' He peered through the fingers of his hands, saw the look of disdain on the older cop's face. 'The nights frighten me,' he simpered, 'I get scared on my own.' The younger one smirked, nudging his partner with an elbow. Bryce bowed his head further, sniffing loudly between his fingers.

He started at the sound of a metallic voice, filling the kitchen with its indecipherable babble. The younger policeman cocked his head to the side, adjusting the radio's volume and listening intently. He turned to his partner. 'We have to go.'

'We'd best leave you to it then,' the older cop announced, ushering his partner out into the hallway.

Bryce looked up, his eyes red-rimmed. 'Are you sure I can't tempt you with a hot drink? I could do with the company.'

'Afraid not,' the cop replied. A cold draught barrelled around the kitchen as the front door swung open. Bryce got up, scuttling after them.

'Thanks for stopping by. Feel free to pop in for a coffee anytime,' he shouted over the revving engine. The Toyota started to back up the lane, wipers beating off the falling sleet. The younger one stared at Bryce from behind the glass, turning to his partner to mutter a comment. Bryce couldn't lip read but he doubted it was flattering. As the vehicle neared the main road Bryce waved a limp wrist then closed the door. He took the stairs two at a time and peeked from the window as the Toyota backed out onto the main road, emergency lights pulsing into life. Bryce prayed Mac was nowhere in sight as the Toyota disappeared and the wailing siren faded into the distance.

He sat on the carpet, back to the wall, breathing heavily. That was close, so very close, but he'd bluffed his way out of it without a single check. Convincingly too, he thought. The cottage was silent once more, save for the patter of sleet on the window. He sat there for a while, until his heart rate had returned to normal and his stomach had ceased its nauseous churning. Then he climbed to his feet. There was no time to waste.

He marched into the master bedroom, quickly stripping the bed and bundling the sheet, pillowcases and duvet cover into a black bin liner. The duvet he squashed into another bag. The only spare clothes he had, a navy blue sweatshirt and sweatpants, plus underwear and a few toiletries, went into another bin liner. After that, Bryce made a start on the cottage. It had been a long time since he'd picked up a duster or pushed a vacuum cleaner around – not since university and only then very occasionally - but he threw himself into the task that would've made a professional housekeeper blush with shame. For the rest of the afternoon Bryce attempted to erase all traces of his stay in the cottage. Every door handle, every light switch, every tap, every surface touched, sat or leaned on, every utensil used, every glass, every mug, every plate, every carpet walked on or tile traversed was dusted, vacuumed, scrubbed, scraped, wiped, washed or sponged until, when the grey winter skies gave way to darkness and the sleet had thinned to a fine drizzle, the cottage was as clean as it had ever been.

Sitting in the dark at the front bedroom window, Bryce recognised Mac's familiar gait as he headed up the lane towards the cottage. By the time the key turned in the lock, Bryce was waiting for him in the hallway. Mac snapped on the light and Bryce immediately reached out and dimmed it.

'What's going on?' Mac asked. He wasn't angry anymore, Bryce realised. Maybe because he'd accepted the situation for what it was, realising that Bryce had no choice, and was making the best of it. Or maybe it was because Bryce was stood in front of him, rubber gloves on his hands, plastic carrier bags tied around his feet, raincoat zipped to the neck and a woollen hat pulled low over his forehead. Behind him, everything he'd worn or slept in was tied up in black bags, arranged in a neat row in the hallway.

'I think it's time I left,' Bryce said.

Whitehall, London

The aide leaned in close and spoke softly in Saeed's ear. 'Prime Minister, Miss Jackson has arrived. She's waiting outside.'

'Show her in.' Saeed stood up from behind his desk and snapped the front of his jacket out, his hands smoothing the green silk tie that complemented the fine wool of the navy blue Ede & Ravenscroft three piece suit. In addition to his blossoming qualities as a statesman, Saeed also had an eye for bespoke attire, a trait not gone unnoticed by the British press. He was often seen gracing the covers of magazines and in newspapers, handsome, elegant, the celebrated blue eyes, dark hair and neatly trimmed beard giving him the aura of a movie star. Gossip columns loved him, men envied him and women wanted to be with him, despite the fact that he was married with children. Saeed privately loathed the attention, the media that revered vanity and superficiality above all things, but he encouraged it none the less, knowing the opinion polls reflected well on him after every public appearance. An expensive suit and a smile had more media cache than a fundamental change in the law, a state of affairs that Saeed had every intention of exploiting.

He walked around his desk and waited. The room where he now stood was just one of the Prime Minister's suite of new offices, situated in the Old War Office building in Whitehall. Standing at the junction of Great Scotland Yard Street, the building had barely been grazed by the Downing Street bomb and had been recently refurbished to accommodate Saeed and his administration whilst more permanent offices were considered. Too many bad memories at Millbank, Saeed had forlornly declared to a sympathetic media.

His office was well appointed, maybe a little too ostentatious some had advised, but Saeed ignored them. A huge desk sat at the head of the room while massive picture windows ran its length, flanked by thick red drapes. A row of sculpted columns stood opposite, another feature of the building's neo-baroque design. A large ornate cupola above the centre of the room cast rays of coloured light onto the white marble floor, and at the far end were the impressive double doors through which visitors were shown. It was a long and intimidating walk to the chairs in front of Saeed's desk, footfalls echoing across the marble, passing through the god-like rays of light cast from the cupola above. It sent a subtle message of course; the British respected power and status, the importance of occasion, the gravitas of ceremony, none of which could be conveyed successfully in an air-conditioned, carpeted office where an important meeting usually commenced with statically charged handshakes.

Saeed didn't use this room all the time of course, only when the occasion justified it, and today was such an occasion. The audience was small, a few of Saeed's personal staff and a photographer from his media team stood off to the side, nestled between the room's impressive plaster columns. There was to be no audio or video footage today, just a few poignant still shots for the official record - Saeed shaking hands with the injured and infirm, quiet words of condolence and support for the survivors of the Downing Street bomb, official recognition of their suffering and bravery, culminating in a small reception to be held later that evening. Today's initial meet and greet was to be kept deliberately low key, the Prime Minister unwilling to make political capital or to intrude on people's privacy. That would be the official story, anyway. Unofficially, Saeed would choose the photograph to be leaked, and he had no doubt which one that would be. As the doors at the far end of the room opened, Saeed glanced down, subtly checking that the toe of his shoe hit the small marker taped to the floor, the spot where the photographer declared the light most flattering. He waited patiently, hands folded in front of him, as Ella Jackson whirred across the marble floor in her battery powered wheelchair.

Bryce's former Special Advisor was the thirty-third and last Downing Street survivor to meet the Prime Minister that morning. The others, mostly kitchen staff and domestic workers, had already been whisked away and were now enjoying the hospitality of the Park Lane Intercontinental before this evening's reception.

'Miss Jackson,' Saeed bowed, holding out his hand, 'it's good to see you - ' he nearly said *on your feet* but quickly shifted gear ' - back with us.'

Between the columns the photographer went to work, capturing the handshake, the benevolent smile, the compassionate tilt of the head, his camera clicking softly, the remote light stands flashing. Ella blinked before the halogen spots.

'Oh come on Tariq, don't be so stiff. Ella's fine.'

Saeed glanced towards his people. He saw the photographer pause and look up over his viewfinder, the duty press officer's pen poised above his pad. The others stared silently. No one had called him by his given name for some time, not since Hooper had offered his resignation to the pavements of Millbank. He smiled a little wider, dropping her hand. This would be short and sweet.

'How are you?'

'Tired of going to funerals. Today is a welcome change.'

'How's the treatment?'

'Never ending,' she smiled, although Saeed could see the smile was strained, the pain evident behind her eyes, magnified by the glasses perched on the end of her nose. Saeed had never liked her, her irritating tenacity, her brusque manner, the way she'd protected Bryce like a faithful dog. And the fact that she was a woman, of course. He had no respect for career women, particularly those hard bitten hags who struggled to hide their bitterness towards men, taking every opportunity to exert their authority over the poor eunuchs beneath them. Saeed would have no such creatures in his government, only willing supplicants or women of the faith like Rana Hassani. Rana had been a loyal servant and had gone to her death unwittingly, but she had played her part. Then there were others, strong women, like his wife for example, who'd given him three healthy boys, who kept home, and kept quiet. That was her role, as a woman, as a wife, and she accepted it without question, the media warned to keep their distance, their pictures never taken nor published. It was Saeed's will.

Jackson had changed, however. Physically her appearance wasn't up to the high standards that Saeed recalled. Her hair was still tied back in a familiar pony tail but the ends were split and straggly, dark roots clearly evident on her scalp. She wore her familiar trouser suit and shirt but the suit was crumpled and the shirt devoid of its usual crispness. Saeed could see that her legs were as thin as matchsticks and her feet shod with comfortable shoes rather than the inappropriate designer heels she previously wore. Her tired face bore no makeup, the lines a little more pronounced around the eyes and mouth, a pale ghost of the woman she once was. It was to be expected of course, the initial hopes of a lesser injury dashed, the failed spinal surgery, her acceptance of a life bound to the chair she now occupied. The fire was gone from her belly. In another life Saeed might have felt some pity.

'Your suffering has been well documented, Ella. You've been very brave.'

'Brave? Oh, I don't know about that,' she snorted. 'Scared, yes, angry, most certainly. And then there's the self-pity, I've wallowed in plenty of that. But no courage, I'm afraid. That's been in short supply.'

'I'm sorry to hear that.'

'Can we not talk about my injuries, Tariq? Can we talk about something else?'

Saeed spread his hands. 'Sure.'

'Can we talk about Gabriel?'

His eyes flashed angrily but the smile remained frozen across Saeed's face. 'Your devotion is to be commended, Ella, but now is not the - '

'I'd really appreciate it. Just a few words. In private.' She turned towards Saeed's staff and smiled. Saeed saw one or two of them return the smile, their expressions sickeningly sympathetic. The camera flashed again, capturing the frail figure in the wheelchair. He'd have to tread carefully here.

'My schedule is full. It may be more appropriate to talk later, at the reception. It'll be a lot less formal.'

Ella shook her head. 'I won't be attending, I'm afraid. I get very tired in the evenings.'

'That's regrettable,' he simpered. 'Perhaps another time then?'

'You can't give me five minutes, Tariq? For old times' sake?'

She adjusted her useless legs and glanced toward his assembled staff once again. Saeed seethcd. Despite her disability the bitch still knew how to play the game. He nodded, the smile frozen on his lips. 'Of course I can.' He ordered the assembled personnel to leave the room and took a seat behind his huge executive desk. It was uncluttered, just a computer pad and a telephone occupying its surface, the polished mahogany reflecting Saeed's face like a mirror as he pulled his seat in. Footsteps faded and the doors at the far end of the room were closed. They were alone.

'Nice picture,' Ella said, looking over Saeed's shoulder. The Prime Minister turned, following her gaze. The painting was in oils on a huge canvas, a camel train snaking across the bleached white sands of the Arabian desert, the dawn sky a mixture of pink and red hues, the dark fingers of the Sawarat mountains in the background. When Saeed had seen it in Cairo he had to have it, and he felt it matched the period features of the room perfectly, lending it an almost colonial feel, something that bothered his more politically correct staff than himself.

'Sunrise over the western desert,' he announced proudly. 'An emerging Egyptian artist, Ahmed Lufti. A very gifted young man, wouldn't you say?'

'It's very you,' Ella replied. Her wheelchair whirred as she guided it closer to Saeed's desk with her joystick. 'Can we talk about Gabriel?'

Saeed swivelled around and placed his hands on the desk. 'Sure.'

'I want to visit him, Tariq. I've tried going through your office but you've been frustratingly unavailable. Did you get any of my messages?'

'Some,' he admitted, 'but with Cairo and then poor Jacob's suicide things have simply been chaotic. I did ask my office to make sure you were kept up to speed.'

'Well you may want to kick them up the arse a bit,' Ella advised. 'If there's a loop, I'm not in it.'

Saeed leaned back in his chair. The curtness still lingered, directed straight at him. Now was as good a time as any. 'While we're on the subject of loops and things, I'm afraid I've had to make some changes, changes that have impacted on your own position, Ella.'

'Oh?' Ella's eyes blinked behind her glasses.

'Obviously you've been out of government for some time and the present administration is geared towards new methods of working, new approaches to old problems. It's clear to me now that where once we shared the same vision, Gabriel and I had a difference of opinion on many things. I think it's fair to say that you were very loyal to Gabriel, sympathetic to his political viewpoints. His personal feelings.'

'Guilty as charged,' Ella smiled, holding up her hand.

'Indeed. However, you must appreciate that I've had to make some difficult decisions during your absence. The past must be wiped away, the old guard retired. New blood is what's needed now, fresh minds with fresh - '

'You can cut the bullshit, Tariq. I'm fired, right?'

Saeed stared at the foul mouthed cripple in front of him for a long moment. 'I see you haven't lost your talent for candour, Ella. In any case you'll keep your pension, and your medical benefits of course. And I'd like to take this opportunity to thank you for your hard work during the previous administration. I've no doubt you'll find something else soon.'

'Yes, the job offers are piling up outside my specially adapted front door,' Ella jibed. 'So, now we've got that out of the way let's move on. I want to see Gabriel.'

'Hmm. That might be tricky.'

'I have a right.'

Saeed leaned back in his chair. 'You're not a relative.'

'He hasn't any. Apart from his sister that is, and we both know she's never given a toss about him. Besides, Gabriel hadn't spoken to her in years.'

'There's also the question of security. As you're no longer in government your clearance is invalidated. I'm sorry.'

Ella tugged at the cuffs of her shirt. 'I was his Special Advisor, and up until a few moments ago I had clearance as high as yours. Nothing's changed, Tariq. I'm still the same person, loyal to the party, discreet. Surely that buys me a little kudos?'

Saeed shook his head. 'It's not my decision. It's out of my hands, I'm afraid.'

'Rubbish.'

Saeed wasn't used to being contradicted. He leaned forward, tapping his finger sharply on the table. 'This is no small request, Ella. It's a matter of national security. For your information there have been further threats to Gabriel's life. They come in daily, from a variety of sources, despite his frailty and other health problems.' He leaned back in his chair, draping one leg across the other. 'He's deteriorated quite badly you know, both physically and mentally. You've seen the news.'

'I don't care,' Ella announced stiffly, 'I want to see him.'

'I wouldn't advise it. He's not the man you remember.'

The hand moved and the chair whirred closer until it bumped against Saeed's desk. 'He was my friend Tariq, and I his. Look, the bomb has devastated us both. Maybe I can help him, you know, with his rehabilitation. A friendly face, mutual support, that kind of thing. I know he'd want to see me.' She dropped her eyes, twisting her fingers in her lap. 'I need to see him. Please.'

Saeed heard her voice catch, watched her as she dabbed at her eyes with a balled up tissue, wondering for the umpteenth time if their professional relationship had ever crossed the line. It was an avenue he'd explored in the early days, looking for a chink in Bryce's armour, a way to exploit the man and influence his policies. The rumours and the court gossip had been surreptitiously investigated but nothing was discovered that he could use to his advantage. Yet Jackson had revered the man, and it was obvious she still cared about Bryce in a way that was less than professional. Crippled or not, she was a determined woman. Denying her access might cause more problems than it solved.

He was suddenly reminded of Suleyman. What was it, nearly a week since he'd heard from him? Still, that wasn't particularly unusual. During the run up to Cairo he'd had little contact with his Turkish fixer, knowing the intelligence operative was fully capable of taking care of things in his absence. He'd done a wonderful job with Bryce, the drug dependency, the physical appearance, the carefully staged photographs, all evidence of Suleyman's professional creativity and devotion to the cause. Yet with Hooper dead there was little point now in prolonging the agony. New Years Eve was a date he'd considered for Bryce's disposal, knowing the usual drunken revelry would diminish the impact of the news, the former Prime Minister's death a mere footnote at the end of a particularly bad year for government. Psychologically the public sought closure and Bryce's death would deliver just that, the new year heralding another new start. Stability, that was what was needed now.

'Alright, Ella. I'll see what I can do.'

Ella closed her eyes for a moment, the relief evident in her voice. 'Thank you, Tariq. I really appreciate it.'

Saeed studied her, realising his decision had given her a boost, both physically and emotionally. He had a sudden, mischievous urge to prolong the charade, to add another layer of credibility to the unfolding drama. 'In fact, let me check my diary. Perhaps I'll accompany you.' Saeed picked up his computer pad and flicked through a couple of web pages, settling on the Euro News channel. 'Ah yes, here we are. Let me see...' He looked at Ella. 'Would the second week in January suit?'

'That would be fine,' Ella nodded.

'Don't you want to check your own schedule?'

Ella placed a finger on her lip. 'Hmm, my schedule for January, let me see. Crawl out of bed, stare at walls, partake in pointless physiotherapy session, drink wine until I pass out. Ad infinitum.' The smile was without warmth. 'Don't worry Tariq, I'm pretty sure I'll be free.'

Saeed tapped a news item on the Turkish Parliament's recent announcement to ban inappropriate bathing costumes in its coastal resorts. 'There. We're locked in to the tenth. I'll request clearance for you with the Security Services and the Interior Ministry. You have no idea how close they're playing this one. Gabriel really is in the best of hands.'

'That's good to know. We hear so little about him these days. It's almost as if the country's forgotten all about him.'

'Nonsense.' Saeed leaned back in his chair. As soon as the cripple left he'd call Suleyman and order him to make the necessary arrangements. Time was of the essence now. Ella's next question snapped him out of his thoughts.

'Where is he, by the way?'

'Gabriel? As I said, he's in a secure facility, very private. Round the clock care. And well protected of course.'

'Where?' Ella insisted. 'I need to know.' She tapped the armrest of her wheelchair. 'Because of my condition. The journey?'

'Oh I see,' Saeed realised. 'It's not far. Just outside London. I'll make sure appropriate transport is organised for your visit. '

'Good. Great.' During the silence that followed, Saeed noticed the tension ease from her shoulders. Eventually she smiled and said, 'I'm going to miss all this.'

'What?'

Ella waved a hand around the room. 'This. Working at the heart of government, being part of the team, influencing the decision-making process. And the overseas trips of course, that was fun, mostly. Power can be quite a heady cocktail.'

'I don't drink,' smiled Saeed.

Ella chuckled. 'Very funny. You know what I mean.'

Saeed leaned his elbows on the table and clasped his hands together. 'I'm not sure I do, Ella. Serving the government is a responsibility, both to oneself and to the people. Personally I have little regard for the trappings of power.'

Ella swivelled in her chair, gazing around the ornate room. 'You could have fooled me.'

'It's true,' he insisted. 'All this is just window dressing. For me it's about providing sound leadership, about healing divisions and bringing the country together. Don't take this personally but look where we are today, as a nation, an economy, compared to when Gabriel was making the decisions. The recovery is gaining pace, no?'

'Granted, the Downing Street bomb certainly produced its fair share of winners and losers.'

'Excuse me?'

Ella returned Saeed's unblinking gaze. 'You were on the verge of being sacked, Tariq, remember? That very day, in fact. Now look at you.' Ella shook her head. 'Prime Minister Saeed. Even you must be surprised at the way things have worked out.'

'Some days I have to pinch myself,' Saeed lied. 'I've been very lucky. Both of us,' he added quickly.

Ella lowered her eyes, absently toying with the chair's joystick. 'It's hard to feel lucky when you're trapped in one of these things.'

'Yet here we are, both alive, by the grace of God,' Saeed pointed out.

Ella looked up, 'Speaking of God, I see you've run into a few problems with the amendments to the Religious Freedom Laws.'

'There's been some criticism, but people will get used to it.'

'Not if you live near a mosque.'

'The call to prayer is of fundamental importance to Islam,' Saeed pointed out. 'Besides, church bells are a constant source of annoyance to people of faiths other than Christianity, so the objections are unfounded.'

'Yes, you're probably right,' Ella conceded. 'How's the investigation going?'

'Slowly. Whelan is being uncooperative at present. I suspect that may change in the near future.'

'How so?'

'He's being transferred to Holland, where initial proceedings will be heard in the International Criminal Court. Cairo is particularly keen to play a role in his trial and sentencing.'

'Really?'

'As you know, there were many Egyptian nationals amongst the victims at Luton,' Saeed explained, 'and of course, the bombs were designed to derail the Treaty itself. The Egyptian legal position is one of victim in this case. They have filed a strong argument for jurisdiction and quite frankly Brussels is keen to accommodate them.'

'Even though most of the victims were UK citizens?'

'These terror attacks could have happened anywhere across the continent. It's important that this is seen as a European problem, to be dealt with as a community on an international stage. We're not an island anymore, Ella.'

'True,' Ella admitted. 'Besides, domestically you're going to have your hands full. I've heard a rise in the basic tax rate is on the cards.'

Saeed arched an eyebrow. 'Oh?'

'Something to do with the financial pressures caused by the relocation program, trouble balancing the budget?'

'Where did you hear that?'

Ella smiled playfully. 'I may be out of the loop Tariq, but I've still got friends in Whitehall. I hear these things. The word is the system is buckling under the financial strain.'

Saeed waved the comment away. 'Propaganda, Ella, put about by those who wish to ferment discord.' He fished inside his jacket for a pen and pulled a small notepad from a drawer. 'Their names?'

Ella's smile slipped from her face. 'Excuse me?'

'Their names. The people who gave you this information.'

Ella fidgeted in her wheelchair. 'I really don't – it's just gossip, Tariq. Water cooler rumours, that's all.'

The pen hovered over the notepad. 'Are you sure, Ella? Because these are dangerous comments, guaranteed to play straight into the hands of hate mongers and racists. You yourself are living proof of what these vile people are capable of. These sort of wild rumours only give weight to their cause.'

Ella brushed an errant strand of hair way from her face. 'Look, just forget it, o.k.? I'm sorry I mentioned it in the first place. It was just something I heard, that's all. I won't repeat it.'

Saeed clicked the pen and slipped it back inside his jacket pocket. 'That's the right thing to do. My government is still finding its feet. Going forward the country needs unifying, that's where our strength will lie. A coming together, as Europeans, under one flag, with one purpose.'

'Of course,' Ella muttered.

Saeed watched the cripple drop her eyes and study her useless feet. Maybe he'd been too hard on her. He could see now her fire was well and truly spent, the combative flame she once possessed now reduced to a few dying embers. He was about to wind up their meeting when his cell vibrated inside his jacket pocket. He fished it out, checked the screen. 'Excuse me, I need to take this.'

He got up and walked a short distance away, his shoes echoing across the marble floor. He flipped open the phone, an encrypted Nokia. 'Salaam alaikum, Brother.'

'Salaam alaikum,' repeated the voice on the other end of the line. Saeed stole a glance over his shoulder. The cripple sat quietly, her hands draped over the arms of her wheelchair. He walked a little further away.

'Everything is well, I trust?'

'We may have a problem,' warned the voice. Saeed thought he could hear the hiss of the sea in the background. No doubt the man was calling from his remote villa perched on Turkey's rocky Lycian coastline. 'Our asset has failed to make scheduled contact with his station chief and he's not answering his cell. Have you heard from him?'

Saeed kept his voice low. 'It's strange you should mention it, I was only just thinking about him. The answer is no, I haven't heard from him in nearly a week. Leave it with me. I'll check and get back to you.' Saeed ended the call then speed dialled another encrypted device in Hampshire. It answered after three rings.

'Yes, Parry here.'

'I need to speak to Sully urgently,' Saeed ordered, the phone's sophisticated voice-altering software distorting his familiar timbre. There was a pause on the line, a nervous clearing of the throat.

'Sully, yes. I'll have to go and find him. He's not answering his cell.'

'Why not?'

'I don't know, I haven't seen him. I've been away for a few days, at a conference in Bristol.' There was a pause on the line and Parry said, 'Come to think of it, I haven't seen that nurse for a while either. She was supposed to pick up some medication from me before I left for Bristol. What was her name again? Malloy? No, Malone, that was it.'

Saeed took a deep breath to calm himself. 'Have you finished?'

'I, er - '

'Good. Here's what I want you to do. The patient is your main priority, so check on him first. Find out the last time he was attended to by either Sully or the nurse. Once you have that information, call me back immediately. Is that clear?'

'Yes.'

Saeed ended the call. He took a moment to compose himself, to quell the sudden feelings of doubt, the tiny butterflies of apprehension taking wing inside his stomach. He adjusted the knot of his tie and turned back to his desk. The cripple was gone. Then he heard the rustle of material and the squeak of her rubber wheels on the white marble. He took a few paces, his eye drawn towards the window, to the large object that stood near it, the one that was normally covered with a dust sheet to guard it from prying eyes, to be drawn back only when in the company of trusted friends and colleagues.

And the cripple was staring at it.

Saeed stepped smartly across the room to where Ella was circling the exposed architectural model. It was set on four large stone plinths, surrounded by a small glass border and Ella whirred slowly around it, examining the glass towers, the flag lined avenues, the giant domes, with an approving eye. It was too late to stop her, too ridiculous to try and bluff it out. She was too smart for that. He folded his arms and watched her expression as she continued to circumnavigate the giant model.

'What do you think?'

'It's beautiful,' she gushed, 'amazing. A real work of art.'

'Isn't it? A personal gift,' he explained, 'commissioned by the Sultan himself and built by Abbas Architects in Riyadh. It's a conceptual piece on a scale of one to two hundred. Notice how they've used photo-etched phosphor bronze to represent most of the important buildings. The modellers have worked day and night for weeks to have it finished.'

Saeed watched the cripple study it a while longer. Then the look of amazement melted from her face, replaced by cold realisation. The chair whined to a stop a few feet away from Saeed.

'Is this – is this supposed to be Whitehall?'

'Correct,' confirmed Saeed, 'the new Whitehall in fact, stretching from Trafalgar Square to Lambeth Bridge. You'll note that Nelson's statue on the column has been removed, along with those ghastly lions. In fact, all traces of Britain's imperialist past along the length of Whitehall will be replaced, including many of its buildings.'

Ella stared at the model a moment longer then looked up at Saeed. 'You're not serious.'

'On the contrary, I thought you might approve, Ella. After all, Whitehall's construction, its whole history, is nothing less than a sordid celebration of warfare and an embarrassing nod to the era of colonialism. A theme you've alluded to once or twice yourself, if memory serves.'

Ella's voice faltered. 'Well yes, I'm sure I've said things to that effect, but what you're proposing here is simply unacceptable.'

Saeed ran a finger along the smooth edge of the glass border. 'As I said, this is a conceptual piece. A final design has yet to be agreed, but what you see before you is a modern, purpose-built administrative and state capital complex that will better serve the business of European and regional government. At the same time it will help to sever psychological links to Whitehall's past, specifically to the recent attacks. We're moving forward, Ella.'

'Why?'

Saeed leaned close, his eye never tiring of the exquisite detail. 'It is felt by many that the recent devastation has presented an opportunity to start again, to build something that all Europeans can marvel at. There'll be no more Defence Ministry, no more Horse Guards or soldiers on horseback. Long dead generals will be removed from their plinths, replaced with more contemporary pieces.'

Ella frowned. 'But the current restoration works - '

'Have been halted.' Saeed slowly circumnavigated the model, his hands clasped behind his back. 'London needs a new vision, one that better reflects its place in a new Europe.' He pointed a slender finger towards a particularly well-constructed miniature building. 'The architects in Riyadh have naturally included a mosque, complete with a magnificent bronze dome and full-sized minarets, each one a full thirty feet higher than Big Ben. It's footprint will encompass the existing bomb site, and what remains of Downing Street. The Foreign Ministry and the Cabinet Office buildings will also be demolished to make way for it. It's a necessary addition for those of us of the faith who are unable to find adequate facilities during the course of their working day. And particularly during Ramadan.'

Ella manoeuvred her chair closer, studying the fine detail of the miniature building. 'It's huge.'

'Of course.' Saeed squatted down to peer along the length of the model's impressive flag lined avenue. 'Britain's Muslim population is flourishing. Many of my own government are of the faith and visiting dignitaries will expect to be able to worship in the heart of London, close to their embassies and the seat of power. As a modern city we cannot expect important visitors to shuttle back and forth to the existing facilities at Regent's Park. Besides, the sheer scale and traditional design of this new construction means it will become an attraction in itself, much like the Blue Mosque in Istanbul.' The cripple's silence was deafening. Saeed straightened up. 'You seem troubled.'

Ella shook her head as she continued to inspect the model. 'It just doesn't seem right. You can't just wipe away Britain's history because of a bit of bomb damage.'

Saeed looked down at her, choosing his words carefully. 'And progress cannot be hindered by misplaced sentimentality, Ella. Many people in this country have little or no interest in history. It's economic opportunities we must provide now, not the preservation of old stone. In any case,' he soothed, 'the whole of London is steeped in antiquity, so the loss of a few buildings will soon be forgotten.'

'Where's the money coming from?'

'Various sources, including Brussels, of course. The Gulf States have agreed to make a substantial contribution.'

Ella hit her lever and whirred past Saeed toward the desk. 'I think it's misguided, offensive even. Gabriel would never have allowed it,' she muttered.

'Gabriel isn't here,' Saeed reminded her. The Nokia trembled in his pocket; it was Parry. Saeed strode past his desk to another door set between two columns. He held it open. 'Would you mind, Ella? An important call. Someone will take care of you.'

Ella manoeuvred her wheelchair into the outer office where several of Saeed's staff were busy working. 'We'll talk soon,' he promised. He slammed the door behind her and sat down at his desk. He lifted the Nokia to his ear. 'Speak.' Nothing, only the faint crackle of static on the line. 'Hello?'

'Oh my God,' the voice whispered, 'Oh Jesus.'

'Parry? What's the matter?'

The administrator's voice trembled with emotion. 'There's been a terrible accident. At least I think it's a... oh, Jesus.'

'Listen to me,' hissed Saeed, 'get a grip on yourself and tell me exactly what's happened.'

'They're dead.'

Saeed bolted upright in his chair, his thought processes kicking into overdrive. Bryce dead? How? Never mind, that wasn't important right now. It was imperative he got hold of Sully, get this mess cleared up, keep the corpse on ice until he figured out a plan.

'Where's the body?'

'Bodies. Plural.'

Saeed held his breath. 'Come again?'

Parry's voice cracked. 'There's blood everywhere, all over the floor. And the smell, Jesus Christ. The room's full of flies.'

Saeed laid the phone down on the desk and took several deep breaths, steadying his hands on the mahogany surface. He could hear Parry's tinny voice calling to him from the Nokia's earpiece. After a moment he picked it up. 'Listen to me, Parry. I want you to start from the beginning. When you went to check, the accommodation was secure, yes?'

'That's right. I used the master to gain access,' Parry explained. 'Place is swarming with flies. Like a bloody horror movie.'

'Focus, you idiot!' Saeed hissed. 'Then what did you do?'

'The patient's room was secured from the outside. I had to slip the bolt to get in. Sully and Malone were lying on the floor. I didn't go too close but it's obvious they're both dead. What shall I do?'

Saeed's eyes widened. He shot out of his chair, sending it bouncing off the wall behind him. The camel train wobbled above his head. 'Wait! Where's Bryce?'

'Gone.'

Saeed could feel his heart pounding inside his chest. 'What do you mean, gone?'

'Gone. Escaped,' Parry blurted down the line. 'I've checked with security. An unidentified male used Sully's card to access the main gate some days ago. It must've been Bryce. He's gone.'

Saeed stared at the phone in his hand.

'Listen!' Parry hissed, 'whoever you are, I need help here! I didn't sign up for this! I've done what you asked, now I want - '

Saeed stabbed at the Nokia and dropped it back into his pocket. Bryce gone? How was that remotely possible? He was permanently drugged to the eyeballs, locked in a secure wing, monitored by two professionals. How did he overpower Sully? Where was he now? What was he planning? So many unanswered questions. And so much failure, not his, but that of others. Like Parry.

He stood there for several moments, fighting the panic, the rising anger that swirled inside him, threatening to choke him. He ground his teeth and bunched his fists, filled with a sudden urge to break something, to smash it into a thousand pieces. He reached for the phone on his desk, picking up the receiver and hammering the base unit until it cracked open, spilling its electronic guts across the polished surface. A shard of plastic stabbed him beneath the nail and Saeed roared with fury. He tugged at the phone once, twice, until the cable snapped and the shattered device came free in his hands. Without thinking he hurled it across the room with a scream of rage. It sailed through the air and hit the glass lip of the model, the battered instrument tumbling end over end, cutting a path of destruction through the miniature streets of the new Whitehall.

'No!' Saeed wailed, and bolted across the room. He cringed, a hand held over his mouth, surveying the damage to the model's intricate and pains-taking construction with abject horror. Behind him the outer office door burst open and his staff rushed in, their faces bewildered, anxious. Saeed ignored them all.

He leaned over the ruined model and saw the crumpled buildings, the shattered streets, the magnificent mosque, now destroyed. He reached out with a finger and gently touched its crushed dome, the delicate minarets severed and scattered into several pieces across the tiny but perfectly manicured lawns of St. James' Park. Then he heard the whirr of the wheelchair, the squeak of the rubber wheels as Ella Jackson came to a stop beside him. Saeed, his face in his hands, turned to look at her.

'Oh dear,' she said, the smile creeping across her face, the fire once again dancing behind her eyes. 'What a terrible shame.'

ICC Detention Centre, Scheveningen, Netherlands

Danny sat at the table, a tobacco stained finger tracing its scarred surface, wondering for the thousandth time how he'd ended up in his present position. He'd run all the scenarios over in his mind, all the theories and possible outcomes, and arrived at one inescapable conclusion – he was fucked. His only option now was to make a run for it but the chances of escape, like his future, looked bleak. His wrists were secured with a pair of rigid handcuffs, the windowless interview room was locked and two Dutch policemen stood outside, occasionally peering at him through the small spy hole. Even if he managed to get out of this room, he was still locked within the interrogation wing of a high security prison in Holland, so escape wasn't exactly a practical option.

He brought his hands up to his mouth and sucked deeply on the self-rolled cigarette, exhaling the smoke in a long, thin plume. He watched it billow up toward the ceiling in a blue cloud, before being sucked violently out of the room by the extractor in the ceiling. It hummed quietly overhead, its once-white plastic housing now stained brown, its gentle rattle the only sound on the dead, insulated air.

He took another drag then coughed violently, the unfiltered rollup catching at the back of his throat, the nicotine slowly regaining its poisonous hold on his lungs. He'd started smoking the day he was captured, because he knew he'd pick up the habit again in prison. There was nothing else to do when you're banged up. Watch TV, read, eat, sleep, smoke – that was about the strength of it. He'd be an old man by the time he was fit for release so fuck it, he might as well start now.

He stared at his reflection in the mirror that made up most of the opposite wall. He looked like a tramp. His hair was a greasy mess, the beard even worse. As soon as they let him have a razor that would come off, he promised himself. Even the healthy outdoor glow he'd developed back in Hertfordshire was gone, replaced by the pasty pallor he'd been accustomed to for most of his adult life. The old Danny was back, the one from the Longhill estate, not the mug who thought life might just turn out alright. That bloke was long gone.

He wondered who was behind that mirror. There had to be someone there because the two coppers who were interviewing him turned around every so often, as if getting the nod from someone behind it. Then one would leave the room and the other would continue to question him, then after a while the other bloke would come back and – fuck it, it didn't matter. He'd told them a hundred times about the drink with Sully, about the truck in Kings Cross, but he wasn't sure if they believed him. It was hard to read these Counter Terrorist types, but Danny thought he'd managed to persuade them that some of his story was true. Occasionally they would look at each other, then disappear outside for a chat. At one stage he thought he'd heard them arguing in the corridor. Or was that a dream? He wasn't sure because they'd questioned him day and night for four days and he'd got little sleep. Start recording, stop recording, tell us about this Danny, tell us about that Danny, in your own words, Danny – it was never ending. Still, at least they were English. For Danny there was no more depressing scenario than being banged up in a foreign jail, but European law trumped English law so here he was. The good news was that Human Rights legislation meant he wouldn't have to serve his sentence here. He hoped he'd end up somewhere close to London, so dad could visit.

He turned at the sound of raised voices again, muffled behind the acoustically insulated door, like men shouting with socks in their mouths. He sniggered at the mental image, stubbing his cigarette out in the cheap metal ashtray. The table was well-worn, its plastic surface scored by years of graffiti. Danny couldn't read any of it, the confusing swirls of Arabic and God knows what else meaning nothing to him. He briefly considered adding his own name using the metal edge of the cuffs but decided against it. Someone lurked behind the mirror, watching him, studying him, probably recording his every movement. He stared at his reflection a moment longer then looked away, his eyes roaming the sound proofed walls. He studied the posters again, some of which were in English. One showed the Euro flag, the ring of stars flying above the Pyramids in Egypt; *Working to build a better Europe,* it announced. Another showed a smiling Dutch policeman kneeling in front of a young boy as he recorded his details. *For Your Security.*

Once again, Danny's eyes came to rest on the poster to his right. It was a black and white still photo of the Luton mosque, taken right after the explosion. The building was in ruins, smoke and flames belching from inside its shattered walls. In the foreground a young Muslim boy, about six or seven years old, his clothes burned off, his skin peeling, screamed silently at the lens; *Hate crime – Suspect it? Report it!* Danny thought they put that one up just for him.

He turned away as the door swung open and the two Brit cops filed back into the room. In the corridor behind them he caught a glimpse of a group of people, robed judges, suited lawyer-types and a couple of bearded religious characters, deep in discussion. Then the heavy door closed and the officers sat themselves down in two plastic chairs across the table. They placed their files and folders in front of them, but they didn't start flicking through them as they usually did. Danny thought that was unusual. They were always referring to notes or statements. Nor did they activate the Audio Visual recording systems. In fact, they both sat there, staring down at their folders, silent.

'This is a first,' grinned Danny, looking at each man in turn. 'What, no questions?' Then he stopped smiling. He studied their faces again, thought he saw disappointment in the eyes, the slope of defeat in the shoulders. Something was up. A ray of hope suddenly burned through Danny's lingering cloud of fatalism. New information, that must be it. Someone had come forward, a fresh witness maybe, someone who knew the truth about Luton. He leaned forward on the table, his hand slapping the surface triumphantly. 'You've got something, new evidence, yeah? Proves I'm telling the truth? That's it, isn't it?'

The senior officer, Harris, glanced up. He was older than Danny, mid-fifties, his dark thinning hair combed back off his high forehead, his cheeks sunken, his scrawny neck disappearing inside an open necked pale blue shirt. *You look worse than me,* Danny decided.

'Your father was released this morning from Wandsworth Prison. No charges will be brought.'

'Really?' Harris nodded and Danny felt as if a huge weight had been lifted from his shoulders. 'That's great news, Mister Harris. Like I said, he never had anything to do with this.'

Harris paused a moment, then he said, 'There's been a development, Danny.' He glanced at his younger colleague who caught the look and sighed heavily. Danny's eyes flicked from one man to the other.

'What development?' The clouds began shifting, gathering once more to snuff out the light.

'It's a serious one. Concerning your case.' Harris folded his hands together and squirmed in his chair, the red plastic creaking beneath his backside. 'Look, I've been doing this job a long time, almost thirty years in fact. After a while you get a feel for people, Danny. It becomes easy to spot a liar - '

'I'm not fucking lying!' Danny blurted.

Harris held up his hands. 'Take it easy, mate. Let me finish.' Danny slumped back into his seat, his white forensic one-piece overall rustling against his skin. Harris continued slowly, deliberately. 'I believe you, Danny. So does DS Stubbs here. But what we're faced with, what the prosecutors are in a feeding frenzy over, is the sheer weight of evidence. Let's go over it again.' He held up his hand, tapping each of his spindly fingers in turn. 'The truck bomb was delivered to the Luton mosque by you, you've admitted that.'

'For the millionth time, I didn't know it was a bomb.'

Harris tapped another finger. 'Architectural drawings of the mosque were found in your father's apartment.'

'Planted.'

'You used to work for the Government Mail Service, from where a vehicle was procured and used to detonate the Downing Street bomb.'

'I don't know anything about that.'

'You were dishonourably discharged from the British Army for possession of explosives - '

Danny jerked out of his chair. 'This is all bullshit!' he raged, 'I told you a thousand times, I was set up! I'm innocent!'

DS Stubbs shoved a folder across the table and swept it open. The photo was in black and white, the body slumped on the ground, the floorboards soaked with blood. 'You killed this enforcement officer in Battersea with an unregistered firearm. When arrested you had an ID card with false details in your possession, plus access to a clean vehicle. Yet you expect us to believe that you spent your whole time on the run in a railway siding in Neasden? You want to talk bullshit, Danny? There's a bucket load, right there.'

Danny slumped back into his chair, defeated. 'I told you,' he mumbled, 'Sully got me the gun, and the ID. He organised the car too.'

'What else did he do?' snapped Stubbs. 'Come round and wipe your arse? Read you a bedtime story? Why did you need a gun if you're not a murderer?'

'For protection, Sully said. I wasn't gonna argue with him, was I?'

Harris shook his head. 'There's another problem, right there. This Sully person, we can't seem to find him. No surname, no known address, no record of a man matching his description being released from Winchester Prison. And when you met him in the Kings head, when he came to visit you in your little hideout, he managed to avoid every CCTV camera in the area. Man's like a ghost. Almost like he never existed.' Harris moved his folders to one side and leaned forward on the table. 'Look, we know you're not a murderer Danny, but that fact is you're heavily involved in a major terrorist atrocity and you're not telling us everything. You've had help along the way, serious help from serious people.'

'It was Sully - '

Harris held up his hand. 'That's enough.' He pulled the folders towards him again, slowly flicking through their contents, his fingers pinching the bridge of his nose. When he looked up he glanced over Danny's shoulder, towards the mirror, then shifted focus. 'Listen to me very carefully, Danny. I'm out of options here, so, if you've got anything you want to tell us, anything at all that will help your case, then now's the time. Because this is your last chance, Danny, right here, right now. If you stick to this fairy tale you've given us then we can't help you. It's out of our hands.'

Danny's mind raged as Harris stared across the table at him. He buried his head in his arms to escape the cops' eyeballs, to buy some time, to think. *Last chance, Danny,* Harris had said. Or what? Was it a bluff? Probably not. No, if he kept stum then he'd be formally charged with mass murder, that's what this was about. A voice screamed inside his head; *tell them about Ray, about Hertfordshire! Tell them everything!* But what if they raided the estate only to discover the device gone? Tess was no mug, she had powerful friends, influential types with money and means. The place would've been cleaned up by now, the device spirited away. And what if someone used it elsewhere? He'd be done for withholding evidence, probably charged with conspiracy for that too, not to mention the killings of Ray and Joe. *So keep your mouth shut,* another other voice urged, *wait until you get to court, so the jury can see the truth in your eyes, hear it in your voice.* It was a plan – well, not really a plan, more of a roll of the dice – but it was worth a shot. They couldn't find Sully, no trace of him anywhere, but the cops knew he existed because the barman in the Kings Head had verified his story, that much he knew. Danny could implicate Sully in just about everything.

He lifted his head, then leaned back in his chair. 'I've got nothing more to say, Mister Harris. I've told you the truth. I'm innocent.'

'Last chance, Danny.'

Danny shook his head. 'Just charge me.'

Neither policeman answered and Danny studied them from across the table. There was a definite change of atmosphere in the room, one that didn't exactly fill Danny with confidence. Harris looked uncomfortable, embarrassed even. No, it was more than that, he looked nervous. Danny began to sweat beneath the paper suit.

'Well? You gonna charge me or what?'

Stubbs swore quietly under his breath, lumbered to his feet and stamped out of the room. Danny watched him go, his puzzlement quickly turning to unease.

'What's going on?'

'I warned you, Danny. Like I said, it's out of my hands now.'

The door opened again, Stubbs holding it wide for the judges who marched into the room, his court-appointed solicitor slinking in behind them and taking up position behind Danny.

'Stand up,' he whispered. Danny did as he was told and the judges lined up across the table facing him. There were three of them, all wearing black robes with blue piping and funny looking white bibs that Danny thought made them look a little like waiters. But it wasn't a menu the senior one held in his hands.

'Mister Whelan, I'm going to read you a statement,' he said in heavily accented English. Whatever colour was left in Danny's face drained away.

'I don't understand - '

The judge silenced Danny by clearing his throat. 'Daniel Morris Whelan, born the tenth of January, two thousand and three, currently being detained at Scheveningen Prison, Holland, you are indicted at the instance of the Prosecutor's Division of the International Criminal Court and the charges against you are that, between the twenty fifth of September and the thirtieth of December two thousand and forty one, in the United Kingdom, you did conspire together and with others, namely the use of explosive devices in the commission of an act of terrorism, in particular the attack on the Luton Central Mosque, Bedfordshire, England, including the murder and attempted murder of said building's occupants - '

Danny shook his head violently. 'I already told you I - '

' – and in addition, that you did conspire together and with others to further the purposes of a banned organisation, hereto known as the English Freedom Movement, by criminal means, namely the use of a biological device in a further act of terrorism directed against the aforementioned community, and the additional murders of Raymond Carver, Joseph Stephen Wallace and Eugene Patrick Cleary...'

Danny's heart thumped in his chest. He swallowed hard, his fingers trembling. *They know about Ray. About the nerve agent. They've known all along.*

'...after legal consultation with the Grand Chamber of the European Court of Justice, it is the decision of the Presidency and the Office of the Prosecutor of the International Criminal Court that the case be referred to the Sharia Supreme Court in Maadi, Egypt, for concluding testimony and sentencing. Custody is to be transferred to Egyptian authorities at the earliest opportunity.'

The judge refolded the statement then marched from the room with his subordinates, Danny's solicitor scuttling out after them.

Harris shook his head. 'Tess Carver reported you for the murder of her husband the night you killed him and his estate manager. She testified that you brought the nerve agent with you, that you killed the others when they didn't go along with the plan, that you tried to kill Mrs. Carver.'

'That's complete bullshit,' Danny blurted. 'They wanted me to gas some place up in Birmingham.'

'Doesn't matter now,' Harris sighed, 'you've had your chance. Now it's up to the court in Egypt.'

Danny fell back in his chair as if he'd been slapped. He shook his head, his voice trembling. 'But that's a Sharia court. I'm not Muslim.'

Harris shrugged and scooped up the folders from the table. 'There's nothing anyone can do, Danny. My advice? Listen to others, be respectful, observe local customs. Give yourself the best chance possible.'

'Jesus Christ, they'll hang me!' Danny shrieked, slamming his hands on the table. As Harris moved towards the door Danny stumbled after him, grabbing his arm. 'Please Mister Harris, I'm begging you, don't let them take me. I didn't do it, I swear to God I didn't.'

Harris turned around, his back to the mirror, his voice low. 'I don't know how you got mixed up in all this Danny, but I honestly believe you never meant to kill anyone.'

'Then tell them!' Danny begged, 'Please!'

'It doesn't matter what I say. The decision's been made at the highest level. Look, just stick to the truth, whatever happens. In the end, that's all it boils down to.' The policeman gently prised Danny's fingers from his arm then left the room, closing the door behind him.

Danny's mouth was bone dry, his heart beating so loudly in his chest that it threatened to punch through the paper suit. He stumbled across the room towards the mirror, swaying in front of the smoked glass, hands cupped around his face. He couldn't see anything beyond his own mocking reflection. He balled his fists and banged against the smooth surface.

'I didn't do it!' he screamed. 'I'm innocent! You can't do this!

The door to the room flew open and Danny spun around. A scrum of black uniforms charged towards him, knocking him to the ground. He lay still, unable to move, his limbs paralysed by fear. He stared at the black boots that ringed his body and squeezed his eyes shut, drawing his knees up and curling into a foetal position. He wanted them all to disappear, willed himself to wake up from the nightmare he was trapped in, to find himself back home, the sound of his dad pottering in the kitchen, the grey urban sprawl of the Longhill estate beyond the high-rise windows. He wanted so desperately to hear those sounds, to see that view again.

Strong hands gripped his arms and yanked him to his feet. Danny's eyes snapped open, seeing the circle of hard faces around him, uncaring, alien faces that spoke in a rapid fire tongue that Danny didn't understand. They marched him from the interview room along the corridor, his feet barely touching the floor. He felt the tears run down his cheeks then, tears for a life squandered, a life played out on the fringes of society where only bitterness and hate existed, his only true companions these last few years.

In the walled compound outside a prison van waited, exhaust smoking on the cold air. A phalanx of heavily armed policemen and prison staff watched his progress silently, the former clearly part of the escort team, the latter in coats and scarves, huddled together out of sheer curiosity. But it wasn't their presence that caused Danny to tremble, nor the salt tinged winds that gusted in from the nearby coastline, piercing the thin paper suit around his body. It was the voices of hate that drifted over the high walls and the barbed wire, the fury of the religious mob that lay siege to the building, calling for justice, demanding vengeance. And now they were going to get it. His eyes wide with fear, Danny was bundled inside the van and locked in a small transport cubicle.

The engine rumbled into life and sirens wailed across the sky. The van lurched forward then swung to the right, accelerating out of the prison gates. The poisonous chants of the mob filled the air, battling with the sirens for supremacy, assaulting Danny's ears as he sat locked inside his own private hell.

As the convoy swept past the baying crowds, no-one heard the pitiful wail of the man inside the van. Nor would they have cared.

The South Coast

Bryce glanced up at the ceiling as the sound of Mac's voice drifted below decks. The orders were unintelligible barks, fused with the purposeful stamp of feet and the gentle throb of the engines. Bryce smiled. Mac, his saviour, appearing out of that rain swept night to snatch him away from danger, whisking him towards the south coast where sanctuary waited. Short-lived, as it turned out. He'd told Mac about the police patrol, as he promised he would, and in a perverse way their arrival had been beneficial for him, encouraging Mac to make speedier preparations for their departure. But it also triggered the guilt again, reading the tension on Mac's face when he discovered that the police had entered the cottage, that the visit might have been recorded somewhere. Bryce had assured him that they'd left in a hurry, that no notes had been taken, but it didn't make much difference. He hated himself for what he'd put Mac through, making a silent promise that he'd make it up to him someday, somehow.

The roads were empty as they left the cottage behind them and made the short trip south to the deserted marina in Hamble. Beyond the security gate and the chain link fence, a large boat shed loomed out of the darkness. A single lamp glowed above the Judas gate, casting its dull yellow light over a small sign bolted to the corrugated metal door: *Marine Movers*. Just before he ducked through the gate, Bryce noticed a boat tied to the adjacent dock, a very large sailboat that glowed ethereally in the darkness like a ghost ship.

Inside the shed was dark, the only light a portable lamp on a nearby worktop, and the stale air tasted of seawater and oil. As his eyes grew accustomed to the shadows, Bryce could see that most of the shed was taken up with sailing paraphernalia; ropes and wet weather gear hung from hooks around the cinderblock walls and piles of sails and rigging were stacked neatly across the floor. It was indicative of a slick, well organised operation. Professional was the word that sprang to Bryce's mind and it gave him considerable comfort.

In the centre of the shed was another vessel, smaller than the one outside, squatting on metal hull supports like a stuffed whale in a museum. Bryce jumped when he caught sight of the shadowy figures gathered beneath it, men who watched him intently. The crew, Mac explained. All three were former Royal Marines, none of whom batted an eyelid at the identity of their latest crew member. Hands were shaken, quiet greetings exchanged. Bryce was relieved to escape their combined scrutiny.

Mac escorted him to a suite of offices at the rear of the building. There, amongst the desks and computers, Bryce expressed serious concerns about the others. Mac had assured him that 'the lads', as he constantly referred to them, needed to be told, that they knew about the importance of security, that their loyalty and discretion was assured. They were Royal Marines after all, he'd smiled. And besides, he couldn't do this without them. They were all in it together.

Clearing a space in the office, Bryce bedded down for the night on a surprisingly comfortable cot. He'd spent those first few hours fidgeting in the restricted warmth of his sleeping bag, staring up at the ceiling and listening to the sound of the wind moaning through the masts along the marina, the slap of water against the tightly packed hulls. Again, the sights and smells of his new surroundings gave rise to familiar fears. He started at every noise, expecting a sudden chorus of shouts to echo across the warehouse, for the door to be kicked in, for hard faced men to drag him off into the night, but the new dawn brought fresh hope and he felt a little more relaxed. As the days passed and they prepared for the voyage, the hope that he'd done enough, been smart enough, was quietly strengthened.

It was yesterday morning, whilst packing dried foods into a watertight container, that the words of the TV anchorman drifting across the boatshed floor made his blood run cold:

'*...when he failed to show up for work at Alton Grange, a high security NHS facility in Hampshire, where Duncan Parry held the post of Chief Administrator...*'

Bryce dropped a handful of freeze-dried curry meals and ran to the kitchen area, where the wall-mounted TV broadcast to an empty room. He stood in the doorway, hands braced against the frame. He vaguely recognised the face on the screen; the fair hair, the heavy glasses - it was Parry who'd stood over his paralysed body that first night, nurse Orla who'd blurted his name.

'*...forced entry to the family home in Farnham where they discovered Parry's body and that of his wife Celia, bound and gagged in the main bedroom. Both victims had suffered multiple stab wounds and the house had been ransacked in what police are saying was a particularly frenzied attack...*'

Despite the warm clothing, Bryce shivered. On the screen, a curious crowd stood behind police tape strung across a quiet suburban road, the sound of helicopter rotor blades beating the air overhead. The TV cameras didn't capture much else, only the front of the property partially shrouded behind a white tarpaulin.

'*...with the hunt for the killer now centred around the mental health facility itself. Police are neither confirming nor denying that a further two bodies have been discovered on a* *disused ward and that a patient is involved in the murders. The hospital is now locked down and inquiries are being conducted in the nearby town of Alton, where CCTV footage is being analysed in an effort to trace the killer...'*

Bryce paled. The loose ends were being tidied up. There was no mention of him directly but it was only a matter of time now. He had to assume the CCTV would place him at the hypermarket. The café owner might remember him, and possibly the bored youth behind the bar of the pub. So, the hunt would turn south and that knowledge didn't make the day pass any quicker. He spoke to Mac who, despite his obvious concern, reminded Bryce that the route he took that first night was a random one, using little used country roads and back lanes, his car registration plates smeared with just enough mud and dirt to be obscure rather than suspicious. There were only two CCTV traffic cameras in Four Marks, both in the centre of town, and police blimps tended to stick to the skies over major urban areas. The chance they'd been spotted heading south was remote. Feeling slightly reassured, Bryce had spent the rest of the day packing boxes, ticking checklists and listening to the easy banter of the men around him. Their confidence was infectious and when Bryce began to think where his life was headed he quickly tuned his mind to something else. Escape, that had to be his focus, his only priority. The rest was in fate's hands.

Mac had woken him at five-thirty that morning. He climbed out of his sleeping bag, packed up his personal gear, then joined the others in the kitchen for coffee and bacon sandwiches. Mac held a short briefing and Bryce listened carefully as each man verbalised their last minute checks and preparations. Bryce was no exception. He was part of the crew now and like the others he would be expected to do his share, to steer the boat, to stand watch, to cook and clean. He couldn't wait.

Outside the sky was beginning to pale to the east. Nothing moved on the marina, a vast majority of the boats and pleasure craft laid up until the spring. His breath fogging on the chilly air, Bryce helped the others move the last of their gear aboard, impressed by their quiet efficiency, their meaningful hand gestures and silent whispers that made Bryce imagine he was part of a military operation.

Even before he climbed aboard, Bryce could tell the *Sunflower* was a magnificent vessel. The winter covers had been removed and the boat's rails and brasses gleamed in the pre-dawn light. The superstructure rose gracefully out of the long deck, forming a sleek fly bridge that was wrapped in smoked glass. The tree-like mast rose above it all, its mainsail furled, piercing the star-filled sky.

Bryce waited on deck, hands in his pockets and grip bag at his feet, until Mac had secured the boat shed. When he climbed aboard he motioned Bryce to follow him below, bunking him in one of the crew cabins. On the way they passed through a dining room and entertainment salon, the state of the art kitchen and the guest quarters where the marble bathrooms and emperor sized beds were wrapped in protective plastic sheeting that failed to disguise the sheer opulence of the craft. Bryce could only guess at the cost of such a vessel.

The crew quarters were well forward and as Bryce had expected, quite cramped. Mac advised him to stay below and he made himself busy by sorting out his bunk space and personal gear. He didn't have much; a set of oilskins (you'll definitely be needing those, Mac had grinned ominously), two jumpers, two t-shirts, two pairs of cargo pants and two pairs of shorts. Deck shoes and sailing boots made up his footwear plus a woollen cap, sunglasses and a few basic toiletries. Bryce had looked at it all, barely covering his single bunk mattress. Like most people he'd spent a lifetime accumulating possessions of all kinds, storing them in cupboards and wardrobes, sheds and garages, filling his two houses with a vast amount of belongings, most of which he'd never use or wear. Now he was reduced to this, the bare essentials. As terrifying as the prospect of having nothing was, in another way it felt almost liberating. Still, it must have cost a fair amount of money but Mac had promised him he'd work his passage.

In the crew galley he'd made a large pot of coffee and listened to the radio as the *Sunflower* cruised quietly under engine power along the silent channel of the Hamble river and out into Southampton Water. He felt the chop of the deeper sea as the bow turned south and the twin Cummins engines increased power. After a while a shadow loomed in the gangway, one of Mac's team.

'Skipper says it's alright to come up on deck.'

'Great. Thanks.'

Bryce went to his cabin and tugged his cold weather coat on, pulling a woollen hat down over his ears. He made his way up the staircase and paused before hitting the open air, pulling the hat a little lower over his forehead. He'd been careful so far, why change now? Then he stepped out on deck.

The sun had risen, climbing above the gently sloping ground to the east. In the morning light, under a deep blue sky, the Oyster 125 was even more impressive. He crossed the teak decking and climbed the steps to the fly bridge where he found Mac seated behind the large stainless steel wheel of the vessel.

The wind whipped off the surface of the water but the fly bridge's angled canopy deflected the worst of it. The elevated view was magnificent, staring straight down the keel of the boat as it knifed through the green waters. The land fell away on either side, the refineries and docks giving way to low lying fields and wooded hills. He was gripped with a sense of freedom he'd never felt before, the nightmare of Alton Grange temporarily banished, his pursuers ignorant, frustrated. Bryce took a deep lungful of salt tinged air and exhaled noisily.

'Marvellous,' he smiled.

Mac pointed to the deep leather pilot's seat next to his. 'Take a pew.' He was hatless, dressed in a red sailing jacket and trousers, a turtle neck sweater and rubber boots on his feet. With his dark stubble and wraparound sunglasses, he looked every inch the yacht master he was. Bryce slid into the chair next to him, his eyes drawn to the sophisticated array of instruments spread across the open cockpit.

'Sailing's come a long way since I first got my feet wet.'

Mac laughed, keeping a wary eye on the shipping lanes ahead. 'She's something all right. The owner's a Yank, a heavyweight Wall Street financier. He's got a place in Miami you wouldn't believe. He's putting us up for a few days while he gets familiar with her.'

'Lucky you,' Bryce replied, his eyes roaming the digital readouts and 3D displays. 'What's the traffic like?'

'Reasonably light.' Mac tapped one of the inbuilt colour screens. 'We've got two large freighters steaming up from the south towards East Solent but we'll pass well ahead of them. Here.' Bryce took the offered binoculars. He scanned the water, spotting a huge white cruise ship with a yellow funnel steaming down the channel ahead of them.

'Cold start to their holiday,' Bryce remarked, pointing to the distant ship.

Mac shook his head. '*P&O* transport. The passengers are émigrés, headed south. Australia and New Zealand.'

'How d'you know?'

'Don't you watch the news? That's all *P&O* do these days.'

Bryce refocused the binoculars until the huge vessel filled the lens. He could see people crowding around the deck rails, men, women, children, braving the cold weather in their coats and scarves, ribbons of coloured streamers trailing from the superstructure, rippling in the wind.

'Can't say I blame them,' Mac said, 'especially after everything you've told me.'

Bryce lowered the binoculars. 'Maybe I'm wrong. Maybe it won't be as bad as I fear.'

Mac turned the wheel a few degrees to starboard. His hand rested on the engines' power levers, teasing a little more from the plant below decks. 'Yes it will. You don't have to be a genius to read the writing on the wall. Things have changed, since the bombs, and especially since Cairo. There's an atmosphere on the streets, a lot of tension, especially in the big cities with all those refugee camps springing up in public parks. Every week there's a demonstration of one sort or another in London. Rumour is the army are gearing up for civil unrest.'

'Where did you hear that?'

'I've still got mates in uniform. Military stores around the country are filling up with riot shields and tear gas.' Mac pointed to the ship as it drew ahead of them, the water churned to white foam in its wake. 'A lot of people are getting nervous about the future. I reckon those ships will get busier and busier.'

Two families in our village have already gone...

'God help us.' Bryce lifted the binoculars to his eyes again, watching the tiny figures packed around the railings, the small boats scampering in the giant vessel's wake, the deep bass of the ship's horn as it boomed across the cold waters.

'They're saying farewell,' Mac explained. 'Won't be many dry eyes on board tonight.'

Bryce watched the ship for a short while longer as it steamed south into the Solent. He lowered the binoculars and eased himself off the pilot's chair.

'I'm sorry I put you through all this.'

Mac kept his eyes on the water ahead, his hands making delicate adjustments to the steering wheel. 'Truth is, you've done me a favour. At least I know what's going on now, politically I mean. I never took much notice before. The business came first, plus I wasn't in the country much. Now I know, well...forewarned is forearmed, right?'

'So they say. But they won't stop looking. The danger's still very real, Mac. And it's still out there.'

Mac shrugged. 'There's not much else I can do. The family's at my mum's in Plymouth and I've got someone watching the business in Hamble. Cover story is I'm in Scotland to price a boat move and recce the coastline around Oban. I'm pretty confident our tracks have been covered.'

'What about this vessel?' Bryce asked, tapping the Perspex canopy. 'Someone will notice it's gone.'

'This move has been planned for weeks,' Mac explained. 'We've just brought it forward a bit, that's all. And the *Sunflower* is still registered with the manufacturers, and they take their client's anonymity very seriously. I think we'll be alright.'

He pointed off to starboard, past the sparkling lights and steaming towers of a large power station, where a circular stone castle stood guard over the entrance to Southampton Water.

'That's Calshot Spit. Things can get a little tricky here so I need to pay attention. Once we round the point we're raising the main sail and I'll need all hands on deck. Fancy a job?' Bryce nodded, eager to put distance between himself and the shoreline. 'Good. How about a round of coffees?'

'No problem. I've got a pot on the go already.' Bryce took orders from the rest of the crew, then headed back down to the galley. He filled a tray with five no-spill mugs, made some toast and brought the whole lot up to the wide aft deck. There was a curved bench seat there, sealed in thick plastic, and a table similarly covered and bolted to the deck. Bryce set the tray down and called the others. He took Mac's mug up to him, plus a couple of slices of toast. Mac attacked the toast first.

'Mmm, nice,' he mumbled between mouthfuls, 'sea air always gives me an appetite.'

'Me too,' Bryce admitted.

'But you're not eating. You alright?'

Bryce stared off to starboard, watching the long spit of land curving towards them, like a shingle finger beckoning them to shore. There was someone there, at the water's edge, a boy with a fishing rod, wrapped up in a green jacket and a red and white football scarf. He lifted his head as the *Sunflower* drifted past, then raised his hand and waved. Bryce waved back. 'Thanks to you a lot better,' he said. 'I'm not match fit yet. The nights are difficult, and I'm still suffering a bit of memory loss, but I'm getting there.'

Mac polished off the last of the toast. 'I'm not going to push you on this trip, you know that. If you need a break, if you don't feel well, then let me know. We'll cope. We've all done this journey a dozen times.'

'I want to do my bit,' Bryce insisted.

'Safety first. Besides, my sea burial skills are a bit rusty and we don't have a Bible aboard.'

Bryce cracked a smile but inside his stomach lurched. It was something he'd thought about during the troubled nights he'd just mentioned. What better way for Mac to rid himself of his problems than to toss him overboard, into the dark, cold graveyard of the Atlantic ocean. Bryce shivered, turning to watch the boy at the water's edge, now a tiny figure in the distance. No, Mac wasn't a murderer. He'd killed people, sure – he was an Afghan veteran after all - but not in cold blood. He wasn't the type, Bryce reassured himself. *Try telling yourself that when you're five hundred miles offshore,* his inner voice taunted. Bryce shook his head to clear the thought. It was too late now anyway.

Mac gulped the last of his coffee and handed the empty mug to Bryce.

'Alright, let's get prepped. Tell the lads to stand to. You can keep watch on the bow if that's alright.'

'Sure.'

'Don't forget your safety line.'

Bryce returned the tray to the galley and made his way down to the front of the vessel, getting as close to the bow as possible. As the *Sunflower* drifted past the medieval fort and rounded the southern tip of the spit into deeper waters, he felt the wind strengthen as the boat turned to starboard and headed west. He lifted his sunglasses from around his neck and slipped them on. The sun was behind them now, its strong light dappling the water, making it difficult for Bryce to spot obstacles or debris floating in their path. He screwed his eyes tight, his brow furrowed in concentration as he scanned the sparkling water. Behind him he heard the main sail being lifted out of its protective jib, the electronic motors hoisting it to the top of the mast. It billowed once, twice, then the wind caught it and it snapped taught, taking the boat with it. Bryce held on as the vessel listed a little, then settled in the water. There was nothing quite like it, being on a boat at sea, powered only by the strength of the wind. He no longer felt the steady throb of the engines beneath his feet as wind and tide took over completely.

The land on either side drifted by, the patchwork fields and wooded hills of the Isle of Wight to port, the long, empty beaches and inlets of the Hampshire coast to starboard. Boats of various sizes dotted the waters around them; freighters heading for the shipping lanes, a flotilla of fishing boats, their nets and pots bundled on cramped aft decks, chugging towards their designated grounds. They were out of the ferry lanes and it was too early for the fast boats and pleasure craft. All in all traffic was minimal and the *Sunflower* had the waters pretty much to herself.

Bryce sat on the deck, his legs dangling over the bow, his arms hooked over the rail guard. The water passed beneath him, the odd wave catching the boat and breaking over his waterproofs. It was both exhilarating and soothing at the same time, watching the sea slip by, the wind in his face, the taste of salt on his tongue. He was suddenly reminded of a moment, just before the bomb, when he'd returned to his office to pick up the Heathrow dossier. He vaguely recalled the promise he'd made to himself back then, to take some time off, hit the waters, recharge his batteries. Never in his wildest imagination did he ever think it would be under these circumstances.

Ahead, the land began to crowd the Solent from either side, funnelling the *Sunflower* through the fast moving gap of Hurst Spit. Bryce got to his feet, alert once again as the chalk cliffs and a large, red bricked fort closed in to port, a solitary white lighthouse on the spit's sandbanks to starboard. The waterway was clear and soon they were through the gap and the land fell away. He felt the boat turn a few degrees to port, the bow slicing through the sea on its new course. He heard the squeak of rubber boots on the deck behind him and saw Mac approaching, the wind whipping the collar of his waterproofs. Up on the fly bridge one of the others handled the boat as the wind filled the giant sail above, driving the *Sunflower* westward.

'Everything o.k.?'

'Fine,' Bryce replied, getting to his feet. They stood silently for a moment as the offshore winds began to make themselves felt and the boat picked up speed. 'To tell the truth I'm a little apprehensive,' Bryce admitted.

'About the voyage?'

'About afterwards. This isn't going to end with me sailing off into the sunset.'

'That's for sure.'

Bryce shivered in the sharp wind, thrusting his hands deep into his pockets. 'By the time we get to the Azores I'll be wanted for the murder of three people, and the evidence will be overwhelming. No-one will ever believe I'm innocent.'

'So what will you do?'

'Stay out of sight, get my strength back. Make a plan. It's going to be a long and uncertain road, Mac. God only knows where it will lead.'

They stood in silence for a few minutes, the wind gusting across the bow, the ripple of the sail above them. It was Bryce who finally spoke.

'Tell me what happens, when we reach Tortola.'

The ex-marine braced his feet as the *Sunflower* rode a sudden swell. Bryce wasn't so quick, snatching at a guideline as the bow bucked, then settled. Mac lent him a steadying hand. 'You alright?' Bryce nodded. 'I know the Road Town marina well,' Mac continued. 'We'll use the opportunity to resupply there before pushing on to Miami. Don't worry though, getting you ashore will be easy. We'll do if after dark, when the bars are busy and there're lots of people around. The Immigration bods tend to stick to office hours and marina security is pretty laid back. Getting out onto the island won't be a problem.'

'Good,' Bryce said, 'all I need then is change for a phone call.'

Mac grinned. 'I'll stick it on the bill. This friend of yours, how do you think he'll react when you show up on his doorstep?'

Bryce considered that for a moment. It had been a while since he'd spoken to his long-term benefactor, even before the bomb, but Bryce was certain that Oliver Massey would provide his old friend sanctuary in a heartbeat. 'I've known him for almost thirty years. I've a feeling he'll be pretty pleased to see me.'

Mac nodded. 'Well, you'll get a decent tan while you're there. The Islands are lovely this time of year. A good place to recuperate, recharge your batteries.'

Bryce watched the coastline fall away, the foamy wake of the *Sunflower* spreading out across the waters behind them. 'It's not just physical, Mac. I've got blood on my hands.'

'You did what you had to do,' Mac reminded him. 'Look, the important thing is that you've disappeared, dropped off the grid. You know how hard that is to achieve in this day and age? You're the one with the tactical advantage now. Focus on that.'

It was true, Bryce had vanished like an early morning mist, yet he had to keep praying the trail to Hamble would stay cold, that Tariq's wolves would continue going around in circles, following one false trail after another. He had a sudden mental image of Tariq himself, livid with frustration as each avenue of investigation reached another dead end. But it wouldn't end there, oh no. He knew Tariq too well, his determination, his ruthlessness. How he would love to see his face when he hears the news that Gabriel Bryce is alive and well. That would be something.

'One thing's for sure,' Mac added, 'they certainly won't be looking for you in Tortola. Right now we've got the wind behind us and an empty ocean ahead.' The westerly breezes seemed to pick up just then, filling the sail above them and urging the boat towards the distant horizon. 'Come on,' Mac smiled, clapping a hand on Bryce's shoulder, 'let's get aft. There's work to be done.'

As they headed back along the deck, Bryce suddenly turned around. 'The letter, did you manage to post it?'

'One of the lads did it late last night,' Mac confirmed. 'Dropped it in a box in Guildford.'

Bryce nodded, relieved. 'Thanks, Mac. It means a lot.'

'No probs. Who is she anyway? A relative?'

A smile played across Bryce's face as he watched the coastline of England drift by, the boat carving steadily

westwards through the deeper waters of the channel.
'Ella? Just a friend. A very good friend.'

Overhead a flight of black tipped gulls dipped
and screeched, their wings beating effortlessly as they
escorted the *Sunflower* out towards the open sea.

Epilogue

Danny brushed aside the tent flap and stood upright, shielding his eyes against the low sun. He took a moment to stretch his aching limbs, then headed off between the endless rows of white canvas tents that stretched across the flat, sun-baked desert.

He walked slowly, conserving his energy in the oppressive heat. The surrounding terrain was featureless in all directions, except for a thin ridge of hills to the south-west. Beyond those hills were the mines where most of his fellow detainees worked. Danny had yet to see them and he thanked God for that particular blessing. Out there, across the arid desert, thousands of prisoners worked night and day, hacking away at rock faces deep underground, filling carts full of mineral deposits and transporting them to the surface in dilapidated, creaking cargo lifts. It was dangerous work and many had died. Danny had no intention of joining them, preferring his current employment to anything the mine offered.

The workings of the mine, and its recent victims, were regular topics of discussion amongst the prisoners around the cooking fires in the evenings; the nature of the accidents, the injuries sustained, which tunnels were the most dangerous. They talked of ways to improve their chances of survival until exhaustion overcame them and they stumbled back to their tents for a few hours of rest. Others slept where they lay, wrapped in thin blankets beside the fires. Often, one or two remained under the covers even after the sun had come up, the lethal combination of workload and disease finally taking their toll. That was where Danny came in. The dead were his living.

And they were the lucky ones, many said. Their spirits had been released and were free to roam the desert, to travel on the winds, to leave this place far behind – wherever this place was. The southern Egyptian desert, probably near the Sudanese border, Clive had said. Clive knew a bit about birds and once he'd seen some sort of lark that only existed in this part of the world. That was good enough for Danny. Clive was a clever bloke, middle class, educated.

Well, maybe not so clever. In his previous life he'd been a teacher and he'd taken his kids on a school trip from England to visit the Pyramids. One night he'd had a little too much to drink in a city restaurant and had driven back to his hotel across Cairo in a hire car with another teacher. The Imam they hit on a darkened street was one of Cairo's more important scholars and a Sharia judge. Panicked, Clive had tried to drive away, dragging the dying man another few hundred yards along the street. The mob had nearly killed them and Clive said on numerous occasions he wished they had. One hundred lashes, followed by fifteen years hard labour in this hell hole was harsh punishment, but not nearly as harsh as forty years without parole, without visitation rights, where the comforts guaranteed by European penal laws were patently ignored. Here there were no prospects, no hope. That's what Danny had to endure.

The details of his own trial were fading now, only the aftermath remained etched in his memory. They'd dragged him screaming from the court in Maadi and transported him to the notorious Burg-al-Arab prison outside Alexandria, the initial beatings so bad that Danny had to be hospitalised twice, the second time for internal injuries after a vicious gang rape. There the doctors had taken the opportunity to chemically burn the offensive tattoo from his arm, his screams echoing across the prison. During his recovery he'd written to his father and banned him from visiting, afraid that his physical condition and emotional scars would tip the old man over the edge, unable to trust himself and admit that he'd contemplated ending his own life. He spent the first year in solitary confinement, mostly for his own safety. It was during his sixteenth month of imprisonment that they finally came for him.

The sun hadn't yet risen when he was quietly removed from his cell and transported to a military airfield north of the city. There he was frog marched up the ramp of a cargo plane and shackled to the floor with scores of other prisoners. They'd all been hooded and the plane had taken off, the journey lasting over an hour Danny estimated. When they arrived at their destination the hood and shackles were removed and the prisoners were whipped from the plane by guards in camouflaged uniforms, their heads covered with chequered shemagh's, only their cruel eyes visible through the slit of the cloth. Blows rained down, driving the frightened prisoners out onto the blistering heat of the runway where the blast from the massive turbofan propellers whipped the dirt into a stinging, choking storm. Danny cowered amongst the others, burying himself in the middle of the herd of terrified prisoners. They were beaten to the side of the runway and down a steep embankment. Behind them the plane roared and Danny crouched at the bottom of the embankment, watching the huge tail fin flash past in a cloud of yellow dust, his eyes tracking the giant transport as it lifted off and drifted away into the cloudless sky.

When the dust finally settled Danny saw the camp for the first time. Row after row of white canvas tents stretched away into the distance, shimmering in the heat haze. There were no fences, no watchtowers or patrolling guards, just the tents, the flat desert and the unrelenting sun. The leather sticks whipped his arms and legs and he ran with the others as the screaming guards corralled them towards a large military compound, this one surrounded by a razor wire fence. Behind the wire there were Hummer jeeps parked beneath camouflage nets and dozens of air conditioned huts. Inside the compound nothing moved. Danny was the first to faint, only to be brought back to consciousness by the boot of an angry guard. No one spoke English and neither did they try. The man with the large moustache and the pistol strapped to his thigh was the camp commandant and he spoke to them, again in Arabic, from behind the wire. They were ordered to strip and prison uniforms were issued, black cotton smocks and baggy pants. He discovered later that black made it easier for the guards to locate the bodies of escapees against the white sands of the desert. Plenty of prisoners had tried, heading out into the wilderness under cover of darkness, but only death waited for them out beyond the endless horizon. Water was issued, one litre per man, and Danny gulped his greedily until it was finished. Stupid really, because he didn't get his next ration for another day.

They say the first month of captivity is always the worst. For Danny, it was those early weeks in the desert that proved to be the most horrifying. Wracked by his first bout of dysentery, confined to a hospital tent populated with the dead and dying and swarming with flies, he sweated by day, squirming in his own filth, and shivered by night, huddled beneath the thin blanket while his bowels emptied themselves with alarming regularity. Too weak to move or speak, Danny silently begged Death to take him soon.

And He was close by during that first month. Danny had seen him many times, mostly at night, lurking around the hospital tent, the pale skull glimpsed beneath the black hood as he silently circled the dying. As the fever consumed him Danny often saw him in the shadows, the pointing finger, the macabre grin, before melting into the darkness once more.

Waking was the other nightmare, knowing that the tent would heat up like an oven during the day, that the medical staff were in fact fellow prisoners with little or no real training, that as an Infidel, Danny was the last to be treated. There were no drugs, no pain relief of any kind, just survival or death. If you walked out of the hospital tent it was Allah's will and nothing else, so when Danny finally managed to drag himself out of his filthy cot the other inmates were astounded. The word spread quickly. Rarely did anyone survive a stay in the hospital tent, Clive told him later. Those that did were looked on almost reverently, like the hand of God himself had touched them.

Danny didn't know anything about that. All he knew was that one day he'd woken up and felt better. A lot better. The fever had broken, the stomach pains and the chronic diarrhoea gone. Only the thirst remained but that was quickly sated by donations from some of the other prisoners, eager for their charity to be recognised by the same God should sickness befall them too.

That's when he'd first met Clive, while recuperating. They were two of only a handful of Europeans in the camp. The rest were mostly Egyptian, with a sprinkling of Sudanese, Libyans and Arabs. Clive had been at the camp for nearly two years and spoke fluent Arabic. He was tall and very thin, his beard bright ginger, the skin on his bald head constantly burned and spotted with huge freckles. His nose was twisted and his front teeth missing, the result of continuous beatings when he'd first arrived. He had a job teaching the camp commandant conversational English which got him out of working the mine. Clive spent the next few weeks educating Danny on life inside tent city. He explained the rules, the procedures and customs. As the infamous Luton bomber Danny was a natural target for many of the nastier inmates but Clive managed to keep him out of the way, finding different tents for Danny to sleep in, sticking to safe areas within the canvas streets. Danny wasn't as scared as he might have been in the past. He'd looked death in the face, literally, and lived to tell the tale. The prospect of dying just didn't fill him with dread anymore.

Danny was never forced to convert to Islam. In the early days, just before dawn, he'd hear the call to prayer amplified through tall speaker posts dotted across the camp. He'd watch the others in his tent rise quietly and gather their prayer mats, walking out to the dusty square in the middle of the camp where the huge stone *Qibla* pillar rose out of the desert floor to point towards the Holy City of Mecca. Occasionally he'd follow, watching proceedings from the relative coolness of the morning shade as thousands prayed quietly, as one, the low murmur of their voices carried on the stillness of the dawn, their bodies rising and falling in devoted supplication. As time passed Danny began to crave the peace it appeared to bring, the comfort, the knowledge that a higher power had a plan for each and every one of them, for mankind.

In the months that followed Danny spoke to others, in his halting Arabic and through Clive, about a personal discovery. He took the testimony of faith, the *Shahada,* in front of the *Qibla* and a small group of friends, publicly entering the fold of Islam, all previous sins forgiven. Things were different after that. He was no longer looked on with contempt or suspicion, his victory over disease and his attendance at daily prayers granting him the respect of his fellow brothers. Like many of the other inmates he shaved his head but kept his beard, the sun turning his skin a dark brown. He had become one of them, a devotee of the one true faith, the very thing he'd once detested. Sometimes, late at night as he lay on his cot, he thought of the regulars in the Kings Head and wondered what they would make of him now. The thought made him smile.

Clive introduced him to the camp commandant, used Danny to test the man's ever increasing command of the language in a series of verbal exercises that had the commandant clapping his hands with pleasure. As a reward, Danny was given the job of burying the dead. It was hard work, gruesome at times, but it was infinitely better than working the mine. If you died in there your body was hurled down a disused shaft. If you died in the camp, Danny or one of the other gravediggers would be called to transport the body by donkey and cart to the graveyard a mile across the desert.

And business was good. Men here died in a variety of different ways; disease, heat stroke, heart attacks. Then there were the screams that rang out across the desert night, the murders, the knifings and strangulations, the fatal beatings. The mornings always brought fresh corpses. There was never any investigation, no inquiry into the cause of the violence. This was a prison after all, one never visited by officials from Brussels. Or as Danny had begun to suspect, even heard of.

At the end of each day, when the commandant had tired of Clive's teachings, when Danny had fed and watered the donkey, they would eat quietly around the camp fire then disappear into the darkness. Often they would sit up near the runway, on the embankment overlooking the camp. They would watch the fires glowing across the desert and talk about their lives back home, about their families and how they were coping. Clive had a wife and three children in Leeds. Danny fretted about his dad every day.

Clive mentioned it first, the possibility that they were officially dead.

'Not one letter in two years,' he complained in his broad Yorkshire accent. 'I write once a week. Never got a single reply. How about you?'

Danny shook his head. 'Dad's getting on. I don't want him worrying all the time. Best he forgets about me.'

Clive was quiet for a while, then he said: 'I even wrote to my MEP once.'

'Oh yeah? What did he say?'

'Nothing, you daft bastard. That's what I'm trying to say. I think we're both dead. Officially, like.'

Danny swallowed hard. 'I might as well be. I'll be nearly eighty when I get out.'

'You're not getting out,' Clive said. They heard shouting from somewhere in the camp, carried on the night air, then a long, blood curdling scream. 'Sounds like a bit more business coming your way.'

They were quiet for a while, both men staring across the camp, watching the breeze ruffle the tents in gentle waves, the tiny figures gathered around the myriad of cooking fires.

'I don't know how it happened,' Clive said, 'a fight maybe, disease, an accident. Any way you cut it we're dead. I suspect we've been cremated locally and our ashes sent back home. Knowing Jenny my urn is probably sat pride of place on the bloody mantelpiece.'

Danny chuckled, then fell silent as the Yorkshire man continued in a sombre voice. 'He takes a nap every afternoon at two, right after lunch. Flops out on a sofa in a small room next to his office. I usually wait outside, sitting in the shade until he needs me again. There's an IPad on his desk. He watches the BBC sometimes, helps with his English. He doesn't let me near it.'

'So?'

'So I'm going to send a message to Jenny and the kids, let them know I'm alright. Get her to get us out of here.'

Danny turned his head. 'Us?'

Clive flashed his toothless grin. 'You stay here then. Me, I'm getting out.'

'If you get caught - '

'I'm a dead man. After that it's up to you.'

'Me?'

'One of us has got to get out.' Clive scooped up a handful of sand and let it run between his fingers. 'His English is coming on a treat. Pretty soon he won't need me and I'll end up in that bastard mine. I'll be dead in a month.'

'We could work together,' Danny suggested. He feared loneliness more than death. He had friends around the camp, yes, but they were no substitute for one's own kind.

Clive shook his head, his thick beard rustling against his smock. 'And what if the boss man decides otherwise? I can't take that risk. Listen Danny, even if both of us live long enough to see out our sentences, they'll never let us go, especially you. They'll find a way to knock us off, European laws be damned. We don't even know where we are, for God's sake. I'll bet you anything you like, this place doesn't officially exist.

We might as well be wearing striped pyjamas and gold stars.'

Danny looked toward the compound. It was quiet, the accommodation blocks shrouded in darkness, the gentle hum of the air conditioners carried on the air. 'What will you say?'

'To Jenny? Doesn't matter. If she knows I'm alive she'll scream blue bloody murder. She'll camp out in Whitehall or Brussels until someone listens. All we have to do is stay alive, keep out of trouble.'

'That's it?'

'No. There's one more thing.'

'What's that?'

Clive brushed the sand from his hands. 'Pray.'

The hot sun was beginning to dip towards the horizon as Danny wandered between the tents, carefully stepping over the guide ropes that criss-crossed his path. That night on the embankment, the conversation with Clive, it all seemed so long ago now. He clung to the memory to combat the relentless fatigue that assaulted his mind and body, but lately he'd found his recollections fading, his sandals catching the ropes once too often. Exhaustion was starting to become a permanent state of being.

He skirted around the last tent and the empty desert opened up before him. A mile away the burial ground shimmered like liquid in the distance. He shielded his eyes against the setting sun, spotting several other prisoners making their way to and from the gravesite, their elongated silhouettes quivering in the heat haze. He took a disciplined nip from a water bottle, wiped the sweat from the grey stubble of his head, then climbed aboard the wooden cart. He gave the listless donkey a gentle slap of the reins and set off across the desert floor.

By the time he reached the cemetery the shadows were beginning to lengthen, stretching across the sand like black fingers. Danny tugged on the reins and brought the cart to a halt. He jumped down and gave the donkey a pat on its bony flanks. Only two bodies today and luckily there were a couple of Sudanese prisoners close by who gave him a hand hefting the white shrouded corpses to the ground. He thanked them and they went on their way. The small excavator and other tools were behind a nearby dune but Danny didn't have any intention of burying the two corpses this evening. Instead he'd come for another purpose.

The burial ground was kept neat and tidy in accordance with Islam's respect for the departed, and divided by nationality for practical purposes. Many prisoners spent time amongst the rows of graves, praying quietly or reading the inscriptions on the white painted boards that served as headstones. Danny made his way between the neat rows of carefully tended burial plots towards the far edge of the graveyard where the last graves met the empty desert. It seemed more peaceful here, as far from the camp as possible, and Danny would resist any attempts to expand the cemetery in this particular direction. He stepped carefully around the last two rows of peeling headboards and then he was there.

He reached inside the pocket of his loose trousers and produced a handful of black pebbles brought up by some of the mine workers. Kneeling down in the sand, Danny placed them within the stone border that marked the grave's boundary. His aim was to fill the border with shiny black pebbles and give this last resting place a little more permanence and dignity.

It would take a few more trips but Danny would finish the job before long. It was the least he could do. He looked up at the inscription carved into the wooden board and dusted away the sand that had collected in the grooves of the roughly-hewn letters;

Clive Banks, Leeds, UK. RIP.

He'd been caught that day, all those years ago, as Danny feared he would be. His body had hung for three days from the gallows outside the compound, the wire noose stretching Clive's thin neck, his head tilted grotesquely to one side, his face blue, his tongue protruding from his thick red beard. Danny himself had cut the body down and transported it to the cemetery. He never found out if Clive had been successful or not but as the months turned to years, he was pretty sure he'd been caught before any message had been sent. Clive was a brave man though, a man of his word. He'd tried, given it a go. More than most of them had done.

Danny stood wearily, dusting the sand off his knees as he looked around. The cemetery had grown since the early days and wooden grave markers stretched for hundreds of yards in all directions. Here and there men walked between the rows of headboards in silent contemplation or chatted quietly in small groups. There was a sense of peace here, a place where a man could find some comfort in the silence of the desert. For most of them, it was the best they could hope for in a hopeless situation.

He looked out across the flat sands and watched the blood-red sun dip beyond the distant horizon. It would soon be time for evening prayers, then food. The twice-daily meals were deficient of any real nutrition and unsuitable for stockpiling. Water was also carefully rationed, each prisoner receiving not much more than a few litres a day. The whole operation was pared down to the bare bones, hence a constant supply of fresh labour and the ever-expanding cemetery. The longer a prisoner survived, the weaker he got and the less chance he had to make a run for it. Danny had been here for almost seven years now and time and age were working against him. His weight was getting dangerously low, his strength fading. Soon his job would go to someone younger, stronger. He couldn't wait much longer.

The plan would take a little more time to finalise. He'd been watching the runway for weeks now, the cargo flights, the distracted ground crew, the lazy guards. Certain details needed ironing out but there was a chance, a very slim chance, that it could work. If he got back to Cairo, to civilisation, then he had a shot at getting home. He gave himself another month to prepare, to steal a little food, get a little stronger, before he executed his plan. If things changed and the opportunity was missed, well, it wouldn't really matter much then. He'd simply walk off into the desert. Dehydration, coma, death; there were worse ways to go. And at least he'd give Clive a bit of company.

Danny watched the setting sun a while longer then turned back, trudging between the long rows of graves until he reached the last sun-blistered marker. He swatted away the flies and nuzzled the donkey's neck for a few moments, then climbed up on the cart and released the brake.

With a gentle slap of the reins Danny headed across the desert floor, back towards the sprawling encampment that shimmered in the distant haze.

The End

Lightning Source UK Ltd.
Milton Keynes UK

175471UK00001B/1/P